W9-CMO-579

A Love For All Time

Yearning made his voice scratchy. "Lianna, I haven't stopped thinking about you since the moment we met." Rand touched his lips at random over her flushed and startled face. "You make me want to forget who I am, to forget there's a world and a time beyond this moment."

Had he kissed a thousand women, he knew not one of them could seize his soul as Lianna did.

She lay still, naive, accepting. Her lips felt like moist velvet as he brushed them with his own. She tasted of morning dew and mystery, as if her body held some secret just out of his reach. He burned for her, longed to unlock the person she was, to peel away the layers of her outward identity and cast them aside like petals plucked from a daisy.

Madness, he thought, feathering kisses over her brow, into her hair. Madness to indulge in this forbidden tryst. But, oh, how he wanted to explore the insanity.

*   *   *

THE LILY
AND THE
LEOPARD

SUSAN
WIGGS

HarperPaperbacks
A Division of HarperCollinsPublishers

This is a work of fiction. The characters, incidents, and dialogues are products of the author's imagination and are not to be construed as real. Any resemblance to actual events or persons, living or dead, is entirely coincidental.

HarperPaperbacks *A Division of* HarperCollins*Publishers*
10 East 53rd Street, New York, N.Y. 10022

Cover illustration by B. A. Maguire

First printing: February 1991

Printed in the United States of America

HarperPaperbacks and colophon are trademarks of HarperCollins*Publishers*

10 9 8 7 6 5 4 3 2 1

To my sister, Lori, with love,
and to her husband, Graeme Cross,
a "parfit, gentil knight."

With heartfelt gratitude to my boon companions, Barbara Dawson Smith, Arnette Lamb, Alice Borschart, and Joyce Bell;

and to Richard Curtis, slayer of dragons and doer of good deeds.

Special thanks to John Lloyd-Evans, Bob Beck, and Charles B. Sanders of the Kinkaid School, Pat Jones of the Houston Public Library, and to Alice Shields, for her proofreading skills.

Many poor men through their service in the French wars have become noble, some by their prudence, some by their energy, some by their valor, and some by other virtues which...ennoble men.

Nicholas Upton, *De Studio Militari*

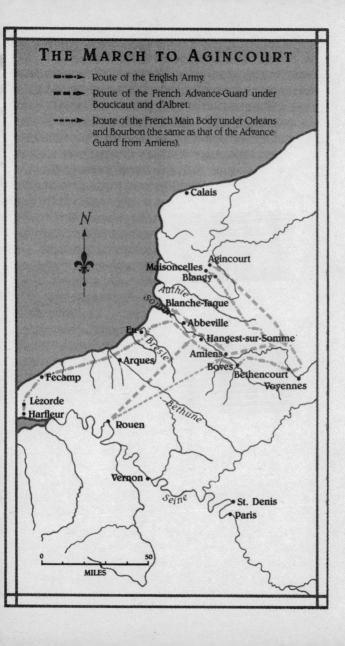

THE MARCH TO AGINCOURT

Route of the English Army.

Route of the French Advance-Guard under Boucicaut and d'Albret.

Route of the French Main Body under Orleans and Bourbon (the same as that of the Advance-Guard from Amiens).

N

• Calais

Maisoncelles •
Blangy •   • Agincourt

Authie

Somme   Blanche-Taque

• Abbeville

Etr •   • Hangest-sur-Somme

Bresle

• Arques   Amiens •

Boves •

Bethencourt

Voyennes

• Fécamp

• Lézorde

• Harfleur

Bethune

Rouen •

Vernon •

Seine

• St. Denis

• Paris

0 ─────── 50

MILES

PROLOGUE

Westminster
January 1414

He sat naked in a wooden tub; the King of England loomed at his back. He shivered, tensed, and awaited a sluice of cold water from Henry V's own hand. The wind whistled, harmonizing with the voices in the shadows of the stone chamber.

"Always thought he'd earn his spurs on the battlefield," remarked Thomas, Duke of Clarence. "Enguerrand Fitzmarc is the king's own avenger. He served us right well at Anjou."

"It was a different dragon Rand slew for the House of Lancaster," said Richard Courtenay. The Bishop of Norwich leaned forward, the rushlight giving his face a ghostly aspect. "A far more deadly dragon," he added. "God in heaven, Tom, if not for Rand, you and your brother the king would be but carcasses carved up and served by the Lollards to the Thames."

Listening, Rand felt pride in Courtenay's tribute. Then he felt shame in that pride. What had he done, after all, save overhear a plot of ill-guided religious fanatics? A peasant could have done as much. But it hadn't been a peasant; it had been Rand, gone a-harping at twilight, stumbling into intrigue, barely escaping with his hide intact to alert the king at Eltham.

"Are you ready," King Henry said with quiet solemnity, "to wash away your former life?"

Rand paused before delivering the expected response. Unlike many aspirants who yearned for the glory of knighthood, he did not want to shed his former life: the quiet sunsets over Arundel keep, the baying of the alaunts on a hunt, the silvery tones of his harp across the heaths of Sussex, the warmth of Justine's hand in his. . . . Jesu, could he wash away Jussie?

The men in the chamber fell silent. The king waited.

"Aye, Your Grace," said Rand.

Water, blessed by the bishop and chilled by the January air, drenched Rand from head to toe, crawling like rivers of ice over his naked flesh. He sat unflinching, although inside he clenched every nerve against the cold.

Jack Cade, Rand's scutifer, stepped forward. Awkwardly Jack held a pair of barber's shears in his maimed hand. He flashed an irreverent grin as he bent to his task, the crude scissors biting into Rand's golden locks. "Enough baths like this," Jack muttered, taking up a razor, "and you'll be well able to hold to your vow of chastity." The razor nicked Rand's chin.

Hearing King Henry clear his throat, Rand swallowed his laughter. "Hush, Jack, and mind that blade. The shearing's supposed to show my submission to God, not to your clumsiness."

Washed clean of his former life and shorn of his former identity, Rand was dressed in shirt, hose, and shoes—black, the color of death, that he might never forget his own mortality. Over this he wore a white tunic for purity, then a red cloak of surpassing richness to show his nobility and willingness to shed blood for God and his king.

Jack secured a white belt around Rand's waist. "Another symbol of chastity," he whispered, disgusted. "Would you like me to loosen it, Enguerrand Sans Tache?"

Edward, the portly Duke of York, sniffed. "Mind your manners, varlet."

King Henry's dark eyes glinted beneath a shock of straight brown hair. "Leave off your scolding, cousin. Tom did contrive the title Sans Tache—the Spotless—in jest. And yet . . ." Henry's sharp gaze assessed the aspirant. "I do find it fitting. By my troth, Rand, were you born with that damned saintly countenance, or is it merely an affectation? Never mind, we've a long night ahead of us. We can talk then." He grinned at Rand's thunderstruck look. "Aye," said the king, "I do mean to sit vigil with you."

Rand sank to one knee. "Your Grace, you do me too much honor to stand as my sponsor."

"We shall see, Enguerrand Fitzmarc, if you think that is so on the morrow." King Henry turned and led the way through the winding passageways of Westminster, up two newel staircases from the confessor's chapel, to the chantry Henry had built to honor Bolingbroke, his father. Rand's new weapons and armor lay on the altar steps, his sword on the altar itself.

Courtenay said mass, then intoned, "Hearken, O Lord, to our prayers, and bless with the right hand of Thy majesty this sword with which Thy servant desires to be girded."

Rand stared at the sword, a gift from King Henry. Girded . . . nay, more likely shackled, he thought. Yet the bright blade, wrought of Poitiers steel, inlaid with gold, its cruciform hilt glinting with the single green eye of an emerald, beckoned to something deep inside him.

Following mass, the celebrants filed slowly out of the chapel. Rand remained kneeling before the altar, pondering the sword and all it meant to him.

Henry sat down on a prie-dieu. "I'll stay hard by, to give you encouragement, to prod you if the temptation to sleep becomes too great." Grinning, he added, "Though you're unlikely to fall asleep on your knees."

Rand resisted the urge to shift restlessly. The cold stone flags pressed into his bones.

The king leaned back and crossed his ankles. "You're well formed, Rand Fitzmarc. My brother of Clarence says you once vaulted a battlement at Anjou without a ladder. How tall be you?"

Remembering that an aspirant should pass the night in tacit meditation, Rand lowered his eyes and kept silent.

"Come, you may speak," said the king. "There are things I would know about the man who saved my neck. Did you indeed vault the battlement?"

Rand flushed. "It was a common wall, not a battlement. I heard a woman crying on the other side, saw flames rising. There was no time to call for a ladder."

"I see. So, how tall be you?"

"A hand . . . nay, two, perhaps, past six feet, Your Grace."

"And did you deliver the woman from the flames?"

Rand glanced at his hands, folded in prayer. The knuckles of the left one were sleek with scars. "Aye."

"How came you to learn your battle skills?"

"From my father, Marc de Beaumanoir. He was captured by the Earl of Arundel's men at St.-Malo, and held prisoner at Arundel. He was never able to raise his ransom."

"So he stayed in England, got a son, and raised him up to be a knight," Henry finished, satisfied.

Rand looked up. The king had spoken in French. Politeness dictated that he answer in kind. "He did, *mon sire,* but never found the means for my initiation into knighthood."

"You've earned it by denouncing the Lollard plot. Damned religious zealots!"

Hearing the quiver of pain in the king's voice, Rand said, "*Mon sire,* I do not believe your friend John Oldcastle was among the conspirators at Eltham." One corner of his mouth lifted in a crooked grin. "Oldcastle would never have let me escape."

Henry nodded. "You're right. You're . . ." His voice trailed off, and his eyes danced with a keen light. "You're speaking in French, by God!" He threw his head back, and his laughter ricocheted through the chantry. "Your French is as flawless as your reputation. Faith, but I see the hand of God in this."

Rand felt a prickle of apprehension in his fast-numbing limbs. God's hand lent convenience to many of the young king's schemes.

Henry's laughter stopped abruptly. He leaned toward Rand, eyes ablaze with an inner fire, brighter than the light from the tapers on the altar. "Have you lands?"

"No, Your Grace. I am bastard born, and Beaumanoir was seized by the French Crown."

"Are you betrothed?"

Rand hesitated. The banns had not been posted; Jussie had insisted on waiting until his campaigning with Clarence was over. Still, their vows had been spoken to the stars above the Sussex heaths, long ago. . . .

"Well?" King Henry prodded.

"Not yet, Your Grace, but there is a girl—"

"A commoner?"

"She is not of noble blood, sire, but there is nothing common about her."

Henry smiled. "Spoken as a true knight. But I've your future in hand now." Rising, he melted back into the shadows at the rear of the chantry. Rand heard him summon his advisers from their beds, heard the whispers of a conference, and felt a thin, cold knife blade of foreboding slice into his heart.

At sunrise Rand preceded the king and his nobles and ministers into the yard where the arming would take place. His mind nearly as numb as his limbs, he was clad in hauberk, cuirass, and gauntlets. A white linen *cotte d'armes,* emblazoned with the gold Plantagenet leopard, was drawn over his head. Around Rand's neck hung an amulet, another of King Henry's gifts. The talisman, too, bore the leopard rampant and the motto *A vaillans coeurs riens impossible.* To valiant hearts nothing is impossible.

Symbols and ceremonies, thought Rand. They seemed so strange to a bastard-born horse soldier.

The Earl of Arundel bent and affixed the golden spurs to Rand's heels. "Your father would be right proud, lad, to see you thus," he said.

"Aye," said Rand, "he would." But not Justine. Jussie would know the cost of his new status.

Spurs whirring, Rand approached the king and held out his hand. Henry laid the gleaming naked sword over his palm.

"On this blade," Henry said, "depends not only your life, but the destiny of a kingdom." He girded the sword to Rand's right side, and Rand knelt before him.

"I do mean that, my friend," Henry said. "I intend to grant you lands and a wife, and style you a baron."

Rand's heart raced. Jesu, a title and lands. And a wife. His heart stilled.

"The barony is Bois-Long—Longwood—on the river Somme in Picardy," Henry said. "The lady is the Demoiselle Belliane, niece of the Duke of Burgundy. Her lands rightfully belong to England. I claim her as my subject, and have the right to order her marriage. Burgundy and I have an agreement."

Belliane. She was yet faceless, soulless. But her name skewered Rand's hopes like a flaming arrow.

Eagerly Henry leaned forward. "Bois-Long guards a causeway where an army can cross the Somme. I need a loyal noble stationed there if my campaign to win back my French lands is to succeed."

Dashed dreams and disillusionment raked at Rand's heart.

Henry said, "With your new rank come privileges, my lord, but also responsibilities." His gaze held the fierce power of royal determination. "This alliance is my will."

The king's will. Nothing was more sacred, more compelling. Not even the promise Rand had made to Jussie. The ground beneath his knees felt as if it were falling away. His will rebelled at the idea of going to a hostile land, of marrying a stranger. As Rand Fitzmarc, he might have ducked the obligation. Yet as Baron of Longwood, he had no choice.

Staring hard at the king, he said heavily, "Your will be done, sire."

The king smiled, bent low to give Rand the kiss of peace, and drew his own blade. Bringing the broad side down onto Rand's shoulders, he said, "Rise, Enguerrand Fitzmarc, first Baron of Longwood. Be thou a knight."

Chapter  1

Bois-Long-sur-Somme, Picardy
March 1414

It was her wedding night.

A breeze from the river teased the flame of a cresset lamp, and the shadows in the room flickered. Having been conducted to the nuptial chamber by a host of besotted castle folk, Lianna stood listening until their bawdy chants faded.

She gathered a gossamer robe about her shoulders and went to sit in a window-alcove. Absently tapping her chin with one finger, she listened to the lapping of the river Somme against the stone curtain walls. The dancing, the feasting, the salutes from Chiang's cannons, the endless rounds of toasts to the newly wedded couple, had left her a weary but triumphant bride.

She considered the marriage her greatest victory. Not because her husband was handsome, which he was, nor because he was wealthy, which he wasn't. Nor even because she had found the mate of her heart. Love and romance, she knew, existed only in the whimsical gesso paintings on her solar walls.

Still, triumph rang through her veins. Her marriage to Lazare Mondragon, a Frenchman, shielded her from the English noble who was on his way to wed her at the command of Henry, King of England and pretender to the throne of France. Her life hadn't been the same since King Henry had set his sights on Bois-Long, the gateway to the kingdom of France.

She felt no regret at having defied the English usurper's orders, no shiver of fear when she considered the consequences of her rebellion, because the sovereignty of France was at stake. Besides, a more immediate matter faced her.

A scratching sounded at the door. She jumped, then calmed herself and glided to answer it. Clutching the doorjamb, the caller sagged drunkenly into the room.

"*Nom de Dieu,*" Lianna said with mingled amusement and annoyance. "Look at you, Bonne."

The maid grinned crookedly, her pretty face flushed to ripeness. "Aye, look at me, my lady." Wine-scented breath rushed from her mouth. "*Sainte Vierge!* That devil Roland, he has torn my best bliaut!" Bonne indicated the gaping garment, her big breasts nearly spilling from the bodice.

Her red-rimmed eyes widened as Lianna stepped into a pool of light from the cresset lamp. "By the head of St. Denis, you're already prepared for bed!"

"Somehow, Bonne," Lianna said dryly, "I knew you wouldn't be much help to me tonight."

The maid stamped a slippered foot; the motion made

her lurch. "You should have summoned me."

"I hadn't the heart to pull you away from..." She tapped her chin, thinking. "Whose lap ornament were you tonight? Ah yes, Roland."

"My first duty is to you," Bonne said, then hiccuped softly. "Roland would wait a hundred years for me, anyway," she added matter-of-factly. "At least let me do your hair."

Bonne drew Lianna down to a stool. With the overcautious motions of a drunk, she fetched an ivory comb and freed Lianna's hair from its coif. "Spun by the angels, I always say," she said, pulling the comb through the silvery curtain of straight, fine locks.

"I'd as soon have it cropped by the hand of man," Lianna said, grimacing as the comb snared in a tangle. "Chiang nearly set my head aflame when we were testing those new charges."

"Chiang." Bonne spat the name. "You're too much in the company of that odd Chinaman, my lady. I trust him not."

"You've been listening to the men-at-arms," Lianna chided. "They're jealous because they know Chiang's gunnery can defend Bois-Long better than their swords."

"I know naught of defending a castle. But I do know of pleasing a man. Tonight you'll play the lady instead of dabbling in warfare like a soldier. Perhaps a woman's pleasures will turn you from a man's pursuits."

Lianna sat still as Bonne unstopped a bottle of fragrant oil and anointed her, secreting the scent of lilies at her nape and temples, between her breasts and at the backs of her knees. Despite her drunken state, the maid's hand was steady as she imbued Lianna's lips and cheeks with a discreet mist of rouge.

Bonne stepped back and gasped in admiration. "By St. Wilgefort's beard!" She took up a polished-steel mirror and angled it toward Lianna. "You look like a princess."

Lianna frowned at her image. The pale robe fluttered against her willow-slim form; her hair hung in drifts around her oval-shaped face. Her customary look of arrogance, worn to hide the intrepid dreamer deep inside, made her delicate features seem hard tonight, hard and bloodless.

"How can you scowl at being so favored?" Bonne demanded.

Lianna shrugged and eyed her maid's ripe bosom and bold smile. "In sooth, Bonne, you have the looks that turn heads. Besides, an agreeable face doesn't win a kingdom, nor does it endure."

"Happily for you, your beauty has endured into your twenty-first year, my lady. You look far younger. I was beginning to think your uncle the duke would have to drive you to the altar at sword point. Think you he'll approve of your Lazare?"

Lianna swallowed. "My uncle of Burgundy will send his spurs spinning into oblivion when he learns what I've done."

"Aye, I've always thought he wanted better for you."

Privately Lianna agreed. She'd often wondered why Uncle Jean had never pressed her to wed but was too content in her spinsterhood to question him. Now King Henry had forced her out of that comfortable state.

A burst of noise from the hall drifted in through the window, along with a breeze tinged by the smell of the river and the lingering acrid odor of Chiang's fireworks. Bonne put away the mirror. "I'd best leave you to your husband. My lady . . . you must be biddable and patient with him. . . ."

Flushing, Lianna raised a hand to forestall her maid. "Don't worry, Bonne." Women's talk made her ill at ease; she had no interest in secrets whispered behind a damsel's hand. She propelled Bonne toward the door. "I daresay I'll survive my wedding night. Go and find your Roland." The girl swayed down the narrow spiral of stairs.

Lianna returned to her solar to ponder that mysterious, much lauded act that would solidify her marriage to Lazare Mondragon. With a stab of loss, she thought of her mother, long dead of drowning. Dame Irène might have guided her this night, might have prepared her to receive her husband.

Glancing at the gesso mural, Lianna watched the firelight flicker over a detail of a young woman reading to a child from a psalter. Again Lianna searched her memory for her mother but found only a whisper of rose-sweet fragrance, the ghost of a cool hand against her brow, the soft tones of a female voice. She might have told stories to me, Lianna mused.

Shaking her head, she tossed aside the useless sentiment. She had no place in her life for pretty stories and games. Fate had left her to learn on her own, to approach every task with calculated logic.

She faced marriage in the same dispassionate manner. When the English king's envoy had arrived three weeks earlier ordering her to marry a baron who styled himself Enguerrand of Longwood, she'd begun a swift, methodical search for an eligible Frenchman who didn't fear her powerful uncle. In Lazare Mondragon, she'd found him. Sufficiently needy to be dazzled by her dowry, and sufficiently greedy to flout the duke, Lazare had proved instantly agreeable. The castle chaplain—aging, senile—hadn't insisted on a lengthy reading of banns.

The door swung open. With stiff movements Lianna inclined her shining head. *"Mon sire."*

Lazare Mondragon stepped inside. He was resplendent in his wedding costume, from the velvet *capuchon* on his graying head to his narrow pointed shoes. The shimmering cresset flame lit his handsome features—a strong nose, angular chin, and dark, deep-set eyes. Taking Lianna's hand, he brushed it with dry lips.

The brief contact ignited a flicker of trepidation in her. She snuffed it quickly and said, "Is all well in the hall?"

"My son Gervais and his wife have won the hearts of the castle folk, Gervais with his bold tales and Macée with her pretty singing." Lazare's voice rang with fatherly pride.

She studied his lined face. The shadowy eyes looked world-weary, the eyes of a stranger she'd met only six days before. He lacked the eagerness of a new bridegroom. She pushed aside the notion. Of course he wouldn't look eager. Lazare was a widower, her senior by twenty-five years. But he was French, and that was enough for Lianna.

She poured wine into a mazer and handed it to him.

"Thank you, Belliane," he said absently.

"Please, Lazare, I do go by my familiar name."

"Of course. Lianna."

Smiling, she filled another cup and lifted it. "A toast, to the deliverance of Bois-Long from English hands."

A frown corrupted the smoothness of Lazare's brow. "That's what you wanted all along, isn't it, Lianna?"

The bitterness of his tone sparked a flash of understanding in her. Crossing to his side, she laid her hand on his arm. "I never pretended otherwise."

He shook her off and turned away. "I was quite cheaply bought, was I not?"

"We were two people in need, you and I. That our marriage answered those needs is no cause for shame." She faced the window and looked out at the beloved, moonlit water meadows surrounding Bois-Long. "We can be well content here, Lazare, united against the English."

He drank deeply of his wine. "Longwood could arrive any day now, expecting a bride. What will he do when he finds you've already wed?"

"Pah! He'll turn his cowardly tail back to England."

"What if he challenges us?"

"He's probably old and feeble. I have no fear of him."

"You're not afraid of anything, are you, Lianna." It was more an accusation than a tribute.

Nom de Dieu, he did not know her at all. Soon enough, no doubt, some loose-tongued castle varlet would tell him of her soul-shattering terror of the water, that childhood nightmare that plagued her yet as an adult.

"I fear some things. But I won't waste the sentiment on this Baron of Longwood." With distaste she recalled his flowery missive, scented with roses and sealed with a leopard rampant device. "In fact, I look forward to sending him on his way." She touched her chin. "I've been thinking of saluting him with Chiang's new culverin, the one on the pivoting gun carriage. . . ."

"It's all a damned game to you, isn't it?" Lazare burst out, his eyes flaring. "We court the disfavor of the two most powerful men in all Christendom, yet you talk of cannon charges and fireworks."

Although dismayed by Lazare's mood, Lianna bit back

a retort. "Then let's talk of other things," she said. "It is our wedding night, *mon mari.*"

"I've not forgotten," he muttered, and poured himself another draught of wine.

She almost smiled at the irony of the situation. Wasn't it the bride who was supposed to be nervous? And yet, while she faced her duty matter-of-factly, Lazare seemed distracted, hesitant.

"We've bound our lives before God," she said. "Now we must solidify the vow." Dousing a sizzle of apprehension, she went to the heavily draped bed and shrugged out of her robe. Naked, she slipped between the herb-scented linens and leaned back against the figured oak headboard.

Lazare approached, drew back the drapes, uttered a soft curse, and said, "You're a beautiful young woman."

Her brow puckered; the statement was not tendered as a compliment.

Cursing again, he jerked the coverlet up to her neck. "It's time we understood each other, Lianna. I'll be your husband in name only."

The sting of rejection buried itself in her heart. Ten years without a father, seventeen without a mother, had left scars she'd hoped her marriage would heal. "But I thought— Is it King Henry or my uncle? Are you so afraid of them?"

"No. That has nothing to do with it."

"Then do you find me lacking?"

"No! Lianna, leave off your questioning. The fault doesn't lie with you." Lazare's eyes raked her shrouded form. "You are magnificent, with your hair of silk and sweet, soft skin of cream. Were I a poet, I'd write a song solely on the beauty of your silver eyes."

The tribute stunned and confused her. He laid his hand, dry and cool, upon her cheek. "You've the face of a madonna, the body of a goddess. Any man would move mountains to possess you!"

The stillness between them drew on. A faint crackle from the fire and the hiss of the ever-shifting river pervaded the chamber.

Lazare jerked back his hand. "Any man..." He laughed harshly. "Except me. One of the wenches downstairs will have to do as a receptacle for the unslaked lust you inspire."

Lianna shivered. "Lazare, I don't understand."

He leaned against a bedpost. "This marriage is one of mutual convenience. No children must come of our union."

"Bois-Long needs an heir," she said softly. And in her heart she needed a child. Desperately.

"Bois-Long *has* an heir," said Lazare. "My son, Gervais."

A cold hand took hold of her heart and squeezed. "You can't do this to me," she said, clutching the sheets against her as she sat forward in anger. "The château is my ancestral home, defended by my father, Aimery the Warrior, and his kinsmen before him. I won't allow your son to usurp—"

"You have no choice now, Lianna." Lazare smiled. "You thought yourself so clever, marrying in defiance of King Henry's wishes. But you overlooked one matter. I am not a pawn in your ploy for power. I'm a man with a mind of my own and a son who deserves better than I've given him. My life ended when my first wife died, but Gervais's is just beginning."

"My uncle will arrange an annulment. You and your

greedy son will have nothing of Bois-Long."

Lazare shook his head. "If you let me go, no one will stand in the way of the Englishman who is coming to marry you. Your uncle of Burgundy has been known to treat with King Henry. He may force you to accept the English *god-don*. Besides, you've no grounds for annulment. We are married in the eyes of God and France."

"But you yourself have decreed that it is to be a chaste union!"

"So shall it be." With a smooth movement, Lazare drew a misericorde from his baldric. Shocked by the dull glint of the pointed blade, Lianna leapt from the bed, shielding herself with the coverlet. Lazare chuckled. "Don't worry, wife, I'll not add murder to my offenses." Still smiling, he pricked his palm with the knife and let a few ruby droplets of blood stain the sheet.

Lianna bit her lip. In sooth she'd never quite understood where a maid's blood came from; it was destined to remain a mystery still.

"Now," he said, putting away the misericorde, "it is your word against mine. And I am your lord."

She clutched the bedclothes tighter. "You used me."

He nodded. "Just as you used me. I'm tired, Lianna. I'll pass the night on cushions in the wardrobe, so that no one will look askance at us. After a few days I'll be sleeping in the lord's chamber—alone."

"I'll fight you, Lazare. I won't let Gervais have Bois-Long."

Giving her a long, bleak stare, he left the solar. A river breeze snuffed the lamp. Lianna crept back into bed, avoiding the stain of Lazare's blood, and lay sleepless. What manner of man was Lazare Mondragon, that he would not take his bride to wife on his wedding night? *Her* wedding night.

Moonlight streamed into the room, casting silvery tones on the pastoral scene painted on the wall. Beyond the woman and her children, a richly robed knight knelt before an ethereal beauty, gazing at her with a look of pure, mystical ecstasy.

An artist's fancy, Lianna told herself angrily, turning away from the wall. An idealized picture of love. But she couldn't suppress her disappointment. The whimsical dreamer she so carefully hid beneath her armor of aloofness had hoped to find contentment with Lazare.

Instead, she realized bitterly, the sentence of a loveless, fruitless marriage hung over her. No, she thought in sudden decision. Lazare was wrong to think she'd relinquish her castle without a fight. She wrested the wedding ring from her finger. "I am still the Demoiselle de Bois-Long," she whispered.

The chaplain's rapidly muttered low mass was sufficient to satisfy the consciences of the castle folk. Grateful for the brevity, Lianna sped to the great hall.

After nudging a lazy alaunt hound out the door, she stopped a passing maid. "It smells like a brewery in here, Edithe. Fetch some dried bay to sweeten the rushes."

The maid bustled off, and Lianna crossed to the large central hearth, where Guy, her seneschal, stood over a scullion who was cleaning out the grate. Guy, a gentle giant of a man, ruffled the lad's hair and chuckled at some joke. Both came to grave attention as Lianna approached.

Once, she thought, just once I wish they'd share their mirth with me. But her aloofness, cultivated to augment the authority she so feared to lose, did not invite intimacy.

"Are the stores in the kitchens adequate?" she asked Guy.

He nodded. "We've yet a side of beef, and fresh eels, too. Wine's a bit diminished after last night, but it'll suffice."

"Are the stables cleaned and stocked?"

Another nod.

She took a deep breath. "Gervais and his wife?" Her tongue thickened over the name of her stepson. Did he know of his father's plan?

Guy's face was expressionless. "Stumbled abed not an hour ago, my lady."

Fine, she thought. Gervais would have no part in running the castle. "My . . . husband?" She faltered over the word.

"Out riding the fields with the reeve, my lady."

He would be, she thought darkly. Inspecting his new acquisitions, no doubt. Stifling a feeling of despair, she turned and spied Edithe returning. The maid dropped a handful of bay leaves onto a fresh bundle of rushes. "*Nom de Dieu,*" Lianna snapped, "they must be spread out, like so." She took a twig broom from the girl and scattered the leaves.

Sulkily Edithe took the broom and set to sweeping. Spying the scullion staggering beneath a bucket of ashes from the grate, Lianna hastened to propel him out the door before he spilled his burden on the new rushes. He made it as far as the stone steps; then the ashes fell in a gray heap. A stiff breeze blew them back in again. Catching Lianna's look, Edithe hurried over to ply her broom.

Lianna leaned her head against the figured stone of the doorway and sighed, thinking again of her mother. It was said that Dame Irène, singularly unattractive but beloved by her handsome husband, had been a gifted chatelaine. Guy, who was old enough to remember her, often said Irène's success stemmed from the devotion her sweet nature inspired in the castle folk.

Lianna knew she possessed no such endearing quality. She directed every task with immutable logic, her manner distant yet implacable. Her thoroughness amazed the devoted members of the château staff and dismayed those who tried to shirk their duties. Yet no one, perhaps not even Chiang, understood that beneath her cool mien lived a lonely soul who did not know how to spark warmth in others.

Troubled by Lazare's duplicity and seeking answers for her dilemma, Lianna rode out alone that morning. She crossed the causeway that spanned the Somme, then paused to look back at the château. The quiet impregnability of the stone keep, stout curtain walls, and limewashed towers comforted her. A month ago she had no adversary save droughts and hard freezes that threatened her crops. Now she had enemies within, enemies without.

She vowed to contend with each. Never would she let the castle fall to Lazare's son. Nor would she allow Longwood's leopard standard to supplant the golden trefoil lilies that now waved over the ramparts of Bois-Long.

As she nudged her horse into the long stretch of woods leading to the sea, the restful harmony of the landscape enveloped her. She found solace in the reflection of cottony clouds in the river, the calm strength of ancient beeches, the deep peace of cows udder deep in grass.

She did not stop until she reached the sheer, windswept cliffs overlooking the roaring Norman sea. Her fear of water held something of a horrifying fascination; simply looking at the churning swells made her tremble. Dismounting, she approached the lip of a cliff. Her palms grew damp; her breath came in curiously exhilarating shallow gasps. She sat on the promontory, hugging her knees to her chest, watching the white spray as it battered the rocks. Behind her reared a cleft of dark gray shale where she and Chiang mined sulfur for their gunpowder.

Yesterday morn, at her nuptial mass, she'd listened to the recitation of the Hours of the Blessed Virgin and dreamed of the children Lazare would give her. Children to bring to this beautiful, wind-worn place, to share the dreams she'd never dared reveal.

No children must come of our union. Lazare's sentence rang like a death knell in her head. Lianna had never felt so alone. She buried her face in her arms and anointed her sleeves with hot, bitter tears.

The ship appeared while she wept. It was suddenly there when she looked up, a beautiful four-masted cog bounding over undulating swells. Sails painted with whimsical dragons and writhing serpents puffed like the breasts of great, colorful birds over the hull. Shields emblazoned with a leopard rampant flanked the ship's sides.

She recognized the device from Longwood's letter and King Henry's written order. Her heart catapulted to her throat.

The English baron had arrived.

Chapter  2

From the deck of the *Toison d'Or,* Rand studied the Norman coastline. Squinting through a dazzle of sunlight against the chalky cliffs, he watched a pale rider mount a horse and gallop toward two dark gray clefts of rock. In moments the lithe horseman was gone, like a fleeting silver shadow.

Unhappy that his arrival had sparked immediate fear, he moved down the decks. Eu, the town where he planned to land, huddled against the tall cliffs. Denuded orchards and burnt fields, remnants of turmoil, lay about the village. France was a hostile, war-torn land, plundered by its own knights and the *chevauchées* of the English. Atrocities committed by the nobility had schooled mistrust into the plain folk of France. Rand resolved that when he took his place at Bois-Long, he would prove himself different from those greedy noblemen.

A swarm of tanned and wiry sailors climbed barefoot up the rigging to reef the sails for landing. The chains of the anchor ground as a seaman studied his knotted rope and called out the depth. Horses in the hold stamped and whinnied. The winds and weather had been relentlessly favorable, shortening the voyage from Southampton to a mere three days.

Rand was in no hurry to reach his objective, despite King Henry's impatience to secure a path into the heart of France.

A moan sounded. His face a sickly pale green, Jack Cade staggered to Rand's side. "I'll never get seasoned to these goddamned crossings," he grumbled. "Praise St. George I'll be on dry land ere nightfall, upon a sound bed . . . and, if I be lucky, between a woman's thighs."

Rand laughed. "Women. You use them too carelessly."

"And you use them not at all, my lord."

"They are meant to be protected, revered."

Jack belched, grimaced, and scratched his unshaven cheek. "Faith, my lord, I know not how you quell your man's body into submission."

"It's all part of a knight's discipline."

"Remind me never to become a knight. I'll get no comfort from golden spurs."

Rand regarded his scutifer with affection. The droll face, the merry eyes brimming with earthy humor, marked a man whose feet were planted firmly on the ground, happily distant from the unforgiving demands of chivalry. "Little danger of that," Rand remarked, "given your complete aversion to anything resembling high ideals and saintly devotion."

"Goddamned right," Jack said, and leaned over the side to heave. The bright, mocking laughter of a sailor drifted across the deck. Turning with elaborate casualness, Jack dropped his breeches and presented his backside to the seaman. A chorus of whistles and catcalls arose.

"You'll not catch a fish on that shrunken worm," remarked a seaman.

Jack hitched up his breeches and thumbed his nose.

Grinning and shaking his head, Rand looked again at the coast rearing ahead of the bounding ship. He'd crossed the Narrow Sea numerous times, under the colors of the Duke of Clarence, and usually he felt a surge of anticipation at the sight. This time he came in peace yet felt only dread, like a hollow chamber in his heart. His arrival heralded the end of the dreams he'd shared with Jussie, changed the path his life would have taken. That it also heralded the beginning of King Henry's grand scheme gave him little enough comfort.

"My lord," said Jack, "you've been too silent these days past. Are we not boon companions? Tell me what troubles that too pretty head of yours."

His hands gripping the rail, Rand asked, "Why me? Why did the king choose me to defend this French territory?"

A grin split Jack's pale face, and the wind ruffled his shock of red hair. "To reward you for exposing the Lollard plot at Eltham. And Burgundy's envoys gave it out that the duke would have only the finest of men for his niece."

Rand held silent; honor forbade him to voice his thoughts on the liberties Henry and Burgundy had taken with his life.

"You should be thankful," said Jack. "Your new rank gives you a rich wife and her château. What had you at Arundel save a meager virgate to plow and a burden of boonwork to the earl?"

Rand looked at him sharply, felt a rattle of longing in his chest. "I had much more than that."

The corners of Jack's mouth pulled downward. "Your Justine. How did she take the news of your betrothal?"

Rand stared at the white breakers exploding against the cliffs. The seascape gave way to Jussie, sweet as cream and biddable as a lamb. As children they'd raced laughing through the ripening wheat that clothed the gentle landscape of Sussex. As youths they'd shared shy kisses, whispered promises. She'd listened to his songs and his dreams; he'd watched her clever fingers at their carding and spinning. He thought he loved her; at least he felt an affection and concern deep enough to control his manly urges and remain loyal. He'd wanted to plight his troth to her years before but couldn't subject Jussie to the uncertain existence of a horse soldier's wife.

Now it was too late. His grip tightened on the rail. Justine had taken the news with surprising aplomb. "'Tis fitting," she'd said simply. "Your father was of noble blood, and French." At first her response had confused him. Where was her outrage, her weeping, her defiance? She had merely bade him adieu and pledged herself as a novice at a convent.

Rand attributed the gentle reaction to her serene inner strength and admired her all the more for it. When he turned to answer Jack's query, hopeless longing creased his fine-featured face. "Justine understood," he said quietly.

"Perhaps it's for the best. I always thought you two a mismatched pair."

Rand glared.

"I'm only saying that you're very different, as different

as a hawk from a songbird. Justine is passing sweet and retiring, while you are a man of action."

"She was good for me," Rand insisted.

Jack raised a canny eyebrow. "Was she? Hah! Other than keeping you to your inhuman vow of chastity, she had no real power over you, offered you no challenge."

"Had anyone save you made that observation, Jack, his face would have swiftly met with my fist."

Jack brandished his maimed hand. Three fingers had been severed to stumps. "You're ever so tolerant of a cripple."

Rand clasped that hand, that archer's hand that had been ruined by a vindictive French knight so Jack might never draw his longbow again. "Soon we will both live in this hostile place."

"Think you the woman will prove hostile?"

"I don't know. But she's twenty-one years old. Why has she never married?"

"You don't want to think about that," said Jack. He extracted his hand and spat into the sea. "You're determined not to like her, aren't you, my lord?"

"How can I, when she stands between Jussie and me?"

Jack shook his russet head. "You know better than that. 'Twas the king's edict that took you away from Justine."

"I know." Rand let out his breath in a frustrated burst of air. Ever loyal, he said, "I cannot fault Henry. Longwood is vital to him. He's trying to secure it peaceably, and this is the best way he knows." Rand tried to fill his empty heart with a feeling of high purpose, of destiny. It felt cold, like a draught of bitter ale after a cup of warm mead. "I suppose winning back the French Crown is larger than one man's desires."

* * *

Presently the *Toison d'Or* dropped anchor in the small, quiet harbor of Eu. Wedged between the granite cliffs, the town seemed deserted. Disembarking with his contingent of eight men-at-arms, his squire, Simon, the priest Batsford, and numerous horses and longbows, Rand recalled the ruined fields he'd observed. His shoulders tensed with wariness.

"Goddamned town's empty," said Jack. "I like it not."

Their footsteps crunched over shells and pebbles littering the road, and the wind keened a wasting melody between the shuttered stone-and-thatch cottages.

His sword slapping against his side, Rand approached a large, lopsided building. Above the door, a crude sign bearing a sheaf of wheat flapped creakily. A faint mewing sound slipped through the wail of the wind. Rand looked down. A skinny black-and-white kitten crouched behind an upended barrel. Unthinking, he scooped it up. As starved for contact as for food, the kitten burrowed into his broad palm and set to purring.

"I puke my way across the Narrow Sea and for what?" Jack grumbled. "A goddamned cat."

"Easy, Jack," Rand said. "Maybe she'll let you sleep with her." The men chuckled but continued darting cautious glances here and there as if half-afraid of what they might see.

Rand shouldered open the door to the inn. Afternoon light stole weakly through two parchment-paned windows, touching a jumble of overturned stools, tables, and broken crockery. The central grate was cold, the burnt logs lying like gray-white ghosts, ready to crumble at the slightest breath.

Absently Rand stroked the kitten. "The town's been

hit by brigands. Lamb of God, the French prey upon their own."

"And leave us naught," Jack said, scowling at an empty wall cupboard. The other men entered the taproom. Jack looked at Rand. "Now what, my lord?"

A chunk of plaster fell from the ceiling and landed squarely on Jack's head. He choked and cursed through a cloud of dust.

Rand's eyes traveled the length of the ceiling. In one corner a small opening was covered with planks. "There's someone in the loft," he said. Ducking beneath beams too low to accommodate his height, he knocked lightly on the planks.

"We come in peace," he said in French. "Show yourselves. We'll not harm you."

He heard shuffling, and more plaster fell. The planks shifted. Rand saw first a great hook of a nose, then a thin face sculpted by sea winds, its high brow age-spotted and crowned with a sprinkling of colorless hair. Sharp eyes blinked at Rand.

"Are you an Englishman?"

Rand rubbed absently behind the kitten's scraggly ears. "I am a friend. Come down, sir."

The face disappeared. A muffled conversation ensued above. An argument, by the sound of it, punctuated by female voices and the occasional whine of a child. Presently a rough ladder emerged from the opening. The old man descended.

"I am Lajoye, keeper of the Sheaf of Wheat."

"I am Enguerrand Fitzmarc," said Rand. "Baron of Bois-Long." Yet unused to his new title, he spoke with some embarrassment.

"Bois-Long?" Lajoye scratched his grizzled head. "I

did not know it to be an English holding."

"All Picardy belongs to the English, but a few thick-heads in Paris refuse to admit it."

Lajoye glanced distrustfully at the men standing in his taproom. "You do not come to make *chevauchée*?"

"No. I've cautioned my men strictly against plundering. I come to claim a bride, sir."

Interest lit the old pale eyes. "*Ça alors,*" he said. "Burgundy's niece, the Demoiselle de Bois-Long?"

Rand handed him a stack of silver coins. "I'd like to bide here, sir, while I send word to her and await her reply."

Lajoye turned toward the loft and rasped an order. One by one the people emerged: Lajoye's plump wife, two sons of an age with Rand, and six children. More noises issued from the loft.

"The others, sir?" Rand said.

Lajoye glared at the men-at-arms, who were shuffling about impatiently. Instantly Rand understood the old man's concern. "The first of my men to lay a hand on an unwilling woman," he said, touching the jeweled pommel of his sword, "will lose that hand to my blade."

Lajoye stared at him for a long, measuring moment, then flicked his eyes to Robert Batsford, the priest. Although he preferred hefting a longbow to lifting the Host, Batsford also had an uncanny talent for affecting an attitude of saintly piety. "You may take His Lordship at his word," he said, his moon-shaped face solemn, his round-toned voice sincere.

Apparently satisfied, Lajoye called out, and the women appeared. Children dove for the skirts of the first two; the second two, their hair unbound in maidenly fashion, stood back, fearfully eyeing Rand and his soldiers.

Lamb of God, Rand thought, they must live like rats scuttling in fear of their own kind. Eager to show his good faith, he turned to his men. "Set the room to rights, send for the ship's stores, and arm yourselves." He handed the black-and-white kitten to a little girl. "We'll ride out after the brigands. Perhaps we can recover some of the plunder."

As the men set about their tasks, Lajoye eyed Rand with new respect. "Your name would be blessed if you could return the pyx those devils stole from our chapel."

"I'll try, Lajoye." Rand moved out into the dooryard, where Simon was saddling his horse.

Lajoye followed. With a gnarled hand he stroked the high-arched neck of the percheron. "So, you lay claim to Bois-Long."

Rand nodded. "Do you object to my claim?"

Lajoye heaved a dusty sigh. "As a Frenchman, I suppose I should. But as an innkeeper seeking a peaceful existence, I care not, so long as you keep your word on forbidding plunder." He spat on the ground. "The French knights, they ravage our land, rape our women."

Rand tensed. "Would the brigands attack Bois-Long?"

"No, the château is too well fortified. Have you never seen it, my lord?"

Rand shook his head.

"The first keep of Bois-Long was built by the Lionheart himself. Your sons will be wealthy."

Rand furrowed his fingers through his golden hair. "As will this district, if I have my way. Do you know the demoiselle?"

"I've never met the lady, but I once saw her mother at Michaelmas time, years ago."

"What was she like?" Rand asked.

Lajoye shook his head. "What can I say of the sister of Jean Sans Peur?" He grinned impishly. "Her face would better suit a horse—and not necessarily its front end. Like her brother, she wasn't favored by beauty."

Rand tried to laugh at the jest. "Pray God she wasn't like Burgundy in character, either," he said under his breath, thinking of the dark deeds credited to the ruthless duke.

"The father of your intended, the Sire de Bois-Long, was a fine man by all reports, and handsome as a prince. Perhaps 'tis he, Aimery the Warrior, the daughter favors."

As he rode out in pursuit of the brigands, Rand clung to the possibility Lajoye had planted in his mind. God, let her be handsome and fine like her father.

Thrusting aside the thought, he moved restlessly in the saddle and waved two of his men toward the south. The hoofmarks on the forest floor were scattered; doubtless the brigands had separated. Rand didn't mind riding alone. The events of the past few weeks had given him a restless energy, a coiled strength. He'd gladly unleash that power on brigands who robbed old men, widows, and orphans.

As he rode beneath the grayish branches of poplars, he noticed a carved stone marker in the weeds. A single stylized flower—the fleur-de-lis—rose above a wavy pattern. With a jolt, he recognized the device of Bois-Long. Burningly curious, he tethered his horse and approached on foot.

Skirting a cluster of half-timbered peasants' dwellings and farm buildings, he walked toward the river until the twin stone towers of the castle barbican reared before him.

He stifled a gasp of admiration. Thick walls, crowned

by finials, encompassed a keep of solid beauty, with slender round towers and tall windows, a cruciform chapel, an iron-toothed portcullis beneath the barbican.

Stone creatures of whimsy glared from the gunports, griffins and gorgons' heads defying all comers to breach the walls they guarded. Like an islet formed by man, the château sat surrounded by water. The deep river coursed in front, while a moat curved around the back, which faced north. A long causeway—the structure Henry so coveted—spanned the Somme.

This is my home, thought Rand. King Henry has given me this; I need only be bold enough to take it. But not yet, he cautioned himself, moving back toward the woods. There is carelessness in haste.

He passed brakes of willows, stands of twisted oaks, and his thoughts drifted back to his bride. Belliane, the Demoiselle de Bois-Long. The lioness in her den. Rand smiled away the notion. He had the might of England and the right of seisin behind him. How could she possibly oppose him?

Her weaponry concealed beneath a long brown cloak, Lianna slipped beneath the archway of the barbican. Jufroy, who guarded the river gate, inclined his head.

"Out for a walk, my lady?"

She paused, nodded.

"I should think you'd stay hard by your husband."

I'd sooner stay hard by a serpent, she thought. "Lazare is out riding again with the reeve."

"Don't stray far, my lady. We've had word *les écorcheurs* hit a coastal village yesterday."

Lianna intended to go very far indeed but saw no need to worry Jufroy. "Then they will be long gone. Besides, no brigands dare approach Bois-Long. Not with our new cannons on their rotating carriages. They'll blow any intruders to Calais."

Jufroy grunted and stared straight ahead at the causeway stretching across the river. Lianna realized she had stung the sentry's pride by implying that the cannon, not the valor of the men-at-arms, was responsible for the impregnable status of Bois-Long. She stepped toward him. "A cannon is useless without strong men and quick minds to put it to use."

Jufroy's expression softened. "Have a care on your forays."

As always, Lianna crossed the causeway without looking down. To look down was to see the dark shimmer of water between the planks, to feel the dizzy nausea of unconquerable fear. She concentrated instead on the solidity of the thick timber beneath her feet and the sound of her wooden sabots clunking against the planks.

An hour's walk brought her to the very heart of the manor lands, far enough from the château to test her new weapon in private. The castle folk feared the cannons; surely this gun would send them shrieking. Another hour's walk would bring her to Eu, where the Englishmen were doubtless billeting themselves among the townspeople. Lianna shivered. No need to venture there. The usurping baron would find her soon enough. She clenched her hand around the gun. She would be ready.

Pulling off her cloak and untying her apron, heavy with bags of powder and shot, she smiled. Chiang had cast the handgun for her as a wedding gift. Chiang alone understood her fascination with gunnery and, like her, believed that firepower in the right hands was the ultimate defense.

She hefted the wooden shaft and curved her fingers around the brass barrel. A bit of Chiang's artistic whimsy, a tiny brass lily, stood over the touchhole. She ran her hand over the slim, angled rod of the gunlock, then murmured the customary blessing for a gun. *"Eler Elphat Sebastian non sit Emanuel benedicite."*

Turning, she spied a plump leveret some yards distant. The rabbit, heedless of Lianna's presence, nosed idly among a stand of sweetbriar. A live target. The perfect test for the efficacy of her gun. If Longwood proved difficult, it would behoove her to learn to use it well.

A little sizzle of exhilaration shot down her spine as she made the sign of the cross over a small lead ball and fitted it into the barrel. Remembering Chiang's instructions, she crumbled a cake of corned powder into the removable breech. The charge seemed so meager that she added more, then lit a slow match of tow soaked in Peter's salt. Fitting the smoking match into the end of the lock, she sank down on one knee and laid the shaft over her shoulder.

Blinking against the acrid smoke that smarted her eyes, she sighted down the stock at her quarry, her hand tensing. Steady, she told herself. A gun is useless in nervous hands. She closed one eye, drew a deep breath, let exactly half of it escape her, and slowly, steadily, began pressing on the lock.

"Poachers do favor the crossbow, *pucelle,* because it has the advantage of silence," said a whisper-soft voice behind her.

Surprised beyond caution, Lianna let her hand clutch involuntarily around the lock. The slow match delved into the firing pan.

The ear-splitting explosion deafened her, seared her

nostrils with the smell of overheated sulfur. The shaft of the gun recoiled violently, catapulting her backward against something large, warm . . . and breathing.

Furious at her stupidity in overloading the charge, she scrambled away on hands and knees, prepared to vent her rage on the man-at-arms who'd dared follow her from the château.

She turned.

He smiled.

The impact of her gape-mouthed surprise and his devastating smile sapped her will to rise. Bracing her hands behind her, she stared upward, her astonished gaze traveling a seemingly endless length of broad, blond man.

He picked up the gun, set it aside, and spoke. She couldn't hear him for the ringing in her ears. Her first thought, if something so absurd could be termed a thought, was that she'd happened upon a mythical Norse deity, a golden forest divinity returned from days of old. For surely a body of such massive power, a face of such sheer beauty, could not possibly be human.

The vision extended a big, squarish hand. Lianna shrank back, afraid that if she touched him, he'd shimmer away like a will-o'-the-wisp from the marshes. His lips were moving; still she could not hear. He cocked his head to one side, his expression mild, quizzical, and perhaps a little amused.

This was no vengeful warrior god from the North, but a more forgiving creature. An angel, perhaps . . . no, an archangel, for surely only one of the very highest rank could be favored with that clean, powerful bone structure, the chaste innocence that imbued his beautiful smiling mouth and eyes with such heavenly character.

His eyes were not simply green, she noted wildly, but

the pure color of a new leaf shot through by sunlight. In their depths she perceived the pain and devotion of the saints in the colored windows of a chapel.

He spoke again, and this time she heard: "Don't be afraid of me." He reached down, grasped her by the waist, and pulled her effortlessly to her feet.

In that instant she realized her reckless flight of fantasy for what it was. His hold was firm, his voice a rich velvet ripple over her scattered senses. It was a man's body pressing against hers, a man's voice caressing her ears.

Alarmed, she pulled back. "Who are you?"

He hesitated, just for the upbeat of her heart. "Rand," he said simply. "And you, *pucelle?*"

She, too, hesitated. *Pucelle,* he called her. A maid. What would this man say if he knew he was speaking to the Demoiselle de Bois-Long? Absently she tapped her chin. The novelty of anonymity intrigued her. The necessity of it, because Lazare had destroyed any trust she might have in a stranger, made her say only, "Lianna."

"Your face is completely black, Lianna."

Vaguely annoyed at the mixture of humor and censure dancing in his leaf-green eyes, she lifted her hand, touched her cheek, and looked at her fingertips. Black as soot. At least the concealing powder hid the hot blush pouring into her cheeks.

"I . . . mismeasured the charge," she said.

"So it seems." He took her hands and drew her down to sit on a bed of dry bracken. "I know little of such things."

"*Nom de Dieu,* but I do," she said with self-contempt. "I should have trusted the precision of science instead of my own eyes."

"*Alors, pucelle,* how does one so fair possess a knowledge so deadly?"

She realized anew that it would not do to reveal herself to this stranger. If he were a brigand, he'd consider the Demoiselle de Bois-Long a valuable hostage. And if he were an Englishman . . . She dismissed the notion. The stranger's French was not corrupted by the broad, flat tones of a foreigner. "My . . . father was a gunner. He indulged my interest."

He frowned at the blackened gun. "Then your father was a fool."

She thrust up her chin but resisted the urge to defend her father and sink deeper into untruths.

"Hold still," he said. "I'll clean you off."

She was never one to obey orders, but, unrecovered from the shock of the explosion and the surprise of meeting this mesmerizing stranger, she sat unmoving. He reached beneath his mail shirt, pulled out a small cloth bundle, and unwrapped a loaf of bread. With the cloth, he began cleansing her face. His light, gentle strokes felt soothing, but the odd intimacy of the gesture revived her anger.

"Why did you sneak upon me? You ruined my aim."

"That," he said, brushing her chin, "was my intent. The leveret was a doe, and nursing."

She scowled. "How could you tell that?"

"Her shape. She was not as plump as she looked, only appeared so because her dugs were full."

Lianna prayed he'd not yet revealed enough of her face to discern her new blush.

"You wouldn't have wished to slay a nursing mother, would you?"

"Of course not. I just hadn't thought on it."

He held out the loaf to her. "Bread?"

"Thank you, no. I wasn't hunting my dinner."

"Blood sport, then?" he asked, mildly accusing.

"*Nom de Dieu,* I am not a wanton killer. I merely wished to test my gun on a moving target."

"I doubt Mistress Rabbit would have appreciated the difference."

She shrugged. "I probably would have missed anyway. My aim is imprecise, the weapon passing crude."

Like a parent wiping away a child's tear, he daubed the delicate flesh beneath her left eye. "Your eyes are silver, *pucelle.*"

"Gray."

"Silver, like the underside of a cloud at dawn."

"Gray, like the stone walls of a keep during a siege."

"Argue not, *pucelle.* I've a sense about such things. Stone does not capture the light and reflect it, while your eyes"—he cleansed beneath her right one—"most assuredly do."

Bit by bit, Rand uncovered the face beneath the soot. As he worked, his amazement and fascination grew like a bud warmed by the sun. He'd come to survey the area for brigands and have a glimpse of his barony. Instead he'd found a beautiful girl and a deadly weapon, two surprises and one of them curiously welcome.

Moving aside a pale lock of hair, he brushed the last of the soot from her cheeks. Black dust clung stubbornly to her brows and lashes, but at last her face was revealed to him. The cloth dropped from his fingers as he stared.

Sitting in the nest of her blue homespun surcoat, she stared back with huge, unblinking silver eyes. Her face was a delicate, pale oval shaped by fragile bones and small, fine features. Despite a lingering shadow of soot, he could discern that her skin was the ivory of a lily, pinkening to the shade of apple blossoms at her cheeks and lips. His body quickened at the sight.

An unexpected thunderbolt of awareness struck him. He desired this girl; he burned for her with a yearning Jussie had never aroused. Calling up all the strength of his vow of chastity, he resisted the idea that they were alone, unchaperoned, far from anyone else.

It was not so much her maidenly beauty that called to him, but the expressiveness in her features. Her eyes held a deep intelligence yet seemed haunted by shadows in their silver depths. Her mouth was full and firm, yet the way she worried her lower lip with her small white teeth hinted at vulnerability.

Years of celibacy faded beneath the onslaught of vivid desire. Rand laid his big hands on her cheeks, letting his thumbs skim in slow, gentle circles. "I've never seen a face like yours before, Lianna," he said softly. "At least not while I was awake."

Alarm flared in her quicksilver eyes. She drew back. "You are not from around here. You speak like a Gascon."

He smiled. His father's legacy. "So I am a Gascon, at least part of me is. And you *are* from around here. You speak like a Norman."

"Are you a brigand? Do you burn, pillage, and rape?"

He chuckled. "Preferably not in that order. Are you a poacher?"

She stiffened. "Certainly not. I've every right to hunt the lands of Bois-Long."

Suspicion shot through Rand. "You hail from Bois-Long?"

"I do."

Sweet lamb of God, Rand mused, she's from Longwood. He had to duck his head to hide a flash of curiosity. A gunner's daughter, she'd said, yet she'd have to be of noble birth to hunt. Despite her homespun garb, her speech and manners marked her as no one's servant.

"Your father was a gunner," he said slowly. "Was he also a man of rank?"

"No." She eyed him warily.

"You're well spoken."

"I am well schooled."

"What position do you hold at Bois-Long?"

"I am . . . companion to the chatelaine."

He nodded. "I see. It's common enough for a gentle-woman to surround herself with younger girls, common for those girls to learn polite accomplishments." One eyebrow lifted. "Gunnery is hardly a polite accomplishment."

"But far more useful than spinning and sewing."

"And far more dangerous. Does your mistress know of your experiments with guns?"

A small, tight smile. "*Certes*."

"She approves?"

A regal nod. "Most heartily."

Rand loosed a long, weary sigh. What manner of woman was his bride-to-be that she'd let this girl, clearly little older than a child, dabble in weaponry?

Lianna was staring hard at him. He sensed his questions had aroused her suspicions and so left off his queries. Instinctively he'd kept his identity from the girl. Now he was glad. Soon enough she'd learn he was Enguerrand Fitzmarc, the English knight come to claim the demoiselle and the château. Until then he merely wanted to be Rand to her.

"You're trespassing," she said matter-of-factly, pointing to a line of blazed poplars in the distance.

"So I am," he replied, looking at the boundary of trees. He took her hand and helped her to her feet. Her hand felt small but strong and seemed to fit his own like a warm little bird in a nest.

"Come," he said, "I want to be certain your gunshot didn't frighten my horse all the way to Gascony." Dropping her hand, he bent to retrieve her cloak and apron. The weight of the apron surprised him. He peered into the pocket, then stared at Lianna. "I don't know why I expected to find winter stonecrop blossoms in here," he said. "You're a walking arsenal."

She picked up her gun and stood while he tied the apron at her waist and draped the cloak about her shoulders. He let his hands linger there. "Your mistress is wrong to allow you to venture forth with a gun." Silently he swore to stop Lianna once he took possession of the castle.

She shouldered her gun as they began walking. "My mistress understands the necessity of it."

"Necessity?"

Her little wooden sabots kicked up her hem. She had a brisk, purposeful walk. "We've had no peace since Edward the Third crossed the leopards of England with the lilies of France."

Rand stared at her in amazement. What a curious mixture of innocence and worldliness she was. At once fragile, forceful, and forthright, she awakened powerful desires in him. Eyeing her with a sidelong glance, he tried to reconcile her with his idea of what a woman should be. She looked like a girl immortalized in a troubadour's lay, yet her behavior contradicted the image. Jussie, he recalled, had never concerned herself with affairs of state.

"France is more at war with herself than with England," he said. "King Charles is drooling mad, and the noble houses bicker like fishwives while the peasants starve."

"And will subjecting ourselves to Henry's usurpation improve our lot?"

"Better a sane Englishman than a mad Frenchman on the throne," Rand said.

She stopped walking, whirled to face him. "You're a Frenchman. Under whose banner will you fight? What cause do you champion?"

He swallowed, then affected a rakish grin. "Widows and orphans, of course."

She sniffed. "A convenient reply."

Discussing intelligent subjects with a woman, he thought, was not altogether unpleasant. "You speak ably of affairs that most men know nothing of."

"I'm not one to hide myself away and pretend ignorance. 'Tis exactly what the English *god-dons* would like, and I'll not oblige them."

It's not what every English *god-don* would like, he thought, watching the sunlight dance in the silvery mantle of her hair.

They found his horse grazing placidly on salt grass in a glade of water beeches. Nearby stood a weathered stone marker, its four arms of equal length marking it as St. Cuthbert's cross. The horse looked up, ears pricked. His dappled flanks gleamed in the heatless light of the March sun.

Lianna stopped walking to stare at the hard-muscled percheron, then at Rand. "I think you should explain who you are," she said. Her quicksilver gaze slipped over him, from the top of his blond head to the spurs on his mud-caked boots. "You are simply dressed, yet that horse of yours is no plowman's rouncy."

Inwardly he winced at the distrust in her tone. She was too straightforward to be easily deceived. "Charbu was a gift." His hand strayed to the lump created by the amulet beneath his mail shirt. Henry had given him Charbu as one of many gifts and another thread in the web of obligation he'd woven around Rand.

Lianna set down her gun and approached the horse. "Charbu," she said softly, stroking the handsome blazed face. "A fine, strong name. Tell me, Charbu, about your master. Does he hail from Gascony, as he claims? Does he ride you on raids with a band of *écorcheurs*?"

The horse whickered gently and tossed its head. Momentarily captivated by the sight of the small girl with her cheek pressed against the horse's neck, Rand stood speechless. At length he found his voice and strode forward. "If you think me a brigand, why aren't you fainting or screaming?"

"I never faint," she replied smugly. "And rarely scream. And you've not answered me."

"I am a . . . traveling knight, Lianna. I swear to you I do not ride with brigands. But I would like to ride with you. Let me take you to Bois-Long."

"No," she said quickly. "I think it best you stay clear of the château."

Why? he wondered. Did the chatelaine treat trespassers harshly? God, did she mistreat Lianna? He touched a strand of her hair; it felt like spun silk. "Is Bois-Long such an inhospitable place?"

"I fear it has become so," she replied, her eyes brimming with unspoken regret.

Rand felt a great urge to fold her against him then, to

surround her with the tenderness that had been blossoming in his heart since he'd first laid eyes on her. "At least let me take you partway," he suggested.

She balked; he persisted and, finally, prevailed. Her gun across the saddlebow, her arms clasped around his waist, she rode behind him and they talked. He learned that she often saved crumbs from her breakfast to feed a family of swallows that nested in the castle battlements. He told her that he invented songs to play on his harp. She confessed to a passion for comfits, and he admitted to holding frequent, absurd discourses with his horse.

Then she was silent for a long time. Glancing over his shoulder, Rand asked, "What are you thinking, Lianna?"

Softly, so softly he could barely hear, she said, "I'm thinking that you've come too late."

The soft throb of sadness in her voice made something inside him ache. His hand stole to hers, cradling it. "Too late for what?"

She withdrew her hand. "For . . . nothing. It matters not."

Although curious about her melancholy, he asked no more of her. If she yearned for a suitor, he could not be the one to court her.

Presently they came to a coppice of elm trees, and Lianna asked to dismount. Rand leapt to the ground and, grasping her at the waist, helped her down.

"Lianna?" he murmured, his voice deep and husky. He placed his fingers under her chin and raised her face to his. "Have a care for yourself, *pucelle*."

"I will. And you, too, in your travels."

Their eyes met and held for a breathless moment. Rand lifted a wisp of pale hair from her cheek and set it aside. She smiled, and her smile made everything inside him clamor with joy and fear. God, he thought, will she look at me so when she learns who I am, why I'm here?

His hands came up to frame her face, thumbs tracing the lyrical lines of her cheekbones. Slowly, like a man moving through a dream, he leaned down, drawn by a force that resisted every harsh rule that had been schooled into him. Their lips touched lightly at first, searching, tasting, and then their mouths fused into a kiss of desperate abandon. High, shattering waves of yearning crested within Rand, lifting his soul. He wanted to fill himself with this brave, winsome creature who smelled of soap and sulfur and who tasted of springtime.

His vows began to waver, but guilt bored a hole in his passion. Like it or not, he was betrothed to another woman. In kissing Lianna, he was betraying his obligation to the demoiselle and belittling his years of devotion to Jussie.

Slowly, unwillingly, he released her and drew his fingers from the shining white-blond hair that cloaked her shoulders. She wore a look of bewildered wonderment.

"I'd . . . best . . . go," Lianna said unsteadily, feeling her every nerve vibrate with exultation. She put her fingers to her lips, to hold the taste of him there, to brand his touch on her memory. Her captivated heart wanted to beg him to come with her, but her cautious mind warned her off. Although a victim of Lazare's treachery, she was a married woman. Trysting with this stranger was the act of an adultress. One day, she thought hopelessly. Had I met him one day before, my life would have been different. This Gascon knight would not stray from her chamber, would not deny her an heir, a child. Quelling a surge of sorrow, she said, "I suppose you ought to get back to your travels."

"I suppose. . . ." He seemed as reluctant to leave as she was for him to go. "Lianna—"

The bright tones of clarions suddenly rent the air. Recognizing the distinctive blare, she froze. The familiar trills could mean only one thing: her uncle of Burgundy had arrived. Reality crashed down around her ears, ripping her mind from the fantasies she'd built around this great, golden archangel of a Frenchman.

"Who comes?" he asked, craning his neck to see the distant road.

"A . . . guest of rank," she murmured, her thoughts already racing. Was the kitchen prepared to serve another feast? Was the hall presentable? A soft curse dropped from her lips.

"Did your father the gunner teach you to swear, too?" asked Rand.

She flashed him a smile. "I learned that on my own." Her grin faded. Burgundy was coming to see her, and she was covered with soot and reeking of gunpowder.

"I must make haste," she said. She pulled her hand from his, grabbed her gun from the saddlebow, and sprinted toward the château.

"Wait!"

"I cannot tarry," she called back.

"When will I see you again?" he asked.

"I . . . we can't . . . I shouldn't . . ." Torn by indecision, she slowed her pace and turned, walking backward. She had too much to explain, and too little time.

"But I must see you again."

The urgent, compelling note in his voice brought her to a complete halt. She stared at him, a sun-spangled vision surrounded by blue sky and budding trees, and her heart turned over in her chest. His eyes shone with a deep, inner light that she knew would haunt her for the rest of her days. He looked as if his very life depended on her answer.

"Meet me," he said, "at the place of Cuthbert's cross. . . ."

The clarions blared again, startling her anew and driving a hot arrow of hopelessness into her heart. "*Nom de Dieu,* why?" she asked raggedly.

His face opened into that magical, mesmerizing smile. "Because," he shouted, "I think I love you!"

Chapter 3

Her mind reeling with apprehension at her uncle's sudden arrival, and her heart snared by Rand's parting words, Lianna raced over the causeway and bounded into the bailey.

Don't let him see me, she prayed silently. Please, Lord, not until I make myself presentable. She skirted the band of ducal retainers, ducked beneath the flapping standard of a blood-red St. Anthony's cross, and headed for the keep. A flock of chickens wandered into her path, panicking as they tangled in her skirts. Shrieking, the chickens scattered, winging up dust eddies and leaving Lianna on her knees.

A vivid oath burst from her as she blinked against the dust. When her vision cleared, she found herself staring up at the unfaltering blue eyes, stark face, and uncompromising figure of her uncle. A wide-cut, squirrel-trimmed sleeve gaped before her as he extended his hand and helped her up.

"You stink of sulfur."

She blushed. A ripple of mirth emanated from the retainers. Burgundy silenced them with a single powerful scowl.

Abashed, she indicated her gun. "I was out shooting."

He rolled his eyes heavenward, took a deep breath, and said, "Five minutes, Belliane. You have five minutes to present yourself to me in the hall—as a lady, if you please, not some ragged hoyden from the marshes."

She dipped her head in a submissive nod. "Yes, Your Grace," she murmured, and fled to her solar.

Exactly four minutes later, clad in her best gown of royal blue, her head capped and veiled in silvery gauze, Lianna careened down the stairs toward the hall. Bonne had doused her with a generous splash of rosewater and had scrubbed the last traces of gunpowder from her face. Lianna glanced down at the heavy velvet swishing around her slippered feet. The anonymous *pucelle* who had enchanted Rand was no more. She longed to fold his image into her heart, to cherish in private his avowal of love. But her uncle was waiting.

Nearing the hall, she slowed her pace, lifted her chin, and glided in to confront the most powerful man in France.

Styled Jean Sans Peur—the Fearless—by friend and foe alike, he kept a stranglehold grip on the political pulse of the kingdom. A ruthless man, Burgundy possessed stone cold ambition and a penchant for intrigue and deeds done in secret. Men lived at his sufferance and sometimes died at his command.

Yet when Lianna greeted him, looked into his blue

eyes, she saw only affection. Pressing her cheek to his chest, she felt the chain mail he always wore beneath his ducal raiments. But the hand he lifted to stir a lock of her hair was gentle. Burgundy's cold, suspicious heart housed a small, warm corner for his orphaned niece.

"Better, *p'tite*," he said. "Much better. You're lovely."

She nodded to acknowledge the compliment, although she would have preferred that he notice the new gun emplacements she and Chiang had worked so hard to build. "Come warm yourself by the fire." She took his wind-chilled hand.

But Burgundy gestured toward the passage at the back of the hall. "I would speak to you in private, niece."

She preceded him into the privy apartment, waited until he sat, then perched nervously on the edge of a stool.

His eyes full of dark fires, Burgundy looked at her for a long, measuring moment. He sucked a deep breath through his nostrils. "Your disobedience would not hurt so much," he said quietly, "did I not love you so, Belliane."

An unexpected lump rose in her throat. "I had no choice. King Henry would have made an English bastion of Bois-Long."

"Better an English bastion than a French ruin. Where is this husband of yours?"

"Out riding with the reeve."

"I know Lazare Mondragon," Burgundy said, his mouth twisting with distaste. "He came begging favors some years ago. I turned him away." Stroking a long-fingered hand over his Siberian squirrel collar, he added, "They say Mondragon loved his first wife to distraction, nearly grieved unto death when she died. Think you he will hold you in such esteem?"

"I do not need his esteem, only his name in marriage."

Burgundy sighed. "You could have had better, *p'tite*."

"I thought you meant for me never to marry, Uncle."

"Ah, for *certes* I did." Frustration shadowed his face. "By marrying Mondragon, you've cheated yourself out of a brilliant alliance."

Unbidden laughter burst from her. "What mean you, Uncle?"

"I speak in earnest," he said harshly. "By my faith, Belliane, I was saving you for an English noble."

Shock rocketed through her, then gave way to harsh understanding. So that was why King Henry had meddled with her life.

Bleakly she realized that she was her uncle's pawn after all, a minor chess piece in his political game. An alliance with England would bring Burgundy's power to a zenith, enable him to vanquish his hated enemy, Count Bernard of Armagnac, who now controlled the mad French king.

Recoiling from the idea, she took a gulp of air. "My allegiance begins and ends with Bois-Long and France. The promise of winning a title cannot lure me from it."

"You should not have acted without my consent, Belliane."

She could not meet his eyes, because he would see her distrust, her belief that his love for her was less compelling than his affinity for intrigue. "Uncle, your wardship over me ended when I reached my majority December last. I was free to contract for my own marriage, free to flout Henry's directive."

"You speak treason, my lady."

"*He* is not my sovereign!"

"Yet he has styled himself so, claiming the lands won by his grandsire, Edward the Third. Henry will enforce that claim with military might. An alliance with him would be prudent at this time." The duke's face pinched into an expression known to strike terror into the hearts of royal princes. But Lianna didn't flinch as she raised her head. Her silver-gray eyes held him in steady regard, her chin jutting stubbornly.

They sat facing each other, eyes locked. Then Burgundy's expression changed to grudging admiration. "Would that more Frenchmen had your attitude," he mused. "We'd never be under Henry's thumb in the first place." He strode to the hearth, stood before the blaze. Firelight carved hollows in his cheeks, and worry pleated his brow. Sudden tenderness touched Lianna. Her uncle held a difficult position. Caught up in the madness and dissension between the princes royal of France, Jean had spoken for the common people in the Royal Council, made enemies of the nobles. Now, banished from Paris and opposed by the Armagnacs, he had apparently thrown in his lot with the English.

"Young Henry means to regain the throne of France," said Jean. "He's a man driven, at least in his own mind, by divine inspiration. His ambition knows no scruples. Not a man to defy heedlessly."

"That may well be, Your Grace. But I will not cede Bois-Long to him. I'd be doing my king and my countrymen a great disservice if I were to relinquish the ford to Henry's army."

"Your countrymen!" the duke spat. "Who are they, but a lot of quarreling children switching allegiance as capriciously as the winds over the Narrow Sea? And King

Charles, curse his insane soul, is but a puppet manipulated by the Armagnacs. France needs a strong guiding hand. Henry—"

"Is another English pretender," Lianna snapped.

Burgundy sighed. "You may think you've thwarted him. Perhaps you have, for the time being. But Harry of Monmouth is too much like you for my comfort. He's willful, intelligent, energetic." Burgundy returned to his chair and sat in pensive silence. At length he asked, "What know you of Longwood?"

"Only what I could read between the lines of his overblown missive. This Longwood is *un horzain* —an outsider, an upstart bastard," she stated. "His title is barely a month old. And he is a traitor like his father, Marc de Beaumanoir."

"Beaumanoir was no traitor, Lianna. He simply hadn't the means to buy his ransom from Arundel."

"Traitor or not, his bastard will never have Bois-Long."

Burgundy shook his head. "*Parbleu*, but you are an exasperating brat. You constantly meddle in male affairs."

"Only those that concern me and my people, Uncle." Seeing his face darken, she crossed to his side and took his hand. A cold tongue of apprehension touched the base of her spine. In the game Burgundy was playing, the stake was nothing less than the control of France. "What will you do?" she asked.

"I shall do as I see fit," he said simply. His silence made her more nervous than any ruthless plan.

For the first time in her life, Lianna found herself too preoccupied to supervise the feast with her usual meticulous control. Ordinarily she would have chastised the servitor who brought the venison on a poorly polished plate. Her sharp eye would have noticed that the crous-tade Lombard, made with fruit and marrow, was placed too far from the high table, and that the pastry subtlety of the lilies of France was overdone.

Instead her mind worried her problems like a persistent itch. Burgundy seemed determined to undermine the steps she'd taken to protect Bois-Long. The Mondragons were intent on flaunting their new status. And all the while, sweet, lingering thoughts of Rand, his stunning declaration, the goodness that emanated from him, kept her heart in a state of high rapture.

Ignorant of Burgundy's displeasure, the Mondragons feasted with delight. Lazare ordered wine casks to be unbunged and called to the minstrels' gallery for livelier entertainment.

Gervais, darkly attractive and full of confidence, raised his cup. "To my mother," he said, nodding congenially at Lianna. "Two years my junior, but I pray that won't keep her from doting on me." Laughter rippled from the lower tables.

The heat of a furious blush crept to Lianna's cheeks. She darted a look at her uncle, who sat at her right. Only she understood the significance of Burgundy's controlled silence, the tightness of his grip around his glass mazer. Damn Gervais, the *salaud*! He'd not speak so blithely did he realize how tenuous his hold on Bois-Long had become.

Artfully arranging a raven curl over her milk-white shoulder, Macée turned boldly to the duke. "Your Grace," she said, fluttering her inky lashes, "don't you wish for Belliane to perform for us? She has a fine hand at the harp."

Lianna cringed inwardly. Macée had heard her play at

the wedding feast and knew her art was poor. But Uncle Jean, merciful at least in this, shook his head. "I'm content to hear the minstrels, madame."

Macée pouted. Lazare, affecting a dignified air to cover his drunkenness, clapped his hands and called for silence. "My wife will play for us," he said.

Lianna looked from Lazare to the duke. She had no choice but to comply. Lazare was asserting his husbandly control over her; if she wished to prove to Burgundy that she intended to uphold her French marriage, she must act the wife and obey.

Taking her place in front of the high table, she stroked the harp strings with her long, tapered fingers. She performed a *chanson de vole* that she knew to be a favorite of her uncle's.

Her voice rang true, the notes hard and bright with unwavering clarity. Still, her style lacked the deep resonance of true artistry.

Burgundy watched her closely, seeming more interested in her somewhat dispassionate countenance than in her singing. When she finished on a clear, contralto note, he was the first to applaud. *"Enchantante,"* he commented.

She shrugged. "Thank you, Your Grace. Though I gave little character to Petrin's *chanson*."

He nodded. "You are aware of your own limitations and are not ashamed to state them."

She set aside the harp and returned to the table. She couldn't resist whispering to Macée, "You'll have to try harder, *chère,* to belittle me in the eyes of my uncle."

Macée sent her a sizzling look. "Your art would improve did you not spend so much time in the armory, concocting gunpowder."

The gibe hurt more than Lianna cared to admit. Of late her femininity had been called into question—by Lazare's rejection, her uncle's anger. Even Rand, in his kindness, had made a gentle censure of her interest in gunnery. Now Macée—fabulously beautiful, wise in ways Lianna was only beginning to suspect—challenged her.

"I'm defending the castle instead of warming a chair with my backside," said Lianna, keeping her tone light.

Macée spoke slowly, as if to a half-wit. "The defense of the castle is man's work."

Lianna encompassed Lazare and Gervais with a dismissive glance. "The men in charge of Bois-Long have done little to see to its defense." Flames of anger ignited in the eyes of both Mondragons. She stole a glance at her uncle. His mouth grew taut with suppressed merriment.

"Well spoken," he murmured.

"But do you not think," persisted Macée, "that a lady should have polite accomplishments? After all, if she's to be received at court—"

A hiss of anger escaped from the duke.

"I'll practice," Lianna promised with sudden urgency. She prayed Macée, ignorant of Burgundy's banishment, would speak no more of the French court. Inadvertently the foolish woman had stuck a barb in an old wound. Desperate to placate him, Lianna turned the subject. "Guy and Mère Brûlot, folk who remember my mother, say she made magic with the harp."

The hardness left Burgundy's eyes, as if he'd decided to let the offense pass. "Aye, my sister did sing well."

"Perhaps there's hope for me, then. I could send to Abbeville for a music master."

He shook his head. "The feeling, *p'tite,* the passion,

cannot be taught. It must come from the heart." He glanced pointedly at Lazare, who seemed to have discovered something fascinating in the bottom of his goblet. "You have the skill. One day, perhaps, true music will come."

She pretended to understand, because the duke wished her to. But in sooth she knew better than to suppose that passion would improve her singing. Unless . . . The blinding radiance of Rand's image burned into her mind. The scene in the great hall receded, and she saw only him, her vagabond prince. The memory of his gentle touch and caressing smile filled her with a sharp, plaintive yearning that she likened to the ecstasy of an inspired poet. *Nom de Dieu*, could such a man teach her to sing?

"Sing the one about the cat again," cried Michelet, tugging insistently at the hem of Rand's tunic. The boy's younger brothers and sisters chorused a half dozen other requests.

Rand grinned and shook his head. He set aside his harp and reached down to rumple the carroty curls of little Belle. "Later, nestlings," he said, stooping to aim the baby's walker away from the hearth. "I must not neglect my men."

In the adjacent taproom, Lajoye and the soldiers discussed their forays, filling their bellies with bread and salt meat from the *Toison d'Or* and wine from a keg the brigands had overlooked. Some of the men vied, with lopsided grins and faltering French, for the attention of the girls.

Rand had avoided his companions since late afternoon. He was too full of unsettled emotions and half-formed decisions to act the commander. Meeting Lianna had left him as useless as an unstrung bow. One hour with her had threatened everything he'd ever believed about loving a woman. Before today, love had been a mild warmth, a comfortable, abiding glow that asked little of him. But no more.

The arrows of his feelings for the girl in the woods had inflicted a ragged wound, a heat that burned with a consuming, continuous fire. He felt open and raw, as if an enemy had stripped him of his armor, left him standing in fool's attire.

Bypassing the taproom, he walked outside, looked around the ravaged town. Wisps of smoke climbed from a few chimneys. In the rose-gold glimmer of early evening, a woman stepped into her dooryard to call her children to table, while a group of men with their axes and scythes trudged in from the outlying fields. The town was beginning to heal from the wounds inflicted by the brigands. The woman waved to Rand, and he realized with relief that he was now looked upon with trust, not fear. An excellent development. If the Demoiselle de Bois-Long resisted his claim, he'd need to secure the town to use as a retreat position.

He followed a familiar, muffled curse to the paddock. His horses and those of his men occupied the stalls, Lajoye's livestock having been taken by the *écorcheurs*. A bovine shape caught his eye. "Jesu, Jack, where did you find that?"

Jack Cade looked up from the milking stool. "Lajoye's youngsters need milk," he said. "Spent the king's own coin on her, down in Arques." The milch cow sidled and nearly overset Jack's bucket. "Hold still, you cloven-footed bitch." He grasped a pair of fleshy teats and aimed a stream of milk into the bucket. "I made sure Lajoye knows the milk's from our King Harry." Leaning his cheek against the cow's side, he gave Rand a brief accounting of the events of the day.

"Godfrey and Neville ran down a hart and brought it back to Lajoye. Robert—er, Father Batsford, that is, went a-hawking. Giles, Peter, and Darby found the brigands' route and followed it some leagues to the south, but the thieves are long gone, dispersed, probably, after dividing their spoils."

Rand frowned. "I did want to recover the pyx from the chapel. 'Twould mean much to the people."

Jack's eyes warmed with affection. "Always trying to win hearts and souls, aren't you?"

Rand smiled. Was he deluding himself to believe chivalry could achieve such an end? "Always skeptical, aren't you?" he countered.

Jack shrugged. "Take them by the balls, my lord. Their hearts and souls will follow." Wearily he rotated his shoulders. "I worked like a goddamned swineherd today. And yourself, my lord? Any luck?"

Rand swallowed and stared at the dust dancing in a ray of golden twilight. The rhythmic, sibilant splatter of milk against the sides of Jack's bucket punctuated the silence. Presently Jack finished his task and straightened. "Well?"

"I met . . . a girl."

The milk sloshed in Jack's pail. Too late, Rand realized his voice had betrayed the feelings he'd kept folded into his heart since he'd watched Lianna run off toward the castle.

Eyes dancing with interest, Jack set down his pail, picked up a stalk of hay, and aimed it at Rand's chest.

"Has Cupid's arrow found a victim? Welcome to the human race, my lord."

"Her name is Lianna," Rand said in a low voice. "She lives at Bois-Long."

"Better still," Jack exclaimed, rolling the hay between his fingers. "Surely it's a sign from above. The girl has been sent to spare your loss of Justine. Merry, my lord, perhaps life won't be so disagreeable with a ready wench at hand."

Rand shook his head. "The married state is sacred. And I'd not dishonor Lianna."

Jack laughed. "Knight's prattle, my friend. Your commitment to the demoiselle is one of political convenience. No need to be good as gold on her account."

Rand turned away. "If gold rusts, what would iron do?"

Jack tossed a forkful of hay to the cow and picked up the bucket. They walked out of the paddock. "I for one," said Jack, "intend to grow right rusty wooing Lajoye's hired girl. She's got a pair of—"

"Jack," Rand warned, drowning out the bawdy term.

"—to die for," Jack finished.

"I've forbidden wenching."

"Only with *unwilling* females," said Jack. "But never mind. When do we go to Bois-Long?"

"King Henry insists on proper protocol. A missive must be sent, and the bride-price, and Batsford must read the banns for a few weeks running."

"Still in no hurry." Jack grinned. "That hired girl will be glad of it." He walked back to the inn.

Caught in the purple-tinged swirls of the deepening night, Rand left the town and climbed the citadel of cliffs above the sea. A nightingale called and a curlew answered, the plaintive sounds strumming a painful tune over his nerves.

Staring out at the breaking waves, he pondered the unexpected meeting and the even less expected turn his heart had taken.

Lianna. He whispered her name to the sea breezes; it tasted like sweet wine on his tongue. Her image swam into his mind, pale hair framing her face with the diffuse glow of silver, her smile tentative, her eyes wide and deep with a hurt he didn't understand yet felt in his soul. She inspired a host of feelings so bright and sharp that it was agony to think of her.

There was only one woman he had any right to think about: the Demoiselle de Bois-Long.

The nearness would be hardest to bear. To see Lianna's small figure darting about the château, to hear the chime of her laughter, would be high torture.

End it now, his common sense urged, and he forced his mind to practical matters. The Duke of Burgundy was at Bois-Long, but his retainers were few. Clearly he did not plan a lengthy visit. Jean Sans Peur could ill afford to tarry with his niece when his domain encompassed the vast sweep of land from the Somme to the Zuyder Zee.

Aye, thought Rand, Burgundy bears watching.

But even as he hardened his resolve around that decision, he knew he'd go back to the place of St. Cuthbert's cross where he'd met Lianna. The guns, he rationalized. He must dissuade her from working with dangerous and unpredictable weapons. Yet beneath the thought lay an immutable truth. Guns or no, he'd seek her out—tomorrow, and every day, until they met again.

* * *

"Gone!" said Lianna, running into a little room off the armory. "Lazare is gone!"

"Did you think your uncle of Burgundy would let him stay?" Chiang asked, his dark eyes trained on a bubbling stew of Peter's salt that boiled in a crucible over a coal fire.

A warm spark of relief hid inside her. Ignoring it, she said, "Uncle Jean had no right to order Lazare to Paris."

"Not having the right has never stopped Burgundy before."

"Why would he send Lazare to swear fealty to King Charles?"

Chiang shrugged. "Doubtless to keep the man from your bed."

She nearly choked on the irony of it. Lazare had taken care of that aspect of the marriage himself. And now that he was gone, she could not place him between herself and the English baron.

"Burgundy has left also?" asked Chiang.

"Aye, he claimed he had some private matter to attend to," said Lianna glumly. "He had no right," she repeated. She studied Chiang's face, admiring his implacable concentration, the deep absorption with which he performed his task. His eyes, exotically upturned at the corners, seemed to hold the wisdom of centuries. He had a stark, regal face that put her in mind of emperors in the East, a distance too far to contemplate.

"You know he has it in his power to do most anything he wishes. Pass me that siphon, my lady."

She handed him a copper tube. "That is what worries me about Uncle Jean. He also refused to send reinforcements to repel the English baron. He will not risk the King Henry's displeasure."

Carefully Chiang extracted the purified salt from the vat. "Will the Englishman press his claim by force?"

"I know not. But we should be prepared." She sat back on her heels and watched Chiang work, his short brown fingers handling scales and calipers with the delicacy of a surgeon. Sympathy, affection, and respect tumbled through her. Chiang had been a fixture at Bois-Long since the days of her youth. Like the man himself, his arrival was a mystery. Fleeing the capture of a mysterious ship from the East, he'd washed up on the Norman shore, the sole survivor of a vessel whose destination and mission Chiang had never revealed.

Only the Sire de Bois-Long, Lianna's father, had protected the strange-looking man from a heathen's death at the hands of superstitious French peasants. With his timeless knowledge of defense and his meticulous skill at gunnery, Chiang had repaid Aimery the Warrior a hundredfold.

But even now, the castle folk who had known him for years regarded him as an oddity, some gossips falling just short of denouncing him as a sorcerer. The men-at-arms begrudged him this small workroom in a corner of the armory and never failed to sketch the sign of the cross when passing by.

Chiang peered at her through wide-set, fathomless eyes. "And are you prepared, my lady?"

She hung her head. During the two days of the duke's visit, she'd prayed and worried over a difficult decision. "Yes," she said faintly.

He set aside his sieves and calipers and gave her the full measure of his attention. "Tell me."

She tapped her chin with her forefinger. "I've sent a

missive to Raoul, Sire de Gaucourt in Rouen, asking for fifty men-at-arms."

"Did you consult Lazare in this?"

"Of course not. He knows nothing of diplomacy and politics. It matters not anymore. He is gone."

Chiang showed no surprise at her defiance, yet she read disapproval in his calm, steady gaze. In appealing to the Sire de Gaucourt, she had betrayed her uncle. Gaucourt did not openly side with the Armagnacs, yet he was known to be sympathetic to Burgundy's enemy.

"Was I wrong, Chiang?" she asked desperately.

He shrugged. His straight dark thatch of hair caught blue highlights from the coal fire. "You have shown yourself to be a poor judge of character, but Burgundy's niece nonetheless. The duke himself would have done no less. Remember his tenet: 'Power goes to the one bold enough to seize it.'"

Bolstered by Chiang's counsel, she gave him a glimmer of a smile. "Very well. Shall we go try the culverin?" The piece was new and had three chambers for more rapid firing.

He looked away. "I plan to do so. But alone."

"What?"

"Your husband forbade me to work the guns with you."

She leaped to her feet. "The *salaud*. How dare he dictate what I may and may not do?"

"Your laws dictate that you are subservient to your husband—or his son in his absence. Gervais has already said that he will enforce his father's command."

"We shall see," she muttered, and left the armory to search for Gervais and tell him exactly what she thought of his father's interdict.

In the hall she found the women at their spinning. Fleecy balls of carded wool littered the floor, and women's talk wove in and out of the clack and whir of the spinning wheels. Edithe sat by the hearth, idly eating a pasty.

"What do you, Edithe?" Lianna asked, struggling to keep the irritation from her voice. "Why are you not helping with the spinning?"

The girl wiped her mouth on her sleeve. "Lazare released me," she said, a faint gleam of smugness in her ripe smile.

Lianna stared. The wooden sounds of the wheels stopped, leaving an echo of expectant silence in the hall. Lazare had singled Edithe out to vent his lust; apparently all knew of it. Covering her dismay with anger, Lianna ordered the women back to work with a clipped imperative, then turned her attention to the idle maid.

Edithe made an elaborate show of finishing the pasty and licking the crumbs from her fingers. Fury welled like a hot powder charge within Lianna.

"I see," she said, her throat taut as she exerted all the control she could marshal. "I wonder, Edithe, if you know where Lazare has gone."

"Mayhap the mews," the maid replied. "He does enjoy falconry, you know."

No, Lianna didn't know. Lazare had shared nothing of himself, and she had never asked. She didn't care; she had his name, and that was all she needed for now. Still, his open infidelity stung her pride. With great satisfaction she said, "Lazare is no longer at Bois-Long, Edithe. He has gone to Paris."

The maid's eyes widened. Lianna smiled. "Lazare excused you from spinning. Very well, you are excused." Edithe looked relieved until Lianna added, "You will do needlework instead. Aye, the chaplain needs a new alb."

Edithe's face crumpled in dismay. "But I am so clumsy with the needle," she said.

"Doing boonwork for the church is good for the soul," Lianna retorted, and strode out of the hall. Climbing the stairs to the upper chambers, she tried to formulate a speech scathing enough for Gervais. Keep her from her gunnery indeed. Her dudgeon peaked as she arrived at the room he shared with Macée. She raised her fist to knock.

A sound from within stopped her. A moan, as if someone were being tortured. *Nom de Dieu,* was Gervais beating his wife? But the next sound, a warm burble of laughter followed by a remark so ribald Lianna barely understood it, mocked that notion. Cheeks flaming, she fled.

Her fury deepened into an unfamiliar sense of helpless frustration. Shamed by the tears boiling behind her eyes, she rushed to the stables and commanded her ivory palfrey to be saddled. She rode away from the château at a furious gallop.

Please be there, she prayed silently as the greening landscape whipped by. Please be there.

Twice during her uncle's sojourn she had managed to slip off to the place of Cuthbert's cross; twice she'd found the coppice empty. No, not quite empty. The first time she'd found a single snowdrop lying on the cross, its waxy petals still fresh. The second time she'd found the emerald-tipped feather of a woodcock. She kept the flower and feather in her apron pocket, and often her fingers stole inside to touch the evidence that Rand had gone seeking her. Evidence that he wasn't just a dream conjured by her troubled mind. Evidence that one man found her desirable.

But today a token would not suffice. Encased by the icy armor of betrayal and confusion, she needed Rand—his generous strength, his tender smile, the liquid velvet of his voice. She needed to gaze into the same green depths of his eyes.

He was there.

Lianna checked her horse, dismounted, and tethered the palfrey to a bush where Charbu grazed. Rand sat leaning against the cross. His winsome smile reached across the distance that separated them, to beckon her.

Her heart lifting, she hesitated, then approached at a slow walk. The scene was almost too perfect for her worldly presence to disturb. Rand sat cross-legged, surrounded by an arch of trees and meadow grasses that nodded in the breeze. An errant shaft of sunlight filtered through the budding larch boughs, touching his golden hair with sparkling highlights. In his lap he held a harp. The fingers of one hand strummed idly over the strings. Stepping closer, she saw that his other hand cradled a baby rabbit. *I nearly slew its mother,* she thought absurdly.

Rand's eyes never left her. At last he spoke—to the rabbit, not to Lianna. "Off with you, nestling," he said, and set the creature down, giving it a nudge with his finger until it scampered away. Then he laid aside his harp and stood.

She stayed rooted, frozen by new and awesome sensations that pulsated through her like the wingbeats of a lark. Rand was a deity in a dream garden, and suddenly she feared to enter his world. Lazare's duplicity and her uncle's scheming had soiled her. She couldn't belong here.

But that was Belliane, an inner voice reminded her. To Rand she was Lianna, brave and unsullied in her anonymity.

He stepped forward, put out his hand, and brushed his knuckles lightly over her cold cheek, an inquiring gesture, one that demanded a response.

The restrained tenderness and gentle warmth of his touch melted the ice encasing Lianna. Thawed by his kindness, a single tear emerged, dangled on the points of her lashes, then coursed down her cheek. He traced its path with his thumb, caught the second with his lips, and then the broad wall of his chest absorbed the hot floodtide that followed.

Chapter 4

Stricken by her grief without understanding it, Rand wrapped the small, shuddering girl against him. Whatever he'd expected—a shy smile, a tentative greeting—was swept away by the depth of her naked emotions. For long moments he stood holding her, stroking her tense back, her rounded shoulders, bending to touch his lips to the wind-cooled silk of her hair. "Hush, *pucelle*," he whispered. "Please don't cry anymore."

He'd felt guilty coming here, giving in to an impulse he knew he should not indulge. Now her need drove away the guilt and filled him with a powerful sense of rightness. Although pledged to Lianna's mistress and bound to style himself the girl's overlord, he could not withhold his comfort.

He tightened his throat against speaking further, for to speak now would be to admit to emotions he had no right to feel. Instead he cradled her small, quaking body against him and fought the dark, liquid burn that stung his loins.

At length her weeping subsided. She clung to him, kept her face buried in his tunic. When Rand curved his fingers under her chin and lifted her face to his, she stiffened and resisted. But the gentle force of his will won out, and he found himself staring into the battered silver of her eyes.

The pain there was so deep, so vivid, that he felt as if a fist had reached down inside him and squeezed his heart.

"Tell me, *pucelle*," he whispered.

She shook her head. "I can't."

His finger caught the sparkling drop of a tear from her cheek and brought it to his own lips; he tasted the faint, bitter salt of her grief. "I'd break a hundred lances if the deed could drive the sadness from your eyes."

That brought a tiny smile. "I am no damsel in a *chanson de geste*. I need no dragons slain for me."

"What do you need, Lianna?"

"A friend." Her voice sounded faint, as if she were reluctant to confess such a human necessity.

He touched his lips to her hairline, breathed in the light scent of her fragrance. Soon enough he would be forced to betray the childlike trust that softened her features. "I'll be your friend, *pucelle*," he said.

She unwrapped herself from his embrace. Long, loose strands of her hair clung to his arm, linking them. Gesturing at his harp, she said, "Sing me a song."

He smiled. "I was prepared to break lances for you." He brought her to sit by the cross and took the harp in his lap.

Fascinated, Lianna watched his strong hands close

around the frame of ashwood worn smooth by years of handling. Long masculine fingers caressed the gut-spun strings, bringing forth a sweet shiver of sound. The tones lifted to mate with the spring breeze, and Lianna felt an odd sense of intimacy, as if the notes were whispered in her ear. She drew her knees to her chest and wrapped her arms about them.

He sang an old troubadour's lay of unrequited love. His rendition sounded unique, new. He had a voice like none other she had heard—vibrant, clean as rain, powerful as the wind singing through the crags.

Each word was a prayer; each bright cadence echoed the voice of a rill spilling over rocks, washing through her like a healing balm. The slow-circling melody bathed her senses with heat and light, and she sat enthralled until the final plaint shimmered from the harp.

Only when a breeze cooled her cheeks did she realize she was crying again. But the new tears came on a release of pain, as if Rand's singing had drawn a thorn from her flesh.

He watched her expectantly. She swallowed. "How can you sing like that?"

"Like what, *pucelle?*"

She paused, wondering from where to pluck the words to describe the deep enchantment of his artistry. "As if— as if your soul were touched by God."

Laughter rippled from him. "Not by God. By you."

They weren't touching, but Lianna felt as if she'd been caressed. *I think I love you,* he'd called to her, and she'd wondered about that for days, questioning his honesty and her own worthiness of it. No man had ever said those words to her, had those feelings for her. Did he still feel affection for her, or was the emotion only a passing fancy?

She feared to ask, but what she saw in the pure, liquid green of his eyes made her hear the words in her heart over and over again.

He set down his harp and walked to her horse. "Let me guess," he said, stroking the palfrey's satiny neck. "You've stolen a horse and you're running away."

"I am allowed certain liberties," she said quickly, leaping up to join him. His eyes were so clear, so all-seeing. Did he know she lied? She felt guilty deceiving him. Quickly she justified it. This knight-errant would never befriend the Demoiselle de Bois-Long; no one ever had.

He ran his hand over the palfrey's withers and down her leg, pushing aside the grass to examine the iron curve of her shoe. "The horse is well tended."

"Of course." Lianna's chin lifted. She tolerated no sloth in her stables. Catching Rand's curious look, she added, "The marshal is most exacting." Only, she thought, because he knew she'd put him out to the rye fields if he shirked his duties. She tugged at Rand's hand. "Let's walk."

Gratified by her light mood, Rand followed. Her hair played in the breeze like threads of moonlight spun by fairies. As they fell in step together, the hem of her heather smock brushed against his leg, sending a sweet, forbidden thrill to the center of him. The browns and greens of the new season colored the landscape, and he forced his attention to the pollarded willows and stunted poplars that nodded in the wind.

"I'm convinced this was a pirate path of the Vikings," she said, leading him over the hill that sheltered the glade. "I used to play Helquin the Huntsman when I was a child."

He smiled. She spoke as if her childhood were long

past, yet in his eyes she was a child still. "Who is Helquin?"

"Ah, you do not know the legend in Gascony." Her arm sketched the sweep of the landscape. "All the way from the cold white country of the north Helquin came, bearing the shrieking souls of the damned on his shoulders." She shivered and looked as though she enjoyed the sensation. The thought crossed his mind that Justine would never have savored such a gruesome tale.

"When the wild birds cry out over the marshes, the peasants say they echo Helquin's long gallop through the centuries. I'd pretend to see him burst through the woods with all the battalions of hell at his heels."

Rand grinned. "Would you run in terror from Helquin?"

"Certainly not." Adorable obstinance hardened the delicate line of her jaw. "I would pretend to blow him all the way to the Zuyder Zee with a sixty-pound ball."

He stopped walking, took her by the shoulders, and rolled his eyes. "I do not approve of your penchant for gunnery."

Scowling, she struck him lightly on the chest. "Doubtless you would have me cloistered in a lady's bower, carding wool."

I would have you folded in my arms, he thought. Next to my heart. He gave her shoulders a squeeze. "I cannot dictate what you should or shouldn't do. That's not how it is between friends. But I would prefer you didn't work with guns. I've seen the destruction they can wreak."

"Very well, Rand the Gascon," she said, her eyes glittering a challenge, "how would *you* defend a château?"

"With the might of men-at-arms and archers."

"Knights." She spat the word. "They indulge in looting

and ransom." Color rose to her cheeks, and Rand realized he'd discovered a topic she had often pondered, and not happily. She planted her hands on her hips. "Chivalry is but an empty spectacle, an excuse to plunder the weak."

"Unscrupulous men, not the laws of chivalry, are to blame."

"Chivalry is but a cloak to hide the excesses of their *chevauchées*."

A sudden hideous thought struck him. "Have you been hurt by knights, Lianna? Is that why you disdain chivalry?"

She lowered her gaze. "Anyone who has smelled the smoke of a burning orchard, seen a baby spitted on a sword, heard the cries of a terrified woman, has been hurt by these men who call themselves knights."

He swallowed hard. She was French; she'd seen these horrors, lived with them all her life. Still, she challenged everything he believed about knighthood. "Do you include me in your censure?"

She looked up. "Do you do those things?"

"No," he said. "Never. Do you believe me?"

"I think you truly wish to protect the weak and uphold the faith. But I also think you are wrong to believe you can achieve this through chivalry." She softened the blow by touching his cheek, adding, "You are that rare man, Rand, a man who cannot be touched by corruption."

Her statement sent him into a spiral of self-reproach. Every lying word he told her would soon come back to haunt him. Unable to extricate himself from the dilemma, he started walking again, then surprised himself by asking, "What think you of archers?" Jesu, was he truly having such a conversation with a girl?

"Rabble," she said. "Undisciplined rabble."

"Can you dispute the success of the bowmen at Crécy and Poitiers?"

She glared. "A fine way for a Frenchman to speak, lauding English victories."

Fool, he said to himself, she'll find you out even sooner if you don't guard your tongue. "I laud not the victories, only the way in which they were won. How many arrows could a master archer let fly in the time it takes to load and discharge a cannon?"

"A hundred arrows cannot bring down a stone wall. A single gun can."

"What good is a firearm that hides the enemy in smoke?"

"What good is an arrow in a strong wind, a bowstring saturated by rain?"

Her vehemence delighted and disturbed him. Deliberately he sidestepped the challenge. "What good is arguing with a maid too precocious for her own welfare?"

She scowled, but he held her with a look of amused affection until the corners of her mouth tipped up in a smile. "You will never defeat my logic in this, sir knight," she stated. "I am far too quick for you—in more ways than one." She turned and ran down a slope covered by stiff salt grass.

Laughing, he followed, his long, loose strides devouring her path. He held back apurpose and let her lead him past great elms, old yews, giant beeches, over half-buried stones and purplish mud, until he glimpsed the sea through rows of wind-torn hedges.

His caution swept away by her capriciousness and the lithe grace of her movements, he lunged forward and caught her around the waist. Her soft gasp tickled his ear as he swung her in the air. They tumbled together into the spiny grasses, until, with gentle force, Rand pinned her beneath him. One hand bound her delicate wrists and held them above her head, while the other tiptoed in light caresses down her rib cage until she fairly shrieked for mercy.

"Who is the quicker now, *pucelle*?"

She clamped her mouth shut, refusing to yield. His fingers found and tickled each rib in turn, sending little shocks of awareness through him as her form and the warmth of her flesh came alive beneath her homespun smock.

Boldly he teased the flesh of her neck, his fingers rippling beneath the dense silk of her hair. Her skin was as smooth as ivory, as lustrous as a pearl. Wildly he wondered if she could feel the simmering heat of his desire, if she knew how close he was to letting his passion devour them both.

Sudden guilt flayed him. He was betrothed to another. Yet with Lianna his vows of chastity, of chivalry, flew on the wind, beyond the reach of reason.

As of its own accord, his touch changed to searching caresses, his fingers tracing her cheeks, her shoulders, the dainty line of her collarbone. He explored her form and texture, wanting to stamp her image on his soul. She stirred, and a small whimpering sound escaped her. "Who is the quicker now?" he asked again, forcing lightness into his tone. "Who?"

"You . . . oh, you," she gasped.

Immediately Rand released her wrists, but he touched her still with languorous strokes. Bringing his face very close to hers, he studied the clouds of pink color in her cheeks, the sparkle in her eyes.

"There is naught so heady," he whispered, "as a battle won."

"You do not play fair," she replied breathlessly.

"Where you are concerned, Lianna," he said, "I forswear fairness." The wind stirred the hedges, and a shadow drifted over her face, deepening the color of her eyes to opaque silver. She shifted beneath him, the slight movement bringing his every nerve to a state of burning aliveness.

"Lianna . . ." Yearning made his voice scratchy. "I haven't stopped thinking about you since the moment we met." He touched his lips at random over her flushed and startled face. "You make me want to forget who I am, to forget there's a world and a time beyond this moment."

She took a deep, dreamy breath, and he caught it with his mouth, absorbing the warm sweet nectar of her lips. The times he'd held a woman other than Justine in his arms were few, but had he kissed a thousand women, he knew not one of them could seize his soul as Lianna did.

She lay still, naïve, accepting. Her lips felt like moist velvet as he brushed them with his own. She tasted of morning dew and mystery, as if her body held some secret just out of his reach. He burned for her, longed to unlock the person she was, to peel away the layers of her outward identity and cast them aside like petals plucked from a daisy.

Madness, he thought, feathering kisses over her brow, into her hair. Madness to indulge in this forbidden tryst. But oh, how he wanted to explore the insanity. His hand found the sweet curve of her breast. He lifted his head. She eyed him with soft inquiry. Her lips were moist, love-bruised.

"We'd best start back," he said reluctantly.

Wistfulness darkened her eyes. "Why?"

"Because you are a funny little *pucelle* who enjoys guns and tries my convictions, and I am a knight-errant bound where my travels take me." He forced himself to speak easily as he helped her up. "Did your *maman* never teach you better than to consort with strange men?"

"I am an orphan, and you don't seem a stranger to me."

Although she spoke matter-of-factly, he recognized the glint of pain in the sea-silver depths of her eyes. He drew her against him, startled anew by her smallness, her sturdiness. He whispered, "I don't want to hurt you, Lianna."

She nuzzled her cheek against his chest. "You'd never hurt a woman. You told me so."

Desire swelled in him; he choked it off with a fresh dose of guilt. Before long she would learn who he was, and he'd never have the gift of her trust again.

At a leisurely pace they started back toward their horses, easing into a relationship that Rand knew could only flourish for a few more days—even hours, perhaps. He showed her a bittern's nest occupied by four brown-speckled eggs. She showed him a limestone deposit and a ruined Roman aqueduct. He wove a crown of laceweed and placed it on her head. She fashioned a tiny catapult from a green ash bough and showed him how to fling a stone fifty paces.

Rand scowled at the makeshift weapon. Putting it into his belt, he caught her against him. "You are impossible."

"I am practical."

"You are beautiful."

"Prate not about the way I look. I would rather have you admire my skill at weaponry."

He grinned. "Are all at Bois-Long as bloodthirsty as you?"

"Some are worse," she said simply, and turned away.

Some are worse. Could she be speaking of her mistress? As he watched her untether her horse, his throat went tight with apprehension. Taking her by the shoulders, he stared at her. "Will your mistress punish you for taking the horse?"

Confusion, then amusement, chased across her features. "Of course not," she said, flushing.

Relieved, he dropped a kiss on her brow.

"Will you come back?" she asked softly.

He swallowed. "I don't know. . . ."

"Are you leaving, resuming your travels?"

"My plans . . . are uncertain."

She nodded, as if aware that what they had was tenuous, fragile. "I'll come when I can in the late afternoon," she said solemnly, "at the hour of the woodcock's flight."

Wishing the world would fall away and leave them to themselves, Rand hauled her against him and crushed his mouth down on hers.

But by the time he reached Eu, he knew he'd not go to the place of St. Cuthbert's cross again. The selfish joy of being with Lianna was not worth the pain she'd suffer when she learned his purpose.

He rode out to sit alone on the cliffs where the breakers leaped up in an endless assault on the rocks. He longed to yank his dreams out of his heart and cast them into the sea, to turn himself back into the hollow shell he'd been before he'd met Lianna. She made him too human, too sensitive, and those qualities would serve him ill when the time came to take Bois-Long and his new wife.

He went back to the village, walked into the taproom, and found Jack Cade, who had agreed to act as his herald. Cheeks ruddy from too much hard Norman cider, Jack raised a wooden mug. "My lord of Longwood."

Rand nodded curtly. "Tomorrow."

Lianna lay wrapped in the cloud coverlet of a dream. She'd been dreaming of Lazare, her haughty husband. In the dream he'd stood in the shadows beside her bed, a dark, unwanted presence. But then he'd stepped closer. Darkness gave way to golden sunlight, and the figure by her bed was not Lazare at all, but Rand, his face alight with that heart-catching smile, his arms open, inviting her.

She moved toward him, reaching, getting close enough to catch the scent of sunshine and sea winds that clung to him, to feel the warmth emanating from him. . . .

He faded on a shimmer of light, and she felt herself being pulled out of the dream and thrust into the cold gray drizzle of dawn.

Wondering what had awakened her, she stared bleakly at the long, narrow window. A shout sounded. She jumped up, wrapping herself in a sheet as she hurried to the window. The sentry at the barbican was gesturing at the causeway spanning the river.

Spying a lone rider, Lianna suddenly felt the cold of the stone flags beneath her bare feet. The sensation crept up her legs and crawled over her scalp. The traveler wore a white tunic emblazoned with a gold device. The leopard rampant.

Her throat constricted; she swallowed twice before finding her voice. "Bonne! Come quickly." Moments dragged by before the maid appeared. Frowning at the wisps of straw in Bonne's hair, Lianna guessed the maid had been dallying with Roland. Bonne's sleepy, satisfied smile confirmed the suspicion.

"Honestly, Bonne," Lianna snapped. "You're supposed to sleep on your pallet in my wardrobe. Surely it doesn't take the entire night to . . . to . . ." A hot flush rose in her cheeks, and, irritated, she looked away.

Bonne's smile widened. "Not the whole night, my lady, but afterward . . ." She indulged in a long, luxurious stretch. "It is so agreeable lying in a man's arms, you know."

Lianna didn't know, and that fact annoyed her all the more. "In the future, you're to be here by cockcrow."

"Yes, my lady," the maid said, knitting her fingers together in front of her. "What is your pleasure?"

Lianna motioned toward the window. The rider was in the bailey now, his horse being led to the stables. Bonne looked out, then drew back, fully awake now. "By St. Wilgefort's beard," she breathed, "it's the English baron."

"Not the baron, but surely his messenger."

"Gervais was up playing at draughts until the wee hours, but I'll send for him. With your husband gone to Paris, it's Gervais's place to receive the message."

"Don't you dare awaken him," said Lianna. "I shall dispense with Longwood's man myself."

Bonne reached for a comb.

"Never mind my hair," Lianna said. "Just cover it with a hennin and veil. I'm anxious to meet this English bumpkin."

Wearing her best gown and her haughtiest look, she found the man in the hall. He was sucking prodigiously at a wine flask. Then he gaped at her, his mouth slack as a simpleton's.

She refused to ease his task. Flicking her eyes over his ruddy hair, oiled and mercilessly furrowed by a comb, she asked, "What business have you here?"

"I am Jack Cade. I bear a message for the Demoiselle de Bois-Long." His crude French assaulted her ears.

"I am the demoiselle," she said in English. The language, schooled into her by tutors sent by her uncle, tasted bitter on her tongue.

He gave her a sealed vellum letter. Distractedly she noticed his right hand was missing three fingers. A cripple, she thought uncharitably. What must the master be like?

The seal bore the hated leopard device. Breaking it savagely, she scanned the message. Though long and arrogantly worded, the grandiloquent phrases could not sweeten the outrageous proclamation. King Henry, self-styled sovereign of England and France, ordered her to receive one Enguerrand Fitzmarc, Baron of Longwood, along with the customary bride-price of the uncustomary sum of ten thousand gold crowns.

Momentarily dazzled by the amount, she glanced up. Bonne had entered, bearing cups of mulled wine. The herald stared at the maid. His eyes bulged, and mangled phrases of admiration burst from him. To Lianna's disgust, Bonne accepted the tribute with smiling grace and gave him a cup of wine.

Furious, Lianna said, "Move aside, Bonne. I want him to see exactly what I think of his message." She rent the vellum into tiny bits and scattered them among the rushes with her foot. "Your king is a pretender! I reject his edict, and I reject the spineless lackey he has sent to wed me, along with the pittance he mistakenly thinks will make him palatable."

She glared fiercely, like an ancient war goddess, her veil swirling, her silver eyes snapping. "Tell your master that he can take his foul carcass back to England."

Red-faced, the man stammered, "But . . . but my lady—"

"I wouldn't marry that English *god-don* if the moon fell out of the sky." She laughed harshly. "And if he thinks to force me, tell him to think again. I am already married to Lazare Mondragon."

Cade's jaw dropped. He grabbed a second cup of wine and drained it. "Married?"

She nodded. "I've had a copy of the marriage contract drawn up, so there can be no question as to its validity." Drawing the document from the folds of her gown, she thrust it under Cade's nose.

She couldn't resist a slow smile of dark satisfaction. Today she would dispense with the Englishman; now she could turn her mind to the problem of Lazare. "There is nothing your master can do. Even King Henry cannot undo what has been wrought before God. Begone, now. The sooner you and that *god-don* you serve leave our shores, the better!"

With jerky motions he pocketed the contract, sent a look of longing at Bonne, took the last of the wine, and left the hall.

"You were a bit hard on the poor fellow," said Bonne, staring after him. "He's only a messenger, after all."

"He's an English *god-don*."

An impulse of wicked mischief seized Lianna. She ran to the armory, put on her gunner's smock, and climbed to the battlements. The new culverin, on its rotating emplacement, was small enough to be discharged by a single gunner. She loaded a ball and a modest charge into the chamber, lit a piece of tow, and waited until the Englishman passed under the gatehouse and crossed the causeway. She aimed the gun well away from him; the firing would be just for show.

The charge crackled, then rent the morning air with a powerful report. The ball passed wide of the rider and came down harmlessly in the woods. The horse reared; Cade spurred him and disappeared down the road.

The shot brought half the residents of the keep running out into the bailey, stumbling over milling chickens and squealing pigs. Wrapped in a hastily donned robe, Gervais appeared below, red-faced, shaking his fist.

Lianna didn't care. Like potent wine, the heady sensation of triumph warmed her. How good it felt to vent her wrath, even on that worthless messenger. She half regretted that she'd never meet the master; she longed to see that damned *horzain* humiliated, wallowing in the mire of defeat, an Englishman bested by a Frenchwoman.

Gervais was shouting something, but Lianna paid no heed. Clutching herself around the waist, she doubled over and laughed, and laughed, and laughed.

A gray mist drizzled over the *Toison d'Or* as she nosed up the coast from Eu to Le Crotoy, a stronghold of the Duke of Burgundy. Standing at the rail, Rand felt a chill seep into his bones. He barely heard the shouts of the crew as they made ready for landfall, because he was thinking of Lianna. Like a recurring melody, her name played in his mind. How tempting it had been, after seeing the demoiselle's marriage contract, to seek Lianna out, to . . . to what? Locking his hands around the rail, he scowled. He was no more free now than he had been this morning when he'd sent Jack to Bois-Long. King

Henry needed the ford; Rand was honor-bound to secure it—if not by marriage, then by might. Perhaps Burgundy, who had sent a cautious message to Eu, inviting them to come in secret, would provide an answer.

For now, though, Rand needed answers from Jack. The scutifer had returned a few hours ago, too drunk to do more than place the demoiselle's message in Rand's hand. "Fetch Cade for me," he called to Simon.

Hand over hand, Jack Cade struggled along the rail toward Rand. "Please, my lord, not now."

Rand scowled. "From the looks of you, if you put me off much longer, I'll be talking to a corpse."

Gulping air, Jack sank into a crouch. Rand took out a skin flask of wine. Jack waved him away. "I'm still drunk from this morning. Drunk and seasick. Fried to my tonsils."

From his belt Rand drew Lianna's ashwood catapult and a stone. He flung the missile into the sea. "Speak, Jack. Tell me of your interview with the demoiselle. What was she like?"

"Beautiful," Jack mumbled sottishly.

"The demoiselle?" But she was Burgundy's niece.

"Hair like flame . . . breasts like fresh cream . . . God, but she did fling a cravin' upon me."

"The demoiselle?"

Jack blinked. "Oh, that one. I was speaking of her maid. Bonne, that's her name; means 'good,' don't it? I'll wager she's very good indeed."

His patience gone, Rand snapped, "It's the demoiselle I want to hear of."

Jack hiccuped. "Oh. Well . . . she's . . . cold, my lord." He grimaced. "Cold as the teat of a cockatrice."

Unbidden but welcome, relief spilled through Rand.

Thank God she'd married another. "What did she look like?"

The ship listed. Jack closed his eyes and began to tremble. "Like . . . a cockatrice?"

"Jack—"

"My lord, what know I of the high nobility?" Jack opened his eyes. "She looked upon me with scorn. She was all tricked out in gauzy stuff, such as we saw on the ladies at Eltham."

Rand could see the line of questioning was going nowhere. "What did she say?"

"She called you a *god-don*. What the hell is that?"

"A nickname we Englishmen have earned among the French, referring to our habit of calling upon God to damn whatsoever displeases us."

"Well, she's wrong about you. You've never taken the Lord's name in vain. I do so often enough for us both."

Rand sent another stone flying. It skittered across the iron-gray swells and was swallowed by a white-crested wave. "What else did she say?"

"She said she wouldn't marry you if the moon fell out of the sky." Jack watched him curiously but did not comment on the little weapon.

Robert Batsford, who had been standing nearby, joined them. "Her defiance is impressive," said the priest. "Few men, still fewer women, would dare flout a king's edict. Your bride is certainly bold-spirited."

Jack mumbled, "She's got the damnedest maid. . . ."

Furious, Rand squinted through the stinging mist. He'd been duped by a woman; he'd failed in his knightly duty. "Oh, she's a bride all right, Father. But not mine. She wed some Frenchman called Mondragon."

"Good Lord, is the woman mad?"

"Having never met her, I wouldn't know."

Batsford let loose with a low whistle. "Married. Blessed St. George, I'm beginning to feel a grudging respect for the woman. What will you do now?"

Like ghosts in the mist, the four round towers of Le Crotoy hove into view. "Burgundy and I will find a solution," said Rand.

Chapter 5

Rand was gone. For two weeks the glade where St. Cuthbert's cross stood had been empty, save for the lonely presence of a confused young woman. Still Lianna went there; she waited at the hour of the woodcock's flight, hoping to see Rand.

Over the days her remembrance of him turned to longing, and longing to obsession. She couldn't forget that smiling face hewed by angels, his lips whispering endearments before closing over hers, the rich caress of his voice as he sang her a love song. Standing in the glade, she moved her hands over her ribs, her neck, her breasts, remembering, wanting, needing. Her body cried out for him with a passion so strong it hurt. He'd plumbed a well of deep, secret longings inside her—longings that only he could fulfill. A timeless, mystical bond had linked them from the first, and even if Rand never came again, she knew she would never be free of him.

She could think of only one reason for his disappearance. The Englishman had quit the coastal town of Eu; obviously her Gascon knight had known about the invading foreigner and had gone after him. He'd wanted to break lances for her. Perhaps, unwittingly, he was doing just that.

Swathed in a vague, dreamy sadness, she returned to the château one day and walked her horse to the stables. Absently she noticed a gilt leather bridle had been left in the yard. Roland, the marshal, snatched it up.

"Sorry, my lady, I must have overlooked that," he mumbled, and scurried aside as if to escape the expected dressing down. But she said nothing as she gave him the reins of her palfrey. What mattered the loss of a bridle when her own heart was breaking?

An excess of equine noise penetrated the sorrow-spun web of her thoughts. Looking about, she saw that every empty stall was now occupied.

Catching her curious look, Roland said, "The Sire de Gaucourt has arrived, my lady. Best soldier in France, and right fussy about his horses, he is."

Lianna froze inside. She'd expected Gaucourt; the château was prepared for his visit, but now that he was here, her defiance against her uncle was real, irrevocable. Swallowing a feeling of uncertainty, she went to the hall to greet her guest.

Raoul, the Sire de Gaucourt, sat by the hearth with Gervais. The knight had a strong, arrogant face and an oddly lashless stare of deep calculation. His eyes were pale stones washed by the ice of command. The sight of him sliced through Lianna's defiance with a blade-sharp sense of apprehension.

Spying her, Gervais smiled. Unexpectedly, Lianna had

discovered a tolerance for her husband's son. He'd relaxed his father's interdict against her gunnery and lately seemed content to leave the running of the château to her. "Come greet our guest," he said. His eyes lingered on her stained homespun smock, but she saw no disapproval in his gaze.

She swept toward Gaucourt. "Welcome, *mon sire*."

He took her hand and leaned down, brushing his lips over the backs of her fingers. "Madame," he murmured.

She extracted her hand from his. "Thank you for coming to my aid."

His chilly, pale eyes crinkled at the corners, and she realized he was smiling in his own bloodless way. "I could not but come when I learned of the brave deed you did for France."

Despite her instinctive distrust of Gaucourt, Lianna was pleased that the knight offered none of the warnings and recriminations her uncle of Burgundy had dealt her. "Under the circumstances I had no choice. I couldn't possibly wed the Baron of Longwood and cede Bois-Long to the English Crown."

"I agree, madame. Bois-Long is precisely what King Henry needs, a stronghold on the Somme to give him access to Paris. He may have his sights set on France, but thanks to you he'll get no farther than here."

"And thanks to you, *mon sire*," Gervais said, "the English will not take Bois-Long by force."

Lianna sent him a cool look. So, Gervais did have some understanding of the lay of things. She turned to Raoul. "The Englishman was seen to sail away from Eu, where he landed, but I fear he'll be back."

"The presence of fifty of my best men will stay his hand."

Her eyes traveled down the length of the hall. Servitors were setting up the trestle tables for the evening meal. In a far corner of the room, the elderly Mère Brûlot sat crooning to the two babies she held in her arms. At one of the tables Guy, the seneschal, labored patiently over a *livre de raison*, his record of the daily events of the château.

Fear rushed over her like the shadowy wingbeats of a dark bird. Not for herself, but for the many people under her protection. How many of their fields would be burned if Henry acted? How long would they survive if the marauding English leveled their homes and slaughtered their livestock? Even Chiang's guns might not hold back Henry's wrath.

Gaucourt must have understood her unspoken thoughts, for he patted her arm reassuringly. "I've sent a number of *hobelars* out to scout the area. They'll report to me at the first sign of an English contingent."

"I'm deeply indebted to you," she said. But she wished she felt more confident. The greatest battle commander of France had come to safeguard her château. So why did his presence evoke such an odd, ineffable feeling of dread?

Gaucourt lifted his mazer of wine. "There is no price too high to preserve the sovereignty of France, my lady."

"At the moment I can but concern myself with preserving Bois-Long," said Lianna.

"With my help, you shall," Gaucourt promised. His eyes coursed over her, fastening on her waist. "Slim as a willow withe," he murmured with slight accusation. "You'd best call your husband back from Paris and see about getting an heir."

Lianna hoped her light laughter didn't sound as forced as it felt, issuing from a throat gone suddenly tight. "*Nom de Dieu, mon sire*, I wish you'd leave such concerns to my women and the soothsayers who haunt the marshes."

"I jest not," said Gaucourt. "A child is a political necessity. It would solidify a marriage your uncle of Burgundy opposes."

Gervais cleared his throat. His customary congenial smile seemed strained. "Bois-Long has an heir apparent," he said.

Gaucourt shrugged. "Belliane has the blood of both Burgundy and Aimery the Warrior in her veins. 'Twould be a shame to let the line die out."

That night in her chamber, she felt out of sorts as Bonne helped her prepare for bed. "Gaucourt's mention of an heir is all the talk, my lady," said the waiting damsel.

"Fodder for idle tongues," Lianna snapped, stiffening her back as Bonne ran a brush through her hair.

"A child would be a blessing," Bonne said boldly. "Perhaps it would even sweeten Macée's disposition. She's barren, you know."

Lianna stared. "No, I didn't know. Poor Macée."

"Get a babe of your own, my lady. She'd be a devoted nursemaid." Bonne's eyes glinted with a sly light. "But for your womb to quicken, you must lie with a man."

Lianna shot to her feet and whirled, her linen bliaut swirling about her slim ankles. "I'm not an idiot, Bonne. Lazare is in Paris. What would you have me do?"

"Take a lover. Queen Isabel herself has dozens." Bonne moved across the chamber to the bed, whipping back the coverlet and brushing a bit of dried lavender from the pillow.

Lianna shivered. The king's brother, Louis of Orléans, had paid with his life for consorting with Isabel. The Armagnacs credited the murder to her uncle of Burgundy.

"Would you have me present Lazare with a bastard?" she demanded.

"And who could call your child a bastard?" said Bonne. "The bloodied sheets of the marriage bed were duly inspected." The maid brightened. "Perhaps you're carrying a child now."

"That's not poss—" Lianna stopped herself. If word ever reached her uncle that the marriage had not been consummated, Burgundy would waste no time in getting it annulled and forcing her to marry the Englishman. "Enough, Bonne," she said. "It is not your place to speak to me so."

"As you wish, my lady," the maid said without a trace of contrition. She patted the pillow. "Come, to bed with you. Doubtless Gaucourt and the fifty extra mouths he's brought to feed will keep you busy on the morrow."

Lianna slipped beneath the coverlet and lay back on the pillow. Wisps of gullsdown drifted around her.

Bonne brought her lips together in a tight pout of irritation. "By St. Wilgefort's beard," she declared, "I told that slattern Edithe to mend the pillow."

Lianna patted her hand. "Leave Edithe to me, Bonne." The maid looked so outraged that Lianna tried to turn the subject. "Who, by the by, is St. Wilgefort?"

Bonne sat on the edge of the bed and leaned forward eagerly. "A new one, my lady, that Father LeClerq told me of. Wilgefort, it seems, was a matchless beauty. Growing weary of having so many suitors, she prayed to God for help." Bonne hugged her knees to her chest and giggled. "She woke up the next morning with a full beard."

Though she laughed, Lianna drew a painful parallel with her own dilemma. People lauded her beauty, but they kept their distance. She needed no beard, not with her domineering uncle, her scheming husband, and her own nature—a coolness born of confusion and ignorance—keeping men at bay.

Bonne started to withdraw, then returned to pick up a mug she'd left on a shelf. "Mustn't forget my tonic," she murmured, lifting the mug and draining it.

"Are you ailing?" Lianna asked.

Bonne laughed. "No, my lady, 'tis a draught of rue and savin." She flushed. "Prevents conception."

Knowing the substance to be a mild poison, Lianna frowned. "Is Roland so careless with you, Bonne?"

The maid shrugged. "Men. They are all alike. They spread their seed like chaff to the wind, heedless of where it takes root."

That night Lianna had the dream again, the now familiar fantasy in which the husband who approached her bed transformed from Lazare into Rand. She awoke the next morning with a vague but compelling sense of new purpose.

During the three weeks since Rand had gone in secret to Le Crotoy, spring had pounced like a golden lion upon Picardy. Bees droned over the clover-carpeted meadow through which he walked, bearing hard for Bois-Long. In a distant field, cows stood motionless in the shimmering sunlight, and the scent of the salt marshes tingled sharply in his nose. Travel would have been quicker on horseback, but with Gaucourt's *hobelars* about, Rand couldn't risk detection.

As his long strides carried him across fields and through forests, he discovered a deep appreciation for the beauty of the land. To the east a field of blue flax and budding poppies waved in restful harmony; to the west loomed the highlands bordered by chalky cliffs and stunted trees. The Somme coiled inland, fed by scores of tributaries. A forest of beeches and elms, their powerful trunks nourished by rich earth, sprang from the marshy valley. Ahead, a line of blazed poplars nodded in the breeze. The gateway to Bois-Long.

His French heritage linked him to this land. His English title made him master of it. Yet Burgundy's new plan made secrecy necessary. The duke had promised that the demoiselle would soon be free to wed; he seemed confident of an annulment of her marriage to Mondragon. Rand was only too happy to leave the intriguing to Burgundy.

Cautiously he approached his destination. He misliked stealth; he had no prowess at it.

As he edged along the bank, keeping to the shadows of great water beeches, he saw, for the second time, the impregnable magnificence of the château. Only now he looked at it, not as his future home, but as a fortress to be breached. He calculated the height of the walls and determined the route he'd take when he came for his bride.

With a bit of charcoal he made a sketch on parchment, noting the locations of the sentry towers, the number of windows in the keep proper, the merlons in the battlements.

The idea of sneaking into the château and abducting an unsuspecting woman filled him with distaste, but he had no choice. Gaucourt's presence made an overt attack ludicrous; the idea of returning unsuccessful to England was unthinkable.

The clopping of hoofs on the causeway snared his attention. Muscles coiling, he pressed back against a thick tree trunk and watched a small contingent of men-at-arms emerge from beneath the barbican. At their center rode a woman.

The Demoiselle de Bois-Long.

It could be no other, for she perched on her saddle with an air of haughty authority and was robed in a gown of sumptuous red. King Henry's gifts of cloth and jewels should please her, Rand thought. She favors rich dresses.

Feeling both detached and uneasy, he studied the woman who would become his wife. Her face was milk pale; she had ripe red lips, sleek black hair, and fine-drawn brows that swept high above eyes too distant to discern the color. Beauty, not warmth, was the chief impression Rand gleaned from his glimpse of the demoiselle. She was Burgundy's kin, he reminded himself. Why look for kindness in her?

She reined in and snapped an order to one of the men. When he made no move to respond, she gave a little screech, produced a stout riding crop, and laid it about the man's shoulders until he dismounted and adjusted her stirrup. Then they were off again, crossing the causeway and turning east along a dirt road.

As he stared at the narrow back and raven locks of the demoiselle, Rand felt each breath like a harsh rasp in his throat. This woman, with her hard red mouth and cruel white hands, was to be his wife, the mother of his babes. Not only was he condemned to asserting his control over a French keep; now he knew his wife had a temper he'd have to tame.

Troubled, he glanced up at the westering sun. *I'll come in the late afternoon each day, and wait until the hour of the woodcock's flight*. Lianna's words drifted into his mind, pulling him to the place he knew he should not visit, the place of St. Cuthbert's cross.

Lianna visited the glade with less and less frequency, for her hopes of meeting Rand again had begun to wane. He's a knight-errant, she told herself. His home is where he pitches his tent and tethers his horse.

But the spring-soft afternoon and the terrifying goal she'd set for herself brought her back to the glade. Bonne's words haunted her: *Men. They spread their seed like chaff to the wind.* At last Lianna was ready to admit that Bonne was right; Gaucourt was right. She needed an heir to prevent her uncle from tampering with her marriage to a Frenchman and to prevent Gervais from inheriting Bois-Long.

Walking through the long stretch of woods, she pondered her plan. Surely Rand, if she could find him again, would plant a child inside her, and Lazare would be too proud to deny the babe was his own.

So simple, she thought. So cold-blooded. So damnably necessary. She wondered if she had the courage and callousness to bring her attraction to Rand to its natural conclusion.

She did. But not by virtue of her courage, which she doubted, nor by virtue of her callousness, which had been soothed to tenderness by Rand's loving hands. For she was motivated by more than the simple need for an heir. She wanted Rand to make love to her, to fill the void that had gaped like an open wound in her heart all her life. He'd awakened the dreamer within her, given her the will to reach out with both hands for the love that had ever eluded her.

Since she was accustomed by now to finding the glade

empty, her heart hammered in surprise when she spied Rand through a frame of budding willows. Filled with gladness and fear, she approached him from one side. The woods craft schooled into her by Chiang gave her a light, silent step. Rand didn't notice her; he appeared deep in thought.

His back against the stone cross, his sun-gilt head bowed over his chest, he put her in mind of a sleeping giant, his power unsprung, hovering beneath a patina of repose. Hazy, diffuse light showered over his profile. His hair, she noticed with affectionate attention, had grown longer, the ends curling like a halo around the unspoiled beauty of his face.

His guileless pose, his pensive attitude, made her regret her intention to take advantage of their attraction, yet the heart-stopping magnificence of his long, muscled body filled her with guilty excitement.

She expressed her agitation with a soft gasp, a whispered greeting.

With a start that sent her stumbling back, he jumped to his feet and yanked out a pointed dagger. Recognition, then undiluted joy, blossomed on his face. The weapon disappeared back into its sheath. "*Pucelle*, you gave me a start." His smile touched her heart like the shimmer of a sunbeam.

She flushed. "I didn't mean to." Studying the tender ferns on the forest floor, she felt suddenly shy.

"You always startle me, sweet maid," he said, a strained note of longing in his voice.

Her throat constricted at the sight of those leaf-green eyes, that rugged face far more animated, more compelling, than the one she saw in her dreams each night.

With one swift movement he swept her into his arms.

"Oh, God, Lianna, I have missed you." He hugged her close with his powerful arms, buried his face in her neck, and plunged his hands into her hair. The plaited locks yielded to his fingers, and soon her hair lay loose around her shoulders.

He smelled of the sea and the sun. She felt as if she'd come home, with his arms tight around her, his chest solid against her cheek. "Where have you been, Rand?"

"Nowhere. I am nowhere without you." He cupped her chin and tilted her head up. His lips began a slow descent onto hers.

Trembling, she clung to him, relished every tingling sensation that shivered over her as their lips melded into a long, slow kiss. Her hands ranged up his sinuous torso, feeling the sweat-dampened skin beneath his mail shirt. She twined her fingers through his golden hair and pulled him closer, her lips parting, inviting the velvety sweep of his tongue. He filled her with masculine sweetness, wrapped her with steel-tempered hardness, and kindled the fuse of her passion.

Seared by yearning, she pressed closer. He dragged his lips from hers. His eyes glinted jewel-bright with an inner torment that tore at her heart and filled her mind with questions. "Why did you stay away for so long?" she asked.

He touched her cheek, her brow. "Because it is wrong for us to meet like this, in secret. Lianna, I can offer you nothing."

"How can you say that? How can you belittle the friendship you've given me?" He started to pull away. She grasped his hands, leaned up on tiptoe, and kissed him hard on the mouth. Then she stepped back and let her hair fall forward to hide the fire he'd ignited in her cheeks. Peering uncertainly from between her locks, she wondered if her bold behavior appalled him. He'd certainly been disapproving enough of her interest in gunnery. Doubtless she violated every image this knight-errant had of feminine ideals.

He parted her hair with his fingers. With relief, she saw only affection in his smile.

"Would that I could give you more than friendship," he whispered.

Hope billowed in her chest. "I've come here almost every day," she admitted.

Taking her hand, he pressed his lips to the pulse at her wrist. "Testing your guns?" He sounded both teasing and annoyed.

She shook her head. "Looking for you. You know that, Rand. And I asked where you've been." He didn't speak. Raising one eyebrow, she ventured, "Doubtless on knightly business of utmost secrecy." She fixed him with a probing stare. "But I've guessed your secret."

He fell still, seemed not even to breathe. "Lianna—"

"Don't worry," she said, smiling softly. "I'll not put it about that you've chased the Englishman from Eu."

He blinked. "Chased the—"

"Aye, we heard that the *god-don* has sailed away." Excitement danced in her eyes. "Did you fight him, Rand? Did you slay the man who came to conquer Château Bois-Long?"

"The Englishman left . . . of his own volition. No blood was spilled."

"Did he run back to England like the coward he is?"

"I don't know, Lianna. I just don't know." He sounded weary, immeasurably sad.

She touched his sleeve. "You wear no colors, my Gascon. Are you for the Armagnacs or the Burgundians?"

"I could ask you the same of your mistress. She is of the blood of Burgundy, yet she houses a supporter of Armagnac."

Her eyes widened. "How do you know about Gaucourt?"

"His presence at Bois-Long is no secret."

She regarded him with mock severity. "Perhaps you're a spy for Burgundy . . . or the English."

He grinned. "Suppose I were?"

"Then I would steal your dagger and use it on you." Sadness crept into his eyes again. She took his hand and laid it alongside her cheek. "Talk to me, Rand. I want to know you."

"There is much I would share with you . . . if I could."

"Have you a family?"

His expression softened. "If you could term a band of motley men a family."

"Your men?" She turned to scan the area.

"My comrades. But you won't find them here."

"Tell me about them, Rand."

"They are men like any other. They have mothers, sweethearts . . . except for the priest, of course."

She smiled. "Somehow it seems fitting that you would keep constant company with a priest."

Laughing, he said, "You'd not think so if you knew *this* priest. He's more likely to be found ranging the fields on a hunt than in a chapel hearing confessions. He often says mass in muddy boots and falconer's cuffs."

"What of your other friends?"

A guarded look made him seem suddenly distant, unapproachable. "I think it is better for us both to keep silent about certain matters."

Wanting to draw him back to her, she leaned up and kissed him lightly. It wasn't fair to question him, not when she was full of her own secrets. She couldn't tell him now that she was the Demoiselle de Bois-Long, and married, with the wrath of the Duke of Burgundy and the King of England down upon her. This glade was their private garden, a place to forget they were each part of someone else's plan.

"Times are uncertain. I'll badger you no more," she said.

Cloaked in wildflowers, the fields beckoned. As they walked, Rand stooped to pick hepaticas, fire-pink gay-wings, early yellow violets, and bluets barely furled from their buds. Lianna loved to hear him talk. His rich, musical voice revealed ideas as fine and fanciful as the flowers he gathered. With enchanting whimsy he told her improbable tales of gallantry, unconquerable villains, damsels in distress.

Stopping on a little rise in the middle of the field, he offered her the flowers. She shook her head. "What would you have me do with them?"

"Smell them, for God's sake. Let them pleasure you."

She laughed. "Pleasure me? What a silly notion." She plucked a single stalk of mayapple from his bouquet. "Now this is useful in making a decoction for the grippe."

He tucked it behind her ear. "You sorely try my patience, *pucelle*. To you, everything needs must have a practical use. Why is that?"

"I know of no other way to look at things." Taking a violet, she stared intently at the blossom, then at the waving profusion of flowers all around her. "In sooth they all seem alike to me."

He cupped her chin in one hand and rubbed the silken

petals over her lips. "Then let me show you, Lianna."

Sitting down, he spread his hands and scattered the blossoms. The scent soon brought a tumble of butterflies.

Lianna stepped back, her breath snared in her throat. He was so beautiful, so true of heart. She yearned for a measure of his charming insouciance, the self-assuredness that made him capable of exalting even a lowly mayapple. But, tainted by intrigue and secrecy, she knew she could never share his clear-eyed wonder. Stiffly she sat down beside him. A butterfly flitted between them.

"My sad girl," he said softly. "Why do you look so sad?"

"I wish I could be like you, Rand. So . . . whimsical."

"Whimsical! Dear maid, you unman me."

"But it's true. You're so full of unexpected delights. . . ." She let her voice trail off and frowned. "I am clumsy with words. I know not how to say what I feel."

"Try, Lianna."

"I have an emptiness deep inside me, a darkness. In studying weaponry I learned high-flown ideas of science, the timing of fuses, the use of priming irons, but no one ever taught me how to—" She swallowed hard. "You have said I am beautiful, but I cannot believe it because I don't feel it in my heart. I've never thought the attribute of any value."

She heard the rasp of his quick-drawn breath, saw the unsteadiness of his hand as he picked up the flowers in his lap. He plaited the blossoms into a circlet, put it on her head, let chains of lavender hepatica trail over her shoulders. Placing his arms around her, he lifted her up, out of her wooden sabots, so that she stood with her bare feet on the cool ground.

Her head and shoulders festooned with flowers, her

heart pounding with a sense of new awareness, Lianna saw desire flare in his eyes. His admiration made her truly beautiful for the first time. The idea gave her a sudden, deep sense of self-worth.

As if he understood, Rand caressed her cheek. "Do you see now, *pucelle*? You are lovely, sacred, worthy."

Shaken, she closed her eyes. Slowly she spread out her arms, opened her hands as if to grasp the very air around her. Filled with the scent of flowers and the enlightenment Rand had given her, she tasted the quiet exultation of a dream fulfilled. She opened her eyes and looked at him.

Her thoughts tumbled over one another. It was right. It had to be right. She wanted him now, not just for the child he could give her, but to satisfy the yearning in her newly awakened heart, to unleash the desire she recognized in his taut body and emerald-bright eyes. His hands were hard fists at his sides, as if he were clenching them against the urge to touch her.

How to tell him? she wondered wildly. She could not possibly blurt it out: Excuse me, but I cannot contain my passion for you and I need a child, so would you please make love to me?

Gripped by shyness, her tongue thick and clumsy with words she'd never thought to utter to any man, she snatched a yellow violet and rolled it between her fingers. "Rand...I have been thinking on...a matter."

He cocked his head; his smile grew endearingly warm. "Would you like to speak of it, *pucelle*?"

"Yes. Yes, I would. You see, I think that it is time we were honest about...certain things."

His eyes dimmed almost imperceptibly. "What things?"

Lianna inhaled a gulp of air. "Well . . . our feelings. I confess I have feelings for you. *Nom de Dieu*, but I am graceless with words. I know you have certain desires, Rand. I have felt it in the way you hold me, and kiss me." A blush suffused her face with hot color. "Doubtless you hold the favor of many women," she rushed on, growing more embarrassed with each word, more entrapped in her own awkward speech.

"You presume a great deal," he said.

She blinked, discomfited by his easy, bemused tolerance. "Of course, you might have been with a woman these weeks past."

Suppressed laughter gave his voice a compelling richness. "Why don't you ask me?"

She couldn't bring herself to frame such a question. "You are free to do as you will. But I was wondering, Rand, if you could see your way, perhaps, to act on these feelings." She lowered her head. "Do you not feel some . . . some measure of desire for me? That is—"

"Lianna," he broke in, "I love you."

Her head snapped up. "So you said," she whispered. "At least, you said you *thought* you loved me."

He stepped forward, brushed a wisp of silver-gilt hair from her temple. "I no longer think so, *pucelle*. I know."

Pulse beats of emotion thudded a hot, heavy path through her body. Why did his declaration mean so much to her? She needed only his seed. Still, there was that deep agony within her that had nothing to do with procuring an heir and everything to do with the gorgeous, golden man standing before her.

Sudden doubts pricked at her. She was married; she could never share more than stolen trysts with Rand. Yet she wanted him so desperately. . . .

He regarded her with a steady gaze. His lips curved into a tender smile. A smile she trusted.

The doubts vanished.

"Well," she said, wondering if the raw inner tenderness she felt could truly be love. "Well. 'Tis settled, is it not?"

His smile widened. "What is settled?"

She forced herself to face him squarely. "Why, the matter I was trying to speak to you about. You'll make love to me now, won't you?"

Chapter 6

The thrust of an enemy lance could not have pierced Rand more deeply. Her earnest request singed his every nerve with a longing so hot, he burned with it, a frustration so sharp that he could scarce draw breath.

His mouth was dry, his tongue thick, when at last he found his voice. "Lianna, sweet maid, you know not what you ask."

"Yes," she whispered, her breath warm as she leaned toward him. "I do." A pucker—innocent, adorable—turned her lips to a sweet bud. "I suppose you think no worthy lady would ask such a thing, but I want you...." She stepped closer, brought her thighs brushing against his. "And I think you want me."

Indeed, he thought wildly, how could she mistake the iron-wrought bulge in his braies that reared against her soft, yielding form? "I am a knight," he said, less forcefully than he would have wished. "I took an oath...."

She fixed him with a steady silver stare. "Every true knight," she said, her finger tapping lightly against her chin, "is a lover." She smiled. "So say the troubadours' lays."

"The troubadours preferred the sweet torment of yearning to the passing joy of a conquest won." He spoke quickly, desperately, for his resolve flagged with each wild beat of his heart.

Her gaze touched his face, his shoulders, his torso. "And you, Rand. What do you prefer?"

He kept his hands at his sides, for to touch her now would be to lose the last shreds of self-discipline he possessed. "You are far easier to reckon with in my dreams, Lianna. There, you are only a shadow, the object of worship." Aye, he thought, in his dreams he could control her . . . and himself.

She sent him a whisper-soft smile. Her eyes shone, her face glowed, the curves of her flower-strewn body were evident beneath the plain smock she wore. Yearning wrapped around his groin like a steel claw. Disconcerted, he moved away.

She set her hands on her hips. "I am not some madonna to be set on a pedestal or enshrined in a crypt," she said impatiently. "Professions of knightly devotion might be enough for ladies of legend, but such lofty regard is not enough for me."

"In person," he conceded, "you are a more earthly goddess." He met her steady gaze. "Demanding, complex, difficult."

"Oh, Rand. Will you let your scruples get in the way of something we both want and need? How can it be wrong?"

He looked down at his big, rough hands, the left one

sleek with scars. Too soon, he must put a ring on the finger of another. "I can offer you nothing."

"You say you love me. Will you call that nothing?"

"I don't want to dishonor you."

"You dishonor me by denying my womanhood," she said, her eyes flashing like quicksilver. "You refuse to acknowledge that I have a mind of my own, a body that sings for yours."

"That is precisely what I've been fighting. Lianna, already I love you too much, more than I should."

An errant breeze caused a blue flower to drift across her cheek; she caught the blossom with her hand and rubbed the petals thoughtfully over her chin. "Before I met you, I knew no love at at all. Now you speak of loving too much. I do not understand."

In her voice he heard all the hurt and bewilderment of an orphan left to the care of castle folk. He yearned to gather her into his arms, to teach her love, yet at the same time he felt a terrible futility, for she would also suffer betrayal from him.

He drew a ragged breath. "All my life I have had self-restraint schooled into me. A man who cannot control himself is doomed to be controlled by others. That is why I turn away from the *chevauchées* of my fellow knights." Looking up, he met her wide, unblinking eyes. "Now you've catapulted into my life and shaken everything I've ever believed in."

"Touch me," she said, and her compelling tone caught at his heart. "Touch me, and know that I am a woman, nothing more. Flesh and blood and bone—"

Her words disappeared as, with a groan of fragmenting will, he closed his arms around her and pressed his mouth against hers. He tasted a powerful sweetness, felt the warmth of her awakening body as she slid her fingers into his hair. His own hands charted the supple curves of her fragile frame while his tongue discovered the shape of her lips, the silky moistness within. Over the course of their long, slow kiss of surrender, Rand felt his resistance being peeled away like layers of heavy garments. He abandoned the knightly scruples, the painful vows, the allegiance to an overambitious monarch, the woman who'd erected a military stronghold against him. He set his sights on a fair maid who'd confessed her desire, who'd asked nothing more than the meager gift of friendship, who'd stolen his heart with her unusual ways and sweet, sad smile.

He lifted his mouth from hers but still held the warm, willing girl in his arms. She needed him, she wanted his love, and his heart closed exultantly around the knowledge. It was a relief to shed his ill-wrought principles—principles of a man who, until this moment, hadn't understood so deep a love. With Justine, devotion and duty had held him in check. With Lianna, love and desire pushed him past the bounds of reason.

He pulled back and stared into her passion-bright eyes. He owed her a chance to change her mind. "If I make love to you now, you'll hate me for it one day."

"I could never hate you."

"In sooth you could."

"Is lovemaking truly so disagreeable?"

"No, it's not that; it's—" He broke off, then began again, loathing the necessity for secrecy. "You and I can never have more than these trysts. What if I get you with child?"

Rather than looking alarmed, she smiled. "A child is a gift from God."

He thought of the cruel, raven-haired demoiselle. "Your mistress would beat you, cast you out."

"She'd never do that. Believe it."

"What about me, Lianna? *I* want more than secret trysts."

Her confused gaze caught his; he sucked in his breath. She spoke a single word, so softly that the breeze nearly snatched it from his ears. Yet he heard: *"Please."*

A groan of abandonment rumbled up from deep inside him. He said, "Yes." He caught her against him, kissed her hard. "Yes, Lianna, I'll make love to you."

Roses bloomed in her cheeks, and a smile curved her lips. "We won't be sorry," she said. Yet a shimmer of uncertainty glinted in her eyes. "But there is something I must explain."

As he plucked the flowers one by one from her hair, he asked, "What is that, *pucelle*?"

"I've had a scholar's training in science and gunnery. But I know naught of pleasing a man." Looking down at her hands, she added, "And I would please you."

With gentle fingers he lifted the rest of the flowers from her head. Bending, he inhaled the perfume that lingered there. "You please me simply by being Lianna," he said. "By giving me the gift of your trust, your innocence."

Her smile had the power to steal his soul and plunder his convictions. Battling the urgent clamor in his loins, he slowly plucked at the laces of her smock, drawing the string out, parting the neckline. Her eyes were steady, calm, yet the glints of battered silver never quite left those misty depths. She was like a wounded bird who could not speak her pain to him, but who deserved all the tenderness he could offer.

Aye, he thought, slipping the smock over her shoulders. He would be careful with this fragile creature. She'd fallen from a nest; he'd not be the one to toss her to the cat.

The wide, square-cut neckline of her shift revealed the delicate lines of her throat and collarbone, the sheen of dew on her ivory flesh. He gulped a quick breath; the unique essence of her wafted to his soul.

Reaching behind her, he loosed the laces of the shift and pulled the garment down. A dainty chemise remained. He bent and kissed her. All his life he'd envisioned this as an act performed in the darkness of a cool nuptial chamber. Yet here he was in full, glorious light, unveiling beauty beyond words.

The chemise came away in his hands. She stood motionless, uncertain. The sight of her body, shining with purity, snatched his breath away. She was a harmonic poem of loveliness, a miracle of symmetry and form, from the rich mantle of her hair to her small bare feet. Shoulders and arms sleek and sturdy with delicate muscles. Small high breasts adorned with dawn-shaded tips. Hips flaring with a subtle femininity, a down-soft thatch of womanly curls above her thighs. Her legs were long and finely made, the flesh pale yet kissed by roses.

She smiled. Love blazed high in his chest; desire burned like dark, liquid fire in his loins.

Rand was a stranger to a woman's body. Tavern wenches and noblewomen visiting Arundel had often tried to seduce him, their desire honed by a challenge to possess the unattainable. Passionless, detached, his man's body had resisted.

But now, when he looked upon Lianna, he saw with his heart and soul as well as his eyes. And with his hands.

He traced the curves of her torso, fingers grazing her breasts, her belly. A blush misted her throat and cheeks, but yet-to-be-discovered promises softened her lips and glazed her eyes with a lustrous sheen of passion.

"Well?" she asked, folding her arms across her chest.

Rand grinned at her almost childlike expectancy. "You are passing fair."

Her chin lifted a notch. "Is that all?"

"You have a fine mind."

"Well!" Her pale eyebrows clashed, affronted.

"You once bade me not to prate about your beauty."

"I've changed my mind. I would know what you think."

He took her by the shoulders and lowered his mouth to the curve of her neck. "In sooth, *pucelle*, I think you are magnificent." His mouth moved lower, teeth grazing the ridge of her collarbone. "Your skin is like ivory, but warmer, more yielding"—he cradled her breast in his hand—"than the first lily of spring." He lifted his head and stared into her eyes while his hands continued to caress her, reaching around to cup her hips. "I see something wild and fay in you, as if you were a creature conjured by a skilled sorcerer." He bent again and took her lips with a hard, biting kiss, leaving them love-bruised and glistening.

"Well," she said again, breathlessly. "Well, sir knight." Her fingers shook as she touched the edge of his tunic, fingered the mail shirt beneath. Frowning, she plucked at the lace points. "Who the devil dresses you?" she asked. "Your laces are done up with knots like a friar's scourge."

Rand yearned to share every aspect of his life with her, to tell her of Jack, his scutifer; of Simon, his squire; of all the people who belonged to his other life. He nearly choked on the words crowding into his throat. He'd already said too much, lied too much. All he could offer Lianna was this flower-studded meadow, the tender spring grass beneath their feet and the gulls wheeling overhead, and the passion of a man's body tested far past the tenets of knightly discipline.

Driven by the need for secrecy, he tucked her head into the lee of his shoulder, tugged off King Henry's amulet, and shoved it into a pocket of his tunic. He couldn't allow her to see the talisman, to guess his mission. With bitter irony he recalled the motto carved around the jewel: To valiant hearts nothing is impossible. Yet like a distant comet, a future with the woman he loved eluded him. No, he thought. I'll have her. I'll find a way.

He shed his clothes, the garments skimming down his marble-hard body. The late afternoon sun bathed his skin with honeyed warmth—or more likely the fever came from within.

Wide-eyed, she subjected him to unabashed scrutiny, and he had to remind himself of her empirical bent of mind. With a gaze of melting radiance she touched him, and with one finger, too, tracing the ridges of muscle banding his chest, arms, shoulders, following the path of golden hair down his middle, hesitating, hovering over the fevered, engorged part of him. Her eyes found his and her finger moved on, upward again.

"I always thought you unconquerable, yet you bear half a hundred scars," she said, finding a deep crescent at his shoulder.

"Nicks," he said gruffly. "Pinpricks." In sooth neither sword nor arrowhead could inflict the exquisite agony imparted by Lianna's slender finger. She continued to map the contours of his body; he bore the torture like a martyr in the steely grip of an inquisitor's iron maiden. His gaze searched her face, seeking the emotions written there, dreading to discover fear, regret.

Instead she seemed wild with passion and endearingly curious as her hands discovered the way he was made.

Need stormed his senses. He took her hands and drew her down so that they were both kneeling, thigh to thigh, chest to chest, like supplicants in some pagan rite. He kissed her, a deep, wet, mating kiss that left them both breathless.

"What now?" she asked unsteadily.

He wrapped her against him. *What now?* In wartime he'd seen women raped. In peacetime the act had been described in minute, lusty detail by Jack and scores like him, archers and noblemen alike. Yet Rand could not know if he had the finesse, the substance, to put the force of his feelings into his caresses.

His hands glided down over her shoulder blades, her backside. "I want to touch you . . . all over . . . your body, your mind, your heart." As he spoke, his fingers took flight, winging over her throat, her breasts, her belly, her thighs. Moving his mouth along the curve of her jaw, he added, "I want to fuse my soul with yours, Lianna, to make you forget where you end and I begin." His manhood pressed against her soft flesh.

"*Nom de Dieu,*" she gasped. "Can you do that?"

He pulled back, cradled her chin in one hand. "I mean to try, *pucelle.*"

Swept up in a great wave of wanting, Lianna wove her fingers into his sun-spun curls. His naked body blazed with power. She felt a clamoring need to be engulfed by this man, his noble goodness, the purity of his passion, the enchantment of his masculinity. A small inner voice reminded her that she was breaking her marriage vows. Aye, this was wrong by the laws of man and God, yet her heart knew it was right. Rand made her feel clean and brave and womanly all at once, and the promise he'd voiced, his promise to make her forget, was nigh as potent as the love words that spilled from his lips as he scattered kisses over her face, her neck.

All the kissing, the touching, startled her. How much longer would he torture her with lusty words and loving hands? All ignorant, she didn't understand this arousing loveplay. She knew only what Bonne had said, that men spread their seed like chaff to the wind.

But there was hardly a breeze today. How was he going to plant his seed?

His breath came in quick gasps; he stirred against her thigh. With an abrupt flash of insight, she envisioned a stallion covering a mare. *Nom de Dieu*, she thought, would Rand invade her body in that way? She fixed him with a rapt, helpless stare. Oh yes, said a voice deep inside her. Yes, she wanted him to.

Pressing gently on her shoulders, he brought her down to the grass so that they were both reclining, she on her back, he on his side.

His strong fingers glided over her breasts in a touch so light, so compelling, that suddenly she knew why his harp sang so sweetly for him. She heard a similar note of helpless yearning in her own voice. "Rand . . ."

"I want to make you mine. Only mine."

An unwelcome remembrance of her other life, her life away from here, parted the hot, silken fog of desire shrouding her. King Henry's edict, Lazare's betrayal, her uncle's disdain—all the hurts of the past weeks, all the years of living without love, welled up into a great, aching cannonball of pain. A small sound erupted, soblike, from her throat.

He drew back, his princely face drawn with concern. "Lianna, what is it?"

She turned her head away and swallowed back the tale that threatened to barrel from her lips. "Nothing," she whispered. "Just . . . love me."

He embraced her, and she felt as if he'd wrapped her in a mist-soft web of satin. "I wish," he said, "I could pull the wounds from your soul and take them unto myself."

"Why?"

He kissed her eyelids. "You know why. Because I love you with all the might of my soul." His mouth closed over hers with new, prodigious force. His kiss was no longer sweet, but heavy with powerful emotions, demanding with a powerful need. The hot nectar of his lips seemed, like a sorcerer's philter, to draw the hurt form her, to heal her.

She sighed. Her eyes fluttered shut. He'd freed her, at least for this breathless moment, from the haunting troubles that plagued her. Now she could give to him openly, without restraint. "Yes," she said. "Love me."

"All over, *pucelle,*" he said, repeating his pledge, his fingers rounding her breasts, grazing her nipples. "Aye, all over." He bent his head, and she clenched her eyes more tightly, awaiting the welcome pressure of his mouth on hers; but she didn't feel his kiss on her lips.

Her eyes flew open. "Rand!"

"Hush," he murmured, and closed his mouth back over her breast.

She felt like a slow match soaked in lime and sparked

by red-hot steel. She shut her eyes again as something inside her began to burn. Ignited by his unexpected and intimate kiss, the inner match sizzled with gathering brightness and heat. Its core seemed to be in her belly, but the long, sparkling fuse of passion radiated in a hundred divergent directions, touching all of her with scintillating warmth. All of her. . . .

His tongue roughened the peak of each breast until her flushed nipples blossomed into buds of pure pleasure. Ablaze with sensation, she dragged her eyes open to look upon him—upon them both. His sun-gold cheek contrasted with the ivory paleness of her breast. The mouth drawing on the peak was soft yet seemed to possess a chained hunger about to be unleashed. Then his mouth found hers again, his tongue flicking hotly at her lips until she opened fully to him.

Rand sensed the change in her, the change from profound interest to unthinking passion. "Oh yes, love," he whispered. "Let me touch you. . . ." His hand moved downward, stroking, and he knew the wonder he saw in her eyes was reflected in his own. *Flesh and blood and bone*, she'd said, but she was so much more. She was magic and mystery, fire and fury, full of secrets he longed to unlock, one by precious one.

He pressed gently at the inside of her thigh. She gasped, stiffened. He sipped the sweetness of innocence from her mouth and forced away a tiny, sharp blade of uncertainty. This was uncharted territory, this woman's body of hers, its peaks and valleys unfamiliar to him. Yet his hands, guided by the timeless wisdom of a man deeply in love, skimmed and stroked and explored in a way that heated her flesh to a radiant glow and filled him with a rightness of purpose such as he'd never known before.

There was the milk-pale skin of her belly, smooth and rich as cream, the lush, heavy warmth of her thighs, yielding at last to his gentle pressure, the silk-spun nest of her womanhood.

She gave a little yearning plea, wordless yet alive with the eloquence of her desire. He braced himself on one elbow, the better to see, to touch. She was wondrous there, the magic, the secrets of her, so powerful.

"You are so beautiful," he said unsteadily. Her breath caught as he anointed his fingers with the essence of her. Her breathing stopped altogether as his palm caressed her. She was fine, lovely, mysterious. Petals within petals of soft, soft womanhood, all springing from a tiny, moist bud that blossomed at his touch.

"Rand!" She grasped his shoulders hard. Her eyes grew wide with wonderment.

He bent to feather kisses up her throat, to her mouth. "Aye, love?"

"I . . . I don't know. I just felt so strange all of a sudden, as if I were about to burst from my body when you touched me—" She flushed. "There."

A sharp, clear joy washed over him. He moved his hand. "Where, *pucelle*? Tell me. Teach me. Was it here . . . or here . . . or . . . ?"

"There," she breathed, her body arching, lithe as a willow wand. "Aye, there."

Always he'd thought this moment would drive away all thoughts of anything but his own need. Yet like a supplicant bowed before some woodland divinity, he spared no thought for himself, but only for her, seeking her pleasure before his own.

Loving her with his mouth and hands and heart, he watched her pleasure crest, felt it explode on a tide of warmth, caught and tasted her gasp of surprise.

"Rand," she whispered, "is that how it is between a man and a woman?"

He smiled. She was so naïve, so fresh. She brought light to the discontented darkness in his soul. "Aye, sweet love," he said, "that is part of it."

She flushed. The clarion blue of the sky found a shining home in the pale-lashed silver of her eyes. "You mean . . . there's more?"

"Aye," he said, bracing himself above her. "Much more."

She shivered. "*Nom de Dieu.*"

"I shall be as gentle as I can, Lianna." Staring into the bewildered depths of her eyes, he realized she didn't quite understand. With a tender caress of his finger, he showed her.

"Rand," she breathed as he pressed against her, "you have been as gentle as the melodies you stroke from your harp— Oh!" Something hard and hot, yet smooth as velvet, touched her. Then the tide of sensation that had been ebbing within her changed course, surging with fiery urgency to her center. Renewed desire washed through her, gathering force. She dug her heels into the ground and arched, crushing the grass with her shoulders.

He probed, quested, touching her with fire. Comprehension dawned in her with explosive force. He was about to fuse himself with her in a way she hadn't dared dream about. She wanted that, wanted to draw him into her body, her soul. With her hand she guided him to the place that throbbed for him.

"Oh, Lianna," he whispered. "Oh, love." Above her she saw only Rand and the sky, the jewel tones of his eyes and the soft hazy blue of heaven. He became the archangel she'd once likened him to, lifting her to a mysterious firmament. He filled her with his passion and whispered, "Lianna, this gift you give me, this gift of yourself..." His voice veered off on a ragged path. Astonished, she tasted the salt of a single tear on his cheek.

Emotion flooded her. She closed her eyes, spread wings of abandonment, and began to soar.

At first he moved with oddly clumsy, questing movements. Emboldened by longing, she tilted her hips, and a new, smooth rhythm took over, a tempo as wild and free as the waves beating upon the shore. She felt herself rising, rising, to a fearsome, irresistible height. Underneath her tightly shut eyelids the world seemed to fold into itself, to implode with a fiery report like the fiercest shot of a cannon.

His movements quickened, deepened, and then heat and life pulsed into her with throat-catching force. She heard her name slip from his lips, a wisp of sound that settled over her like gentle rain. Her eyes fluttered open.

He was staring at her with the stunned adoration of a man who'd caught a glimpse of heaven. "Oh, God," he whispered. "God. You are so—"

She stopped him with a fierce kiss, and when it ended he seemed to sense her need to lie quiet. She gave silent thanks for the gift of his love. Shivering from raw, new sensations, she felt him move to her side. She tucked her head into the curve of his shoulder.

A meadowlark raised its voice in a liquid trill of sound, and a breeze stirred the flowers into a catherine wheel of moving color. Lianna gave the softest of sighs and felt Rand's lips bow into a smile at her temple. A welling of emotion, too painfully sweet to name, gathered in her breast. She'd asked him to make love to her, but he'd done much, much more. He'd made a temple of her body, he'd laid her heart open to feelings she had never dared believe in. He'd taught her that dreams could be touched.

At last she broke the powerful spell of silence that bound them. "Rand, I never knew . . . that loving could be like this."

She felt that smile again, warm against her face. "Nor did I, *pucelle*."

She twisted, propped her elbows on his chest, her breasts brushing against him. His pure, noble features looked different somehow. Softer. "Truly?" she asked. Remembering Bonne's mention of Roland's carelessness, she frowned. "I thought it was different for a man."

He shrugged, the glowing breadth of his chest rippling with movement. "I wouldn't know. I can speak only for myself." His knuckles grazed her cheek. "Lianna, you have brought me more joy this day than any man has ever felt."

Remembering her clumsiness, her ignorance, she lowered her eyes and toyed idly with the thatch of golden hair on his chest. "But I did nothing to . . . to see to your pleasure. Surely you've been with women far more skilled in the arts of love than I."

He lay silent. She dragged her gaze upward to stare into his face. His smile was lazily amused. "Always you speak of knowledge and skill," he said teasingly. "You overestimate my experience, *pucelle*. You are my first, my only."

The meadow seemed to fall into a heavy, expectant stillness. Astonishment rocketed through her. "*No,*" she breathed.

The warm, self-assured murmur of his laughter made her smile. "Please, love, don't join the ranks of my comrades who think me a great oddity of nature because I don't indulge in wenching." His hand stirred the wisps of moon-silk hair by her cheek. "I think that I've done well to wait."

Drifting in a lush cloud of amazement, she leaned down and whispered a kiss on his mouth. She glowed at his words, feeling special somehow, that she was the first upon whom he'd bestowed the gift of his body, his love. He'd come to her clean, unsullied . . . chaste. As her mind took hold of the idea, cold talons of guilt clutched at her. She'd come to him for no better reason than to get a child, an heir. She'd taken his love, stolen his heart, his seed, his honor.

No, she told herself fiercely, it was more than that. She had come to him for a greater purpose. He, too, had a need, and she'd answered it. Still, her innocence had driven him to tears when he'd entered her body; her goal placed a taint on their love, made her feel unworthy of him.

Rand saw regret seep into her eyes, and suddenly the enormity of what he'd done struck him like a bludgeon blow. He'd broken a vow sworn before God, cheated a woman he had yet to meet. But most unforgivable of all, he'd dishonored Lianna. He might have done worse. He might have gotten his bastard on her.

"Blessed lamb of God," he whispered, taking her face between his hands. "I let myself believe it was enough that I loved you." Sharp, jagged pain mangled his heart, clawed at his throat. "But it isn't enough. I've ruined you, Lianna, ruined you for a man who can offer you more."

Her big, solemn eyes crinkled at the corners. Incredibly, she gifted him with the treasure of her smile. And then she was laughing—desperately, uncontrollably, her small frame trembling in his arms. He heard an edge to her laughter that told him she was inches from tears. Her vulnerability alarmed him. "You . . . have done nothing . . . of the sort, Rand the Gascon," she said between gasps of mirth.

"But I—"

She landed a firm kiss on his mouth. "Believe me, sir knight, I am not saving myself for my husband." A thin ribbon of irony wrapped around her words. Her gaze was steady now, and still amused. "Believe me, do. I knew from the start that we could never be more than sometime lovers, never have more than stolen trysts. 'Tis all I want, Rand. 'Tis everything I want."

He took the sincerity of her statement into his heart, and he believed her. His vows lay in shreds around him, mocking him with guilt. A guilt he ignored as he made slow, tender love to her, again, and again, until the shadows lay long upon the meadow and a woodcock beat its wings high overhead, loosing its mournful, chittering cry to the gathering evening.

Chapter 7

Lianna paraded through the halls of Bois-Long, leaving in her wake a trail of slack jaws, shaking heads, and inquisitive whispers. Gone were the critical eye and determined gait of the diligent chatelaine; now she had the dreamy look and light step of a woman in love.

"How goes the boonwork, Edithe?" she called as she passed the girl in the great hall.

"'Tis passing tedious," Edithe grumbled, jabbing her needle into the white linen of a priest's alb.

Lianna suppressed a grin. "Perhaps in the future you'll not find spinning so tiresome." She moved on, meeting Macée at the big central doorway. "Good morrow," Lianna said, her smile all the brighter for Macée's dour expression.

"I cannot countenance this unpredictable Norman weather," Macée complained, shaking the thick overskirt of her red velvet gown. "Already the heat of summer seems upon us."

Laughing, Lianna lifted the hem of her thin smock. "I never hesitate to sacrifice fashion for comfort."

Macée fixed her with a hard, critical stare. "Your dress is appropriate, perhaps, for work in the rye fields. Truly, your face and arms are quite disagreeably brown from too much sun. One might easily mistake you for a peasant."

The insult rolled unheeded off Lianna. She was deliriously happy—precisely because a certain knight-errant *did* mistake her for another. In the three weeks since suppressed passion had exploded into ardent lovemaking, she'd spent many splendid hours in Rand's arms. Thinking of him, the long, lazy afternoons in the sun-washed glade, she felt a warm spasm of remembered pleasure. She lowered her head to hide a sudden blush, then impulsively took Macée's hand.

"I know my ways seem strange to you," she said. "I do not mean to offend."

Macée looked surprised; then caution shuttered her eyes. "Nor did I," she said slowly. "'Tis just that this weather, and other small things, have brought a mood upon me."

Sympathy tugged at Lianna's newly tender heart. Macée was barren; perhaps her woman's time had come to remind her of her shortcoming. Now that Lianna knew a man's love, she understood Macée's pain. Sometimes Lianna glimpsed a darkness in Macée that was disturbing. "I'll send for some cool cider," she said. "If you like, I'll come and read to you at eventide."

Still cautious, as if she did not quite trust Lianna's

overture, Macée nodded and went into the hall. Lianna ordered the cider, then walked to the armory to find Chiang.

The master gunner stood brooding at the window, his narrow back stiff, his jet-black hair mussed as if he'd worried it with his fingers. His hands, creased from years of work with caustic substances, were braced on either side of the embrasure. Lianna joined him, followed his gaze. Several knights were in the greensward, practicing lance thrusts at the quintain. Better there, she mused, than in the hall. To her dismay, Gaucourt allowed his men excessive drinking, gambling, and wenching.

"I thought you'd be testing that new batch of corned powder," she remarked.

Without looking at her, he said flatly, "Gaucourt's men have learned about my forge."

Now she understood his glum mood. Years ago he'd perfected a process of tempering steel, and his blades rivaled those the Crusaders brought from the East. But Chiang's interest lay in gunnery, and he resented any task that drew his attention from that passion.

"Doubtless they've been clamoring for you to forge them new blades," she said.

"Every last one of the louts."

"Your swords could make you a rich man, Chiang."

"And plying your body as a courtesan could make you a rich woman. I am no more interested in sword making than you are in whoring."

Her stomach lurched with the bile of guilt. No, she told herself firmly, I do not play the whore. What I do with Rand, I do for love.

"... especially not for Gaucourt's unruly knights,"

Chiang was saying. "They use their blades against peasants."

She pressed her lips together. She'd heard the rumors of Gaucourt's plundering, but necessity forced her to ignore the gossip. "I'll tell Gaucourt your services are not available."

He turned dark, narrow eyes on her. "Your 'stepson' says otherwise."

Anger prickled over her. "Gervais has not the right."

"In his father's absence, he claims it."

"The devil take him on his back," Lianna swore. Cupping her chin, she watched the knights practice. Saddles creaked and soldiers grunted as they drove their sweat-soaked bodies and lowered their lances at the quintain. At length she asked, "What about blades to use against Englishmen?"

"I'd not forge those either, my lady."

She looked at him sharply. "*Nom de Dieu*, Chiang, one would think you favor an invasion from King Henry."

"I favor peace and order. That raving idiot in Paris has not given us that. The only man I trust less than mad King Charles is the man who controls him—Bernard of Armagnac."

A strange feeling of despair gripped Lianna. Chiang had always been her ally, her friend. "You begin to sound like my uncle of Burgundy," she said with forced lightness.

Chiang shrugged. "He's a reasonable man. Ruthless, but reasonable."

"He's trying to force me to submit to the Baron of Longwood."

"At least the baron does not come equipped with a grown son who means to steal Bois-Long."

Her hand stole to her belly. Not if I can help it, she thought. "I'll worry about Gervais later. For now, I must set my mind to keeping Bois-Long out of English hands."

"Would it be so very bad?" Chiang asked with uncustomary vehemence.

"How can you speak so? I thought the blood of Asia ran in your veins, not the blood of Lancaster."

He fell completely still. His eyes grew hard and bright. His hands began to tremble. She sensed she had struck at the heart of a long-hidden secret. Taking his slim, rough hands in hers, she asked, "What have I said? Why do you look at me so?"

"If I told you, we would both be in danger." His voice was soft, urgent, terrified. Then his face closed, and she knew he'd say no more. He forced a smile. "Let's test that powder."

Clamping her jaw against probing questions, she followed him to a marble-topped table. Lighting a small paper cornet of powder, they discovered the explosive to be of the very highest quality. Lianna's mood had regained its lightness by the time she walked out into the garden behind the kitchen.

"I've been thinking, Mère Brûlot," she said to the old woman bent over her weeding, "could we not grow some flowers here?"

Mère Brûlot looked up in wary surprise. Lianna, too, felt a little jolt. Mère Brûlot had been a member of the household for nigh on threescore years, yet Lianna regarded the woman with new awareness. She had crinkles etched around cornflower-blue eyes, long, stark creases below strong cheekbones, a weary set to her mouth. What had placed those lines there? Tragedy? Triumph? In sooth Lianna had never wondered before, but she did now.

Lest Mère Brûlot think her prying, she put aside her questions. "I've been so busy feeding the soldiers of Gaucourt, I've neglected the garden. What about a border of harebells over by the turnips, perhaps a bed of gillyflowers near the pease."

Confusion clouded Mère Brûlot's eyes. "You've oft said flowers serve no practical purpose. They merely clutter a garden, leaving less room for growing food."

Lianna knit her fingers in front of her homespun apron. Her own words touched her like the cold fingers of a ghost, haunting her with a sense of loss. She'd lived her life in an empty chamber of duty and pragmatism, never pausing to reflect on the small but significant beauty around her. She felt different now, unable to detach herself from the joys and sorrows of others. An ache, born of the love she'd found with Rand and of regret for all she'd missed in her life, throbbed inside her.

"I've changed my mind," she said. "Every garden should have room for flowers."

The old woman's eyes twinkled. "I'll make you a pleasure garden fit for the Dauphin Louis himself."

"Good." Lianna gave the frail hand a squeeze. A movement on the sentry walk snagged her attention. Garbed in a mantle of rich, royal blue, Gervais strolled with the Sire de Gaucourt toward one of the gunports. "I must go," Lianna said. "Tell Guy to get you whatever you need. I'll have the tables in the hall graced by your blossoms ere the turn of summer."

"*Certes*, my lady." The kindly face grew soft with a smile Lianna had never seen before. She wanted to hold the warmth of that smile in her heart, but as she hastened up to the ramparts, Gervais's speech annoyed her.

"What we have here," he was saying, "is an array of

artillery that will blow the English back across the Narrow Sea." He swept a gaudy gold sleeve toward a large framed cannon. "This one can hurl a hundred-pound charge."

Amused at Gervais's ignorance, Lianna stepped forward. "Gervais makes much of the gun," she said. "In sooth this cannon holds but a sixty-pound charge."

The two men turned. Gervais spread his hands. "Do tell. We learn something new of you with each passing day."

"I'd not have to tell you such things if you'd but take the time to find out for yourself," she said haughtily. "Chiang has a gunner's table for determining calibers. I'm sure he'd share it with you, did you but ask."

Gervais grimaced. "I mislike laboring over figures."

Smiling innocently, she asked, "Would it overtax your brain to learn numbers?" She touched her chin lightly with a finger. "Guy did tell me you've yet to learn your letters."

All pretense of civility left Gervais. "Sheathe your talons, Lianna. You forget your place." He flung the words like a gauntlet at her feet.

Challenged, she eyed him coldly. "My place," she said, edging her words with ice, "is as chatelaine of this castle, as it ever has been."

"See here, my lady," Raoul said in placating tones, "you should consider yourself fortunate. In gaining a husband you've not only protected yourself from King Henry's manipulation." He smiled at Gervais. "You've also gained a Frenchman to oversee Bois-Long for you."

"'Twas not why I married Lazare," she snapped. She glared at Gervais. "And well you know it."

"Think hard on it, my lady," Gaucourt said. Disapproval hardened his mouth and narrowed his pale, lashless eyes. Oh, God, Lianna thought, had she invited yet another snake to Bois-Long? "Because of your uncle's sufferance, you've held sway over the castle folk. But in calling upon me to defend Bois-Long, you've alienated the Duke of Burgundy. And all here know of it."

Gervais nodded with slow certainty. "Without Burgundy's backing, the castle folk will refuse to swear fealty to a woman." He gave her a dismissive glance. "I hope you plan to wear a decent gown to supper. From the looks of that stained apron, you've been grubbing about that heathen Chinaman's lair again."

She glanced down at her sleeves, smudged by soot from the powder she and Chiang had been testing. Her defiance of Lazare's interdict was a sore spot with Gervais, yet she couldn't help saying, "I do as I please."

"So," he said, smiling, "do I." He pivoted toward Gaucourt. "The Chinaman will forge your swords. We need only await the shipment of steel from Milan."

She fixed Gervais with a keen look. "We'll buy no steel with funds from the coffers of Bois-Long. And Chiang will forge no swords."

"My father—your lord husband—will doubtless approve the project," Gervais shot back.

"Your father is in Paris, and he'd best be begging favors of Bernard of Armagnac and Charles of Orléans, trying to keep my uncle from undoing the marriage."

Gervais's dark eyes kindled. "And *you* had best hope my father succeeds, else you'll find yourself and your keep in the hands of an Englishman."

She ground her teeth. "In Lazare's absence, I rule here. I'll decide the matter of the swords."

Realizing that Gaucourt, an outsider, had heard quite enough of their quarrels, she marched away. The argument and the new worry about Chiang left her hollow and discontented.

Lifting her gaze to the sun, she realized with a throb of anticipation that she would soon see Rand again. Her need for him was strong today; she needed to taste the clean breath of his approval on her cheek, to feel the sheltering strength of his embrace. She needed him, with his sanity and humor, to wash away the sticky web of intrigue spun by the Mondragons.

"Then she starts a-tearin' at me trews like good King Harry's crown jewels was inside, and I says, Hold there, darlin', you'll exhaust me too soon." Jack Cade peered at Rand over the bosom of the woman in his lap. He grinned down at the ample shelf of soft flesh. "They don't call 'em milkmaids for nothing."

Sitting in the *grande salle* at Le Crotoy, Rand listened to Jack's drunken speech with mild annoyance and grudging amusement. The Duke of Burgundy had extended a fair welcome indeed, to Rand and all his men. Jack and the others availed themselves freely of women and wine. Despite Rand's insistence that they drill at war games each day, they were becoming overfond of comfort.

Jack said something in mangled French to the milkmaid, who giggled.

Robert Batsford, the priest, drained his cup and called for more ale.

"Aye, don't deny the pater his ale." Jack chuckled. "It's his way of tempering the needs of the flesh."

"I understand not what she sees in you," Batsford slurred, aiming a glassy-eyed glower at Jack. "The chit doesn't understand a word of English, and your French sounds like the braying of an ass."

"Ha!" Jack laughed, toying with the hem of the maid's kirtle, "you know not your head from your nether end, Batsford. You stem your manly cravings with drink." He tweaked the girl's buttocks. "Minette and I, we speak the language of love. A man's tongue is of better use when applied to a woman's throat, her breasts . . . and elsewhere. . . ." As he spoke, his hand crept more deeply beneath her skirts.

The bawdy talk was familiar to Rand, but of late he listened with more than passing interest. Jack delighted in describing in elaborate detail his methods of seduction and lovemaking.

Lately Rand had become an avid student of the arts of love. He gleaned information from Jack and others, but real enlightenment came in Lianna's arms, her urgings soft in his ear, her willing body pliant in his hands. Each time they made love he discovered something new in her, in himself. It was as if her body and soul held secrets that, once unlocked, only led to new wonders. Still, there were things the heart could not teach, and these he gleaned from Jack's banter and the soldiers' lusty talk.

As he listened to Jack's discourse on reviving a woman's ardor after she protests that her passion is spent, Rand shifted uncomfortably on his bench, discreetly moving his braies to accommodate a sudden, uncomfortable swell of desire. Glancing out the window, he checked the position of the sun, calculating the hours until he would meet Lianna again.

Worries ate into his anticipation. She was a young woman, and hale, and the possibility of her conceiving a child was real. Like his father before him, Rand would insist on acknowledging the babe. But unlike his father, Rand would have a resentful wife to contend with. The demoiselle could not be as tolerant as Lianna believed her mistress to be. Still, a magical force drew him to Lianna; he could not resist it, come what may.

The troubadours warned that winning a conquest removed the excitement of the chase. Not so, he reflected with awe and chagrin. If anything, his love for Lianna grew with each passing day, nourished by ardor in the charmed privacy of their forest bower. Their passion was like a song that had no end, an unquenchable fire: all-consuming, everlasting. Were he to have centuries to be with her, Rand knew he'd not have time enough to love her with all the power of his soul.

But he didn't have centuries. He had only one more day.

The Duke of Burgundy's preparations were nearing completion. He claimed he'd had the marriage of Belliane and Mondragon stricken from church and civil records. He'd summoned the Bishop of Tours to officiate at what was fast becoming a ceremony all out of proportion with the enthusiasm of the parties involved.

Rand shook his head. It seemed a sham and a sin that he would have to speak vows of love eternal to the cruel-voiced, black-haired woman he'd glimpsed on the causeway. She didn't want him and he didn't want her. But King Henry needed the ford, and so they would join their lives for the greater good of England and France. The prospect was far from ennobling.

". . . if that be the case," Jack was saying with the authority of a scholar at a lectern, "then perhaps a man would do well to study the beasts of the fields. Ah, I can think of no greater bliss than a woman's arse a-bobbin' against me—"

"Prate no more of your lusty exploits," Batsford exploded with a frustration Rand could well understand. "'Tis not as if you've conquered a kingdom."

"Jealous?" Jack asked, fondling Minette's knee.

"Women, like falcons, are easily tamed," Batsford stated, and turned to stroke the young gyrfalcon leashed to a perch on the back of his chair. He loosed the jesses binding the bird and tethered her to his leather-clad sleeve. "I'm going hunting." He listed drunkenly as he walked to the door. When he turned back, Rand thought he meant to fire off a parting shot at Jack.

But the priest's face had changed into that startling attitude of saintly piety. Straightening his shoulders, Batsford intoned, "His Grace, Duke Jean of Burgundy. His Excellency, the Bishop of Tours." He swept into a deep obeisance as the two men entered the *salle*.

The gathering took on a sudden change. Women who had been draped across soldiers' laps melted like wraiths into the shadows. Soldiers and servitors stood to pay their respects, and all talk ceased.

The expression on Jean's face told Rand that Burgundy was not fooled by the transformation. With a wry and knowing curl of his lip, he approached.

"I take it you and your men found the midday repast quite . . . fulfilling, my lord?"

Jack belched and tried to excuse himself with a graceless grin and a mumbled apology.

"Yes, Your Grace," Rand said, tightening his throat against an onslaught of humor. "The bounty of your kitchens is unsurpassed."

"As is," Burgundy muttered, eyeing Jack, "the bounty of my maids." He waved his hand dismissively. "I blame your men not. These weeks of waiting have been wearing to men of action. Happily, the waiting is over now."

"Happily," Rand echoed, and steeled his shoulders against slumping. "The annulment is in order?"

Burgundy faced him expressionlessly. "It turns out the annulment wasn't necessary, my lord."

A chilly finger of apprehension touched the back of Rand's neck. "Why not?"

"Lazare Mondragon is dead."

Rand shot to his feet. "Dead!" Batsford and the bishop crossed themselves. "I think you'd best explain, Your Grace."

Burgundy shrugged. The mail beneath his robe clinked with the motion. "Mondragon met with an accident. He fell in with some bad company in Paris, got drunk one night, and drowned in the Seine."

"Was it an accident?" Rand demanded, clenching his fists. "Was it?"

"Don't question an act of God," snapped Burgundy. "Especially since you stand to gain from it."

Rand turned away. Obviously the duke had had trouble securing an annulment and had resorted to violence. Yet it was futile to accuse him of causing Mondragon's death. Burgundy had been nowhere near Paris, though his arm had a long reach. Jean the Fearless accepted daggers and deceit as normal means of conducting business. Lazare Mondragon, poor dupe that he was, had been a victim of Burgundy's brand of ruthlessness. And I, thought Rand, am about to marry into this clan. He turned back to stare at Jean. Will I suffer an accident if I fall from favor?

Burgundy motioned him to a table and waved for the bishop to join them. The churchman, decked in velvet and gold, gave Rand a wide, fleshy smile. Completely bald, his head gleamed like a globe. The almsplate around his neck sagged under the weight of gold, and Rand suspected the bishop had profited handsomely from his association with Burgundy.

Jean laid out an array of documents, all so covered with official seals and signatures that they resembled a battle plan. "Everything is in order. We've but to bring my niece here tonight, and you'll be wed on the morrow." Rand nodded. Burgundy must have seen the tautness in his face, for he added, "I know you are a stranger to stealth, my lord. But since my niece has seen fit to call upon my enemies to fortify her château, we must abduct her. Caution your men to be gentle, though. Much as Belliane has offended me, I would not see her harmed. She is . . . fragile, in her way."

Fragile, thought Rand. The she-cat he'd glimpsed on the causeway had looked about as fragile as tempered steel. "She'll come to no harm. I shall see to her safety myself."

Burgundy gave him the precise location of Belliane's chamber, which would have to be reached by scaling a curtain wall, edging along a battlement, and climbing to the inner apartments. "I trust you'll send someone in advance to secure a rowboat close to the keep," he said.

"I shall see to that myself as well," Rand stated, and his heart leapt high in gladness, for he'd been granted another day with Lianna.

They came together in a tangle of urgent limbs, thirsting mouths, hungry bodies. Rand captured her lithe form in his arms and swung her off the ground. Her laughter caught at his heart, for even as he joined her merriment, some doubting part of him wondered if she would ever laugh for him again after this day.

"Oh, Lianna." He set her down and untied the white cap that covered her locks. "I love you." Pale hair shimmered over her shoulders, grazing her slim hips, slipping like quicksilver through his fingers.

She grasped him around the waist, stood on tiptoe, and clamored for a kiss. "I missed you sorely, Rand." As their bodies melded closer, she gave a soft gasp, then a knowing smile. "And you missed me as well, I warrant."

Chuckling, he moved his hips to give her an even greater impression of the extent of his longing.

"*Nom de Dieu*," she murmured as his mouth descended toward hers, "has it truly been only one turn of the sun since we were last together?"

"A turn," he whispered. "An eternity." He gave her a melting kiss, exulting in the eager sweetness of her mouth.

She pulled away and trailed her fingers in a gossamer-light caress over his face. "And how did you pass the time away from me? Did you bandy tales with your brother knights by the fireside?"

"But of course. I told them a wood witch had cast a spell on me."

"Wood witch!" Feigning indignation, she stepped away and presented her back to him.

"In sooth," he said, lifting the heavy silk of her hair and leaning down to graze her dew-soft nape with his teeth, "in sooth I did naught but dream"—he pulled the laces of her smock and removed it, her heavy apron as well—"of this." He disrobed her from behind until the entire glorious length of her was bared to him.

"Lamb of God," he murmured, "but you are lovely." Ignoring the clamor in his loins, he planted a row of slow, erotic kisses from her shoulder to her neck. She gasped and tried to turn, but he held her away from him.

"*Doucement, pucelle*. We've hours before we must part."

She sank against him and lifted her face skyward as if to assure herself that darkness was far away. His hands crept around her waist, then higher, cupping her sun-warmed breasts. His mouth hungered for a taste of those rose-hued crests; he tormented himself with anticipation.

The valley of her spine invited his kisses and the heated moisture of his tongue. He took a moment to free himself from his clothes, then leaned against the soft swell of her buttocks.

Again she tried to turn; again he urged her to be still. His hands sought the flesh of her womanhood and found her warm and ready. A moan of pleasure seeped from her lips.

Fever-hot, he pulled her to the ground and turned her in his arms. The beauty of her face, the trust he saw there, made his eyes sting as if he were staring at a too-bright flame.

"Lianna." He dipped his head to her breasts and tasted the hard, ready points of her nipples. Vaguely he noted that her bosom seemed fuller today, more womanly, as if swelling with passion. A raging impulse to possess her consumed him like wildfire. It was not enough just to hold her, to kiss her. He wanted more, so much more. . . .

His lips skimmed downward, over the taut, fine skin of her middle and then lower, until the warm honey of her womanhood beckoned him and invited a kiss of such passion that Rand felt as stunned as the gasp that hissed from Lianna's lips.

She stiffened. He stroked. And kissed her again. "It's all right. I love you." He caught a tiny bit of flesh between his teeth and drew on it, tasting, abandoning himself to sensation. Only distantly did he hear her cries of pleasure, feel her tense and arch her body. Her release flooded his very being, flowing through him like a potion concocted by the wood witch he'd named her.

He moved forward and joined their bodies with a swift, sure stroke. "I love you, Lianna," he repeated raggedly. Knowing their time was so short, he was desperate to have her—all of her, completely, her heart, her soul. "Say you love me, sweet maid. Say it."

Her entire being ablaze with passion, Lianna felt the answer crowd into her throat. Words of love clamored to be set free, but she steeled herself against the impulse.

The adoration he showered on her evoked a sudden throb of shame. One day, she thought, he would learn that she had used him to cuckold her husband and get a child. He would learn that she had placed the security of France above her love for him. That was why she could not allow herself to be moved by his gentle urging. The more she gave him, the more he stood to lose.

"Rand, if I could, I would love you 'til the end of time."

As if aware of the cost of her admission, he settled her back against the grass and stroked her soothingly. Her breasts tingled with new sensitivity, creating an ache so heavy and sweet that she nearly wept. "I am selfish to ask for what you cannot give," he said. "Lianna, it is enough that you accept my love, the gift . . . of my . . . body. . . ." As he spoke he began a magical rhythm, and sharp, bright joy welled in her.

This, thought Lianna, is the *joie d'amour* of the troubadours' lays. A feeling that spanned every emotion from the ecstasy of a martyr to the searing fires of physical release. *Joie d'amour*. As much a product of love's wounds as it was of love's boons.

He swept her to a hot, sharp pinnacle of sensation until she burst into myriad shards of misty sweetness. Always, she thought with awe, always he postponed his pleasure until hers was complete. Clenching her hands around the knotted muscles of his shoulders and gazing up into his love-fevered face, she knew that restraint was dearly bought.

When he finally unchained his passion, she felt it rocket through her, almost too hot to touch, almost too bright to look upon. The powerful charge of his love left her shuddering. For long moments they lay silent, damp with the sweat of passion, suffused with contentment.

At length she moved away. "Sing me a song," she breathed, slipping back into her clothes.

Smiling, he pulled on smallclothes and tunic and took up his harp. But he didn't play it; he held it out to her. "No, Lianna. I want you to play for me."

"Don't be silly. I've told you many times my art is poor."

"Most probably because you neglect it." He pushed the ashwood harp into her hands. "Play for me."

"Only if you promise you won't scorn my efforts."

"Oh, Lianna. You know better than that."

"Aye, Rand, I do." The instrument felt heavy, a man's harp, its frame worn smooth by her lover's hands. Timidly she stroked the strings. As if it yet held the charm of Rand's art, the notes rang clear through the sunlit glade.

"Again," he urged. "Be not shy of the music."

She strummed with a surer hand, and the sound pleased

her. She picked out an old minnesinger's melody, then set the words to it:

> The meadow path was soft and easy
> For there my love awaited me.
> Ah, Blessed Mary, he received me. . . .

Dismayed, she let the last word trail off into silence. "You see," she complained, staring at the ground, "I've a voice as flat as yesterday's ale."

"You've a voice of surpassing sweetness. I hear it in your laughter, in the things you whisper in my ear when we are joined as man and wife." He took her chin in his hand and brought her gaze to his. "Do you understand, Lianna? Let the song come from your heart. Give your feelings a voice."

She began the song again. Her voice faltered, wavered, and then her eyes locked with Rand's. The love she saw in those leaf-green depths, on those firm, sun-browned features, gave her the strength to continue. The throb in her heart welled to her throat, and then she was singing, singing as she'd never done before.

> All his kisses seemed one kiss,
> A bed from meadow flowers and grass.
> Except for us, none shall know that game;
> Except for us, and one small bird,
> Tandaradai, see the place where my head lay.

Each sweet phrase rang with the joy of Rand's love; each mournful strain vibrated with the sorrow of not being free to return that love.

She flung the last words to the breeze and looked out

across the clearing, as if she could see the music dancing in the air. Her vision blurred with a sudden shimmer of tears.

"I can sing now."

He took the harp and laid it aside. "Aye."

"Thank you, Rand, for teaching me."

He leaned forward and kissed the tears from her face. "I taught you nothing. The music came from you."

"But you unlocked it, Rand. You—" She closed her mouth and clenched the fabric of his tunic in her fist. No, she told herself with a feeling of unspeakable sadness. She would not—could not—love him. She would not subject herself to the torment of loving a man who could never be part of her life. The only hope she would allow herself was that he'd give her a child. His child. Someone to live for, to fill the long, lonely years ahead and carry on her heritage.

Willfully drawing her mind from the maudlin thoughts, she stood. "You may not take credit for teaching me to sing," she said, "but I certainly mean to see to *your* education."

Looking bemused, he leaned back against the gnarled trunk of an ancient oak. "Do you now?"

"Yes." Her mouth firm with resolution, she reached into her apron pocket and took out a dirty cloth bag. "Gunpowder."

His face hardened. "Lianna, you know I don't approve of your dangerous work with weaponry. You could be maimed, blinded."

"And if you don't learn, you could find yourself with a cannonball through your chest."

"Why must you be so stubborn about this?"

"It's important to me. As important as your knight-

errantry is to you. You've devoted your life to champi-
oning causes you hold dear. Should I do any less simply
because I am a woman?"

"You endanger yourself."

"Gunpowder is only a danger to those who are ignorant
of its uses." She yanked open the bag and showed him
the grayish-yellow mass inside. "Look, it's no more than
a simple substance drawn from the earth and mixed by
my own hand. Carbon, sulfur, and Peter's salt. As common as the wild lilies that bloom in the fields."

He still looked angry. "But a flower has not the po-
tential to wreak unholy harm on those who tamper with
it."

"I do not tamper with gunpowder. I use it. Now watch
closely." With her fingers, she broke off a bit of the substance. "This is called corned powder. It's been mixed
with wine in order to prevent the elements from sepa-
rating." Her gaze alighted on a small hollow log nearby.
"Let's use the powder to explode that."

He shook his head. "Why would you want to burst a
perfectly harmless log?"

"It's in the interest of science, sir knight. Do you not
practice tilting at the quintain?" She pointed to the open
end of the log. "Say this is a tunnel a miner has opened."
She plucked a flower and stuck its stem into the lichened
top of the log. "This is the keep proper, and here is the
curtain wall."

He moved closer, his breath grazing her cheek. He
rested his hand on her shoulder. Ignoring a familiar sensation of arousal, she continued to work. "This stick rep-
resents the barbican, and . . ." Her voice trailed off as his
fingers played across her neck. "Are you quite sure you're
listening, Rand?"

"Oh, yes," he said in a low, lazy voice.

She slid a suspicious glance at him, then turned back to her work. "There. We have our stronghold."

"Not quite." He began adding pebbles and leaves to her structure. "You've forgotten the cow byre and stables. And here, a nursery."

"That's really not necessary," said Lianna.

"Why attack a keep that houses no people or livestock?" He glanced at her. "They know not that your science could kill them at any moment."

She scowled. "How would you breach the walls?"

He nibbled her ear. "I might charm my way inside."

"Rand!"

"Very well." He flipped aside a bit of bark. "I'd storm the gate."

"Ha! With fifty archers shooting at you? You'd never make it."

"It's been done before, *pucelle*."

"Well, I've a better way. Anything is possible with gunpowder." Working diligently, she tunneled a path up inside the log. "The miners clear a passage."

"What about the moat?"

A shiver of fear passed through her. "They'd swim it. With proper wrapping in wax-boiled leather, the powder would stay dry." She put some powder in a bit of parchment, fit the tiny charge under the log, and took out a piece of hemp. "Slow match. It's been soaked in quicklime so it will burn evenly until it reaches the charge. Here, you do it."

He surprised her by placing the slow match perfectly. She realized that, while he disapproved of explosives, he was a man well versed in military matters. Despite his inattentiveness, he'd been quick to grasp each detail of the operation.

"I've used a very small charge, for corned powder explodes fiercely," she said, her eyes fastened on his deft fingers. "We don't want to destroy the keep, only provide a way inside. Now, light the slow match."

He smiled and took the flint, steel, and charred linen from her. Striking a spark, he held the smoldering linen to the end of the fuse. It ignited with a crackle and a plume of sulfurous smoke.

Lianna got quickly to her feet and gave his arm a tug. "Come away. We must get ourselves clear of the explosion."

He continued to crouch, staring at the sizzling fuse.

"Nom de Dieu," she snapped, "move, Rand."

When it became clear he meant to stay close and watch, she threw herself on him, counting on the force of her motion to override his solid strength. They tumbled back onto the grass just as the charge exploded in the log. Chips of wood sprinkled her back.

"Damn you, Rand," she said fiercely, "why did you not move?"

He stared at her with sad and serious eyes. "Does the miner have an equal chance to get clear of the explosion?"

"Yes."

"Always?"

"No."

He moved toward the log and examined the destruction. The pebbles, sticks, and standard lay in disarray on the forest floor. "So," he said, "you've breached the castle."

She looked with satisfaction at the ragged hole in the

log. "Much more effectively than storming the gates would have done."

He cradled her chin in his palm, her jaw between his fingers and thumb. "But at what cost, Lianna?"

"What do you mean?"

He released her and began picking up the leaf bits, one by one. "When an army storms a stronghold, men kill and they die. When a gunner blows up a wall, the dying is not just for fighting men. Your charge could have killed women and children, livestock—"

"Only if improperly placed and ill timed," she said defensively. "Only if the besieged are foolish enough to leave the keep."

"There is much room for foolishness in battle," he said quietly.

Feeling guilty and chastened, she looked down at her hands. "Such concerns do not trouble the generals of today." She brought her eyes up to meet his. "Chivalry is dying, Rand. You are a rarity these days. You were born some two hundred years too late."

"Honor and humanity will never be outmoded, Lianna."

"Aye, but there are no more dragons to slay, no more damsels to rescue. *Grâce à Dieu*," she finished thankfully. "Woman fare far better defending themselves than waiting for a man to come along."

"Are you truly as fearless as you would have me believe?"

"No. But neither am I helpless."

"What do you fear, Lianna? Tell me."

She could have given him a list as long as her uncle of Burgundy's muster roll. She was afraid her control of Bois-Long was slipping. She feared the English baron would return to claim her. She dreaded her uncle's reaction to Gaucourt's presence at Bois-Long. Most of all, she was terrified of losing Rand, because one day they would be discovered, or worse. He might learn the truth about her.

"I'm afraid of water," she said simply.

He started to smile, then stopped, as if he understood how much she loathed the unreasonable weakness. "Are you? Why?"

Knitting her fingers together, she said, "Someone I loved very much drowned in the Somme. I've never been able to bear any water that's not confined in a jug or a shallow tub."

"*Pauvre pucelle*," he said gently, smoothing a lock of hair back from her brow. "Who?"

"My mother."

"Oh, God," he breathed. "Did you see it happen?"

"I . . . yes. I was but four years old at the time. I remember so little—just fragmented images and things later told to me. My mother used to take me on frog hunts down by the river. She . . . slipped, fell. I screamed for help, but *Maman*'s heavy skirts hauled her under." Lianna shivered as a faint, half-buried image blossomed into horror. "Her hair was all spread out around her like the fronds of a fern. Someone came, dragged her out. Her eyes and lips were wide open. I remember thinking, She can't be asleep, because she looks so still, so afraid. . . ." Lianna swallowed. Rand held out his arms, and she moved into his embrace and cried, and cried, until she'd spent her tears of loss and despair against the warm fabric of his tunic.

Much later, his body throbbing with love and sadness, he felt her go still. He thought she'd drifted off to sleep.

Then a faint movement of her hand startled him. Her fingers began a light, suggestive caress over his chest, his thighs, his loins.

Passion and a yearning to heal the hurt she'd revealed rocketed through him. In moments they were naked again, entwined on the grass, their bodies surging together with life-affirming joy.

She gazed up at him, the sky flecking her silver eyes with shards of blue. "I do fear water," she admitted. Then she smiled. "But I am not afraid to soar."

"Oh, Lianna." With a gentle movement he pressed her thighs apart and knelt between them. He tried to pretend that the moment would last forever, that tomorrow they would meet and love again. But hopelessness gave a keen edge of desperation to his passion. Tomorrow he would marry the Demoiselle de Bois-Long, and soon after that Lianna would learn betrayal at his hands.

He entered her, caught her gasp of pleasure in a deep, hungry kiss. "Lianna," he said, moving slowly as he spoke, "always remember one thing."

"Yes?" She tilted her hips to meet his thrusts.

"I love you, and come what may, I shall ever love you." He bent and kissed her face, her neck, her breasts. "Take my love, and keep it with you always." He gave of his heart and then his body, beginning with a hot, hard beat that became a thundering pulse. He opened his eyes when he heard her sounds of release. He imagined seeing the heat of his love spreading through her, touching her everywhere. He wanted to give, and give, and give, until she held all that he was, so that Lianna—and not the other—had the best part of him.

Afterward he had to resist pouring out all his regrets, his sorrow. She nestled sweetly against him, trusting him and, he suspected, loving him in her way, although she protested she could not.

"Where do you go each day, Rand?" she whispered.

He held her tightly. "In these uncertain times I'd not burden you with the knowledge. Just remember that I am near."

"For how long?" she asked, sounding fearful. "There is sure to be fighting soon between the Armagnacs and Burgundians. Will you go?"

"No. That is not my feud."

A curlew wheeled in from the sea and cried out. Lianna stirred, looked up at him. "How loath I am to leave you." She sighed. "But we have tomorrow, do we not?"

Nay, sweet maid, he thought. Today I am your lover. But tomorrow I needs must become your lord.

As always, he waited until she had left. Sitting in the nest of crushed grass where they'd made love, he brooded upon his fate. A faint jingle drew his attention to his discarded baldric. Inside the folds of the belt was the jeweled talisman King Henry had given him—the token he'd always kept hidden from Lianna.

He pulled it out, examined the winking emerald, the image of the leopards of England. The lofty motto mocked him: *A vaillans coeurs riens impossible.*

Enguerrand Sans Tache. Who had that "spotless" knight become? Chivalry dictated that he champion his lady, do deeds in her honor. Yet his heart commanded him to crush her against him, to love her without caution. Now he was doomed to lose her.

He stood. With a bellow of rage, he hurled the talisman away, not caring where it landed.

Chapter 8

"**Y**ou've been taking too much sun," Bonne said as she removed Lianna's smock. "Your skin is turning as brown as a walnut." Tossing the garment aside, the maid led Lianna to the bath, which sat steaming in front of the hearth in her solar. A log dropped, the fire flared, and Bonne gasped. "By St. Swithin's entrails, you be brown all over!"

"Stop gawking," said Lianna. Sinking swiftly to her neck in the tub, she felt a hot blush turn her body from sun brown to mortified red.

Avidly curious, the maid pulled Lianna upright. "It's true," she said wonderingly. "Your breasts, your belly—*Sainte Vierge*, mistress, what have you been doing?"

"Working in the garden," Lianna snapped.

"In the altogether?"

"Mayhap I was bathing in a stream."

Bonne shook her head. "Not you, my lady. You'd sooner dance on hot coals than go near the water."

Glumly Lianna hugged her knees to her chest. Bonne crouched down and patted her shoulder. "I spoke out of turn." The maid leaned closer. "But you're keeping something from me, aren't you?"

Part of Lianna longed to share her joy; another part wanted to keep Rand folded into her heart, her secret, her private ecstasy. "Why do you think I'm hiding something?"

"Because you're much away in the afternoons. And you seem untroubled by Gervais's presumption that Bois-Long will one day be his. It's as if you know something.... You've been meeting someone, haven't you? Tell me about him. Who is he?"

"He exists only in your unwholesome fantasies."

Bonne jumped up and clapped her hands with glee. "No, a lover explains too much. Your new contentment, your desire to grow flowers, the way you sing in the hall when you think no one is listening... Could he be one of Gaucourt's men?"

"Certainly not!"

"Aye, they're louts, and would boast of it." Bonne squinted. "Are you with child yet?"

Lianna gripped a cake of soap hard. In sooth she had thought little of the goal that had first propelled her into Rand's arms. "I... I don't know," she said.

"You can tell me," Bonne reassured her. "I've a reputation for being loose, but not with my tongue."

Lianna tried to smile but failed. Then she tried to look stern and succeeded. "You know the danger I court."

Bonne shivered. "Aye, Gervais wishes nothing to stand in the way of his usurping, and your uncle seems intent on driving Lazare from your life."

Quelling an inner flutter of trepidation, Lianna rolled

the soap in her hands. "Do you really think I could be . . ."

"With child? From the look in your eyes, I'd say your lover's done his manly part," Bonne said sagely. "And judging from the amount of time you've spent lolling in the sun, you've been at it more than once."

Blushing again, Lianna dipped her hair in the water and began soaping it.

Bonne took over the scrubbing. "Women say the first sign is a subtle tenderness, a heaviness in the breasts. I know these things. I'm the eldest of nine, and my mother was ever noisy about the discomforts of childbearing."

Lianna stifled a gasp. Had she not experienced the odd feeling just that afternoon with Rand? At the time she'd thought that new ache a product of their ardor. Drawing a deep breath, she gripped the sides of the tub.

Bonne gave a lusty laugh as she sluiced water over Lianna. "Perhaps 'tis true. You'll miss your monthly time. Then comes a fierce hunger and retching sickness."

Lianna must have been wearing a mask of awe and fear, for Bonne laughed again. "Your Lazare will come home to a surprise. He'll be too proud to deny the child is his."

"It's not his," Lianna said fiercely, settling her soapy hands protectively over her middle. The idea of pretending Rand's child was Lazare's filled her with distaste. But was it not what she'd planned all along? Rand had said he could offer her nothing; she'd accepted that. "My child will have but one parent," she quietly vowed.

After the bath Bonne braided Lianna's hair. Lianna sent the maid for a calming draught of hippocras. A flicker of light from the window promised a storm soon; the lightning brightened the gesso mural on the wall. Lianna felt a new kinship with that painted knight and his lady.

Smiling, she quaffed her honey-flavored drink, crept into bed, and fell asleep.

"Easy on those oars, Jack," Rand whispered. Through a gloom of cloud-shrouded moonlight, he watched his scutifer angle the oars with more care, slicing them silently into the inky surface of the water.

"Silent as a goddamned pall," Jack grumbled under his breath. Sudden lightning glazed the château in silvery light. "Sweet Mother Mary," said Jack, "no wonder good King Harry covets such a prize."

Rand's eyes traveled up the outer wall of the stronghold. The slender finials that decorated the merlons glinted, daggerlike, against the sky. "'Tis more imposing by night than by day. The Lionheart did know how to build a castle."

"Aye, that's one thing he did like a man." Jack's sneering words echoed in the watery gloom. "Bloody poofter."

Rand grinned.

"Quit smiling, my lord," Jack warned. "Your teeth gleam like a beacon."

A breeze soughed through a willow at the water's edge, and Rand's smile disappeared. His cheeks, stiff with the mud he'd smeared on them for camouflage, felt dry. The back of his neck prickled; he imagined the scrutiny of unseen eyes. His soldier's instincts alerted, he scanned the shores on either side, then the causeway and walls above.

"*Hobelars?*" Jack asked, massacring the word. "Goddamn it. I thought we'd given Gaucourt's scouts the slip."

"Piers and Dylan were to distract them. But a few—"

"Might be aiming their crossbows square at our backs." Jack shivered and applied his oars more diligently.

As they neared the château, Rand made a silent check of their equipment. A coil of thick hempen rope, a generous supply of hopsacking, steel grapples for securing a hold on the wall, a folded square of linen for a gag. The instruments of abduction raised a burn of distaste in his throat. He yearned for the knightly exploits of pitched battle. Instead he was about to steal into the castle, stuff an unsuspecting woman into a sack, and spirit her away in this leaky rowboat.

A sudden image of Lianna turned his bitterness to aching sweetness. Shifting restlessly in the boat, he pictured her as she would be now, sleeping on a pallet alongside the castle women. Then he envisioned her as he'd last seen her, lying on the grass in their forest bower. Of all the victims of this unholy plot, she was the most innocent, the least deserving of his betrayal.

It had taken all the strength of his will not to spirit her away with him today, to find some corner of the world where they could live and love in peace. His need for Lianna challenged his loyalty to King Henry—the man who had raised him from bastard to noble, who had given him title and lands. Only the certainty that Lianna deserved more than marriage to an outlaw, a dispossessed knight, had stayed his impulse.

"That way," he whispered, dragging his mind from the punishing thoughts. He pointed. "There's a stand of reeds to conceal the boat."

Jack rowed toward the angled batter at the base of the wall. Moments later they had the craft secreted away. Laden with gear, they stood. The boat listed with their motion; Jack emitted a bright blue oath.

"By St. George," said Rand, "don't tell me you're seasick."

Jack swallowed hard. "Damned if I'm not, my lord."

Rand splayed his legs to steady the boat. Its rocking gentled. The night seemed more still, more dangerous, than ever. The air supported a heaviness, the smell of rain. Well enough, he thought. A storm would surely drive the sentries to the shelter of the barbican. Thunder rumbled and lightning seared the night sky with cold white light. The flash briefly illuminated Jack's face, and Rand saw that his scutifer's eyes showed white around the irises, his mouth drawn tight, unsmiling. Jack was afraid, and rightfully so.

Drawing a deep breath, Rand tied a grapple to the end of the rope. Counting silently, he found the fifth merlon of the south wall. According to Burgundy, one battlement there had been damaged some years ago when a gun exploded. Who had manned the gun? Rand wondered. A stubborn and precocious maid? The thought sluiced like brine over a raw wound.

The sentries avoided that damaged section of the wall walk. Therefore it made a perfect point of entry for two English invaders.

Hefting the coil of rope and holding the grapple, he took aim at the spiky finials. The hook shot skyward, the rowboat lurched, and Jack sat down with a grunt. The grapples scraped down the outer wall and splashed into the water.

Sucking in his breath with a hiss of frustration, Rand reeled in the wet rope and stood still, listening intently. He heard only the rattling of the reeds and a distant burr of thunder. But no call to arms, no tramping of sentries' boots on the lofty wall walk, reached his ears.

He tried again, failed. The third time the hook caught between two finials and held, as if Rand had willed it there with the sheer force of determination.

"Well done, my lord," Jack whispered.

Rand gave a firm tug on the end of the rope, then hoisted himself, testing its hold with his weight. He slashed a humorless grin at Jack. "We're off, my friend." He paused, glanced at Jack's maimed hand. "Can you make it?"

Jack puffed out his chest. "You'd be surprised what this hand can do, my lord."

Scaling the towering curtain wall, Rand gained a full appreciation for the grandeur of its height. The rough rope burned his palms; the cold wall pressed against his feet as he hauled himself up. The muscles of his neck and shoulders bunched and strained. He clamped his jaw against an explosive sigh when he gained the top at last.

The wall walk was indeed crumbled, just as Burgundy had warned. Rand found himself hugging the edges of a merlon, his toes clinging to the narrow ledge of an embrasure. He turned to scan the battlements and bailey. Finding them deserted, he jerked the rope to signal for Jack to follow.

Long minutes later the scutifer appeared, sweating mightily and swearing softly. His eyes widened with dizziness as he gazed down at the inner ward. "Lady Mary," he said through clenched teeth. "We'll likely plunge to our deaths."

"God be thanked that Burgundy told us of a safer way to get out of here once we have her." The duke had spoken of a secret passageway leading out through the water gate. Normally reserved for escape in times of siege, the passage would aid their abduction tonight—but only if they could reach the apartments.

"You'll have to subdue her, my lord."

"I'm prepared to do so." Rand felt a familiar wave of distaste. His hand strayed to the inner pocket of his doublet. A wooden pommel, wrapped in lamb's wool, hid there. He'd learned to wield the weapon during campaigns with the king's brother, but he'd never struck a woman. By applying the pommel to a vulnerable spot behind the ear, it was possible to subdue a victim in silence, imparting unconsciousness but little harm. It was for her own safety, he told himself. The demoiselle, so free with her whip, would surely fight. Yet he despised the idea of overpowering her. Pulling a gulp of rain-heavy air into his lungs, he looped the rope around one shoulder. "Let's go."

Moving gingerly, they edged along the walk until they'd passed the ruined section. Clouds shrouded the moon, snuffing the light. Rand moved by touch, calling upon the plan of the château he'd studied until the map was stamped upon his brain.

Cloaked in shadows, they ran across the inner ward. A dog barked somewhere. Rand and Jack slammed themselves against the wall. Neither breathed until quiet took hold again. Jack skulked off to wait at the base of the inner gatehouse while Rand made another harrowing climb to the window of the demoiselle's solar. This time he could use no rope, as the sound of the hook might awaken her. Reaching, he grasped the stone corbels projecting at intervals from the wall.

Streaking knifelike from the sky, lightning dogged his progress. He prayed no one was about. At last he gained a tenuous hold on the window ledge. Silently he hauled himself up.

On light feet he dropped into the room and stood still as a marble effigy on a tomb. It was dark; no coals glimmered in the hearth. His eyes were wide open, yet he could see nothing beyond a dense, inky shape. The bed.

Moving like a wraith, he stayed hard by the wall. The plaster felt cool beneath his fingers; the wood of the door seemed rough to the touch. He nearly stumbled over a heap of clothing. A faint aroma wafted to him—that of lilies and, sweet God, sulfur. An image of Lianna came crashing into his mind. Had she been attending her mistress? Dear Lord, what if she slept in this room? What if she saw him?

No, he thought. Burgundy had assured him that the demoiselle's servants slept outside the solar.

His steps slow with caution and reluctance, he withdrew his blunted weapon and approached the bed. Pulling back the curtain, he saw only darkness. As his eyes adjusted, he picked out a small shape.

A wisp of sound issued from the sleeping figure—the softest of female sighs. Leaning forward, Rand discerned the sweet scent of hippocras and knew she slept soundly.

With fingers as light as cobwebs, he brushed aside a length of braid. By the rood, but it was soft. He gritted his teeth. Swiftly, emptying his mind of all thoughts of honor, he brought the pommel down.

Pain and terror ignited an explosion of awareness. Putting together shards of sensation and fragments of foreboding, Lianna realized that she was bound, gagged, and blind. A whimper of horror erupted from her throat, stanched by the dry cloth clogging her mouth. She moved slightly, felt the rough fabric of hopsacking on her face, smelled its dampness. *Sainte Vierge*, she wasn't blind, but trussed and bagged like a plump partridge. She stiffened in alarm.

"She stirs, my Lord."

Lianna went still. Her heart flopped over in her chest. *She stirs, my lord.* English words. Furious, she bucked and writhed. The surface began to lurch curiously. Heavy hands reached out to subdue her; the rope binding her wrists bit into her flesh.

"At last," whispered the voice. "Here's where we land."

Land. Lianna froze. Starting somewhere deep in her center, a trembling began. The rocking, bobbing motion made sense now. She was on the water. *On the water.* Terror clenched her stomach and raked her senses until her entire being felt ripped open, raw.

"Gaucourt's men." A new whisper filtered through the shroud of Lianna's horror. A bizarre sense of awareness tickled at her mind. The boat listed. Fear invaded her again.

The Englishmen fell silent; even through her cold cocoon of horror she sensed their tension. Gaucourt's men. Hoping wildly that the *hobelars* were close enough to hear, she drew a deep, musty-scented breath, coiling a scream in her throat. She let loose with a furious burst of sound that, despite the cloth filling her mouth, came forth as a desperate cry.

"Woman's got a goddamned pair of lungs," came the cautious whisper. "Rants like a fishwife. Think you we can reach the horses, my lord?"

"Think you I mean to sit here and wait to be found?"

Again Lianna felt a faint shock of nebulous familiarity. But she spared no time to ponder the sensation, for a pair of arms like thews of iron wrapped around her.

Thunder cracked the air. She heard the splash of rain and a string of English oaths. "It's a bad landing, my lord. Too goddamned deep here to wade ashore. We'll have to swim it."

"No!" Lianna screamed against her gag. Strong arms lifted her.

Water.

Cold and merciless, the liquid wet her feet, her backside. Terror clawed at her gullet with talons of steel. She saw herself drowning, the water closing over her head, stealing her breath and her life.

Her life . . . and the new life she suspected was growing inside her. She'd never see Rand again, never bear his child. The thought made her fight harder. She jammed her elbow against her captor's body. A gust of breath whooshed from him.

"Jesu, don't drop her. She'll sink like a millstone."

"Don't tempt me," he grunted.

Hatred added force to her movements. She twisted, struck out with her bound feet. The men began whispering urgently, but she couldn't hear their words above the hammering of fear in her ears. Just when death seemed a certainty, the movements steadied. The water receded.

Panting and sobbing, she felt the strain of hard muscle wrapping her tightly. The jogging motion of running feet jarred her. A distant shout rose. Hope surged within Lianna. Perhaps the *hobelars* would come to rescue her. Yet the powerful swiftness of her captor soon drowned her prayers.

"No time to unbind her, my lord, and she fights like the devil anyway."

Deft, iron-tempered arms lifted her onto a horse, slinging her like a sodden sack of grain over its withers. The Englishman mounted behind her. The horse jolted forward. Hoofbeats rumbled. She tried to discern the number of horses and men, but pain and remembered fear overwhelmed her reason.

Bouncing against the saddle, she wondered with horror if she might lose the child. Her terrified mind clung to thoughts of Rand. He'd be waiting for her tomorrow in the forest. She gathered memories of him, the sun bright on his hair, his hands gentle on her body. Her heart nearly burst with the pain of loss. Her mind seethed with rage at her captor.

How long they rode she did not know but expected a catalog of bruises to tell the tale.

Something hissed overhead. One of the men said, "Sweet Mother, that arrow was damned close, my lord!"

Lianna longed to tear the sacking from her face. More frightening than arrows was the fact that she could not see, might at any moment be skewered.

"Just keep riding," said a gruff voice behind her. The English sounded so crude, yet that voice . . .

Shouts rang out. She heard a grinding sound, then the clamor of iron-shod hoofs on wooden planking.

"Hurry, my lord! We must secure the gate against them."

Lianna heard more hissing, a slashing sound, a gasp of indrawn breath. The gate groaned closed. The horse drew to a halt. Strong arms pulled her from the saddle, and her battered body was transferred to another pair of arms. She bent like a bow, fighting still.

"Your niece, sir," said a grim, ragged voice.

Walking blindly into the night, Rand strode across the courtyard of Le Crotoy. Jack followed, his gamin face bright with the gleam of victory and streaming with the sheen of rain.

"We did it, my lord," he exclaimed. "I never doubted for a moment..." His voice trailed off when he caught a glimpse of Rand's face. He offered a skin flask. "Drink. 'Twill help you forget."

Wordlessly Rand grabbed the flask and stalked away, deep into the shadows of the courtyard. Leaning against a wall, he unstopped the wineskin and drew deeply at its rich contents.

He felt sick with the deed he'd done. The stealth, the betrayal, the murder of the elder Mondragon, and the loss of Lianna all combined into a wave of nausea that nigh overcame him. He sucked at the flask, tried to assure himself that the demoiselle would emerge unscathed from the indignity he'd forced on her. But the outrage he'd committed might scar her for life. She'd defied a king, opened her home to outlaw knights; yet she didn't deserve what he'd done.

He flattened his lips into a grimace. Only when the burn of wine entered his vitals did he look at his arm.

In the gloom, the blood looked like ink. Peeling away his tattered sleeve, he stared with cold disinterest at the angry slash of an arrow wound. He squirted wine on the gash as he'd seen surgeons do in battle. It might have been another man's arm, for he felt no pain. And then he knew why.

He did not know himself at all.

The damp sacking fell away. Lianna squinted against the light. Her first sight was the rich, figured velvet of ducal raiments. The first word she uttered when her mouth was unbound was an oath so vile that her uncle blinked.

His face, illuminated by cresset lamps, quickly assumed

a chilly mask of power. "*Tais-toi*. I'll not have you railing at me like a beggarwoman."

She made a sound of impatience as someone behind her fumbled with the ropes binding her wrists. Soreness engulfed her. Looking about, she recognized a well-appointed hall. *Nom de Dieu*, she was at Le Crotoy, twenty miles from home.

"You did not hesitate to have me trussed and dragged from my bed." She cast her eyes about the *grande salle*. "Where is the English *god-don* who jumps like a spaniel to do your bidding? Has he skulked away like the coward he is?"

Burgundy propelled her toward a staircase. "He found his task every bit as distasteful as you did. Doubtless he didn't want to add to your indignity by seeing you in such a state."

She gripped the wet fabric of her bliaut. "It is because of him that I am in this state!" She wanted to weep, to scream, to run. But although retainers in Burgundy's livery stood in deferential silence, she knew they'd not hesitate to restrain her. She would escape, *certes*, but not at a wild, headlong run. Still, she vowed that nothing would keep her from returning to Bois-Long...and Rand's arms. With stiff, resentful steps she followed her uncle up the stairs.

The chamber, high in the round Tour du Roi, dripped with opulence, from the arras cloth on the walls to the fluted posts of the massive bed. She stared at the duke. He looked less fierce in the subdued light of the hearth fire. Lines of care creased his face. Taking a deep breath, she sought to forget that this was her uncle Jean, the man who had taken her into his lap and dazzled her with tales of his exploits in Paris and at Nicopolis. Childhood indulgences belonged to the past. The Demoiselle de Bois-Long and Jean Sans Peur were enemies now.

"What do you mean to do with me?" she demanded.

Burgundy eyed her coldly. "I intend to see that you do your duty. You will marry the Baron of Longwood tomorrow."

She laughed humorlessly. Her throat ached from screaming. "Would you force me into bigamy, Uncle?"

"Bigamy? I think not."

The certainty in his voice chilled her. A stiff sea breeze blew in through the window. She chafed her arms. "I am still married to Lazare Mondragon."

Burgundy leveled an implacable stare at her. "He's dead."

She stumbled back, groping at a bedpost. "You *killed* him?"

"I did not. He drowned by accident in the Seine."

In an ice-cold voice she said, "An accident. I wonder, Uncle, if the mishap was anything like what befell King Charles's brother, Louis of Orléans?"

He sucked in his breath as if she'd struck him. Anger burned brightly in his eyes, and she knew her words had reopened the wound of an old disgrace. "You have ever forgotten your place. I suggest you remember it now."

Deep inside, she wanted him to deny that Orléans had died at his command, but his fury confirmed what she'd never wanted to believe. And now Lazare. She pitied the man. He'd used her, betrayed her, yet his life was too high a price to pay for his scheming. Damn you, Lazare, she thought. You should have known better than to go to Paris at the command of Jean Sans Peur. Guilt swept over her. And I, she thought bleakly, should have tried harder to send after you, to call you back.

"So I am a widow," she said hollowly.

"Tomorrow you will be a wife." He took her chilled hands in his. "You were promised to Enguerrand of Longwood first."

She yanked her hands away. "A pretender's lackey. I spit on him. You pledged me to him without my knowledge, against my will."

"Your own stubbornness brought this about. Soon after the wedding Longwood's forces and my own will ride out to take Bois-Long back from Gaucourt."

She drew herself up despite the indignity of being in wet bedclothes, her hair in disarray. "You presume much, Uncle. Thing you I'll go meekly to the altar?"

"Of course." He smiled, yet his eyes glinted with sadness. "I am the Duke of Burgundy."

"I will not allow you to do this to me. I will not marry him."

He froze her with a stone-cold stare. "If you refuse the marriage, then I will have you sent to a nunnery and gift Bois-Long to the baron."

Her heart pounded. "You cannot take my home."

He said nothing, only fixed her with a powerful stare. The meaning of that look seeped into her. She stood still, empty, unfeeling, for she knew her uncle's will would prevail. She leaned against the bedpost. "I don't suppose," she said tonelessly, "you'll allow me a mourning period."

The mail shirt beneath his raiments rustled as he took a step toward her. "You gave up any right to my indulgence when you garrisoned Gaucourt at Bois-Long."

"You gave up any right to my loyalty when you forced my betrothal to an English *god-don*."

His manner thawed the slightest bit. "Calm yourself, *p'tite*. I'll send for a bath and a sleeping draught."

A haze of bone-deep exhaustion settled over her. The baby, she thought. Dear Lord, was she bringing Rand's child to this forced marriage?

As Burgundy turned to leave, she spoke again, softly. "How can you do this to me, to France?"

He turned back, and in his eyes she recognized—and tried to discount—a deep, abiding concern. "Because I love you, *p'tite*, and I love France. I would not see you wed to such a man as Mondragon, and I will not see France sink into despair because the Armagnacs control King Charles and play upon his madness." He opened the door. She caught sight of two guards placed like stone stanchions outside the door.

"Rest," Burgundy said. "Tomorrow is your wedding day."

Chapter  9

"**I** will not wear the clothes the Englishman has foisted upon me." Lianna pulled away from the waiting damsel who was attempting, with sorely tried patience, to plait a string of pearls into Lianna's hair.

"You have no choice." Margaret of Bavaria, Lianna's aunt by marriage, stood beside a huge open chest. Noontide light from the chamber window streamed over the duchess's handsome Germanic face.

Lianna glared. "It was not my choice to be dragged here in my bedgown."

"That is neither here nor there, Belliane. I should think you'd be grateful that the baron has brought such a magnificent trousseau." With a wave of her bejeweled hand, the duchess indicated the contents of the chest. Venetian silks, brocaded velvets, and fine linens crammed the coffer. Stooping, Margaret picked up a royal blue cloak trimmed with gray fur. "The miniver on this must have cost a small fortune."

"More's the pity for the squirrels whose bellies were robbed of their fur for the sake of fashion." Lianna yanked her arm away from the lavish cotte a servant held out to her.

Margaret's wide, noble face darkened. "I'll not see the House of Burgundy shamed by your stubbornness. A woman's lot is to obey. My own daughters never defied me. My Margaret wed the Dauphin Louis. She stands to become Queen of France."

"She'll have no kingdom to rule if I give Bois-Long to the English."

Margaret set her hands on her hips. "Neither you nor I may judge that. You will let my ladies dress you, Belliane."

Lianna stared hard at her aunt. Years of marriage to Jean Sans Peur had honed Margaret's will until it rivaled that of her husband. "And if I don't? . . ."

"I thought your uncle made the consequences clear last night. Surely you don't doubt him."

Lianna fell silent. The alternative to submitting to the Englishman was banishment to a nunnery. Unless . . . She slid a glance toward the window of her round tower chamber. Wooden shutters opened to an iron grille. Beyond lay a sandy peninsula, the meeting of the Somme and the Narrow Sea. The grille looked narrow, yet she might squeeze out.

Her mind snatched at the thought, caught it, and held fast. Lazare was dead. If she could escape, if she could get to Rand, she could convince him to marry her. He was an honorable man who loved her, who'd not refuse her—especially if she told him of the baby. Love stirred in her breast; then fear invaded her. What if her uncle tried to dispose of Rand as he'd done to Lazare?

The duchess's ladies took advantage of Lianna's utter stillness. Her mind racing, she barely felt the deft hands that dressed her hair in pearls and silver netting, the tug of lace points encasing her in a cotte of silver and ice blue. Full sleeves, gathered at the wrists, rustled as she turned again toward the window. The moat lay far below. The thought of water made her shudder. Could she hazard the climb?

An ungentle jab to the ribs jarred Lianna from her planning. "My lady, your aunt speaks."

She looked up to see Margaret smiling. "You look passing fair," said the duchess. "How do you keep your hair so pale? Chamomile? Saffron?"

Her hopes bolstered by the chance of escape, Lianna returned the smile. "Perhaps 'tis the result of exposure to lime or Peter's salt, Aunt."

Margaret pursed her lips. "I'd hoped you'd abandoned your ridiculous interest in explosives."

"Never," Lianna stated. She chafed as a maid covered her head with a silver veil and secured it with a jeweled chaplet.

"Come, my lady," said the brisk maid. "See what a princess you look." Unresisting, Lianna allowed herself to be led to a gilt-framed standing mirror of polished steel.

She stared at herself. The hasty needle of her aunt's seamstress had tailored the gown to perfection. Ice blue overlaid with stiff cloth of silver outlined her slim form. Pearls and aquamarines winked within the folds of her veil; one blue-green jewel descended in a teardrop on her brow. Flowing sleeves and a hem that rang with dozens of tiny bells gave her the aspect of a well-dressed courtier. But these were the gifts of the English *god-don*. The sumptuous costume imprisoned her as surely as the sentries who dogged her footsteps, even when she visited the garderobe.

Margaret started off for the chapel. Wildly Lianna considered leaping for the window. But the servants within and the sentries without made her squelch the impulse. Still, the hope of seeing Rand again burned high in her heart; this forced marriage would be a minor hindrance, nothing more.

She straightened her shoulders. Coldness swept through her. Rand had changed her, softened her, yet the Englishman was bound to turn her back into her former self. She'd revert to being the soulless chatelaine, the intrepid dreamer who hid herself from people for fear of being hurt. So be it. She might have been maneuvered into this position, but she resolved to fight back. She would wed the Englishman, aye, but he'd not find her a willing wife. A terrible smile curved her lips. If her suspicion were correct, she'd present the baron with a French heir. And the final triumph would be hers to savor. For the child was Rand's.

Resolute, she raised her chin. She was the Demoiselle de Bois-Long, daughter of the warrior Aimery. She'd not allow the English king's minion to wrest power from her.

With a last look at her own haughty face, cold eyes, and stubborn chin, Lianna followed her aunt to the chapel portico to await her bridegroom.

Walking through a cloistered upper gallery on his way to the chapel, Rand paused. Rain had cleansed the air, scented it with springtime. He peered through the open stonework at the courtyard below. A group of women stepped from the door of the Tour du Roi and moved toward the chapel.

His eyes flicked over the group; coldly he noted that the blue-and-silver costume looked lovely on the bride. Then he recalled his first glimpse of her, whipping a servant. Red had suited her better.

His hand went to his throat. He felt for King Henry's talisman, then remembered he'd flung the jewel away. Grimly he continued walking. After two steps he froze. In abrupt disbelief he reeled back to stare. Something about the gowned and veiled woman beckoned to him. Her back was to him, yet her movements seemed oddly familiar. Why the devil did the demoiselle remind him so poignantly of his Lianna?

His hands, suddenly cold and damp with sweat, gripped the stonework ledge of the cloister. Leaning forward, he squinted through the sunlight and felt an unexpected yet undeniable attraction. Small and trim, she walked with light, purposeful steps at the head of the women. Disjointed images swam into his mind: Lianna walking beside him, her feet kicking up the hem of her smock. Lianna defending her mistress to him. Lianna tapping her finger against her chin in that appealing gesture of deep concentration.

Jack Cade appeared at his side. "All is ready, my lord. I've the rings here—" He stared down at the group in front of the chapel. "I see your bride awaits."

His face alight with cautious joy, Rand faced his scutifer. "My bride . . ." His voice trailed off as he swung back to stare at her. She reached the chapel and turned.

Jewels flashed in her veil. Her finger lay poised delicately at her chin.

"*Sweet lamb of God.*" Rand's heart leaped. Golden spurs clattered over the flagstones as he began to run.

Armor, ill concealed by Burgundy's scarlet raiments, glinted in the sun as her uncle strode forth and took both her hands. "Belliane, you look so—"

She snatched her hands away. "Do not think I go willingly to this marriage." Her voice and eyes were glacial.

Burgundy took hold of her arm more forcefully. Leaning forward, he said with quiet menace, "My patience is spent. You will behave cordially."

Feigning indifference, she turned a disdainful glare to the crowd outside the chapel. The Bishop of Tours stood solemnly in his rich vestments. English men-at-arms, their garb bearing the hated leopard device, gaped at her, as did the castle folk. Beside the bishop stood another cleric, who bore the blunt features of a Saxon and a look of piety Lianna did not quite trust. Peeking from the sleeve of his robe, she noticed, was a bit of leather oddly like a cuff used in hawking.

Hawking...A memory emerged from the confused thoughts stewing in her mind. Rand had once mentioned a priest who had a fondness for hawking and hunting. Her stomach plummeted to her knees, and her head began to pound. Rand. The name might be a diminutive of—

"Enguerrand of Longwood comes," said her uncle.

She turned.

He smiled.

It was all she could do to choke off the scream that

climbed from the horrified depths of her heart into her tormented throat.

Blazing with power and confidence, wearing a white tabard adorned with a golden leopard rampant, he approached. His massive chest rose and fell quickly as if he'd come in a hurry. His face wore the look he'd given her a hundred times, the look that had the power to melt her soul. His clear, leaf-green eyes danced with elation; his golden hair shone in the noontide sun.

Dear God in heaven, Rand. Enguerrand of Longwood. She trembled all over, inside and out, as Burgundy propelled her forward. Her hands, balled into fists at her sides, were ice cold. So, she hoped, were the eyes with which she raked him from head to toe.

"*You . . .*" Her voice was a harsh, tortured whisper.

"Neither dreams," he murmured as he bent, adorning her cheek with a kiss, "nor even prayers could have so happy an answer."

Stung by his kiss, his words, and her weak-kneed reaction, she pulled away. Betrayal burned in her heart. The man who had pledged his friendship, who had made her life bright with promises, was the *god-don* who had abducted her, who meant to steal her home and her dignity. And, sweet Virgin Mary, she might be carrying his baby. No French heir, but an Englishman's child.

Staring hard at his face—so alight with joy, so devoid of guilt—Lianna heard her uncle speak: "Let the ceremony begin."

In a ringing voice the Bishop of Tours blessed a pair of jewel-encrusted rings, held on a velvet pillow by Jack Cade, the mawkish herald Lianna had driven from Bois-Long. She cringed when the deed of settlement was read. All her worldly goods—her property, even her body—

were given unto Enguerrand Fitzmarc, first Baron of Longwood. She belonged to him—but desperately, silently, she vowed he'd never own her heart.

The bishop called for the common consent. She nearly spoke her protest aloud. Catching a look of dark fury from her uncle, she quelled the impulse.

"Then let him come who is to give away the bride."

Burgundy's fingers closed around hers.

"And let him give her to the man as his lawful wife."

Dazed by fury and heartache, she felt Burgundy place her hand into Rand's keeping. A shock of sensation stung her. Recoiling like an exploding cannon, she pulled away from him. His touch had lost none of its potency. She was shamed by her reaction to the man who had duped her, used her, mangled her heart, and stolen her innocence. Ah, said a niggling voice at the back of her mind, but you were only too eager to give him that innocence. Such are the wages of the deception you practiced.

His face soft with an affection she now knew to be false, Rand took the smaller of the golden rings from Jack. He slipped the ring on and off three successive fingers of her right hand, in the name of the Father, the Son, and the Holy Ghost, then placed the ring on her left hand.

His voice echoed across the crowded yard. "With this ring I thee wed, with this gold I thee honor, and with all my worldly goods I thee endow."

Resentment surged within her; she bit her lip. He proclaimed his vows like a love song, striking a chord of response in Lianna that rang in her soul and left her shaken.

Duchess Margaret's women sent up a collective sigh.

With annoyance Lianna heard their whispers of admiration for the handsome Englishman.

Her fingers numb, she took the other ring, repeated the empty gesture and unfelt vows in a flat, lusterless voice. Rand stiffened beside her. So. She'd managed to communicate her displeasure, to penetrate his armor of self-confidence.

When she reached the end of her vows, Lianna went still. She knew well what was to come next—knew and resisted it with every fiber of pride she possessed.

"We are waiting, my lady," Burgundy said icily.

"No," she whispered. "No, I won't—"

"You will prostrate yourself before your husband." His eyes told her that this was her punishment for defying him, for bringing in his enemy to defend Bois-Long.

Cheeks flaming, she sank to her knees and bowed her head in a deep curtsy of submission. She clenched her eyes shut. She had lost all to deceit and treachery. The utter humiliation of the gesture sapped her of strength.

The crowd buzzed. A strong hand closed around hers. Slowly, as if waking from a bad dream, she dragged open her burning eyes and lifted her pounding head.

And found herself face to face with Rand.

Amazement flooded her mind. Rand had knelt before her, proving to all the celebrants that he and his wife were equals. Like a warm balm, the display soothed the sting of her mortification.

No, he lies even in this, she thought. Still, he'd saved her honor, her dignity. She let him raise her to her feet. Burgundy's face pinched with displeasure as he led the way into the chapel, where the bishop's clean white hands blessed the couple and lifted the Host in a mass of celebration.

"You've a right to be angry, my love," Rand whispered. "But remember, I, too, have the right. You've installed an outlaw knight at the castle given to me. Now I must risk myself, my men, wresting it from Gaucourt and Mondragon."

"My heart bleeds for you, my lord," she said scathingly.

He glanced at her; his eyes glinted with the soft, diffuse light of many candles. "You are not the fawnlike creature I met in the glade, but a warrior-woman. I must get used to that." Firmly he took her hand. "And so I shall. Lianna, this marriage is what we have both wanted."

"I wanted to be loved by the man I believed you to be," she stated. "Not used and betrayed by a *god-don*."

"We will be happy together."

"We will be enemies forever."

The music of timbrels and viols rang through the *grande salle*, mingling with the lively sounds of celebration. Despite his anger at his niece, Burgundy had spared nothing in staging the wedding feast. Sideboards groaned under the weight of puncheons of wine. Trenchers of boar's meat, roasted onions, and spring pease littered the trestle tables. The wedding guests exclaimed over a subtlety of pastry and spun sugar, fashioned into a replica of lilies and leopards.

All during the feast Rand had wanted to shout his elation to the rafters. Even Lianna's coldness and the fact that she'd spared but one dance for him could not dampen his spirits. He had forgotten her deceit; she would forgive his. Once they were alone in the nuptial chamber, he'd show her they were not meant to be enemies, but lovers. Husband and wife.

Blessed by destiny, he lifted his cup to acknowledge

yet another toast given by one of his men. He drank deeply, then leaned back to savor a keen joy as he watched his wife sweep through the processional steps of a *ductia* on her uncle's arm.

"You look like the fox guarding the henhouse."

Rand set down his cup and grinned at Jack Cade. "I've found better than that." His attention drifted back to Lianna. Her face, expressionless yet unutterably lovely, glowed in the light of the chandelier suspended above the dance floor. Slim as a willow, she moved with natural grace. The thought of reclaiming her body sent anticipation burning to his loins.

"By St. George," said Jack, "I cannot credit this change in you. Only yesterday you were stalking about like a chained lion, cursing the fates that linked you with the demoiselle."

"That was before I realized who she was."

"I thought you saw her when you went to secure the boat at the river." Jack slid an admiring glance at Lianna. "How the hell could you mistake a face like that, a body like—"

"No, Jack, I realize now it wasn't her I saw. That woman was the wife of Gervais Mondragon, not Lianna."

Jack set down his mazer with a clatter. "*Lianna?*"

"Aye."

"Holy Mary."

"You were the one who saw her, Jack, when you took the letters to Bois-Long." Pain twinged in his upper arm: the arrow wound. "All you could prate about was her maid. Why didn't you tell me of Lianna's beauty? You might have spared us all a harrowing night."

"By the rood, it was all I could do to bear her insults and save my hide from her cannonade."

Rand frowned. Lianna's gunnery was sure to be a source of contention between them. But not now. Not tonight. He sipped his wine. "I had her in the palm of my hand and knew it not."

"How the devil did she conceal her true identity from you? And you your own from her?"

"When we first met, she would say only that she was Lianna, a gunner's daughter, an orphan. She knew better than to reveal to a stranger that she was the demoiselle."

"Aye, she'd be a valuable hostage, were you of a mind to seize her."

Rand nodded. "I had reasons of my own for not revealing myself to her. She heard the echoes of my father's native Gascony in my speech, and so dubbed me Rand the Gascon."

"Bones of St. Peter, and you trysted with her all these weeks. What in the name of heaven did you talk about?"

Nothing, Rand reflected, and everything.

Jack stared. "I warrant you did little talking at all."

Rand laughed loudly. The sound brought a glare from Lianna, her eyes flashing silver fire.

"God in heaven, but she's passing fair," Jack breathed. "Yet were that look a naked blade, you'd be a dead man, my lord."

Rand met her furious stare, smiled, and waved. "She is still distraught." Guilt stole the smile from his face. He remembered the way she'd fought when he'd dragged her through the water. Unknowingly he'd plunged her into the danger she feared above all others. Half to himself he said, "When her heart catches hold of the idea that we are well and truly wed, she'll come to see the wonder of it."

"I'd not taint your elation with doubts, my lord, but

think on it. 'Twas the knight Rand who won her love, not Enguerrand of Longwood."

"We are one and the same, Jack." But even as he spoke, he felt dread pushing into his mind, thoughts he'd fled from ever since finding his bride on the church steps. He stared at her, saw resentment in her stiff posture, defiance in her marble-hard features. Reluctantly he admitted, "She loved a man who exalted her—her mind, her body, her soul. But she will resist the man who comes to take her castle, her lands."

His face grim, Jack nodded. "You can't trust a word she says or a move she makes, my lord."

Avoiding the troublesome thought, Rand remembered the pleasures they'd shared, pleasures they would repeat for a lifetime to come. As he finished his wine, a new notion entered his mind—an idea that had until this moment been lost amid the drama of surprise and excitement. Lianna was married when he'd first made love to her, yet she'd been a virgin. With a shaking hand he set down his cup. Had she? Or had he been so ignorant of womanly matters that he hadn't known the difference? Angry at the thought that Lazare Mondragon might have been her first, Rand resolved to discover the truth . . . tonight.

At the end of the great hall a man burst into the room. Bearing an urgent look and the dust of a long and frantic ride, he approached the Duke of Burgundy. Seeing Lianna left without a partner, Rand strode across the hall.

She aimed a haughty look at his proffered hand. "I am weary of dancing and must visit the garderobe." She sounded so different when she spoke English—harsher, a stranger. She swept past him.

Annoyed by her blatant snub, he moved to follow her. Burgundy's voice stopped him. "A word with you, my lord."

The harried messenger left to avail himself of the lavish fare. Rand followed the duke to his privy apartments. Light from a taper picked out Burgundy's stony features. Rand studied his host. Crafty and manipulative, Burgundy was a man to be respected . . . but not trusted. By chance or by design, he'd dispensed with Lazare Mondragon as if Lianna's first husband were no more than an annoying mayfly. Although Jean the Fearless lived up to his title, Rand recognized tenseness in the man's shoulders, shadows of trouble in his blue eyes.

"Ill news, Your Grace?"

Burgundy's lips thinned. "Aye. The Armagnacs are en route to lay siege to my town of Compiègne." Anger simmered beneath his calm speech. "If I don't reach Compiègne with a sizable army, the town will be lost." He scowled. "I must leave here by dawn. My men will have to ride hard to intercept the Armagnacs coming from Paris."

Like a sudden frost, understanding gripped Rand. "You'll need, of course, every available man at Le Crotoy."

Burgundy nodded. Rand's heart sank. Instead of spending his wedding night with the woman he loved, he would be busy preparing to join a feud of foreigners. "I'll alert my men."

"No, no." The duke made a dismissive gesture with his hand. "You've but ten men. I was speaking only of those directly in my service. I wanted to inform you of Armagnac's treachery because it changes your plans."

Rand's hand curled into a fist. On the morrow he was

to have ridden for Longwood with a hundred of Burgundy's men to retake the château. Impatience niggled at him. Burgundy might not return for weeks, even months.

"I mean to take Longwood," he stated. "If I've but ten men at my disposal, that number shall have to suffice."

Burgundy's eyes lit with a mixture of admiration and annoyance. "What madness is this? Ten men couldn't take so much as a single stone of that keep. Stay, my lord, at Le Crotoy. Your men are well content here."

"Every day Mondragon holds Longwood, his claim strengthens. I won't sit idle while my castle is usurped."

"You'll do as you must, then. But I cannot help you."

Rand stared at him thoughtfully. An uncertain ally, the duke. Ever quick to duck obligations, commitments. Burgundy had promised to support King Henry's claim to the French throne. Would he avoid that alliance, too?

The chamber door banged open. Wild-eyed and panting, Jack Cade burst inside.

"My lord, your wife—" He gulped for air, sketched a stumbling obeisance to Burgundy. The sounds of shouts and running feet filtered into the room.

"What, Jack?" Rand demanded urgently.

"She's *gone*, my lord!"

The wind soughing through the eaves chilled Lianna. She'd shed most of her clothing in order to make her climb to freedom. Her feet clad in thin slippers, her hair freed of its gem-encrusted veil, and her body garbed in a tunic purloined from the laundry, she edged along the wall of the Tour du Roi.

Glancing up, she saw with satisfaction that the window of her room loomed far above. Glancing down, she saw that the moat shimmered far below. She pictured herself falling into that inky maw. Fear gripped her. She began to sweat. Her heart pounded and her breathing quickened. Then, focusing on her goal, she exerted a stiff control over her terror.

The stone of the limewashed wall felt cold. Already her fingers were raw. Her limbs shook from the effort of climbing. She had to get to the south face of the tower; torchlight from the bailey would not reach her there. Tamping back a thrill of fear, she concentrated on moving downward swiftly, silently, and—God will it—safely.

From the sounds emanating from the *grande salle* and bailey, she realized her disappearance had been discovered. She'd have to move quickly.

Perhaps she should have waited for a more opportune time. But, their senses dulled by drink and revelry, the sentries assigned to watch her had lowered their vigilance. Excusing herself to visit the garderobe, she had seized her chance to escape now, before the wedding night.

Because she did not trust her response in the nuptial chamber.

She hated Rand for making her believe he loved her, even as he'd plotted to abduct her and steal her home. Still, some undisciplined part of her responded to his touch, his nearness, the warmth of his smile, and the scent of sunshine that clung to him. The feeling of desire was so strong that, in spite of her hatred and hurt, she feared she might yet succumb to him.

But not now. There would be no wedding night, no consummation of this sham marriage.

He already gave you a consummation such as most women only dream about, said a traitorous voice in her heart. And the proof of it lives within you.

With a convulsive grip she clutched at a rocky outcrop. She pushed the thought from her mind. Babe or not, she would never submit to Rand.

Shouts rang from her chamber window. A renewed sense of urgency seized her. She hugged the curved wall and prayed the eaves and the night shadows would conceal her. She held her breath until the voices faded. Relieved, she moved on. Mortar crumbled beneath her fingers. The ledge narrowed. Sweat and fear left her cold. Only when her dangling foot found purchase on the edge of an arrow slit did she pause for breath.

She glanced down. The moat lay fifty feet below, she gauged. Her eyes avoided the murky waters, avoided the thought of what she must do. Scaling the wall seemed but child's play when compared to the trial ahead. She could not swim. Pray God she could steal across the flimsy rope bridge that spanned the moat.

Voices drifted up from the bailey. She started moving again and found a series of iron loops and stone corbels protruding from the wall. Put there to aid masons at their repairs, they now helped her to freedom. The footholds lay few and far between. The stone and mortar grew more difficult to grasp, and her muscles began to scream with fatigue. Keep moving, she commanded herself. You are the daughter of Aimery the Warrior. You've made more harrowing climbs in search of sulfur deposits.

The shadowy bailey disappeared as she rounded the tower.

And made an alarming discovery.

Moss, slickened by the sea air, coated the stones.

May you roast in hell, Enguerrand Fitzmarc!

Her mind barely registered a scraping sound. She scrabbled wildly for a purchase. Her hand found an iron loop. She grabbed at it desperately, only to find it, too, beslimed with moss.

She curved her fingers around the loop, her feet dangling. Loosened by her weight, the mortar crumbled. The rung began to move.

As her anchor gave way, Lianna had time for but one unthinking, throat-tearing scream.

"Rand!"

Chapter  10

Her frantic scream echoed in his ears. Horror leaped in his throat as he saw her handhold loosen, felt a shower of mortar on his face. Had he found her only to lose her?

His chest tight with dread, he teetered precariously on the topmost rung of a scaling ladder. He reached for the flailing, falling figure, grasped her waist. His heart pounding wildly, he held her against him. Motion and impact nearly overset the ladder. But for his steel grip and iron will, they both would have pitched into the moat.

Rand pressed against the wall, steadied his feet on the ladder. He buried his face in the cool, fragrant silk of her hair and thought, Thank God. Thank God Burgundy guessed her escape route in time. "I've got you, love," he murmured.

Far below, torches bobbed, casting long, eerie shadows against the tower. Shouts of victory and scattered applause drifted from the banks of the moat.

Lianna made not a sound for a moment; her fall into his arms had knocked the breath out of her. Frantically Rand touched her face, her neck, dreading to find her injured. His own breathing came in sharp, tense gasps.

"Sweet lamb of God," he said, "you might have been killed." He grasped her more tightly as she sucked in her breath with a great *whoosh*. Revived, she struck out at him. Her elbow landed on his ribs.

"Let me go!" she cried.

Alarmed, he leaned into the wall. "Cease your squirming, else you might kill us both yet."

"If I had died, know that it would have been you, *Englishman*, who forced me to it."

The remark drove a shaft of guilt into him. But now was not the time for explanations. "Not I," he said, wrapping her arms against her sides to stay her movement. "But your own recklessness, Lianna. By the rood, will you be still?"

"Never! I'll never stop fighting you, Englishman."

"Will you force me to subdue you again? Do you relish another swim?" He knew not how else to convince her of the peril she courted in struggling on the rickety ladder.

"Ha!" she said, twisting to face him. "I'd like to see you climb down with my dead weight in your arms. You'd probably nigh drown me as you did before."

He met her hostile glare with a look of hard-eyed determination. In the past he'd held her as a lover. Now he gazed upon her as an adversary. His lover's heart gave way to the cold implacability of a soldier's discipline.

"Listen well, Lianna." Steel edged his words. "I once climbed a scaling ladder with Greek fire burning my back and a hail of missiles raining down on me. If I survived that, I can survive your resistance."

She went still. He felt blood welling hotly from his wounded arm; the struggle had opened the arrow gash.

Heedless of his pain, she demanded, "How did you find me?"

His stare calm and steady, he said, "You called my name. I'll always hear you, Lianna, no matter how faint your cries."

"I'd have succeeded if the loops had held," she said peevishly.

He shook his head. "You might have fooled a stranger." He brushed a wisp of moon-silk hair from her brow; she flinched from his touch. "But I am not a stranger. I know every inch of your body and every corner of your mind."

Her shoulders drooped. Feeling the fight go out of her, he knew, with infinite regret, that his reminder of their intimate past hurt her deeply. "You *knew* me well," she stated dully. "Loose me, and I'll follow you down."

He searched her face for a trace of deception but saw only weariness, resignation. Still, the latent fire in her silver eyes reminded him of Jack's admonition: *You can't trust a word she says or a move she makes.*

His eyes never leaving her, Rand climbed to the bottom of the ladder. She followed. Jagged pain seared his arm, but worse, his heart ached with the knowledge that she loathed him enough to endanger her life escaping him. God, he'd almost lost her; he'd nearly gone insane looking for her. The waiting damsel assigned to her chamber doubtless still shook from his rough interrogation; the man-at-arms who'd fallen asleep at his post probably suffered a cracked rib when Rand had kicked him awake.

He reached the bank of the moat, stepped into the boat tied there. The vessel rocked as he took her by the waist and turned her. Clinging to the ladder, she stiffened.

Through the darkness, the heat of her resentful glare burned him.

"You needn't . . ." Her eyes widened when she spied the boat. "*Nom de Dieu*, I won't get into this leaky skiff."

Impatient, he pulled her down from the ladder and into the boat. "Had you not tried such a foolhardy escape, you'd be safe in your bed," he snapped. Her gasp, ragged with terror, reminded him that once she'd trusted him enough to confess her fear of water. His annoyance lessened; he lowered her gently. "You'll come to no harm. You have but to stay put." He wanted to kiss the frown from her pale face. "How would you have crossed the moat if I'd not come?"

She tossed her head. "By the same means by which I've lived my life. Sheer determination, Englishman. I'd have crossed the rope footbridge."

"The bridge is down," he said.

"I'd have found a way," she insisted. Her haughty expression, her confident posture, convinced him that she would have braved her greatest fear in order to flee her husband.

Angry, his pride wounded, Rand took up the oars and began to row. She suffered the brief voyage in silence, her knuckles white as she gripped the sides of the boat. When he took her hand at the other shore, her flesh felt cold, bloodless.

As soon as they reached the top of the bank, Lianna scrambled ahead. With annoyance and dismay, he realized she meant to flee him yet. He gained her side with an easy bound and caught her wrist.

She glared. "Unhand me, Englishman."

His gaze flicked to the crowd of avid watchers gathered

on the bank. "You'll come willingly, Lianna, else I'll drag you."

She began to twist in his grasp. "Drag me, then," she spat. "Show yourself for the abusive coward you are."

Given no choice, he gritted his teeth, scooped her into his arms, and strode toward the bridge leading to the keep. The crowd parted. Torchlit faces grinned; English and French voices murmured lusty suggestions. Lianna felt stiff, unyielding, and oddly fragile. Her face shone white and immobile as polished alabaster.

"I'll never forgive you for this, Englishman," she said through clenched teeth.

"Burgundy gave you a choice."

"Ha! A choice between my home and a nunnery is no choice at all. Never," she repeated peevishly.

"Never is a long time, Lianna."

"Eternity is not long enough to prove my hatred."

Pain sat as cold and hard as a stone in his gut. Even the warmth of Lianna, held fast against his chest, failed to thaw the feeling. He crossed the yard and climbed the stairs of the Tour du Roi. A much chastened man-at-arms stepped aside to let them enter the bedchamber. Within, a waiting damsel folded away Lianna's discarded wedding finery. One fierce look from Rand sent the maid scurrying outside. He closed the door with a backward kick.

An oil lamp ensconced on the wall and two tapers on a polished oak table lighted the chamber. A private wedding supper lay in readiness: roasted capon, apples, dates, nuts, and cheese, a pitcher of wine.

Lianna, however, seemed disinclined to celebrate her marriage with feasting and toasting. As soon as Rand set her down, she lurched away, leaving him standing against the door. Before he realized her intent, she ran to the table. Frantic hands plundered the crockery and cutlery. With a strength belied by her size, she hurled a wine goblet at him.

"Lianna . . ." He ducked the sailing disk of a salver. "Lianna, stop that, listen." An earthenware ewer shattered just to the side of his head.

"I'll not listen to you, Englishman!" She threw the bowl, still filled with apples. "Damn you!"

A knock sounded. "My lord," someone called through the door, "is aught amiss?"

"Leave us," Rand roared.

Like a tempestuous goddess, his bride stood amid the jagged shards of glass and pottery littering the floor. With a sweep of her hand she knocked aside the tapers, plunging the chamber into half darkness. As she picked up the second goblet, her slippered feet danced perilously close to a piece of broken crockery. "Lianna," he said, "have a care, you'll cut—"

The clatter of breaking glass stopped his speech. Hearing her gasp, feeling a slicing pain, the wetness of blood on his brow, he realized her missile had found its mark.

Furious, he wiped the blood from his eyes. The motion scraped a sliver of glass into his cheekbone. He flinched at the pain. By the time his vision cleared she was at the window, one leg slung over the ledge.

"Devil take you, woman," he yelled, "are you twice a fool?" Grimly, grinding glass beneath his boots, he crossed the chamber with long, swift strides. Closing his hand around her arm, he yanked her back into the room.

She kicked, struggled, pummeled. His wounded arm throbbed, his eyes stung, and his patience reached its limit. He jerked her to the bed and flung her down.

"Since you wish to play rough, my lady," he said, "then I must oblige you." Pinioning her wrists with one hand, he ripped a cord from the bed curtain.

She squirmed. "What are you doing?"

"Protecting us both from your temper."

"You're barbaric."

"You haven't always thought so."

Incensed by the taunt, she kicked at him.

He sucked a deep breath. "You're beyond any Christian's control." Using two of the curtain cords, he bound her, arms splayed, to the posts of the bed.

Lianna bit her lip to keep from weeping. The warrior looming above her was a stranger. His golden hair wild, his face flecked with blood, and his mouth grim, he looked as fearsome and merciless as Helquin the Huntsman.

She clamped her jaw against a plea for mercy. She would never plead with him, never show him anything but contempt.

After jerking the second cord tight, he withdrew into the shadows of the chamber. She heard the crunch of glass and twisted her head to glare at him. He put aside his sword; then his fingers worked at the lace points of his baldric, unfastening the belt.

Alarm raced through her. "What are you doing?"

His mouth curved into a heartless smile. "I'm coming to bed, Baroness"

"*This* bed?"

"I see no other available."

A hot flood of anticipation ignited her loins, yet a cold gust of indignation froze her heart. "Stay away," she breathed. "Plea—just stay away from me, Englishman."

He made no reply. His eyes, alight with sensual promise, raked her splayed-out form. Kicking a path across the littered floor, he found an unbroken cup and filled it with wine. He indulged in a long, unhurried pull, then wordlessly offered her the cup. She jerked her head in sharp refusal.

Her gaze crept back toward him in time to see him unlace the full murrey sleeves of his tunic. She yanked her gaze free of his powerful arms, only to feel her attention immediately drawn back. An ugly, bleeding gash marred the smooth muscles of his upper arm.

"You're wounded," she said, trying to hide her concern.

He glanced without interest at the bloody cut. "A *moulinet* from one of Gaucourt's crossbows."

She remembered the hissing sounds that had dogged their flight the previous night. *Nom de Dieu*, she thought, watching his graceful, easy movements, he seems to feel no pain at all.

Noticing her stare, he smiled slightly. "Think you an Englishman does not bleed?"

Suddenly, absurdly, tears gathered in her eyes. She demanded, "How can he, when he has no heart?"

The smile vanished. Shadows fluttered like small dark birds across his face. "I have a heart, Lianna. I feel it breaking when I see the contempt in your eyes."

"What in the name of God did you expect?" she asked, half-sobbing. He held her with a sad, steady stare until she conquered her shameful tears and said, "How long do you mean to keep me trussed on this bed?"

"Until you listen to what I have to say and agree to cease fighting and running." He dipped a corner of his sleeve in a fingerbowl and wiped the blood from his face and arm.

Oh, God, she'd hurt him. Her hands, though bound,

itched to salve the wounds; then she banished the thought of succoring her enemy.

He finished his task. Then, the rowels of his spurs whirring, he approached the bed.

A sense of familiarity pricked at her, the memory of the dream that had plagued her since she'd wed Lazare. The husband coming to her bed had had Rand's face, Rand's eyes. Always the dream had filled her with longing. Now the reality filled her with hopelessness, for the device emblazoned on his tabard was the leopard rampant.

With swift, easy movements, he discarded the *côte d'armes* and his undertunic. She tried to shrink from him, but the cords held her tight. The low light picked out details of a body she used to cherish with her own. She shuddered at the remembrance. A glow from the oil lamp struck golden highlights into the fine hairs on his musclebanded chest. Shadows carved the powerful bone structure of his face into a visage so compelling, she ached just looking at him. His mouth, tender yet firm, curved into a smile. Heat pounded through her; she shifted restively.

As he bent to remove his spurs and boots and hosen, she closed her eyes. *Nom de Dieu*, what manner of woman was she, that she'd still desire this betraying Englishman?

A gentle hand stirred the hair at her temple. Flinching, she clenched her eyes all the tighter.

"I'd have you look at me, Lianna."

She opened her eyes, glaring. "I look upon a scoundrel and a betrayer."

"You look upon a man who loves you with a power stronger than eternity. A man who is ready to forgive *your* deception."

"Prate not to me of love. You love only your usurping sovereign and your foul ambition to steal my castle."

He shook his head. "I love you without regard for King Henry or Bois-Long."

"You lie," she said, battening fury against the awful hurt that clawed at her heart. "You *knew* who I was all along. You deceived me with coy questions about my 'mistress' and false declarations about your hallowed knight-errantry."

He drew back, his eyes wide with shock. Did she not know him for a deceiving *god-don,* she would have believed his surprise was genuine.

"What's this? Do you truly think I realized you were the demoiselle?"

She strained against the cords binding her. "Why else would you have met me day after day, plagued me with sly questions and half-truths?"

He touched her cheek. She recoiled from the caress. "You know me. You should trust what you know. I did not mean to spin such a web, Lianna. It started innocently, and with you. Remember, you asked me if I hailed from Gascony. It was then that I decided, for both our sakes, to let you believe I was a French knight-errant."

"'Tis well you guarded you identity, for I'd have turned my firepower on your miserable hide."

"Lianna," he said quietly, "I didn't know who you were. When I learned I was betrothed to a French lady of twenty-one years, I pictured a woman too flawed to have married at a proper age."

"Aye, I am flawed," she said bitterly. "Flawed by an uncle who cares more for intrigue than for me."

He laid his hand on her shoulder. She fought against

the comfort offered by the warm, steadfast pressure of his fingers.

"I went in secret to Bois-Long," he said. "I spied a black-haired woman riding across the causeway. I now know her to be Macée Mondragon, but I mistook her for you." His jaw grew taut with distaste. "Do you wonder that I did not connect the fair *pucelle* in the woods with the dark woman beating a servant?"

The cords chafed her wrists. Churlishly she said, "Even if that were true, that disrespectful valet you sent to announce you would have proven you mistaken. Surely he gave you a rudimentary description of the demoiselle."

Humor flared in Rand's eyes. "Jack did describe you, Lianna. He said you were cold, hard-hearted, arrogant. I'm afraid he was a bit too put off by your cannonade to admit that you're also angelically lovely."

"His wits are as numb as his master's," she snapped.

"You did spin a fair tale yourself."

She wanted to flee the affectionate look he cast upon her. But his calm, steady eyes, flecked with gold from the lamp, held hers like the mesmerizing flame of a conjurer's lantern. He laid a warm hand on her cheek. "The castle orphan, true. But a gunner's daughter, a gently bred companion to the demoiselle? You were convincing. How could I have believed otherwise?"

"You *knew*, Englishman," she said, twisting in her bonds to escape the firebrand of his touch.

"I did not." He leaned forward. "Besides, Lianna, you are forgetting the most convincing evidence of all."

"What might that be?" she asked loftily.

"The Demoiselle Belliane was a married woman by the time I arrived in France." Ever so gently, his hand coursed down the length of her. "But the woman I made love to at the place of St. Cuthbert's cross was a virgin."

A dreadful darkness pressed in on her. God, he knew her so well; he struck so close.

"No," she denied wildly, struggling. "I was not, I—"

"Oh, Lianna, yes," he said. "I had a moment of doubt tonight, at the feast, but then I thought of the first time we lay together and loved, and my uncertainty vanished." His fingers drew a pattern on her thinly clad thigh. "Even before I saw your maiden's blood, I knew. Don't pretend you've forgotten. You were so sweet, so adorably bewildered. Even in my own inexperience I recognized your purity."

She squeezed her eyes shut to stave off an onslaught of memories. Yet she couldn't forget. His hesitation, her ignorance. His tenderness, her response. His gentle hands teaching her untried body the ways of physical love.

"Tell me why," he quietly urged. "Tell me how it came to be that you were married, yet chaste."

She gazed at him through narrowed eyes and strained against her bonds. "I'll not be interrogated like a prisoner on the rack. I owe you no explanation." A sudden dark suspicion barreled into her mind. "But you owe me one."

"I hold no secrets from you, Lianna. Not anymore."

Oh, Rand, she thought with silent pain, I was so much happier when you did. Her voice cold, she stated, "I find it entirely too convenient that Lazare Mondragon happened to die at the moment you sought to force me to wed you."

Rand went still. He gave her a furious, scorching look. For long moments he seemed not to breathe. Finally he said, "You go too far in accusing me of murder."

"Do I, Englishman? You sneaked into my home, abducted me, braved Gaucourt's *hobelars*. You do much in the name of King Henry. Why not murder?"

"Your uncle assured me a hasty annulment was being secured." Bitterness tinged his voice.

She couldn't control a twinge of empathy. Her uncle of Burgundy had taken in kings and emperors with half-truths and empty assurances. Why should she have expected Rand to see into the intrigue-ridden soul of Jean Sans Peur?

Yet she couldn't allow her thoughts to show. Her voice still cold, she said, "You went away for a fortnight in March. How do I know you didn't journey to Paris, that Lazare didn't die by your own hand?"

His face went taut with anger. Then, seeming to conquer it, he traced his finger over her jawline, her throat. She tried to imagine that hand in a murderous grip around a defenseless man's neck. Tried . . . and failed.

"You will only know that for certain, Lianna, when you decide to trust me," said Rand.

"Then I will never know. For I shall never trust you."

He toyed with the cord binding one of her wrists. "Can I trust *you*, Lianna?"

Although she knew he offered her a chance to be loosed from her bonds, she couldn't help retorting, "You can trust that I will do everything in my power to thwart you."

His fingers left the cord tied securely. He sat silent while she tried to tear her gaze from the entrancing motion of his bare chest, rising and falling with each breath he took.

At last he spoke. "We're together now, Lianna. Isn't that what we wanted all along?"

"I wanted Rand, not Enguerrand Fitzmarc!"

"We are one and the same." He leaned down; his lips

lay but a whisper away from hers. "It is our wedding night."

Alarmed, she jerked her wrists and turned her face away. "No."

His tongue traced the curve of her ear. "You may rail at me 'til kingdom come, but in your heart you know our destinies are entwined. I wanted you as my wife. Now I have you."

Appalled at the tangle of desire and fear roiling within her, she forced herself to regard him squarely. "You wanted my castle, not me."

He smiled; clearly he heard the lack of conviction in her voice. He touched the pulse at her throat. "I want you, Lianna. Always."

She tried to pull away. "Then you'd best keep me shackled with ropes, else I'll never bear your advances."

"I'd hold you with affection, not bonds," he said, kissing her face, her neck.

She fought to will away the hot, liquid flames of desire stinging through her veins. The light flickered, limning his princely features in gold. The commanding beauty of his face, the compelling power of his caresses, raised a tingle deep in her center. The sensation radiated outward, filling her breasts, softening her woman's flesh.

"You are lovely in the lamplight," he murmured, his kisses fast and merciless on her face. "In sooth I always likened your coloring to silver, but tonight you look as precious and shining as new gold." He caught her face between his hands and laid his lips upon hers. Fiercely she vowed that if her hands were not bound, she'd slap him away. Or would she?

Seared by the heat of his mouth, she found herself a prisoner of bonds stronger than velvet cords. His voluptuous kiss grew keener, sharp with sensual abandonment, and heavy with an allure that threatened to claim her wholly. Summoning her will, she turned her head aside. "Do not do that," she said unsteadily.

"I mean to do much more, Lianna." His hands coursed down her sides, touching her with fire. He found her breasts through the fabric of her tunic, his fingers moving in ever-tightening circles. An intolerable ache rose in her. She bit her lip to keep from crying out.

A certain ruthlessness lay beneath the tenderness of his caresses, as if he sought to prove his sexual power over her.

"We've never made love in the dark before," he mused. "Always we celebrated our love in sunshine."

"It is doomed to be mourned in the dark now," she snapped.

"Lianna . . ." Briefly he pressed his lips to hers. "We need not be adversaries."

"We are, and ever shall be. Think on it, *Enguerrand*. You are English and would give my castle to King Henry. I am French and would hold it until my dying breath."

"I love you."

"I despise you."

"Do you?" He shook his head, smiled, and took her breath away with the swift and knowing stroke of his hand on her thigh. "Tell me you despise this." His fingers played a familiar tune upon her flesh. "You love me. Someday you'll tell me about it."

"Never," she swore, and would have launched into a fierce tirade had his mouth not stopped hers. Weak with wanting, she found it easy to pretend this was Rand, her lover. He took her lips in a deep, drinking kiss while his hands—hands that knew her so well—aroused her body to an overwhelming level of sensitivity. His fingers made a slow, meandering path up her bare leg, under her tunic, stealing her will to resist him as his thumb brushed her softness.

Against all reason, she rose to a state of helpless desire. Perhaps the lamb's wool she'd drunk at the wedding feast had been laced with some drug. For surely she must be drugged, else she'd not lie still and countenance this sensual assault from her enemy.

Her body played the traitor, warming to an adversary's alluring touch. Despite a growing sense of despair, she let her limbs go limp upon the bed while his hands and lips teased her thighs and breasts to burning arousal.

Deep in some hidden part of her she was glad of the bonds at her wrists; they took the decision to fight away from her. Rand, and not her own weakness, would be responsible for her submission.

She hated herself for yielding to him; she hated him for bringing her to this weakened state. Yet even while she tried to bolster her flagging will with contempt, she surrendered to the gentle insistence of his hands and mouth.

"Oh, love," he murmured, his lips following his fingers as they unlaced her tunic, "I've dreamed of making you my wife . . . you taste so sweet. . . ."

Vaguely her mind took in the fact that he'd spoken in French. We battle in English, but make love in French, she thought fleetingly. When his hands parted her tunic and bared her breasts, she ceased to think at all.

She could feel only the fire of his caresses as he removed the rough garments she'd stolen from the laundry. He touched and teased until her every nerve went taut.

Naked and bound, she should have felt humiliated. Yet

instead she felt wild and free, wanting him so badly she nearly wept.

His powerful body loomed like a craggy mountain, luring her to the summit.

"You want me, Lianna," he whispered against her mouth.

"Yes . . ." she breathed.

He braced himself above her. The heat of his kiss went straight to her core. He reached for her bound hands, laced his fingers with hers, and joined their bodies with a slow, aching stroke.

She arched toward him, meeting his thrusts, forgetting he was her enemy, bedding her as a conquest. She thought her hatred had banished the knight in the glade. But he was still there, forcing out the love she'd always felt for him, turning her from intrepid dreamer to a woman fulfilled. She closed her eyes while her body drank in the essence of him—his powerful movements, his vibrant warmth, the taste of the love words that spilled from his lips.

She seethed inside, roiling violently like a full cauldron heated by his lovemaking. The feeling rose and then boiled over, spilling through her senses. A cry of release exploded from her lips, and she clasped him with her legs. He tensed, then surged into her with a final, lingering pulse.

His body covered hers; their hammering hearts beat as one. Sighing, she brought her arms around his neck.

And froze.

"Damn you." She tried to squirm from beneath him. Humiliation misted her cheeks and neck with red. At some point during their lovemaking he'd untied her bonds and freed her hands. She could have fought him;

the old Lianna could have resisted. But the person he'd made her had succumbed, too spellbound by his ardor to notice. Now she realized she was bound by something more formidable than velvet cords. Her own unreasoning passion tied her to this man.

She summoned anger, but the fury was directed more at herself than at him. She'd dubbed him her enemy, yet she was a prisoner of desire. She'd vowed to resist him, yet she'd become his willing bedmate. He'd achieved his domination over her—not by force, but by tenderness.

You love me, he'd said. *Someday you'll tell me about it.*

"Get off me, Englishman," she commanded.

He moved aside, although he cradled her in his arms. She knew she should pull away, but she felt weary, lethargic. His body was so comfortable, circling hers with masculine warmth.

Propping himself on an elbow, he stared into her eyes. "Lianna, I do mean to be husband to you."

"And vassal to King Henry."

"Aye, that too." He gripped her shoulders. "Henry has brought order and prosperity to England. He can do the same for France."

"So could the devil himself. But France will not countenance a foreigner on the throne." She narrowed her eyes. "And I will not countenance an Englishman at Bois-Long."

"You do not have a choice, wife."

The cold certainty in his voice jarred her. A vision of Burgundy's implacable face swam into her mind. "What does my uncle mean to do?"

"He leaves for Compiègne at dawn, taking all his men with him. The Armagnacs are on their way to besiege the town."

A shiver rippled through her. Damn Bernard of Armagnac and her uncle for ripping France into splinters with their ceaseless bickering. And damn Rand for having the knowledge before her. Then relief took hold. A satisfied smile curved her lips. "So my uncle leaves. I counted but ten men wearing your colors. Gaucourt will hold Bois-Long for me yet."

He eyed her sharply. "For you, Lianna? Or for Gervais?"

She suppressed a twinge of alarm. "Gervais Mondragon has no claim on Bois-Long."

"Save for the fact that he is Lazare's heir, and installed at the château. Possession is the better part of the law."

"So. You've styled yourself Baron of Longwood. What do you propose to do about Gervais and Gaucourt?"

"I propose to send them fleeing into the salt marshes."

"With ten men against Gaucourt's fifty? Your male pride is prodigious," she scoffed.

Her sarcasm seemed to make no impression on him. He merely smiled and toyed with a discarded velvet cord. He lifted it, watched it spin slowly, then dropped it on the floor. "I'm sorry I tied you," he said. "I'll not do it again . . . unless you force me to it."

She tried to pull away. "It is the only way you'll get me to submit to you again."

He bent his head, brushing his lips over the peaks of her breasts. "Is it, Lianna?" he asked softly. His hand strayed downward, heating places on her body that had barely cooled from the last time. "Is it?"

Every wanton part of her strained toward his stroking hands and moist lips. Every rational part of her dredged up all the agony he'd caused her. He'd taken her innocence, deceived her heart, and had set his sights on her home. His body offered but fleeting moments of passionate forgetfulness, hardly enough to excuse his betrayal.

She went stiff with resentment. "Stop," she said, but he seemed not to hear as he nuzzled her throat. She put her hands flat against his chest and pushed with all her might. He drew back, his handsome face framed by hair of beaten gold. His masculine beauty was intolerable.

"Don't fight me, Lianna," he said.

Ice formed around her heart, and suddenly she wanted to hurt him with all the fury she felt. "I never wanted you, Englishman, not even when I thought you were Rand the Gascon."

"You did," he countered impatiently. " 'Twas you who invited—"

"Did you never wonder why, you great fool?" Her voice rose and quivered, but she was powerless to control it. "Or were you so self-important that you thought yourself irresistible?" She lashed him with the words, watching his face, seeing the certainty of his domination waver. Hurting him gave her disappointingly little satisfaction.

"You wanted to know about Lazare," she forced out. "Then I shall tell you about him. He refused to lie with me, his wife, because he didn't want to get me with child. Aye, he wanted his beloved Gervais to inherit." Tears coursed down her cheeks and sank into the baudekin bolster. Angrily she wiped her face dry. "I needed an heir for Bois-Long. *That* was why I sought your attentions." The incredulous look on his face nearly silenced her. Cruel words didn't come as easily as they should. "It was my *only* reason," she finished.

With a swift motion he clasped her wrists in his two

hands. His eyes glinted fiercely. "You can lie to yourself, but the heart doesn't lie. You may claim I played stud to your mare, but I know better. I've seen your face ablaze with rapture, felt your legs wrapped hard around me, heard endearments spill from your lips—"

"Only because I didn't want you to know my real reason for trysting with you."

His fine, mobile mouth suddenly hardened. He released her, turned away, and yanked on his smallclothes and undertunic. "And did you," he said over his shoulder, "achieve what you set out for? Are you carrying my babe?"

She kept her face impassive, her voice even. "I do not know. But I wonder if any budding life could have survived the perils you've foisted upon me in the past two days."

The hiss of his indrawn breath sounded like an arrow slashing through the air. "What of your foolish climb down the tower?" he shot back. His voice sounded ragged with pain.

She turned toward the wall. It should have felt good to hurt him as he'd hurt her. Yet a cold well of emptiness opened in the pit of her belly—and a rattle of nothingness echoed where her heart used to be.

Chapter  11

His tabard flapping around his athletic form, Rand crossed the yard of Le Crotoy and headed for the barracks. The wave of unseasonable heat that had baked Picardy gave way to a swift bluster of chilly air from the north.

A curlew wheeled overhead and greeted the morn with a plaintive cry. Then the bird beat its wings toward the sea.

Idly he watched the curlew battle the wind. He had not eaten. His stomach was clenched in knots. Lianna's resentment ran as deep and strong as a dangerous tide, straight to his heart. She was convinced he'd duped her from the first, and she had tried to convince him that she'd done the same in using him to produce an heir for Bois-Long. His loins heated with the remembrance of their passion the night before; his spirits sank at the memory of her withdrawal and angry words.

An ambitious monarch divided them. Loyalty to King

Henry compelled Rand to secure and hold Bois-Long for England; her loyalty to mad Charles obliged her to retain the château for France. Setting his jaw, he vowed to win her back. All of her.

Today his goals were twofold: he had to set about wresting Bois-Long from Mondragon and Gaucourt and he had to prove to Lianna that their love was mightier than political disputes. The former he hoped to accomplish within a fortnight. The latter could take weeks, months, even years.

He'd left her sleeping—or more likely feigning sleep in order to avoid him. Simon and Batsford were stationed outside her chamber. The window had been shuttered, the latch slid into place. He'd told his men to permit her the run of the keep but cautioned them not to allow her out of their sight.

Just as he reached the barracks, one of his men-at-arms came hurrying through the main gate.

"Good morrow, Dylan," Rand said. Seeing anxiety in the Welshman's dark, pointed features, he asked, "You've seen something?"

Dylan nodded. The arrows in his baldric bobbed. "Gaucourt's men. The woods beyond the town fester with them."

Rand scowled. No doubt the Frenchmen had seen Burgundy leaving Le Crotoy with all his men.

"Think you they'll try to take the castle?" Dylan asked.

"Nay, Burgundy told me the walls of Le Crotoy have never been breached." He eyed the row of cannon on the battlements. The duke's new firearms were a formidable deterrent to invaders.

Dylan said, "They skulk about the area like night vermin."

"Were you seen?"

The Welshman grinned and stroked his mustache. "Nay, my lord. I am more stealthy than any Frenchman."

Rand placed a hand on his shoulder. "Go get something to eat. I'll send Piers Atwood to relieve you."

"Thank you, my lord." Dylan shouldered his longbow and started toward the hall.

Rand made for the steps to the barracks. A feminine giggle issued from behind a sheaf of wheat straw in the stables beneath the raised soldiers' quarters.

"Jack," he called out. "Jack, I would speak with you."

He heard a high-pitched gasp, a masculine oath; then Jack and Minette emerged from the stables. Jack fumbled with the laces of his trews while Minette finished stuffing the ample flesh of her bosom into the bodice of her homespun blouse. She sent Rand a wide, wet smile and a sultry glance.

"What's this?" she asked in her nasal, peasant French. "*La baronne* has released you from her bed so early?" The milkmaid laughed. "I've heard it said blue blood is cold. Now I know it must be true." She sauntered closer.

Battling annoyance and ignoring Minette's nearness, Rand forced a laugh. "Speak not of what you know not."

"*La barbe,*" she swore. "You are handsome as the sun, *mon sire,* but as cold as ice."

Jack chased her off with a none-too-gentle slap to the backside. "Later, my little bird," he said in mangled French. "I'll make you forget my master's too-pretty face."

"Sorry, Jack," said Rand. "You won't be here to scratch her itch."

Jack shrugged. "It won't be the first time you've spoiled my bed sport. What's amiss, my lord?"

"I want you and Dylan to go to Eu. I mean to engage our friends there to help us take Bois-Long."

Jack started to laugh; then he bit back his mirth when he saw Rand wasn't smiling. "You be in earnest, my lord."

"Aye."

"But the men of Eu are farmers, fishermen. Not fighters. And they are French."

"They are men whose homes have been plundered by French brigands, whose women have been raped by knights."

Understanding dawned on Jack's gamin face. "And," the scutifer said, "they are beholden to you for succoring the town after that raid. You armed them with Welsh longbows."

"Exactly. Gaucourt's knights might be the ones who raided them. If we can prove that, the people of Eu will not turn away from the opportunity to take captives, to charge ransoms."

Jack's face fell. "How does a peasant make a captive of a trained knight?"

Rand smiled. "How did our king win Shrewsbury when he was but a princeling of sixteen summers?"

Jack slapped his thigh. "With bows and arrows, by God, not lances and shields."

"Aye. You and Dylan will train them." He paused. "Speak not of my intent, Jack. Simply say you mean to see them well prepared if brigands should strike again."

Jack looked relieved. "It is best coming from you."

"Have them ready to march inside a fortnight."

"You ask much of me, my lord."

"You have much to offer, Jack."

"Dylan and I will leave today."

"Watch your back. Gaucourt's men are all around."

Jack drew himself up. "Not even the squirrels will note our passing, my lord."

Lianna glared at Rand from her chair by the hearth in the *grande salle*. The late afternoon sun shimmered cold light over his golden hair, his smiling face. She wished her hammering heart would remember that this man was English, and her enemy.

He leaned down and kissed her cheek. The scent of sea breezes clung to him. The rest of her nearly forgot, too.

"How are you, my sweet?" he asked.

The frown she sent him was anything but sweet. "You forced me into a marriage I protest, you hold me against my will, you keep me guarded by your lackeys, and you ask me how I fare?" She gave a dry, bitter laugh and slid a malevolent look at Simon and Batsford, who were playing at backgammon nearby.

Rand sank to one knee before her, took her hands in his. The casual touch reminded her of the powerful attraction they shared. Her pulse leaped; she avoided his eyes.

Lowering his voice, he said, "A foolish question, considering your state of mind." She tried to yank her hands away. He tightened his hold. "I mean to enforce my claim on Bois-Long."

"You mean to turn my home into an English bastion."

"Lianna. King Henry is coming to Normandy. With or without Bois-Long, he will dominate France and take the crown he rightfully claims. Your castle—our children—will reap the rewards of an English monarchy."

She suppressed a shiver. Her uncle had described Henry as a driven man who dealt swiftly and ruthlessly with those who defied him. What if Rand were correct?

What if Henry did win France? Her stomach fluttered. How would a Frenchwoman fare under English rule? Whose subject would her child be?

"You ask too much of me," she stated. "I will not open my home to the English usurper."

His eyes hardened. The chilly look seemed strange on a face that had always been soft with love for her. "Yet you would open it to a usurping Frenchman."

She looked down at their entwined fingers, the bands of new gold. An idea niggled at her. The laws of entail might allow Gervais to inherit the property Lazare had gained through marriage. "I shall perish of boredom here," she snapped, turning the subject and extracting her hands.

He stroked her cheek, then let his hand trail to her neck and lower, poised over her breast until she ached for him to touch her there. He said, "We'll be back at Bois-Long soon."

Her head jerked up. "How?" she asked. "You've but a handful of men."

He started to speak, then seemed to think better of it. Aye, she thought, if we kept secrets from each other before, we keep new ones now. Angry at the yearning of her body, she pushed his hand away.

"I thought you wanted to get home," he said at length.

"I do, I . . . The spring planting must be supervised. 'Tis nigh time to sow the hemp and flax." She tapped her chin. "The shearing must be done. . . ."

He touched her again, stroking her shoulder. He was relentless in exerting his power over her. "I'll get you home."

She tried to ignore the tender promise in his words and the sensual thrill of his caress. "Aye," she said, "no doubt you're eager to settle yourself, to make traitors of my people."

"Our people, Lianna. I would see us as husband and wife, working together—"

"I shall only work against you."

"Then you work against yourself as well." Reaching up, he brushed a wisp of hair from her brow. A leap of attraction surged in her breast. Unconsciously she leaned toward him, hungry and resentful of that hunger. His lips drew closer, a whisper from hers.

"My lord!" An English soldier, an oversized man called Darby Green, clattered into the hall. " 'Tis Piers Atwood. He's come back from patrol, and he's been wounded by gunshot."

"Is it grave?"

"No, the ball only grazed his leg."

"Is the bridge drawn up?"

Darby shrugged. "I'm not sure. There was such confusion."

"Shall I come, my lord?" asked Father Batsford.

"I'll send for you if I need you." Rand jumped to his feet. "Look well to my wife," he said; then he and Green hurried out.

Lianna, too, stood. Wounded by gunshot. She turned the idea over in her mind, wondering . . . Of course, she decided as the truth dawned on her. The gunner could only be Chiang. Chiang, whom she could trust above all others.

She approached Simon and Batsford, who sat glaring at each other across their game board. "I weary of sitting. I'm going out for a walk in the bailey."

Wordlessly the men followed her from the hall.

✳   ✳   ✳

Two hours later, Rand stepped from the barracks. Duchess Margaret, trained in the healing arts, had cleaned and bound the leg wound and pronounced that Piers would mend nicely.

Yet Rand felt grim. The men of Gaucourt overran the countryside. Doubtless Burgundy's absence had emboldened them to act aggressively. Darby Green descended the stone steps behind Rand. Darby's spurs spun with haste, and his tunic, emblazoned with the Longwood crest, fluttered in a chilly gust of wind.

"I'm going out on patrol, my lord."

Rand put a hand on Darby's shoulder. "Not dressed like that you aren't."

Darby spread his hands. "Is aught missing from my livery?"

"No; you're dressed precisely as a knight of Longwood, and that's the problem." Darby shook his head in confusion. Rand went on, "Find yeoman's clothes, and a cloak to conceal your sword and bowstave."

Darby drew himself up. His voice, thick with the accents of his native Yorkshire, rang loudly. "My lord, I am no peasant, but a knight in your service."

"I prefer you as a live peasant rather than a dead knight. Under guise, you can move freely. Your French is good. If you're questioned, say you hail from Flanders. Take along a sheep from the byre. There's a ewe in season. You can say you're taking her to St.-Valéry for breeding."

Darby's face cleared as the plan began to make sense to him. "Aye, my lord, a handy ploy." He hurried off.

A sense of helplessness, of danger, gripped Rand. He hated being hemmed in by his enemies and abandoned by his allies. He ached to share his fears with someone. Wistfully he remembered the long, earnest talks he'd had with Lianna before she'd learned his true identity. Now, despite the presence of his wife and his men, he felt completely alone.

He crossed the courtyard, paused when he heard Batsford crooning in a singsong voice. Rounding the Tour Gobelin, he spied the priest at the mews. A pretty gyrfalcon perched on his wrist. Murmuring softly, he stroked her with a finger.

"What do you here, Batsford?" Rand demanded. "You're supposed to be watching my wife."

"Lovely woman . . ." Batsford's lips bowed into a smile. "Aye, lovely," he continued in a slurred voice. "Sweet as the Virgin herself, and ever so agreeable."

Lianna? Sweet? Agreeable? Suspicion tore through Rand. She'd never behave so toward an Englishman, even a cleric.

"Aye," Batsford said, "found me a flagon of Burgundy's best calvados, and said her uncle'd not mind if I had a look at his hawks. Isn't this a fair bird?"

Rand gripped the priest's shoulders hard. The gyrfalcon squawked and flapped its wings. "Where is she, Batsford?"

The cleric nodded at a long, low building at the opposite side of the yard. "She asked Simon to take her to the armory. I know not why a woman would be interested in weapons, but she asked so prettily. . . ."

A dull explosion rent the air. Pivoting toward the armory, Rand began to run.

The acrid scent of burnt sulfur hung in the air, mingling with a blue-gray haze of smoke. A door leading to the outer wall hung open, its iron hinges mangled. Dazed and frightened, Simon sat slumped in a corner of the armory.

Rand crossed to him. "Are you hurt?" he asked urgently.

Slowly the squire shook his head. "I don't think so. My ears are ringing."

"What happened?"

"I'm sorry, my lord," Simon began, pushing on the heels of his hands, trying to rise, "but I didn't know she could..."

Rand didn't wait to hear the rest. He sprang to the forced-open door and scaled the outer wall in time to see Lianna racing across the drawbridge. Damn, no one had remembered to secure the bridge. His first impulse was to leap after her; then he remembered Piers and the woods choked with enemy knights. It would serve nothing to deliver himself, defenseless, into their hands.

He bellowed at Simon to fetch his sword and dagger, then sprinted across to the stables. Moments later he emerged, hauling his saddleless horse by the reins while Simon buckled on his sword. Rand leaped on Charbu's back and shot from the castle.

Exertion tore at Lianna's throat as she ran headlong beside a canal leading from Le Crotoy. To her left lay a band of woods; beyond that the town proper. Surely Burgundy's niece would find protection there. Fully aware that Rand would immediately know the cause of the explosion, she pressed on.

Gasping, she plunged down a narrow ravine. She noted with fleeting satisfaction that the steep, rock-strewn passage couldn't be negotiated by a mounted man. Gorse and brambles ripped at her green cotte and plucked at her braids. The ravine led to a wide, dry creek bed, a dead estuary of the canal. She followed the dusty path inland.

From the corner of her eye she spied an approaching figure. Fearfully she shot a glance over her shoulder and recognized the blue-black hair and lithe form of Chiang.

They met at a clearing beside the creek. "God be thanked," she breathed.

Chiang grabbed her hand and began pulling her into the woods. "We must away," he said urgently. "They are all around us."

"Nay," she said, hurrying along behind him. "Longwood has but ten men—nine; one's wounded, as you well know—"

"I speak of Gervais," Chiang said impatiently.

"Good. We must find him. Have you a horse?"

Chiang stopped and spun around, his almond-shaped eyes troubled. "Find him?"

"Of course. He'll help me get away from the English."

"But for what? I trust him not. Nor should you."

"What talk is this?" she asked, laughing shortly to cover a sudden thrill of nervousness. "I have no love for Gervais, but I must depend on him to take me home." She frowned. "You came alone, didn't you?"

He nodded. "I thought to take you to Soissons. 'Tis your uncle's town. You'll be safe there." His gaze darted here and there. He held his spare frame taut. "Come, my lady."

"Soissons! I am going home, to secure Bois-Long."

"What of Gervais?"

She touched her chin. "I'll worry about him later." Aye, she thought, he was easier to handle than Rand. Gervais did not have that dreadful emotional power over her. She looked at Chiang, who continued to scan the woods.

"What is it with you? Surely you'd not have me stay with the Englishman."

His mouth went tight. A wild look glinted in his eyes. She'd seen that expression before, that veiled fear. Some secret linked him to the English, she was certain of it. "Well?" she demanded.

"My wishes are unimportant . . . for now."

Her eyes flicked to his long, narrow handgun.

He caught the look. "Aye, I shot him," he admitted grimly. "But only in defense. He'd drawn an arrow on me." Chiang's dry brown hand tightened around the rod of the gun. "If I'd wanted the Englishman dead, he would be."

A thud of hoofs resounded. Chiang glanced from side to side. "Come," he said urgently. The hoofbeats grew louder. Like a smear of blood, the scarlet oriflamme appeared at the head of the clearing. Chiang yanked her arm. "Run, my lady!"

She tried to pull away. " 'Tis only Gervais," she said in annoyance. "I fear him not at all." When Chiang made a sound of impatience, she added, "His father is dead. Gervais might not yet know of it. I must tell him."

"Well done, Chinaman." Like a swift, black lash, Gervais Mondragon's voice cracked across the clearing. "You've found the woman."

Chiang stepped in front of her.

"No," she said, "I need no protection from Gervais."

He sat proud and erect in the saddle, his breastplate gleaming in the evening sun, his visor raised to expose his hard, handsome face. Four knights cantered up to his flanks. To her horror, Lianna saw that one of them bore a pikestaff spitted with a severed head. A severed head with a familiar face. She turned her eyes from the soul-shriveling sight of Darby Green's gray face, his neck dripping blood and sinew.

Chiang tugged on her arm. "For the love of God, my lady—"

"Leave her," Gervais commanded. "I thought we had an understanding, Chinaman, where your mistress is concerned."

Chiang's hand dropped from her arm.

An ominous prickle danced up her spine. Doubtless Gervais had used some threat to play upon Chiang's devotion to her. Dear God, had she been safer with Rand? No, she decided resolutely, walking toward the Frenchmen. Gervais would take her home. Once there, she would settle with him.

"Lianna, no!" Chiang whispered, but she ignored him. She needed to get away, far away, and quickly. She could not trust her treacherous heart to her husband's keeping.

Reaching Gervais, she took his gauntleted hand and allowed him to help her into the front of his saddle. His breastplate pressed hard against her back. He smelled of sweat, metal, and horse. "I knew I could rely on your wiles," he murmured, and she shrank inwardly. Chiang's words echoed through her mind: *I trust him not*.

A sudden wave of compassion drowned her feeling of hesitation. She twisted around to face him, her hand on his arm. "Gervais, your father . . ." She swallowed hard. "He is dead."

One of the knights signed himself with the cross. Gervais went still; she looked away from the pain in his eyes. Fat, jewel-colored flies buzzed slowly around the severed head on the pike, giving the silence a feel of unbearable tension.

"How did it happen?" he asked at last.

"A . . . an accident," she said quietly. "He'd been drinking. He fell in the Seine."

A dry sob gusted from his throat; a single tear slid down his cheek. Lianna realized that he'd loved his father. "You needn't delude me," Gervais said bitterly. "Was it the Englishman or your uncle of Burgundy who murdered my father?"

She stared at the bright metal of his gauntlet. "Neither my uncle nor the Englishman has been to Paris."

He made a hissing noise of coiled fury in his throat. Within the depths of his visor his eyes flashed with rage. "Christ," he said in a harsh bark, "by now I would think you'd know your uncle's arm is long enough to reach the Holy Roman Empire while he sits in Liège."

A crashing sounded in the underbrush. A percheron bearing a golden-haired rider came sailing down the ravine as if the narrow, treacherous cleft were no more than a minor obstacle.

Rand seemed to take in the scene with a single glance. His glittering green eyes raked over Gervais, Lianna, Chiang, and the other knights.

Then he spotted Darby's severed head.

He became a man Lianna did not recognize—a man she'd thought existed only in nightmares. His lips drew back in a snarl, and his sword rasped from its sheath. Hell-wrought anger swelled his unarmored chest and flared in his emerald eyes. Knees hugging the horse, he charged at the man who bore the pikestaff.

She knew with cold, fascinated dread that the French knight was finished. The knight let go of the pike and jerked his reins in readiness to flee.

A bellow of rage tore from Rand's throat. He raised his blade. The air sang with a whipping sound as the sword sliced downward, finding the crevice where the spandlers at the knight's shoulder joined the armholds. A scream rent the air. A fount of blood welled from the knight's wound. Horrified, Lianna realized his arm had been riven from his shoulder.

As the doomed man fell from his bucking horse, Gervais yelled, "Charge him, damn your eyes!" His voice rang loud in her ears. The three remaining men drew steel, yet they hesitated. She could taste their fear, could hear it in the panting breaths that issued from behind their visors. Surely they knew, as she did, that they could soon join the bleeding, twitching man on the ground.

Rand plunged toward the nearest of the three. He'd drawn a dagger; he guided his horse with his knees alone. If anyone had told Lianna an unarmored man riding bareback could face down three steel-clad knights on destriers, she would not have believed it. But with Rand she was learning to believe in many improbabilities.

Like a mantle of sunlight, fury swirled around him. Even Helquin, the horseman of legend, seemed no match for the raging, godlike creature Rand had become. He slashed out. His opponent's shield crashed to the ground. A second knight appeared, sword raised, at Rand's flank.

An involuntary scream of warning erupted from Lianna's throat. With a warrior's instinctive timing, Rand pivoted to ward off the deadly blade.

"Hold!" Gervais bellowed. The knights backed off.

Rand went after the nearest of them.

"Hold, I say," Gervais repeated, "or the woman dies."

Lianna froze as the cold edge of Gervais's misericorde caressed her throat. *Nom de Dieu*, she thought in horror, Chiang was right. Gervais is not to be trusted.

Rand wrestled his blood-crazed mount to a standstill.

Breathing raggedly, he brought his tortured, fiery gaze to Lianna. The scraping sound of the fallen knight's death throes punctuated the long, tense silence.

"Drop your weapons," Gervais ordered. Lianna held her breath and offered up a silent, disjointed prayer.

Rand's sword and dagger thudded to the ground. Gervais lowered the blade from her throat. She began to breathe again.

Her heart pounding, she felt her gaze drawn to Rand's outspread hands. She'd always thought he had such wonderful hands. Yet today she'd learned that the hands that imparted pleasure so gently were also capable of killing without hesitation. He was a man who could hate as hard as he loved.

She raised her eyes to his face. He sat expressionless, his eyes dull, his mouth drawn. He spoke to Gervais in a monotone.

"I like not the shield you use, Mondragon."

"Yet she is more impenetrable than steel." Gervais lifted his arm. "Kill him," he said to his men.

"*No!*" Lianna's voice sounded strange—desperate, pleading, full of feelings she'd battled for two days. Behind her, Gervais stiffened. She fumbled for a more even tone. "Really, Gervais, you are too rash. It is dishonorable to attack an unarmed man." Her face haughty, she stared at Rand. "The man is a baron, and for some reason I cannot fathom, the English king values his hide."

"All the more reason to cut him down, to see the flower of English chivalry wilt under the heat of a French blade."

A knight lifted his sword.

"Hold, damn you," she snapped. Rand's death would end their marriage and keep him from seizing her home, she realized. But to see him cut down, bleeding his life away because she had lured him into his enemy's snare . . . "Don't be stupid, Gervais. Would you sacrifice a fortune for the momentary thrill of spilling English blood?"

"A fortune?"

Rand made a sound of disgust.

"Aye." She turned to Gervais, forced a smile. "You're angry, distraught over your father's death. But think, losing my uncle's patronage and supporting Gaucourt's knights has depleted our coffers. King Henry is sure to part with a goodly sum for my . . ." She hesitated. An inner voice warned her not to let Gervais know Rand was her husband. "This man's ransom."

Summoned by the blast of a hunting horn, Gaucourt's *hobelars* arrived one by one. Lianna felt ready to burst with tension. She looked at Rand; he stared back at her with a stranger's eyes. She could not guess what thoughts he hid behind that calm, icy mien, but she knew they were not kindly.

Finally Gervais spoke. "Bind his hands and take his reins. We ride for Bois-Long."

Chapter  12

Rand stared into a blackness so complete that it mattered not whether his eyes were open or closed. Mildew and decay pervaded the chamber and soured the air. He likened his surroundings to the state of his heart: cold, dark, and empty. He could not sleep; waking nightmares tortured his mind.

He loved a woman who hated him.

He'd lost a man and slain another.

He was prisoner of a man who would soon learn that he'd not extract so much as a sou in ransom money from a king whose every resource was applied to mounting an invasion.

Rand's filth-encrusted hand strayed along the slick, wet wall until he found the set of scratches he'd made in the stone with one of his lace points. One, two, three ... He'd counted off each day of confinement, marked by the regular arrival of silent jailers who brought him a bucket of swill and emptied the chamber pot. Four, five, six . . . The wall seeped, indicating that the chamber sat below the waterline. Seven, eight . . .

I'm here, Harry, he raged silently at the young monarch across the Narrow Sea. I've come to Bois-Long at last.

Sitting back on his haunches, he scowled into the dense blackness. Eight days since he'd felt the sun on his face and the wind at his back. Eight days since he'd seen Lianna's face. His last glimpse of her drove like an arrow into his heart. Crouched in the arms of Gervais Mondragon, her face a cool, beautiful mask, she'd dismissed her husband as if he were no more than a common poacher. True, she'd called a warning to him during the fight; she'd bought him a few extra days with the ransoming ploy. Yet she was obviously content to let him rot in the bowels of her castle.

The darkness turned red as his anger simmered, then boiled over. He should have killed them all. He could have. But Gervais's knife at Lianna's throat had stayed his sword. He'd once dreamed that she would be his strength; instead she was his vulnerability.

The thought brought him surging upright, weakened limbs creaking sorely with the motion. His head cracked against the ceiling, raining moldering mortar upon his shoulders.

Cursing, he brushed away the debris. His hair hung about his face in matted hanks; his body held the stench of neglect; his hands felt gritty.

While slowly rotating his aching shoulders, he brooded upon his dilemma. His attempts at overpowering his jailers had earned him bruises from their bludgeons, cuts from their pointed daggers, even a burn on his hand from a torch. Unarmed and weakened by poor food and confinement, he prayed his men would find a way to gain his freedom.

But that was impossible, he conceded. Gaucourt's knights and Lianna's guns would foil any rescue attempt. And Burgundy, ever riding the fence, was off at Compiègne.

He found himself thinking of his father. Marc had been a prisoner, too. Nineteen years he'd lived at Arundel, a captive of the English and of his wife's disregard. Year after year she had ignored her husband's pleas to tender the ransom. So he'd made a new life in England, gotten a bastard son on a peasant woman, and died in obscurity.

Rand picked idly at the rotting wall. Now it seemed that he, too, was destined to fulfill a legacy of neglect. But under these conditions he'd not survive nineteen years.

He drove his fist into the wall, barely flinching when the flesh of his knuckles split. Like his father, he had a wife who cared nothing for ransoming him. But unlike Marc, he intended to get free.

"Eight days," Lianna said to Gervais. "*Nom de Dieu,* it has been eight days."

He paused in his midday meal, one dark eyebrow slashing upward with cynical coldness. "Aye."

"I wish to see him."

"For the last time, no. He's no high-minded knight who claims Bois-Long for England, but a dangerous outlaw."

"Damn it, Gervais, he'll die down there."

"He's strong as a bloody rouncy. Relieved a guard of two of his teeth just this morning." Gervais pulled a succulent leg from a capon and bit into it.

She clenched her fists at her sides. Time and time again she'd told herself Rand was her enemy; he'd betrayed her and deserved no better than to be tossed, forgotten, into the cell. Yet images haunted her sleep, and memories plagued her wakeful hours. She could not rid her mind or her heart of Rand. His tender lovemaking had suffused her with new, exquisite sensations. His undemanding friendship had filled a pain-edged void in her life. Even his betrayal could not obliterate remembrances of a sunny glade and a man who had pledged his love to a confused, disheartened girl.

She knew him better now, of course. He was a lover, but he was a warrior, too. With nightmarish clarity she recalled his attack on the French knights. She pictured him fighting his jailers, and realized why Gervais sent them to the cell in groups of four or five.

But did Rand deserve to die for his betrayal?

"Why did you send Chiang to Agincourt?" she asked suddenly.

Gervais looked away. "I told you, to buy hemp."

"Eight days is long enough to do his trading and return."

"Perhaps he was detained."

She pressed her lips together in frustration and fear. She knew why Gervais had sent Chiang away. Gervais feared the master gunner, for Chiang alone seemed to understand that Gervais meant to enforce his claim on the château. Lianna understood that now. But too late. She glanced around the hall, seeking allies. Instead she saw only the indolent men of Gaucourt and the confused knights of Bois-Long, who knew not which master to serve.

"I wish to see the Englishman," she repeated.

Gervais eyed her closely. "I find your pangs of conscience tedious."

"'Tis not my conscience," she said defensively. "I merely think we should adhere to the rules of chivalry in our treatment of a prisoner of rank." She heard the echo of Rand's words in her own. She was defending the very conventions she'd scorned.

"Why?" asked Gervais. "He's worthless."

She went cold, inside and out. She stared at Gervais, saw the flash of a secret in his dark brown eyes. "What?" she demanded. "What are you hiding from me?"

A smile slid across his face as he reached into his doublet and removed a parchment scroll. With a trembling hand she unfurled it, angled it toward the weak, misty light filtering in through a high oriel window. She recognized at a glance the royal seal of the King of England.

"You've read this?"

Gervais nodded complacently.

"But you don't read French, much less English."

He shrugged. "Guy does."

She tried not to let her dismay show. Always when a scurrier arrived with news, Guy, in his capacity as seneschal of Bois-Long, apprised her of it. Lately, though, the castle folk deferred to Gervais—swayed, no doubt, by his lenience and the promises he made of reducing boonwork and increasing rations.

Her eyes darted to the page. A quick perusal told her what she already knew, what she'd known since she'd pleaded with Gervais not to slay her husband. King Henry would not ransom Enguerrand of Longwood.

The paper dropped from her numb fingers and drifted to the rush-strewn floor. Rain drove relentlessly against the castle walls. Like the dampness weighting the air,

despair pressed on her heart. Rand's life was worth nothing now.

"What will you do?" she asked.

Gervais shrugged again. "I'm through harboring an
enemy."

"You will not murder him!"

His hard, glittering eyes narrowed. "Better the murder
of one Englishman than the slaughter of scores of Frenchmen when Henry launches his attack." He finished his
meat and tossed the bone to an alaunt hound under the
table. Glancing up at the open window, he said, "It's
been raining steadily. The river is rising."

Shaken by the implied threat, she fought for control.
"I am chatelaine, Gervais. The decision is mine."

"Think again, Lianna," he shot back. "With my father
dead, the estate is entailed to me."

"Not if . . ." She bit her lip. No, she thought. Not now.
Gervais must not know yet of her marriage and the babe
she carried.

"If what?" he prompted.

"If you continue with your foolhardy spending and
idle ways, you'll not have an estate to manage at all."

He smiled and shook his head slowly. With an airy
gesture of his hand he indicated the lower tables. The
castle folk and Gaucourt's knights crammed the trestles,
their laughter and conversation made bold and raucous
by the extra wine Gervais allotted them.

"You're wrong," he said. "I have the land. I also have
the loyalty of the people, and their love."

"Love," she snorted, hiding her pain. "You play lavish
with the stores and excuse them from their work."

"You presume to tell me of love?"

He was right in questioning that, at least. Until recently

she hadn't known how to love. Now she knew it well, for its loss left a hollow chamber deep inside her.

In the kitchen, maids dipped candles from a vat of bubbling beeswax while Bonne supervised and Lianna tallied the work on a notched stick. The scent of wax and woodsmoke mingled with the rain smells from outside. Macée had offered to take a hand in the chore, but she'd been distracted by a wandering tinker whose Spanish lace and Venetian beads had sent her off to cajole Gervais for a bauble. The scene was warm and homey, the perfect task for a rainy spring afternoon.

"Another dozen, my lady," said Bonne. When Lianna didn't react, the maid spoke louder. "Another dozen."

"Yes," Lianna replied, marking her tally stick. "Of course."

"I doubt Gervais allows him a single taper," Bonne muttered.

Lianna stiffened. "Who?"

"Your husband. Don't pretend your mind's not on him."

"Keep your voice down, Bonne," Lianna whispered. "I did not tell you the truth about Rand only to have you sow gossip."

"Sorry, my lady. Your secret's safe." Turning away from the other women, Bonne spoke in a hushed voice. "Will you let him die, then?"

Lianna bit her lip. "He's the Englishman who betrayed me."

"He's the knight who won your heart."

"He used me in the basest manner. Manipulated my affections to conquer my castle."

"You did the same to him, my lady. You used him to get yourself with child."

"I hate him."

"Do you? Or is it yourself you hate for having lost your heart, for feeling compassion for him still?"

"Your tongue is too bold." Lianna stalked to the window. Sheets of rain smeared a smoke-colored sky; the riverbanks swelled with rising water. Soon high tide would roll in, and...

A vision of Rand, trapped in his cell while the water closed over him, set her mind ablaze. Her own terror of water brought the image into sharp, deadly focus.

No, she thought with sudden decisiveness. It was not simply a question of who had wronged whom; mere human decency propelled her from the kitchen toward the cellars. She stopped in her solar to draw on a deep-pocketed cloak.

Hurrying across the greensward, she ducked her head to avoid the rain. Dodging puddles, she stepped beneath an archway. The long open corridor was deserted save for a few stray chickens. Rounding a corner, she came upon Gervais's page, who sat against the wall, whittling a piece of driftwood. At the end of the cloister, an iron-studded door stood open to a black stairwell.

She entered the cellar and paused, sucking in a deep breath of chilly, fetid air. Jesu, how could a man survive even a day under such conditions? She pulled an iron ring of keys from her girdle. Sorting through them one by one, she felt for the key to Rand's cell. She'd seldom used the key but knew it was the one with the cloverleaf top.

The first search did not yield the key. Tamping back a

sense of urgency, she forced herself to sort through them more methodically.

An orange light appeared behind her, casting her shadow against the damp wall. "You won't find it," said a calm, smooth voice.

Startled, she dropped the key ring. Iron clinked against stone as it hit the floor. She whirled to find Gervais and three men-at-arms standing in the corridor.

Gervais smiled. "I removed the key from your ring."

Her heart sank to her belly as she stooped to snatch up her keys. "You had no right. A chatelaine's keys are sacred."

"As is my right to control the castle." With deceptively gentle fingers, he smoothed back her hood so that it fell down over her shoulders. "Although I am certain I know the answer, I suppose I should ask exactly what you're doing down here."

"I wanted to see the prisoner."

He chuckled and withdrew his own cluster of keys. "Did you now?"

Her mind raced. Perhaps if Gervais believed she sought Rand's death as eagerly as he . . . "I wished to be the first to inform the Englishman that his beloved king has forsaken him," she said, forcing a tone of relish into her voice.

Torchlight gave his handsome features a sinister caste. "Perhaps I underestimated your lust for English blood."

"Never underestimate me, Gervais."

"What mischief are you upon?"

She fixed him with a guileless stare. "What could I possibly do?"

He strode into the belly of the cellar, paused at the last door, and fitted a key into the lock. "Very well, I'll let you see him. But I should warn you, he's not nearly as pretty as the man who rode out from Le Crotoy to reclaim you."

She lifted her chin. "No man claims me now."

He motioned for one of the men to come forward with the torch. He turned the key and pushed the door open.

Rand looked up from his crouched position against the far wall of the cell. Momentarily blinded by torchlight, he squinted. Slowly his eyes focused, and he recognized the urbane face of Gervais Mondragon, and then the small, velvet-swathed figure of Lianna.

Agony and love and fury charged through him with the speed of a burning quick match.

"My lady?" he said, the rasping mockery in his voice belying the courteous greeting. He swept into a painful bow. "How do you?"

Hearing her quick intake of breath, he looked up to study her face. She schooled her features into a cold, vengeful mask. But before that—Rand rubbed his eyes and cursed the conditions that blinded him, weakened him—he thought he'd seen a flicker of something not so cold in her eyes.

"I am well," she said icily. "Not that my welfare is any of your concern, Englishman." Her hands came up to worry the drawstring of her cloak.

Pain seared like a hot blade into Rand's gut. Only a short time ago he'd seen affection in the silvery depths of her eyes; now she sliced his soul with a dagger-sharp glare.

"Would you like to do the honors, Lianna, or shall I?" asked Gervais.

She straightened her shoulders, her hand still on the

laces at her throat. "We've had a reply from your devoted sovereign. He will not ransom you."

Rand couldn't suppress a smile of grim irony. He'd known all along that his life was cheap, that the preparations for war had scoured the royal coffers clean. "He's saving his coin to conquer you complacent French," said Rand.

Gervais frowned down at his pointed shoes. Water lapped at the elegant, velvet-clad toes. "The Englishman seems to care little for his hide. Come, Lianna, we must go. When the tide comes in, this chamber will flood to the ceiling."

Rand absorbed the gruesome tidings with the odd detachment of a doomed man.

She tossed her head. "Oh, my, I'd quite forgotten that flooding occurs after a long rain. I must get some men to remove the gunpowder from the chamber just above here, so the ordnance doesn't get wet." She cast a worried look at the low, crumbling ceiling. "Tonight's full moon brings a high tide. . . ."

"Quite so," said Gervais, backing toward the door. "Farewell, my lord. Perhaps when your king learns of your failure, he'll think twice about invading France."

Casting a last, oddly frantic look at Rand, and then at the crumbling ceiling, Lianna turned to follow Gervais. The cloak fell from her shoulders and whispered to the floor.

"*Merde,*" she said. "My cloak."

"Bring it along," said Gervais. "Perhaps the filth can be laundered out."

She shook her head. "Not even Bonne's industrious hand could remove the stink of this place. Leave the cloak.

Perhaps it will keep the *god-don* warm as he drowns." She stepped daintily over the sodden heap.

Gervais smiled at Rand. "The very soul of mercy, isn't she, my lord?"

Fired to mindless rage, Rand lurched forward, his fists doubled.

One of the men levered a sharp halberd at his chest. Rand kept his cold, raw hands at his sides to stay an impulse to drive his fist into that handsome, smiling face. But he did nothing to check the murderous glance he settled on his wife.

His fierce look seemed to discomfit her. She moved back; her throat worked as she swallowed. "What did you expect, Englishman?"

"I didn't expect you to gloat."

She sent him a long, unreadable look. "Curb your temper, Englishman. You'll set the place afire with it."

They left without another word. As he heard the key grinding in the lock, Rand smashed his fist against the wall, wishing it were instead the face of Gervais Mondragon. Coldness stole into his veins; the walls seemed to close in on him. Half-crazed with impotent rage, he snatched up Lianna's cloak and rent it in two with a savage tug.

But as he prepared to shred the garment further, to destroy it as she had destroyed him, something made him hesitate.

"Oh, God," he said raggedly, burying his face in the velvet folds. "It smells of her." Memories washed over him. Could she have changed so quickly, so completely? Before their marriage they had celebrated their love with sweet embraces, intimate kisses. Now she reveled in the thought of his demise.

As he crumpled the garment, his hand closed around something hard and sharp. At the same moment, water seeped through the cracks in the floor, swirling with the chill of death around his ankles.

He clawed through the folds of velvet until he found a pocket. Inside lay a length of steel, curved to fit around the knuckles of a clenched hand.

Somewhere in the depths of his soul, a faint spark flickered.

Working by touch, he discovered a square of flint and a tinderbox with bits of charred material inside.

Lianna's preoccupation with gunnery accounted for the presence of the flint and steel. No doubt losing her tinderbox would vex her more than losing her cloak.

"By the rood . . ." he breathed, his feet shifting restlessly in the deepening water. He remembered her conversation. *I must get some men to remove the gunpowder from the chamber just above here. . . .*

The spark of hope inside him flared.

The idle taunt from a vindictive woman was actually a deed of mercy from a wife who possessed a heart after all. She'd spoken to him, had secretly shown him a way to save himself. His mind closed exultantly around the thought. The woman in the woods still lived in her, still cared.

Shoving flint, steel, and tinderbox into his baldric, he reached up and worked at the loose mortar on the ceiling.

What else had she said in malice, yet meant in warning? *Leave the cloak. Perhaps it will keep the god-don warm. . . .*

By the time his raw, bruised hands had loosened a large chunk of stone, the water was swirling around his knees. He burrowed his hand upward, scraping his wrist. He felt the taut bulge of a full sack, like a sack of flour. Yet it wasn't flour; it reeked of sulfur.

Curb your temper, Englishman. You'll set the place afire with it.

The spark of hope sizzled to the brightness of a signal flare.

With a powerful tug, he rent open the sack and drew forth a handful of sticky gunpowder. The water crept higher, soaking him, lapping at his hips.

Thank God, he thought as his shaking hands blindly measured a charge. Thank God for Lianna and the war game she'd played in the woods. He'd criticized her interest in gunnery. Now he blessed her for it. *Anything is easy with gunpowder. . . .* He waded to the door.

The flare inside him climbed to a high, steady flame of triumph.

Lianna strained to keep her attention on the conversation at the high table. Gervais and Gaucourt debated politics; both men were firmly in favor of the Armagnac ruling party in Paris yet in conflict over minor points.

"The king is not whole," Gervais said in annoyance. "He should be compelled to abdicate in favor of his son."

Gaucourt yanked a portion of meat from the joint of mutton in front of him. "Mad he may be . . ."

"Raving mad," Gervais muttered. "Stark, slobbering, staring-at-the-sun mad."

"But he is still a king anointed before God and France. He needs only able advisers to govern properly."

"Able advisers? Queen Isabel is depraved, fickle. She and the Dauphin Louis are mere puppets manipulated by Armagnac, while Burgundy has gotten away with murder."

Gaucourt's pale, lashless eyes went wide, then narrowed. "Consider whereof you speak."

"Murder," Gervais repeated. "I'll call it nothing else."

Lianna heard rage in his voice, and fear, too, and knew he dreaded that Burgundy would treat him as he had treated Lazare. Ordinarily she would have joined in the conversation. She hated the dissension among the princes of France, deplored the failures of justice, the corruption that caused the income of her country to be sucked dry by warring factions.

But she couldn't speak out now, tonight. Above the murmur of conversation and the clatter of cutlery she heard the hiss of rain, and she thought of Rand. Her enemy . . . but no man deserved the dark, drowning fate that was the stuff of nightmares.

Had he, she wondered feverishly, discovered the tinderbox in her cloak? Had he understood the message she'd tried to relay? Or were her words too bitter, too flippant, for him to discern her purpose? Her throat closed. Dear God, did he hate her too much to hear her warning?

His face—haggard, agonized, yet still heartbreakingly appealing—rose in her mind like the visage of a Hallow's Eve ghost. She didn't want him dead. She merely wanted him out of her life so she could set her mind and her energies to the task of purging the château of Gervais's influence.

She slid a sidelong glance at her late husband's son. Unbidden, a thought tiptoed into her mind. Gervais was as much her enemy as Rand. Mondragon was French, and loyal to King Charles, yet like Rand, he was determined to wrest Bois-Long from her control.

Pressed to discomfort by the weight of indecision, she

let her gaze wander to Macée. She flirted with Gaucourt's master crossbowman, whose bright, avid gaze attested to the allure of Macée's lush figure, raven hair, and creamy skin.

"Did you truly rout a company of mounted knights with your crossbows, *Capitaine*?" Macée asked breathlessly. She leaned across the table toward him, the rounded tops of her breasts visible above her square-cut bodice.

The captain kept his eyes fastened on the velvety bulge of flesh. "Oh, aye. A knight is only as good as the steel that encases his body. An archer depends on subtlety and skill."

Sensible words, thought Lianna, if he were truly speaking of battle. But of course his wet mouth and sharp eyes spoke of other things.

Macée said, "Oh, *Capitaine,* you are so masterful—"

"Macée!" Gervais's stern, commanding voice interrupted her. His eyes glittered with anger, yet he smiled as he patted the empty space on the bench beside him. "Come here, pet, and keep my wineglass filled."

An odd look of satisfaction flitted across Macée's pretty features. She moved to obey.

Lianna glanced away. She understood not the strange bond between Gervais and Macée. He was sparing with his affection, yet she seemed inexorably bound to him. He must hold some fascination for her, some power that drove her to flirt with archers to gain Gervais's attention. Like an unhungry dog with a bone, Gervais only worried about losing Macée when another threatened to take her away.

The thought ignited a startling sense of kinship for Macée. Lianna, too, was at odds with her husband, yet their wedding night had proven that the bond of passion must be reckoned with. Would she one day be reduced to submitting to Rand like a trained spaniel? Never, she decided firmly.

The hiss of the rain rose to a thick, heavy spatter against the oiled-canvas window coverings. Her stomach knotted in fear. What was Rand doing now? Had the tide risen? Did he feel the cold waters closing over him, sucking his breath, stealing his soul? While she sat drinking wine with her French allies, was Rand fighting for his life?

Oh, Rand, she thought, seized by the high torture of envisioning life without him, did you hear my message?

The ear-racking thunderbolt of a distant explosion rent the air.

Startled, the company fell silent. Lianna sat stiff, cold, and unbearably hopeful. Then a murmur rose while the noise was dismissed as a singularly close strike of lightning.

Faint with terror, she clutched the arms of her chair. The impulse to bolt down to the cellars was stayed only by the relentlessly watchful eyes of Gervais. He'd never let her leave the hall unattended.

Pray God Rand hadn't injured himself, she thought wildly. Pray God he'd gotten free.

A guard burst into the hall. His face pale, his clothes spattered with rain, and several teeth leaving his mouth on a stream of bloody spittle, he clambered to the high table.

"My lords!" he said, his words piteously skewed by his wounded mouth. "The Englishman has escaped!"

Half-amused, half-annoyed, Lianna glanced over her shoulder at the mounted knight following her. When

Rand hadn't been recaptured in the massive nightlong search, she'd insisted on riding out with the morning reserves, who had instructions to kill the Englishman on sight. Still convinced that she lusted for English blood, Gervais had consented and sent Roland to accompany her.

In a wild gallop, she'd led the marshal to the reaches of Bois-Long. His massive size and plain, blunt features belied his talent for outstanding horsemanship. He made no complaint about the pace she set.

With every furlong she traveled, her hope grew. She didn't want to find Rand, wanted only to ascertain that he'd gotten away safely.

She contemplated her sudden streak of mercy. She thought to attribute it to the latent sense of humanity she'd recently discovered within herself. Then, in private pain, she admitted the truth. She loved her English husband.

The notion brought her no joy, only a deep, sharp pain. She could never love him without restraint, for he meant to bring English rule to France.

She'd saved her final destination for last. The sun rose to a warm, noontide position. She waved to Roland and urged her palfrey westward, to the place of St. Cuthbert's cross.

As she scanned the place where she and Rand had spent so many passion-filled hours, a choking surge of love engulfed her.

The glade lay peaceful, rain-washed and open to the sun, unsullied by the deception and political machinations that had thrown her life into upheaval. The familiar loamy scent of damp earth and the faint fragrance of wildflowers teased her senses. Larks chittered in the branches of the ancient spreading oaks. A breeze ruffled the dew-damp strands of long green grass.

She halted her horse and looked up at the canopy of branches. The leaves, shot through by sunlight, glowed with a color so pure and so familiar that she clapped both hands over her mouth to muffle a strangled cry of grief. The color matched that of Rand's eyes.

"My lady, are you well?"

Uncovering her face, she lowered her head to hide her tortured expression. "Yes. My head aches a little."

He dismounted and helped her from her saddle. Producing a wine flask, he handed it to her. While she drank, he scouted about, kicking in the weeds. "My lady, look what I've found," he called.

Fearfully she crossed to his side. "What is it, Roland?"

He held up a length of silver chain. Suspended from it was a winking jewel, framed by intricately worked gold. She squinted, made out a design of a leopard rampant and the motto *A vaillans coeurs riens impossible*.

She knew immediately that the talisman had belonged to Rand. When had he lost it? Careful not to reveal what was in her heart, she feigned disinterest. "Possibly a stolen token dropped by a brigand," she said.

"I'd best give it over to Gervais."

She nodded. It mattered not that Gervais would recognize the leopard device on the bauble; his real prize had escaped.

"Odd place, this," remarked Roland. "A bit out of the way for a pilgrim seeking sanctuary." He strolled over to the ancient stone cross and stooped. "But someone's been here."

Lianna's heart jolted to her throat. Quickly she went to the cross. Lying atop it was a single wild lily with raindrops still clinging to its lavender-and-white petals.

Roland scratched his head. "Can't imagine what the devil it means," he mused.

Lianna picked up the lily. Like cool tears, the raindrops anointed her hands.

"But I can," she murmured, too quietly for Roland to hear. She turned back toward her horse. "Oh, I can."

As clearly as if he'd chiseled the promise in stone, she understood Rand's message: *I'll be back*.

Chapter

"**Y**ou're back!" Lajoye stood framed by the rough-hewn doorway of his seaside inn. He had a daub of fresh plaster on one wrinkled cheek.

"*Oui, mon vieux.* Was my return ever in doubt?" Rand grinned—his first smile after two days of traveling by foot and by stealth through the forests and fens of Picardy.

"Only by those who know you not." Lajoye subjected Rand to a close, dubious scrutiny. "What befell you?"

"I paid a visit to my new home."

Lajoye frowned. "A bath, a meal, some doctoring for the burns and bruises," he said. "Have you been to Le Crotoy?"

"Aye, the rest of my men await my orders."

"Rand! Rand!" A gaggle of unkempt children pushed past Lajoye and tumbled into the dooryard.

"Where have you been, Rand?"

"Look how my kitten's grown!"

"Why are you so dirty?"

"Did you bring your harp?"

"I lost two teeth last month!"

He stooped and somehow managed to enclose them all in the circle of his arms. Laughing, he looked up at Lajoye.

The old man sketched a bow. "Welcome back, my lord."

Gently, still laughing, Rand sent the children off with a wink and the promise of a rousing bedtime ballad. He followed Lajoye into the Sheaf of Wheat.

The smell of fresh plaster and baking bread assailed him. His senses reeling with fatigue and lack of food, he put one hand to his head, swayed, and stumbled.

With unexpected speed, Lajoye hurried to his side. *"Merde,"* swore the innkeeper, huffing as he reached for Rand. "'Tis like supporting a falling oak." While he helped Rand to a stool, he bellowed, "Marie, bring our lord food and drink. *Sang de Dieu,* be quick about it, woman."

Chagrined by his weakness and the beads of cold sweat running down his face, Rand let loose with a rare but vivid oath. Only after he'd consumed three trenchers of Marie's stew and then the bread plate itself did he feel himself again.

"So," said Lajoye, eyeing him keenly, "you've been a guest of Gervais Mondragon. We had the news only yesterday."

Rand stiffened. "Who told you?"

"I don't know, and he didn't say. He came down from Agincourt. He was one of those Asian types, or Persian, such as the Crusaders met on their forays in the East."

Suspicion pricked at Rand. He knew no man of that description. He must ask Jack about him.

"How long were you imprisoned?"

"Eight days, in the belly of the château." Remembering how close that cell had come to being his watery crypt, he shivered. But for Lianna...

Tenderly Lajoye touched a swelling on Rand's brow. "You were beaten?"

Rand nodded. "And a stray fragment of stone caught me. I blasted my way out of the cell."

"Blasted? What mean you?"

"I found some gunpowder and made a charge to blow open the door."

"*Parbleu,* you might have been killed!"

"My death would have been a certainty otherwise. I knew what I was doing." A smile played about his lips. "I was trained by a master gunner." A pride he'd never thought to feel barreled through him. Oh, Lianna, he thought, how much we could teach one another if we could but regain the love and trust we once shared.

"Jack and Dylan are well?" he asked Lajoye.

"I fostered them as my own sons. Of course, when Cade heard you'd been taken, he almost went charging off to rescue you. But the Asian said you'd already gotten free."

"The archery training?"

Lajoye's aging face split into a grin. "You'd liken the men of Eu unto the best company of Welsh or Cheshiremen. We'll not lie undefended against brigands again, my lord."

Rand swallowed a gulp of cider. "Lajoye," he said in a low, calm voice, "I ordered the training so the men could defend themselves. But there is another reason, far more selfish, far more dangerous..."

"I know." Lajoye smiled sadly. "We all know." He refilled Rand's tankard. "Drink, my lord. 'Twill ease that startled expression off your face." Rand drank deeply while Lajoye continued. "Burgundy left you to claim Bois-Long without his aid. And you *will* wrest the château from Gaucourt and Mondragon—with the help of the men of Eu."

"God, but Jack has a loose tongue," Rand said ruefully.

"Your man said nothing of the plan." Lajoye laughed at Rand's confused frown. "I'm an innkeeper, for pity's sake. Think you I'm deaf to the gossip of the countryside? Weeks ago I realized the brigands were Gaucourt's men." He pursed his lips and shrugged with Gallic fatalism. "They found a place to bide at Bois-Long, and the attacks ceased."

Rand drove his fist into his palm. "I did suspect Gaucourt." Suddenly the idea that Lianna harbored brigands chilled him. Women of Eu had been raped. Forcing himself to calmness, he drained his tankard. "The others..."

"Are willing. You won their loyalty, Rand of Longwood, by securing the town against Gaucourt's outlaws. We Normans are a cautious lot. We distrust the *horzain*, but once an outsider wins our confidence, he keeps it forever."

"Thanks be to God...and Eu," said Rand. "Where are Jack and Dylan?"

"The Welshman spends his evenings fletching arrows at the home of Pierre, the tanner. Your Jack..." Lajoye winked. "'Tis any man's—or woman's—guess."

Rand went to search for Jack. Geese strolled about the dooryard. He noted with satisfaction that most of the geese were missing a number of feathers—a sure sign of arrows in the making. But likely not by Jack Cade.

Nearing the byre, he heard his scutifer's voice. "Now, lay your body into it," said Jack in his rough French.

Hearing the familiar command of a master archer, Rand smiled. He'd misjudged Jack after all. His scutifer was instructing a pupil to put his weight into the bow.

"Higher now," Jack advised. "Higher! We'll shoot wholly together." He laughed. "That's it. Worry not. I never undershoot. But I always loose quick and sharp."

If Jack's lusty mirth aroused Rand's suspicions, a feminine sigh of satisfaction confirmed them. He rounded to the back of the cow byre.

The hay mow seemed to be in motion. Stepping closer, he spied Jack. The scutifer knelt thigh-deep in hay, buried to the waist in a woman's skirts.

"Oh, lamb of God," muttered Rand.

Chuckling, Jack extricated himself and nonchalantly laced his trews. "I was wondering when you'd get here, my lord. Worried sick about you, I was."

"You sought comfort for your woes, I see."

Jack had the grace to blush. "I'd have rescued you, had I known. But by the time I learned what had happened, you'd already escaped."

Seeing that Jack had apparently forgotten the girl in the hay, Rand reached for her hand. The plump woman leaped up and began smoothing her skirts.

"Run along now," Jack said ungallantly. "We've manly matters to discuss."

The woman looked miffed yet glowing with satisfaction as she departed.

Rand stooped to retrieve a short-brimmed hat from the pile of hay. He set it lopsidedly on Jack's head and said, "Would that you labored so diligently at training archers."

"But I have, my lord. You'll see."

"Tell me first of the man who brought news of me to Eu."

Jack rubbed his chin. "Bloody odd lot, but we've not the leisure to choose our allies." He could tell Rand little more about the man, only confirm Lajoye's description. "Odd," Jack repeated when he'd finished his tale. "And he said one other thing—that we'd all meet again."

While Rand wondered about the mysterious stranger, Jack went to call out the people of Eu for a display of arms.

An hour later twenty men, their ages spanning from four and ten to threescore, their sizes ranging from skinny to brawny, aligned themselves at the edge of a long, willow-skirted meadow. Feet planted, sleeves rolled back, their long yew bowstaves held in front of them, they stood at attention.

Jack paced at the rear of the line, hands clasped behind his back. "The enemy's yonder," he barked in French, "at that brake of willows." Twenty pairs of eyes fastened on the distant woods. Dylan moved among the men, adjusting this one's stance, that one's alignment. Jack plucked a feather from an arrow and tossed it in the air to reckon the force of the wind. "Mild as a virgin's breath," he muttered, then stalked purposefully to the end of the line.

"Draw your arrows," he shouted. "Nock your arrows." As one, the line moved to obey. A satisfied smile slid across Jack's face. "*À St. Georges!*" he bellowed. "Keep your eye to the string and the string to the shaft. Loose gently now. Pluck not the string with your drawing hand. Let fly, lads!"

A high-pitched whine rose above the nasal twang of bowstrings. The arrows flew in a dark swarm toward the willow brake. Shouts of pride and satisfaction burst from the men.

"*Bien fait, les gars,*" said Jack, moving through their ranks, slapping shoulders, pumping hands. "Well done!" Grinning broadly, he approached Rand. "So, my lord?"

Pride and affection surged through Rand. "Jack, I know not what to say. 'Tis a miracle you've wrought, no less. You've transformed a group of farmers into a lance of archers."

"So I have," Jack said with a remorseless lack of modesty. "A few have become crack shots. Come, we'll show you."

Aiming at a painted bull's hide stretched over a wooden frame, the archers displayed their marksmanship. Arrows shredded the hide until the target hung by a thread.

Jack bowed comically. "Now, the pièce de résistance."

Rand watched as his scutifer calmly took up a bow, nocked an arrow, and, with the remaining two fingers of his mangled right hand, drew a yard of string.

His throat tightening with pity, Rand saw blood crease the joints of Jack's fingers. He took a step forward. "Jack, my God—"

"Hush, my lord, you'll spoil my aim."

Jack let the arrow fly. With a hiss it drove straight and sure, its iron-wrought tip neatly severing the last string holding the bull's hide. The target thudded to the ground.

Cheers erupted from the men. Jack planted his bowstave, leaned against it, and crossed one leg, the toe pointed negligently toward the ground. "Not bad for a

crippled scutifer, eh, my lord? They took my fingers, but
not my aim."

High in Rand's heart rose love for Jack, admiration
for his devotion, his skill. Rand wanted to embrace him.
Guessing Jack's reaction should he attempt such an outrage, he merely smiled and said casually, "A scutifer no
more, Jack Cade. That was the work of a master archer."

Gratitude blazed like a banner across Jack's face. He
grinned. "So . . . ?"

"So we take Bois-Long."

An interlude of peace reigned at the château, and
Lianna settled into a numb routine. She rose at dawn,
retched into a basin, then broke her fast with cider and
bread, only to be sick again. Battling the seductive las-
situde of the condition she had once rejoiced in, but now
despaired of, she went about the business of running the
household.

For all his talk of acting the lord of the manor, Gervais
seemed disinclined to attend to the myriad details of stew-
ardship. He preferred hawking and hunting, swapping
yarns with Gaucourt's men, and winning the affection of
the people of Bois-Long through lavish flattery and costly
favors.

Thus the management of the estate fell to Lianna, as
it ever had. She appreciated the distraction. While arbi-
trating a dispute between tenants or supervising the planting of hops near the riverbed, she could banish Rand
from her mind—often for as long as a whole minute.

She rode out sometimes, but never as far as the glade.
To go there was to yield to tender feelings she could ill
afford.

Secretly she'd taken steps to deny Gervais's claim on

Bois-Long. She'd penned missives to the administration in Paris, contesting the entail of the castle and lands. But although her requests for royal indulgence were couched in flattery, she had little hope of a ruling in her favor. The Armagnac party was unlikely to indulge Burgundy's niece.

Not so secretly, Gervais, too, had taken steps. He dictated letters of his own and dispatched them to Paris, begging to be acknowledged as Sire de Bois-Long.

Hunched over her books in the counting house early one morning, Lianna glanced from Guy's *livre de raison* to her own account book. She counted the grain figures and slid the beads of Chiang's odd reckoning device. Rapidly she calculated the yield of rye and notched the figure on her tally stick.

Idly she spun the beads. They were threaded on wooden dowels, set in a rectangular frame. One red stood for ten whites; one white for ten blacks. Figuring could be achieved simply by sliding the beads to and fro, here and there.

She sighed. Would that all problems were so neatly solved. But beads in a frame would not reckon her uncle's treachery, Gervais's presumption, or Rand's determination to take the château for King Henry. Nor would figures on a tally stick lay out an easy life for the child she secretly carried.

What was she to do about the babe? It could be passed off as Lazare's. People would think it only a few weeks late in coming. The necessity of lying bothered her, yet she must do so for the baby's sake, to protect her child's inheritance.

Yanking her attention from the anxious thoughts, she

made another calculation and entered the figure in her books.

The clink of spurs on flagstone made her drop her stylus. Smiling, Gervais entered the room. "How efficient you are," he said smoothly. "Up even before the servants."

She shrugged. "'Tis a time to work without distractions."

"Ah, but I find you very distracting."

She noted his bloodshot eyes, the disarray of his fine clothes. The scent of stale wine and woodsmoke wafted to her. "I was going to remark that you, too, are up early. But I see you've not yet been to bed."

"Not to sleep, anyway." He laughed at her cold expression. "Lord, Lianna, don't look at me so. Longwood had you for two nights." With an idle finger he fished down into his tunic, pulled forth the talisman Roland had found near the glade. Lianna kept her expression carefully bland, although it galled her that Rand's device, his lofty motto, had fallen into the keeping of one such as Mondragon.

Gervais smiled. "Surely the Englishman taught you a woman's pleasure."

She stared down at her books and privately swore not to let Gervais know she'd lain with Rand, married him. Such an admission would ruin her plan to credit the child to Lazare.

Moving behind her, Gervais wove his fingers into the hair at the nape of her neck. She fought the urge to recoil.

"Tell me," he said, pulling her head back gently but insistently, "how was the Englishman? Did he give proper attention to your lovely neck, your beautiful breasts?" His other hand strayed over her shoulder. Although his touch was light, she sensed a latent, hidden brutality in his caress.

"Have you a soft spot in your heart for him?" he asked.

She snapped, "You know naught of what is in my heart."

"I care not," he stated. "I am the Sire de Bois-Long."

Angry beyond caution, she blurted out, "How can you be so certain? Suppose I carry Lazare's child, the rightful heir?"

He laughed harshly. "Impossible. My father swore he'd never lie with you."

"The sheets of our marriage bed were duly examined," she said recklessly. "The marriage was consummated."

The roughness Gervais had only hinted at now emerged. He clamped both hands on her shoulders, squeezed until she winced. "A child would complicate matters. You'd best be lying."

She said nothing. The bruising pressure of his fingers abated. He's a fool, she thought. I'll best him in this. Turning the subject, she said, "What do the *hobelars* report?"

"The Englishman and his sorry contingent have apparently given up on Burgundy's timely return from Compiègne. They've repaired to the coastal hamlet of Eu, where an English cog has docked. Doubtless they'll soon seek their own safe shores."

She twisted to face him. "I'm surprised you and Gaucourt haven't mounted an attack to speed them on their way."

"We decided against it." His eyes shifted restlessly about the counting chamber. "Mustn't divide our forces."

She hid her relief behind the veil of her hair. The true reason, of course, was that both Gervais and Gaucourt feared her uncle. "Why don't you go to bed, Gervais?"

"Why don't you come with me?" He laughed at her

outraged scowl. "Ah, Lianna, we could be good together, you and I. You're so efficient at managing the château, and I am so adept at inspiring loyalty. Think of it. Together we could—"

"Save your dreams for Macée," she snapped.

"Macée. She's become a burr beneath my saddle. If it weren't for her, you and I could be married."

No, we couldn't, she thought darkly. I am already wed. "*Nom de Dieu,* do you never cease your plotting?"

He chuckled. "Never."

Lazare forfeited his life for plotting, she thought, but said nothing.

"I'm off," said Gervais. "'Tis May Day. I'd best go arm myself for the tilting. Gaucourt has called in all his *hobelars* for the holiday." Gervais reached across the table, grasped a lock of her hair, and twirled the strand in his fingers. "And you, I trow, shall be Queen of the May."

She pulled back. "So I have ever been." In sooth she had not the heart for the role this year. But to relinquish the title to Macée would be to admit to a secondary position at Bois-Long. And that Lianna would never do.

"I'll see you at the tilting yard," Gervais said. "I've an announcement to make before the tourney," he added cryptically, and left the counting house.

Bothered by Gervais's cocksure mood, she put away her stylus and corked the inkwell. In a spirit more suited to mourning than to merrymaking, she went outside where, yawning, the castle folk were coming out to greet the May.

Crouched on a weeding stool in the garden, Mère Brûlot watched a group of children as they picked flowers to weave into wreaths. For a moment Lianna stood captivated by the fresh, smiling faces and laughing voices of the children. The golden glow of early morn bathed the scene in soft, diffuse light.

In his eager foraging, one sturdy boy trampled a row of blossoms.

"Mind the pease," said Lianna. Irritation, left over from her confrontation with Gervais, edged her voice.

The child looked down at the vines crushed beneath his bare feet. Quickly he scrambled to Mère Brûlot's side.

"Nom de Dieu," said Lianna, "the flowers all but choke the food."

"You ordered them yourself, my lady," Mère Brûlot reminded her.

"I can't think why," Lianna murmured. But in sooth she knew. She'd been in love when she'd ordered the flowers. Now her dreams had died, strangled by Rand's betrayal. Annoyed at herself for subjecting the child to her temper, she gave him a quick hug and walked away. In the greensward, the maypole stood like a flower-crowned sentinel, ribbons and streamers blowing in the fragrant breeze. Soon the shaft would be a centerpiece for merriment, circled by hand-clasped dancers weaving the ribbons as they sang to the coming of spring.

Dressed in finery, Lianna would be expected to oversee the festivities. People came from the towns of Abbeville and Pont-St.-Rémy to compete at footraces, hoop rolling, and tilting. Costumed chessmen would enact their game on the checkerboard lawn. Others would play at morelles, attempting to win an anklet of bells by aligning colorful balls on the game green.

She must behave, she thought, as if this spring were no different from seasons past. As if she were still Aimery's placid, self-possessed daughter, and not the secret bride of an English invader.

By midmorning guests thronged the western fields. Spectators pressed for a better view of the tournament lists. More arrived on foot, mounted, or in carts. Overdressed, overwarm, and nauseated, Lianna sat with Macée in the open pavilion beside the jousting field. Behind them, Bonne sat eating sweetmeats. The long field was surrounded by a stout fence, which in turn was encircled by a higher fence, the space between crammed with squires and knights.

"Gervais wears my token," said Macée, pointing.

Armed and mounted, he waited behind two cords stretched across the lists. A wisp of ruby silk fluttered on his sleeve.

"Did you give yours to the Sire de Gaucourt?" asked Macée.

Lianna shook her head. "I have no favorite . . . among these men, or anywhere."

Bonne gasped. A fierce look from Lianna held the maid silent. Macée sniffed and turned her attention to the lists. Heralds marched beneath fluttering pennons; horsemen checked their blunted and rebated lances and swords. Here was the spectacle of chivalry at its most colorful, and at its emptiest. Men rode at one another for no better purpose than to knock from the saddle an opponent who was not an opponent. All for the sake of winning a wreath for their heads, a string of bells for their ankles.

Rand would be in his glory here, thought Lianna waspishly.

Spying a lone figure on the distant battlement of the castle, Macée shaded her eyes. "Chiang," she said. "Doubtless he's too busy with his powders and potions to join us."

"Your husband," Lianna said defensively, "has ordered

a *feu d'artifice* tonight. Even if Chiang wished to watch the jousting, he'd be too busy mixing his charges." She lifted her hand to wave at him; distractedly he waved back and disappeared behind a gunport.

Of late Chiang worried her. He seemed withdrawn, uncommunicative, and uncharacteristically obedient to Gervais's whims. And all the while he seemed tense with waiting.

Restless and inexplicably nervous, she shifted her attention to the pageantry of the tourney. Peasants and tradesmen milled about, laughing, eating gingermen and quaffing cider specially brewed for the maying, tinted light green with parsley. Still more visitors appeared on the west road, perhaps a score and ten of them. High-sided, penlike carts lumbered behind stout *haquenée* horses. The newcomers, she noted absently, must feel as hot as she. To a man, they wore long cloaks.

"Here's the parade of arms," Macée said excitedly. She straightened her hennin and leaned forward as trumpets blared a salute. Led by Gervais and Gaucourt, the knights rode down the lists, seventy men crowding the fenced area like a sea of gold. Armor caught the sunlight and magnified the glare so that, momentarily dazzled, Lianna shaded her eyes and looked away.

The crowd buzzed and then fell into an expectant hush; new arrivals moved among them, pressed close to the outer fences. A few, she saw with mild irritation, had rudely jostled others aside. One of them, a priest in brown robe and knotted scourge, haggled with a young boy over a prime seat at the head of the lists. Most unbecoming for a cleric, she thought, as was that gauntlet of leather. . . .

"*Nom de Dieu,*" she breathed. She jumped to her feet.

Macée snatched at Lianna's wrist, pulling her back. "You're blocking my view. Now hush up and listen. Gervais spent hours learning to recite his proclamation."

"He could simply read it if he'd just learn his letters," Bonne muttered.

Macée scowled. "Be silent while your lord speaks."

Lianna barely heard Bonne's cheeky retort.

Trembling in every limb, she combed the crowd with her eyes. Her hands clenched the fabric of her embroidered cotte. With mingled hope and dread she watched the strangers press in on the lists, not with the idle curiosity of spectators, but with the single-minded intent of predators. They perched on the fence or took up positions at the entrance and exit points of the yard. The tallest of the cloaked and hooded men climbed the outer fence, braced himself at the top. She knew that masculine form, the easy grace with which he moved.

Rand.

Obviously he'd come to take the castle. She should act, call a warning. The heavily armed tourneyers could finish him with a few blows.

Gervais droned on heedlessly, enumerating the rules of combat. "Foul play results in forfeiture of the prize. . . . No rushing a man when he's down. . . ."

Her heart pounded. Everyone listened to Gervais; none noticed the secret movements of Rand's men. Warn the knights, she told herself. For the sake of Bois-Long and France, warn them. But the words stuck, unuttered, in her throat. Not even for her home, her country, could she bring about the Englishman's death.

Rand lifted his hand. As one, the visitors flung off their cloaks, planted the bowstaves the garments had concealed, and swiftly nocked their arrows.

"At day's end the champion shall win the hon—" Gervais's voice broke off. A collective gasp rose from the crowd. For a moment the scene froze like a tableau. Then mothers hastened their children to safety; a few men cast nervous glances over their shoulders and slunk away.

The figure on the fence shrugged out of his cloak. Lianna's heart catapulted to her throat.

Sunlight glinted in his golden hair and on the device of the leopard rampant that adorned his *cotte de'armes*. He held his ready bow with strength and assurance. Lianna felt a sudden, involuntary pride in her husband, the father of her child. Behind him, a youth lifted a pennon emblazoned with the motto she'd seen on the talisman: *A vaillans coers coeurs riens impossible*. She was fast learning to respect the words.

To valiant hearts, nothing is impossible. Not even the conquering of seventy armed knights.

Macée clutched frantically at Lianna's sleeve. "It's the Englishman, the one who escaped."

"And that cheeky herald," added Bonne, pointing at Jack Cade. "What in the name of St. Denis is—"

"He cannot do this," said Macée. "Gervais was going to have the people swear fealty to him today, to us—"

"Hush." Lianna cut her off.

"Lay down your arms." Rand's voice boomed like thunder.

Incensed, Gervais spat on the ground. "Never, Englishman. You'll die where you stand."

Gaucourt had gone momentarily tense; then he seemed to relax as he finished his silent tally of the bowmen surrounding him. "Idiots," he bellowed to the fearful crowd. His caparisoned horse sidled beneath him; a light breeze ruffled the long plume on the knight's helm. "What can these motley peasants and English *god-dons* do against our armored strength?"

He turned to his men. "Arm yourselves," he commanded. The knights tossed blunts and rebates off their weapons.

Rand nodded briefly at Jack Cade, who guarded the exit point. Grinning, Jack let fly his arrow. Like a razor borne aloft, it neatly severed the curling panache on Gaucourt's helm. Gasps rose from the onlookers.

Bonne clapped her hands and sent the Englishman a look of pure admiration. She quickly abandoned her applause when several people turned and scowled her into silence.

Gaucourt shook a gauntleted fist. "You'll pay for that, Englishman! You're carrion!" He gestured at the castle. "Your head will rot on that wall."

"Lay down your arms," Rand said again, this time with a biting edge of impatience in his voice.

Rage reddened Gaucourt's face within his helm. "Whoreson!" Snarling, he yanked a pennon from one of the heralds and raised it aloft to signal his men to charge.

Split seconds later an arrow pierced the staff of the pennon, cutting through the wood.

Gaucourt gave a strangled cry of rage. Within the fenced lists, the mounted men shifted warily on their horses. Swearing and spurring his horse, Gaucourt galloped madly toward Jack. The archer leaned far over the fence and yanked a lance from one of the knights. Thighs gripping the rail, he set the lance against his shoulder. The point met Gaucourt's chest; the battle commander fell with a clatter from his horse, and Jack tumbled over the fence. Unencumbered by armor, Jack scrambled to his feet, grabbed Gaucourt's sword, and pressed the point to his face. French knights moved forward but shrank back when the sword nicked their commander's cheek.

"'Tis no game," someone in the crowd murmured.

No, thought Lianna, feeling cold and shivery despite the heat, 'tis no game. My castle will fall to Rand.

"Will you play the outlaw, then?" Gervais demanded. He raised his arm as if to shake his fist, glanced at the broken pennon, and seemed to think better of it. "Bois-Long is mine, I say!" With a flourish he produced a parchment scroll. "King Charles has invested Bois-Long to *me*."

Lianna's heart sank to her knees. So this was the secret Gervais had tantalized her with in the counting house. The French king had proclaimed Gervais Sire de Bois-Long. Damn the madman, she thought. After all her loyalty to him, he thanked her thus. Her life was but one barter after another, from one man to another. . . .

"The letter is signed and sealed by King Charles himself," Gervais yelled, "and—"

Calmly Rand loosed an arrow. It snatched the parchment from Gervais's hand and skewered it, quivering, to the ground.

"That," he said coldly, "is what I think of your king's nonsensical investitures." Nonchalantly he drew a second arrow and nocked it in place.

Macée fainted.

As Bonne attended to the limp form, Lianna stared, fascinated, at Rand. Here again was a facet of him she did not know. Not the lover in the woods, nor yet the raging beast in the ravine, but a cold, calculating warrior certain of victory.

Training his arrow on Gervais, Rand called, "You are defeated. There be but two exits to the lists. You'll trample one another trying to break free. As for being protected by armor, *eh bien* . . ." His eyes flicked to the parchment, then to the helpless Gaucourt. "Your steel serves you ill."

"What do you want, Englishman?"

"What is mine. Lay down your arms." Rand's voice rang with finality. Some of his men, covered by his ready archers, jumped into the lists and set to disarming the knights. Their commander in peril, they made no resistance.

Dear God, thought Lianna, Rand has made French allies. Unable to contain herself any longer, she climbed over Macée's slumped form and ran down to the field. Jostling a path through the crowd, she came to the head of the lists.

"What do you here?" she demanded of Rand.

He impaled her with a jewel-bright stare. "I come to claim my lands and my bride." He vaulted over the fence, swept her into his arms, and planted a fierce kiss of domination on her surprised mouth. She pulled away and was amazed to see some of the onlookers smiling, as if this were a tale enacted for their pleasure.

"You see," Rand murmured, "even strangers see the bond of love we share."

Outraged, she presented her back to him.

Raoul de Gaucourt, the boldest knight in France, was stripped of armor, spurs, sword, and horse. Heads bowed and hands manacled, he and his men were driven into penned carts.

"Traitors," Lianna yelled at the French archers. "Would you make prisoners of the very men sworn to defend France?"

"Better a traitor to the Crown than to our families," an old man snapped. He spat on the ground, gave one of Gaucourt's knights a shove to speed him into a tumbril, and added, "'Twas these same devils who attacked our town, plundered our fields, raped our women. Ransoming is too kind a fate for them, but ransom them we will."

She stared in disbelief. "No," she said hoarsely. "No, 'twas brigands who pillaged Eu."

"The pyx," shouted one of the French archers. "I've found it!" The peasant faced down a disarmed knight. He held aloft a gilt receptacle. The other men from Eu gave a cheer.

"'Twas stolen from their church," said Rand. "Who are the brigands now, Lianna?"

"*Parbleu.*" Guy the seneschal hurried to her side. "We've spent weeks sheltering a band of brigands." His face taut with resentment, he stalked off to aid the peasants in rounding up their quarry. Other men of Bois-Long joined in.

Sickened, Lianna looked at the prisoners in carts or shackled together in lines. The pyx, and their angry, shamed faces, confirmed the truth. *Nom de Dieu,* she thought with revulsion, I opened my home to pillaging outlaws. Like twin scarlet pennons, a flush rose in her cheeks.

The guests from the countryside hied fearfully homeward. The lists lay empty, trampled by nervous horses.

As the men from Eu tied the knights' horses to the carts, she made no further protest.

A shout, followed by curses and the clatter of hoofs, tore her attention from Gaucourt and his men. Turning, she saw Gervais, mounted and fleeing into the forest. Two of the Englishmen followed.

The old man beside her shrugged. "Mondragon. My quarrel is not with him."

"But mine is."

The quietly angry voice of Lianna's husband brought her whirling back around. Finding herself face to face with the golden leopard emblem on his tabard, she raised up on tiptoe to decrease the advantage of his height.

"I suppose," she said scathingly, "your men have orders to hunt him down like a wild boar."

"'Tis a more sporting chance than Mondragon gave me."

Unwillingly, she made a careful study of Rand. His face, though flushed with triumph, was marred by fading bruises and healing cuts. The knuckles of his big hands had scabbed over. She fought a feeling of concern. "He but did as he thought necessary to keep the castle out of English hands."

Rand's smile hardened with chagrin. "I thought you'd freed me to fight another day"—he reached for her, pulled her against him, engulfed her with his scent of woods and sunshine—"and love another night." A scattering of female sighs rose from the pavilion.

Ignoring the onlookers, Lianna said, "And was it sporting of you to hem in Gaucourt's knights from all sides, to aim arrows at them, leaving no chance of fair battle?"

"I but did what was necessary," he flung at her.

"So," she said furiously, "shall I." She spun around and marched off. Rand's squire called him away to arbitrate a quarrel over the right to Gaucourt's sword.

The castle folk hung at the fringes of the field, eyeing the Englishmen with uncertainty and reluctant admiration. Some had already gone into the castle, seeking safety.

And Chiang was within.

She slipped down a path to the north gate. Praying

she'd not been seen, she broke into a run. Her footsteps clattered over the drawbridge, and her gaze locked on the grim iron eyes of the cannon high on the battlements.

Yes, she thought. Yes, even with but two gunners, she might be able to fire on the Englishmen. Their numbers were small, and her skill, combined with that of Chiang, was great.

A hand of steel wrapped around her arm. She was brought up short and once again found herself with Rand. She cast a wild look at the cannon.

"Don't try it, Lianna," he said, reading her intent.

She twisted in his grip; his fingers pressed tighter. "I will not let you simply walk in and take my home. My people will never accept you as their lord."

"I won't give them a choice."

She understood the unspoken message in his gem-hard eyes. Neither would he give her a choice. His clasp on her arm relaxed. "Come, then," he said, striding toward the gate. "The last time I entered these walls it was as a prisoner. Now I enter as lord."

"The French will defeat you," she stated coldly, hurrying to match his strides. "You might have won the day, but France will not yield so easily."

He turned, raised his hand to signal to a distant group of men, and continued forward, Lianna hard at his heels.

"I will never forgive you for this," she said.

"Forgiveness," he replied, "is not one of the vows you made to me at Le Crotoy." He slowed his pace, and his expression grew tender, almost sad. "I would to God you had."

Torn asunder by her longing for him and her loyalty to France, she followed him into the château.

*   *   *

To Lianna's vast resentment, the task of claiming a barony proved easy for Rand. Batsford, the priest, conducted a mass of celebration. He summoned the Baron and Baroness of Longwood to stand before the altar.

To the accompaniment of gasps, whispers, and a shuffling of feet, she reluctantly followed Rand to the front of the chapel. Turning to look upon the people of Bois-Long, she expected to see outrage, anger, disbelief.

Instead the sea of faces showed only surprised pleasure, in the idea that the demoiselle had, in secret, become the bride of the Englishman.

Placing his hand upon an ornate reliquary, which contained a bone sliver from St. Denis, Rand spoke.

"I promise by my oath to be your faithful lord, and to maintain toward you my patronage entirely against every man, in good faith and without deception."

Many of the women, Lianna noticed, were smiling and nodding, clearly enamored of Rand's masculine appeal. Even the twenty knights of Bois-Long, who'd so recently been humiliated by English arrows, stood calm with a fatalism that infuriated her.

His eyes trained on Jehan, captain of the household knights, Rand said, "I shall never ask you to take up arms against a Frenchman. But neither shall you attempt any injury unto myself or my men. Step forward now and give me your oath of fealty."

Jehan approached the altar. Lianna chewed her lip and twisted her hands into the folds of her gown. Half of her was terrified Jehan would offer a challenge to Rand; the other half was terrified that he wouldn't.

The big knight stopped in front of Rand, clasped hands with him, and said, "As you are husband to my mistress,

I grant you my homage, my aid, and my counsel, Lord Enguerrand."

How could he? she wondered fiercely. How could he submit to an Englishman, a foreigner, who would allow King Henry's army to cross the Somme on a march of death?

Murmurs of approval and relief rose from the crowd. Lianna looked at her husband. Dear God, for the life of her, she could not summon the indifference she wished to show toward him. Instead, pride crept into her gaze and love into her heart.

A new banner, fashioned in England as a wedding gift, flapped over the ramparts of Bois-Long. Rand's leopard rampant, quartered with the gilt lilies of France, rose on the spring breeze. The maying continued with a new gaiety. As if they'd forgotten the tourney, Gaucourt's humiliation, and Gervais's flight, the castle folk seemed only too happy to be rid of the deceiving Gaucourt and his hard-drinking outlaws.

"St. Crispin's eyeteeth," said Bonne, finding Lianna at the garland-draped dais overlooking the greensward. "I thought we'd never get Macée calmed down."

"She sleeps?"

Bonne nodded pertly. "Aye, in the *salle* she has always occupied. Mère Brûlot's draught of henbane and poppy did the trick. Of course, now that Macée's position has changed, I suppose I should move her pallet to the women's quarters."

"Leave her," said Lianna. "Losing Gervais is bound to be hard enough."

"*Sainte Vierge,*" said Bonne, staring. "You can't mean you, too, are sorry he's gone?"

With a feeling of futility, Lianna said, "For years this

keep ran as smoothly as the currents in the Somme. Only when men became involved did everything begin to fall apart."

"Yet your husband," said Bonne, looking down at the milling crowd, "seems to have all well in hand."

Lianna sent Bonne a smoldering look, then followed the maid's gaze. Tabard flapping in the cool breeze, Rand walked with Chiang through the bailey. Men doffed their hats to him; women curtsied and whispered behind their hands.

Bonne sighed. "Handsome, he is, and virtuous, too. One of the men from Eu swore the baron never wenches, drinks to excess, or takes the Lord's name in vain."

Jack Cade, who walked behind the two, looked up and noticed Bonne. Grinning, he sank down on bended knee and stretched out both hands, pretending to offer his heart to her.

Irritated by Bonne's girlish giggles, Lianna clambered down from the dais. She approached Rand and Chiang. Her heart leaped; then resentment spread hot and quick through her. Chiang was smiling amiably, gesturing as he spoke.

"That," Rand was saying, his eyes on the dais, "must be Bonne. Jack told me more than I need to know about her."

Chiang laughed. "She's a lusty, life-loving sort. Has an odd habit of swearing by mutilated saints."

"We all have our little quirks," Lianna cut in. She scowled at Rand. "You, for example, abduct unwilling women." Turning to Chiang, she said, "You are quick to embrace the enemy."

He regarded her with placid brown eyes. He drew a deep breath and glanced at Rand.

"Tell her," said Rand. "Tell her what you told me, so she'll understand."

Chiang tensed. His cheeks darkened. "Can it matter?" he asked. "It was all so long ago."

Burningly curious, resentful that Chiang had shared some secret with Rand, Lianna said, "I want to know what you have kept hidden from me."

The master gunner faced her. A deep inner pride Lianna had never noticed before gave his exotic features a princely aspect. Odd, that she should see him as noble after all these years. He said, "I gave out that the ship that brought me here, the *Eastern Star,* was wrecked. But that is not so. The ship, equipped with guns such as the Christian world has never seen before, was seized by the French, and I only narrowly escaped enslavement."

"The *Eastern Star* was a warship?" asked Lianna. He nodded, and at last she understood why he'd never told her, for her next question, automatic, was, "In whose service?"

Chiang lowered his voice. "Henry Bolingbroke, father of King Henry the Fifth."

She began to tremble as pieces of the puzzle fell into place. Bolingbroke had burst upon England from exile and seized the throne from Richard II. *"Par le mort de Dieu,"* she breathed. "You helped the usurper."

Chiang swallowed. "I had my reasons." Muttering something about the evening illuminations, he hurried off.

Lianna conquered the sick sense of betrayal that gripped her. She faced Rand with a fierce glare. "You wasted no time in insinuating yourself into my household."

He smiled. "Our household."

She hated him for making her feel that smile all the way to her toes. "I do not want you here."

"But I am here, Lianna, and here I shall stay." His gaze moved over the crowd of dancers and revelers.

Pipes, drums, and rebecks shrilled and pounded a merry tune for the dancers around the maypole. Children played at hoops and morelles while their elders lazed and chatted around a stack of kegs near the cider press.

Resentment must have shown on her face, for he took her hand and said, "Don't think them disloyal. They are peace-loving folk."

"They are fools taken in by your English lies, your English promises."

"They care naught for politics. They want only peace and security, and don't particularly care where it comes from."

A shout from the barbican interrupted the dancing and gaming. People surged toward the main gate. Lianna threw a distrustful glance over her shoulder at Rand, then went to investigate. She reached the gate in time to see a large cog, its half-furled sails bedecked with dragons and demons, its hull flanked by the leopards of England.

The bottom fell out of her stomach. Pressing her cheek against the cool stone of the gatehouse, she remembered when she'd first seen the ship. It had been the morning after her wedding to Lazare, when she'd fled to contemplate the enormity of her mistake. She recalled blinking her tears away to focus on the approaching cog, remembered the throat-tearing fury of seeing the Norman shores corrupted by the English vessel.

And now it was not merely the rocky cliffs, but her own home that was being invaded.

As she recoiled from the sight, her people marched

down to the river to help unload the vessel. A train of horses and livestock emerged. A parade of chests and coffers borne on the shoulders of stout, dark-skinned sailors followed.

Feeling Rand's presence behind her, she said, "So King Henry means to buy the loyalty of my people with baubles and trading truck."

Almost absently, his hand came to rest on her shoulder, his fingers drifting into her hair. "Gifts of goodwill."

She jerked away from his tender touch and frowned. "They may be impressed by empty gestures, but I am not."

"Such empty gestures," Rand said, his hand claiming a lock of her hair once again, "do fill empty bellies."

Two mounted men rode up from the south and clattered across the causeway. She recognized the pair—the Welshman called Dylan and Piers with his bandaged leg—that had set out after Gervais. She followed Rand out to meet them.

"No luck, my lord," said the dark Welshman.

Piers nodded. "We'd have followed farther, but our mounts are nigh spent."

"In which direction did he flee?"

"He was traveling south, probably to Rouen."

"The important thing is that he has no strength of force."

Lianna whirled on him. "You naïve fool," she said softly, scathingly. "The Dauphin Louis is in Rouen. If Gervais convinces him to come here in force, we'll all be lost."

Rand waved his men into the castle, took her arm, and led her aside. "I have no fear of the dauphin. Although more sound of mind than his father, Louis is fat and lazy.

He'll not bestir himself to accost a minor English baron. More important than that, he's Burgundy's son-in-law, and will think twice before defying the duke." He scanned the battlements with hard green eyes. Lianna wondered how she could ever have thought his eyes as soft and gentle as leaves shot through by sunlight.

"Gervais will persuade the dauphin," she insisted. "And you should fear his might. You are no match for a king's son with the might of France behind him."

"Not all France," Rand said calmly. "Burgundy favors me, and Bois-Long is all but impenetrable. You told me so many times."

"I'll not lift a finger to resist the dauphin should he come seeking capitulation."

"You needn't," Rand snapped. "Such decisions are mine now." He saw her stricken look despite her effort to conceal it. Gently he touched her arm. "Come, let your people enjoy the day. You make a lovely May queen. I would see you enact your role."

"I'd rather go help Chiang with the fireworks."

His hand tightened on her arm. "I've sent Simon to do so. Perhaps the lad will learn Chiang's art. He's still smarting from the way you bested him at Le Crotoy."

She tried to pull away. Instead she found herself a prisoner of his strong, encircling arms, a captive of his low, seductive whisper as he bent close.

"As for us, Baroness, we will forgo the fireworks tonight and make our own."

Suppressing a tremor of unbidden desire, she said, "But Chiang is going to try a new explosive, with blue cobalt added to make it burn hotter. . . ."

Sweet breath stirred the wisps of hair at her temple. "My need for you burns hotter than any gunner's charge.

'Neath your indifference you burn for me as well."

A helpless, drifting sensation reduced her next protest to a weak murmur. "He's obtained some yellow copper to tint the lights...."

Warm lips strayed so close, she could almost taste his kiss. "Hush, Lianna. I mean to show you such lights as have never graced the firmament."

Chapter 14

The keening whistle of an ascending rocket sliced the silence and struck a flash of light in Lianna's solar. She shivered, wrapped her robe more tightly around her. Flames from a pair of candles caused her shadow to dance nervously on the painted gesso wall.

She studied the mural. Familiar images, a frieze of life from another age. The young mother laughed with her infant; the knight on bended knee paid reverence to his lady.

Now she looked upon the scene with new eyes, knowing eyes. Rand the Gascon had made her believe that the painting spoke of real feelings, of dreams answered. Enguerrand the Englishman had shown her that such fancies were the stuff of fools.

Perhaps that was what she regretted above all, at least in her heart. Though she could fight for her home, the loss of her dreams was permanent, irrevocable. Or was it? She had a future with him; she'd have a baby with blond hair and leaf-green eyes. . . . She banished the image. Damn him for making her want a life with an Englishman.

For that she hated him most of all. For that she had barred her chamber door to him.

The crackle of the *feu d'artifice* and the cheers of the crowd grated on her nerves. Everyone accepted Rand and the gifts of King Henry. Everyone except her and Macée. Lianna felt a stab of compassion for Gervais's wife. Tomorrow, Lianna would do what she could to reassure Macée. But tonight . . .

The metal of the door latch grated. Lianna's head snapped around to the thick door, stoutly secured by her own hand. She took a step back, her gaze locked on the door.

"Lianna?" Rand's deep, rich voice called. He worked at the latch again. "Lianna, open the door."

She fell still, mute, and tried with all her might to crush a niggling spark of fear. The long silence, punctuated by fireworks, calmed her. Perhaps Rand had realized she would not submit to him and had gone off to make his pallet elsewhere.

Her sigh of relief became a gasp of astonishment when something heavy slammed against the door. The sound thundered again. She jumped. With horror and awe she watched the iron latch give, rent from its anchoring.

The door crashed open.

His face calm, his hand idly rubbing one shoulder, her husband stepped into her chamber.

He seemed no more distraught than a man entering the hall for his noontide meal. Then he jerked the damaged door shut. Candle flames, flaring in the breeze generated by the motion, lighted his face. And Lianna saw that he was not calm at all.

His eyes glittered, keen and formidable as tempered steel. Never had anger looked so magnificent on a man, nor so fearsome. She forced herself to stand still, her chin jutting defiantly, her eyes unblinking.

"Never," he said softly, fiercely, "never bar this door to me again."

"Did it wound my lord husband's pride?"

His hand stopped kneading his shoulder and dropped to his side. The motion was stiff, forced, as if he were staying an impulse to violence. "Your pettiness wounds us both, and all who serve us. If I lack harmony with my own wife, the poison of dissension will eventually taint this entire household."

"I am not interested in achieving harmony with you."

Anger flashed in his eyes. Again he began rubbing his shoulder; again she had the impression that he was forcing his temper into submission. Despite his dark fury, he looked tired. Mentally she reviewed his day. Up before dawn to make the trip from Eu, surrounding, subduing, and capturing armed knights, unloading a cog, extracting oaths of fealty. That she'd crowned such a day with her defiance left her feeling strangely guilty.

"Salic law is much more stringent in France than in England," he said. "I would be well within my rights if I beat you or punished you publicly for your defiance."

She swallowed. "You'd do that?"

Letting out his breath with a hiss, he came to stand in front of her, rested his hands lightly on her shoulders. She felt the chained power in those hands. "I don't have to."

The gentle pressure of his hands unnerved her, as did

the light, insistent kisses he feathered over her brow.

"But I do not want—"

"You do," he insisted, reaching for the hand she held clutched at her throat. He forced her fingers open. "Lianna, I know you're angry. You feel betrayed. I understand your loyalty to King Charles and your disappointment in your uncle. But I do not see why you stubbornly refuse to admit you care for me, why you deny yourself the pleasure I can give you."

"It's not right," she said desperately. "I shouldn't feel—"

"It is our right as husband and wife to feel all the pleasure we can give each other. It is your right as a woman, a wife." He bent and kissed her briefly, lightly. Passion-heated blood roared in her ears. "We differ over many things, Lianna, but not in this. Let us have peace, at least, in the bedchamber."

Outside, rockets soared and missiles exploded, but Lianna barely heard. Her mind and her heart stayed riveted on Rand alone, on his soft, seductive whisper, his gentle caresses, and the deep, sharp yearning that probed her soul.

His heart full of agonizing love, his arms full of Lianna, Rand blinked in the predawn darkness. He lay still, sorting through his feelings, resurrecting images of the night before. So angry had he been to find the chamber locked against him, he'd barely felt the crunch of bone and muscle as he'd heaved himself against the door. His rage had been so deep, so tearing, that at first he hadn't trusted himself to touch her. Even with Lianna his patience had a limit. Thank God she'd not fought him, for she might have found his limit.

He tightened his hold on her. Pain twinged in his shoulder. She stirred, sighed, and burrowed sweetly against him. He pressed his lips to her temple.

She wakened then, uttered a soft sound of dismay, and pulled away. He caught her against him. "Stay," he murmured. "It's early still."

"You've become complacent too soon," she said, trying to squirm from him. "Gaucourt is not a man to countenance the insult you dealt him."

Her movements revived a fierce surge of desire in Rand. Doggedly he steeled himself; he knew he'd get nowhere with her in her present mood.

"Gaucourt and his men are out of the way," he said, "awaiting ransoming or riding for parts unknown on their repurchased mounts. He'd need weeks to gather the men and mount an attack." Rand toyed with a gossamer strand of her hair. "Thanks to your guns, Bois-Long is no easily won prize. Gaucourt will be reluctant to return. He's too practical to fight merely to salve his wounded pride."

"You know little of Frenchmen, then."

Anger nipped at him. "Would you have him back? Even knowing he allowed his men to sack Eu?"

"They adhere to the same lofty ideals of chivalry you embrace," she shot back, snatching her hair from his fingers.

"Do not liken me to a French raider. I've forbidden my men to practice thievery, chicanery, and rape. Women are not to be accosted unless they earnestly invite attention."

"Oh?" she said harshly. "And was I earnest in my invitation last night, my lord?"

Remembering the ardor that had followed her defiance, he moved his hand gently over the curve of her hip.

"Earnest enough, Lianna." He laid his lips briefly over hers. "You refuse to admit your feelings for me, yet your body tells a different story." His hand moved upward, fingers skimming her breasts. "When we make love, the world falls away."

"So you say." Her voice sounded slightly breathless. She batted his hand aside. "And what of Gervais?"

Rand ground his teeth. "I would have a moment of peace. Let us not discuss politics in our bed."

"Think you he'll stay away?" she persisted.

Rand sighed. "He's doubtless begging an audience with the Dauphin Louis. But surely Mondragon's influence is too slight to merit anything but the smallest show of force, if any."

He stared into her resentful silver eyes. He longed to stay abed and coax her out of her mood, but she looked pale and tired, and other matters called for his attention. He gave her a long kiss, ripe with promise, then rose.

Minutes later he walked through long corridors. The rooms smelled sweet with fresh rushes and verbena polish. Servants moved about in quiet order, pausing to greet him. Pride settled over Rand. What an efficient chatelaine Lianna was. He imagined his children growing up here, learning the tale of how the leopards of England and the lilies of France had been united under this roof.

Unfurling a mental list, he forced his thoughts to more immediate matters. After prime he would acquaint himself with the castle—its defenses and routine. Stores must be laid in and inventoried in case of siege. A letter must be dispatched to King Henry; the cog would be leaving with the evening tide.

As he descended the staircase to the great hall, a female screech stopped him short. Frowning, he veered to the right and spied a man and woman grappling in the screens passage. "St. Appolonia's bloody teeth," said a shrill voice. "Release me!"

Stepping closer, he recognized Jack and the maid Bonne. A tangle of string laced the woman's hands together. Jack took advantage of her defenseless state to caress the globes of her breasts, which mounded high above the bodice of her dress.

"By my troth, Jack," Rand said irritably, "must you bind your conquests? I gave express orders—"

"Hold, my lord," Jack said. "'Tis but an innocent game we play."

Uncomprehending, the Frenchwoman gave a tug on the snarl of string. She muttered a disgruntled curse invoking a bearded saint called Wilgefort.

"My man protests his innocence," Rand said in French. "What say you, girl?"

"He is as innocent as a pig in rut," she snapped, "and slier than St. Louis's physician."

Gently, his face bright with pleasure, Jack began to pluck the strings from her fingers. "There now, *chère,* I but tried to amuse you with the game of Jacob's ladder." He stuffed the string into his pocket and held up his mutilated right hand. "Alas, in this I still have no prowess."

She looked away from the hand, the two sound fingers and the scarred stumps where the others had been. "I suggest," she said tartly, "that you find a task more suited to a cripple."

Rand tensed. For milder insults, Jack had trounced strong men. Yet her fetching figure, her dulcet voice, seemed to amuse rather than incense him. "I am adept at other things," he said. "More than one satisfied woman has dubbed this"—he flourished his hand—"my other love tool."

Bonne gave a little squeak and blushed to the roots of her soft auburn hair. "You shall roast in hell, Master Cade."

Jack pinched her backside. "I'd rather heat things up on earth with you."

Rand bowed slightly to the maid. "If you would see to your mistress . . ."

Still blushing, she scurried off.

Rand and Jack began walking toward the hall. "I want you to go to Rouen," said Rand.

"Now, my lord?"

"Aye, today. It would behoove us to keep close watch on Gervais Mondragon. 'Tis unlikely he'll win the dauphin's ear, but if he does, I would know about it."

Jack looked crestfallen. "Why me, my lord? I was just . . ." With longing in his eyes, he glanced at the screens passage. "I was just getting to like our new home."

"I need to send a man I can trust, a man who understands French."

Eyes lighting, Jack held up his right hand. "Too conspicuous, my lord. I am marked."

"True." Rand wavered on the verge of indulgence.

"Piers Atwood!" Jack said suddenly, slapping his thigh. "He speaks French. Has a bit of an accent; his dam was Flemish, I believe, but he'd do nicely, my lord. And he does so want to redeem himself for blundering upon that Asian chap and getting himself shot."

Rand laughed. "Why is it I'm so loath to say you nay, Jack Cade? Very well, Piers Atwood it is. You may stay and try to entice that feisty maid with your other love tool."

*   *   *

Lianna wished her pride would allow her to stay abed longer. She felt nauseated and achy, and to bestir herself at dawn set her insides to roiling. Still, she refused to have Rand think her lazy and neglectful. She rose moments after he had left. Finding Bonne absent as usual, she shrugged into a tunic and surcoat and pulled her hair back with combs.

Pausing at the door, she swayed. She felt worse than usual today and unhesitatingly laid the cause at Rand's feet. Unlike normal people, he seemed to have little use for sleep. Following a long night of ardent lovemaking, he'd bounded from the bed as if refreshed by hours of slumber. Would he, she wondered idly, still have that drive when his golden hair turned silver?

So much, she thought, for the old Norman saying, "A guilty conscience makes a restless bedfellow." Either Rand had no conscience, or he truly believed he had the right to claim her. Sternly she repressed the tiny qualm brought on by the notion.

She clutched the door frame while the wave of nausea ebbed; then she went to Macée's room.

"The small beer is flat," Macée said to a serving maid. "I'll not break my fast with flat beer." Spying Lianna, the dark-haired woman glowered and waved a hand to bid her enter.

They sat in an embrasure furnished with a laden table. Sunlight streamed in through the window, aiming radiant heat at the back of Lianna's neck. Sounds drifted from the yards; prayers were over, and the workday had begun.

"Well," said Macée, breaking off a piece of pungent goat cheese and stuffing it in her rosebud mouth. "Have you come to gloat over your husband's victory?"

Lianna dragged her eyes from the bountiful table and wished for a breeze to carry away the odor of food. She swallowed. "You know better than that, Macée."

Macée finished her cheese and nibbled on a comfit, licking the stickiness from her fingers. "Do I?" She bit down hard on the sugary fruit. "Gervais had the Englishman well in hand. Yet you helped him get free."

"I did no such—"

"You did. Gervais might have been fooled by your false innocence, but I was not. The Englishman used gunpowder to blast his way out."

Lianna scowled. She remembered Chiang's confession the day before. "The English know much of gunpowder."

Macée eyed her suspiciously. "Why did you not tell Gervais you and Longwood were wed at Le Crotoy?"

"Gervais would have slaughtered him in cold blood and we'd have forfeited the ransom."

Macée's look took on a keen edge. "Ransom? Ha! Perhaps you love this Englishman. He's fair as a prince and doubtless excels at bed sport." She spoke half to herself. "Aye, I know what it's like to love a man so much you'll do anything for him."

"Love has nothing to do with it," Lianna said defensively. "He would have drowned in that cell."

"Would that he had."

Lianna's temper billowed at the cruel remark. Her stomach churned. With an effort she reminded herself that Macée was distraught over Gervais's departure and her own uncertain future.

The woman shoved a salver of ripe, briny-smelling olives under Lianna's nose. "Eat something. You look pale unto death."

Bile rose in Lianna's throat. She pushed the salver away. "I've no appetite lately."

Macée glanced at her sharply. "Why are you here? Am *I* being held for ransom now?"

"Of course not," said Lianna. She and Rand had not discussed it, but she was certain she could speak for him in this. "Gervais has only to come for you, and you are free."

"Free." Macée snorted. "Free to retire to Lazare's crumbling hall in Tramecourt."

"Until he comes, your place here is secure."

"Secure?" Macée chewed an olive. "How mean you?" Her eyes looked as dark and gleaming as the olives she devoured.

"You'll be treated as a guest of rank."

Macée's hand shot out and tightened like a claw around Lianna's wrist. "It's not enough." Her breath was hot and salty. "Lazare is dead. Bois-Long belongs to Gervais."

"Perhaps. Perhaps not." One by one, Lianna loosed Macée's fingers.

"What mean you? What—"

Suddenly the smell of the food, the heat of the sun, and the vehemence of Macée proved too much. Mumbling an apology, Lianna lurched to her feet. Knowing well she'd not reach her own room in time, she knelt over the chamber pot and spilled the meager, bilious contents of her stomach. Groping for a linen serviette, she wiped her face and stood on shaky legs.

Macée had fallen silent. Lianna turned to face her. The dark-haired woman sat still, staring, her expression so furious that she resembled the cockatrice of legend, one of those fearsome beasts that adorned the buttresses of the château.

The rasp of Lianna's breathing and the pounding of blood in her ears punctuated the silence.

Macée jumped up, oversetting the table.

"You're pregnant, damn you!"

"How long have you known?" Irritation and perhaps the smallest hint of hurt edged Rand's inquiry.

Lianna looked about the great hall, at the knights and servitors, the alaunt puppies cavorting under a table. Anywhere but at Rand's face.

"How long, Lianna?"

"I . . . had my first suspicions some weeks ago."

"Some weeks ago!" His fist crashed down on the trestle table. Nearby, a few people stopped to stare curiously. His hand gripping her elbow, Rand drew her into the privy chamber behind the hall.

His anger ignited the fuse of her own. Her head snapped up, and she glared at him. "I will not countenance your interrogations, nor listen to your accusations."

He gripped her shoulders. "You will. By the rood, Lianna, think of all you've done to endanger our child. Climbing down a tower wall, setting off gunners' charges, riding hard and fast as any man—"

"Dragging me from my bed, dropping me bound and sacked into the river, yanking me down a scaling ladder." She took dark satisfaction in his sudden pallor. "Aye, Rand, you too endangered the child."

"Only because you didn't see fit to tell me," he roared, so loudly that she reeled back as if he'd struck her. He stared at her, and she saw the anger drain from his eyes. "No more," he said, hauling her against his chest. "Henceforth you will take care. We both will."

She stood unmoving, torn between fury and sadness,

yearning and defiance. She wished he didn't make her feel protected, secure, cherished. He lifted her hair, leaned down, and pressed his lips to the pulse below her ear.

Dismayed by the sudden warmth that suffused her body, she searched within herself for a means to resist him. Like a general marshaling the last of his flagging troops, she dredged up bitter words. "What . . ." She cleared her throat and battled her guilt. "What makes you so certain the child is yours?"

He went rigid. He straightened and stared hard at her.

She forced herself to continue in a brittle voice. "Ah. I see your male pride has not allowed you to consider the possibility. But think, I gave myself to a stranger in the woods. What was to stop me from giving myself to other men?"

Only when he bent and sipped the tears from her cheeks did she realize she'd begun to cry. "Oh, Lianna," he murmured, "we both know better than that. I have only to look in your eyes and see that the child is my own." He brushed his hands over her shoulders, her breasts. "I have only to remember last night to know you would never give yourself to another. The babe is mine, as is your heart, would you but admit it."

She said nothing, only cursed herself inwardly for being unable to deceive him in this. Finally, her emotions laid raw by his tenderness, she whispered, "I'm scared, Rand. I know not what to do with a babe."

He crushed her against him. "Oh, Lianna. You love it. You just love it." She sobbed into his shoulder. "You wanted a child," he said, "an heir for Bois-Long. Why are you not happy?"

"I wanted a French heir. This child will be torn between

England and France as I am. You'll seek to make him vassal to King Henry."

He shook his head. "I will love him as I love you. I will bellow at him, lavish him with gifts and kisses, fight legions to keep him safe . . . him, and his brothers and sisters to come."

His solemn pledge struck a chord of response deep inside her. Her tears dried; her heart seemed to drift to her throat. He kissed her softly and withdrew to see to his new duties.

Lianna went about the rest of the day in a pensive mood, alternately angry, despairing, confused. She wanted to believe him, to be his wife, to bear his child. She wanted to forget that he meant to hold the castle for England.

That night, instead of barring the door against him, she held it wide for him to enter. She'd begun to feel hope for herself, her child, Bois-Long, and that hope hinged on shutting down all resistance to him—for a time. She'd be the bedmate he wanted . . . for now.

He made love to her slowly. His hands and mouth stroked voluptuously, relentlessly, heating her flesh, stealing her breath. He offered his vibrant masculinity like a gift; she clasped him to her. A sense of aliveness quickened her heart, but with it came the recognition that she would never be the same. Still, she gave herself up to sensual abandonment, to the almost intolerable magic of his caresses. He filled her so completely that he seemed to touch her very soul with tenderness, and when he whispered that he loved her, she believed him.

Aye, she believed him. He may well have deceived her, but she'd begun to doubt it. Before, resentment had gotten in the way of reason. Now she conceded that if he'd known she was his betrothed, he'd not have risked the harrowing abduction. He could far more easily have taken her to Le Crotoy from the place of St. Cuthbert's cross. Yet he hadn't. He hadn't, because perhaps he had truly believed the demoiselle to be the raven-haired woman he'd glimpsed soon after his arrival.

"I love you," he repeated, pressing his lips to her brow, her eyes, her cheeks. "I would have you believe it."

"Yes." The word dropped easily from her lips. "But does that make life easier for us? Must I disavow France as if she were an outmoded gown?"

He stroked her cheek. "Perhaps our captains and kings will come to terms yet. Perhaps there will be no war."

She knew better; the tortured look in his eyes told her he knew, also. "You say you love me, yet do you love my loyalty to France, my resistance to England?"

"It is all part of what you are. I love you for your devotion, your spirit."

An idea burst into her mind. She had Rand's love. Her uncle of Burgundy had once said that love was the most powerful emotion of all. Could she one day call upon that love, test it, find its boundaries?

Yes, she thought, wrapping her arms around Rand in exultation, eliciting a groan of response from him. She'd had the answer all along. Instead of fighting she should have been loving him, binding him to her, body, heart, and soul. They made love again, briefly, fiercely.

Later she felt him drift off to sleep, felt his big limbs relax, smelled the sunshine in his hair.

He's mine, she said fiercely, silently, to the implacable monarch across the Narrow Sea. He's mine, and you'll not have him. For by the time you mount your unholy invasion, Rand will belong to me so completely that he'll turn away from you.

She shivered at the blasphemy of making a bargain with fate. The thought of forcing Rand to choose between the woman he loved and the monarch he served filled her with uncertainty. Even a noncommittal man would find the choice a hard one. Rand, with his deep, abiding emotions and his iron-clad values, could well be rent in two.

I'll make it worth your pain, she promised him silently. She burrowed her head into the lee of his shoulder. Aye, for once you place me above empire, I'll be free to love you. She smiled, remembering his prediction on their wedding night. Someday, she vowed, she'd tell him of her love.

Chapter  15

Autumn blazed over Bois-Long with unseasonable, chest-squeezing heat. The shimmering rays of the Norman sun invaded every chamber and cloister of the château, warming the well water, turning the rooms to ovens, making a frying iron of every surface.

Perhaps, thought Rand, mopping his brow as he glumly surveyed the single sow pacing the stockyard, the heat wouldn't seem so oppressive if they could lower the drawbridge, take advantage of a cross breeze, or ride out into the cool woods and water meadows and bathe in the river.

Rides and river baths were impossible. For the château was under siege.

His big hands tightened into fists. Years from now, bards might sing of the bloodless coup that had placed Bois-Long in the hands of an Englishman. Yet Rand's victory would be meaningless if Gervais succeeded in his current enterprise.

Leading thirty knights of the dauphin's household, Gervais had returned six weeks before. Aware of the castle's defenses, he'd mounted an insidious method of persuasion.

He'd raised not a siege of arms, but a siege of starvation.

Staring at the restive sow, Rand shook his head. A heavy burden of futility settled over him. The sow was in season, yet all the boars had been butchered and eaten. In his own way, he felt as frustrated as the mateless sow.

He turned from the stockyard and strode to the tilting green where Jack was browbeating and cajoling the knights of Bois-Long at their archery practice.

"Aim not with one eye closed," Jack railed at one man. "The good Lord gave you two." Spying Rand, he hastened over. "Shoots like a green youth on his first whore. Quick and off the mark. Couldn't hit the broad side of a goddamned hog."

Rand nodded. "I wonder if Jufroy's aim would be truer did he not fear he was being trained to fight the dauphin's men. I worry that I ask too . . ." His words evaporated and his mouth went dry as Lianna stepped into view and walked to the cistern.

Her body ripe with their blossoming child, her hair flowing behind her like a banner of moon-colored silk, she bent to drink water from a dipper.

Suddenly Rand had no notion of what he had been saying. Always she had this effect on him, the sight of her enough to drive even the most burdensome thought from his mind. No worry held sway over her winsome face, her enchanting demeanor, or the fact that in her beloved body grew the most wondrous and tangible evidence of his love for her.

Jack's elbow landed sharp in Rand's ribs. "My lord?"

"I . . . forgot." Catching Jack's wide, knowing grin, Rand shook his head and borrowed a phrase from his friend. "'She does fling a cravin' upon me.'"

"Things sit well between my lord and lady."

"Aye. More than well."

She turned, sailed a kiss in his direction, and disappeared into the hall. In the months since he'd taken control of the castle, and against all expectations, she had grown to accept him. By day she was devoted and helpful as they met Gervais's challenge; by night she was warm and pliant as they sought refuge in each other's arms. She still refused to speak of love, yet deep emotion emanated from her each time she spoke to him, smiled at him, touched him.

Although conflict hovered on the edge of contentment, they had both agreed, in an unspoken pact, to keep their differences at bay. But what would happen when war came?

Doubt cast an ominous shadow. Her capitulation had come too suddenly. How had he won a woman like Lianna? He glanced up at the banner of lilies and leopards flapping on the ramparts. Someday there would be a price to pay.

A stirring atop the battlements dragged his thoughts from Lianna. A horde of women, their wimples cast off in the heat, had clambered to the wall walk. Guards tried ineffectually to keep the castle dames at bay. Yelling and shoving, they surged toward the wall facing the river.

"What the hell are those crones about?" asked Jack.

Rand was already running across the yard. Vaulting a stone railing, he bounded up the stairs.

"Your pardon, my lord," said Giles. "Mondragon taunts them with food. They clamor to see."

"Get away from those embrasures!" Rand's voice scattered the women like a flock of hens. "Go tend your children."

"He's brought a herd of swine," yelled Mère Brûlot.

Rand rolled his eyes. Taunting a starving host with food could be as deadly as a shower of Greek fire.

He stepped between two merlons and looked down. Gervais and perhaps fifty head of swine milled at the end of the causeway. Sylvain, the castle swineherd, stood nearby, looking confused. Rand cursed under his breath. The lad had made some successful forays for food, but Gervais had him now.

Woods fringed the long meadow beyond the river. As Rand watched, the forest seemed to shift and shimmer in the heat. The knights of the dauphin waited on mounts, ready to charge the gate if Rand were fool enough to open it.

"Greetings," Gervais called. "I bring a gift from the dauphin." He waved his hand to encompass the squirming swine.

"Keep your gift," Rand snapped. "Pigs are fitting company to keep you warm at night."

"I'd not see Frenchmen starve." Hands clasped behind his back, Gervais paced the planks of the causeway. "Open, my lord, and you'll be feasting on pork tonight, not rationing out stale bread and thin soup."

"Get us the meat, my lord," Mère Brûlot urged, and the other women echoed her plea. "You'll not let us starve!"

Rand wheeled on the old woman. "Nay, but neither will I risk the death of our men."

Mère Brûlot faced him squarely. "We've but a week's worth of food left, if that. My niece birthed twins a fortnight ago, and the smith needs fresh meat if he's to heal from the burn he suffered while mending your armor."

Nodding and muttering, the others clustered around her.

Rand's eyes flicked over the thin, weary faces of the women and then back to Gervais, who had planted himself at the head of the herd of fine, fat pigs. A gust of hot wind ruffled Gervais's dark mane and carried the animal smell to Rand.

"Don't forget your wife bides within," said Rand.

"Don't forget I care not," replied Gervais. "You'd never harm Macée," he added with maddening insight. "I smell hunger on the wind, hunger and dissension. Think you they'll follow an Englishman into starvation? Their French bellies say no."

Chiang appeared with a long, narrow handgun. "My lord, perhaps 'tis time for a display...."

Rand waved him away, saying, "'Tis too risky. Sylvain stands in the way." He ground his teeth in frustration. If he kept the gate closed to Gervais, people would starve. Yet if he opened it, people would die.

The hot wind stole over him again, blowing in from the south. As if borne on the heated gust, an idea occurred to Rand, an idea so outrageous that it just might work.

"We will accept your gift, Mondragon," he called.

Behind him, the women murmured words of thanks.

Chiang gasped. Gervais grabbed Sylvain, hauled the lad in front of him like a shield, and said, "Remember, you're in no position to play tricks, Englishman."

Bellowing for the women to clear the battlements, Rand bounded down the stairs.

Her heart pounding in fear, Lianna sped from the hall. Mère Brûlot had warned her that Rand was about to open the gate to Gervais. She reached the outer ward to find the archers ready behind the merlons. Armed knights sat mounted in the yard.

Moving quickly despite the burden of her distended belly, she searched for Rand. There had to be a better way, a safer way. Gervais would offer no quarter to the man who had humiliated him.

Rand appeared from the stockyard. Instead of leading a small force, he pulled a disgruntled, squealing sow behind him. Jack followed, cursing and beating the animal with a switch.

Lianna ran toward them. "What in the name of God do you—"

"Jesu, Lianna, stay away," he ordered, and hauled on the sow's tether. "She could knock you down."

He disappeared beneath the barbican. Like an intolerable itch, the temptation to discover his purpose deviled her. She hastened up to the battlement.

Huffing with effort, she reached the top. Rand gave the order to lower the drawbridge. A withering swirl of heated wind blew small tempests of dust around the river's edge. The stone wall savaged her fingers as she gripped the edge of an embrasure. From the fringe of woods at the river's south bank appeared a line of mounted knights. With the confidence of a victor, Gervais planted himself in the middle of the causeway.

Like a giant maw, the drawbridge yawned open and

connected with the lip of the causeway. Gervais motioned to the swineherd, who reluctantly plied his switch in an effort to drive his pigs back toward the guarded meadow.

"*Nom de Dieu,* we shall starve anyway," Lianna breathed, nearly reeling from the stink of swine.

The pigs at the head of the causeway pricked their ears and lifted their snouts. French knights burst from the wood.

A blur of dust rose. The squealing herd turned, not away from the drawbridge, but toward it. Whooping, Sylvain lunged toward the gate. Porcine screams and the pattering of hoofs filled the air.

Bonne ran up behind Lianna. "Ha!" she shouted at Gervais. "You'll die where you stand, trampled by your own kin!"

Gape-mouthed, Gervais faced the thundering herd for a moment. Bellowing a curse, he dove into the river and swam frantically for the south bank. One animal fell, surfaced, and, jaws snapping, swam clumsily in his wake.

"Even the pigs turn against you!" Bonne shouted gleefully.

The rest of the herd stampeded into the outer ward. Chains rattled as men hastened to pull up the drawbridge. The French knights thundered to a halt and milled outside helplessly. A few of them shook their fists at Gervais before veering from the causeway and heading back toward the woods.

Stunned, Lianna clambered down from the wall walk. Pigs squealed, men shouted, and women ran from all directions. At the center of the confusion, Rand bore a round of much backslapping and hand pumping. The swineherd, who had entered with the pigs, tried frantically to maneuver his herd to the stockyard. Bois-Long's last sow, the tether still around her neck, screeched hysterically as the boars closed in on her.

The sow was in season, Lianna recalled. Carried on the hot breeze, her scent must have incited the stampede. *Nom de Dieu,* she thought, Rand has outwitted Gervais again.

Jack Cade's hearty laughter rang out. Clutching his sides, tears of mirth streaming down his face, he approached Lianna. Seeing her stunned expression, he burst again into hoots of laughter.

"Mondragon will never live this down," he gasped. "From now on he'll be known throughout France as Gervais Sans Sooey."

On St. Crispin's Day, a shower of sparks burst in the night sky over Bois-Long. The weather had turned; the sharp chill of autumn had driven away the stifling heat. A swirl of wind brought the smell of roasting pork.

The victory feast, a week in preparation, had begun. Not only did Bois-Long now have stores to last the winter, but a humiliated Gervais and the dauphin's knights had also quit the area. Frustrated by weeks of idle waiting and impatient for their pay, the Frenchmen had taken Rand's second bloodless victory and the change in weather as a springboard for retreat.

With the siege over, spirits soared. Lianna sat at a table, her hands folded over her belly, and stared contentedly into the bonfire. Three carcasses, hoisted on cranes above the flames, turned slowly, the fat sizzling and popping. Seasonings of rosemary and garlic wafted on the breeze. Rand was in the armory with Chiang, so some of the men started the toasting without him.

"Here's to victory," said Piers, lifting a mug. "Lord

Rand's learned well how to handle a female."

"Learned to think with his pizzle," said Jack.

Jehan grinned drunkenly. "I always knew there was more than one use for a female in heat."

Godfrey said, "If the French follow their battle commanders like those boars followed the sow, our cause is lost."

Pretending to ignore the joking, Lianna looked away. Macée Mondragon hovered at the edge of the crowd.

As a small host of servitors lowered the chains and carved the meat, Lianna studied Gervais's wife. Sympathy and regret welled in her heart. Although Macée had come to accept Lianna's pregnancy, the young woman was far from content. Gervais had all but forsaken her, rejecting the *sauf-conduit* offered by Rand, refusing to allow her to join his travels. As Lianna watched, Macée wandered almost listlessly toward the bonfire, the hem of her red gown dangerously near the flames.

Jumping up, Lianna cried out, "Macée, have a care!" Macée stared disinterestedly at the sparks dancing near her feet, but she stepped away from the fire and wandered off.

Since Gervais's last departure, Lianna had sensed a new level of desperation in Macée, a curious disregard for her own safety.

Guy sat with Edithe and Bonne on a bench nearby. The seneschal lifted his mug, then drank deeply. "A right fair celebration," he proclaimed. "Look, the illuminations are set."

Lianna glanced up at the gunner's walk. Assisted by Simon, who'd vowed never to be bested by firepower again, Chiang commenced a dazzling display in honor of the triumph. Sulfur seared the air; sunbursts of yellow and plumes of cobalt blue lit the night sky.

Guy seemed to have found something of great interest in the cleft of Edithe's breasts. Clearing her throat, Lianna said, "We've spent nigh on a week preparing this feast. Starting tomorrow we must begin plowing the burned-out fields and putting in a crop of winter wheat."

Guy stiffened. "Yes, my lady," he said, chastened. "Of course."

"Guy, I didn't mean to diminish your pleasure in this night. 'Tis only that—"

"I understand, my lady," he said abruptly, and drained his mug of cider. He leaned over and whispered in Edithe's ear. She giggled and edged closer to him.

"Never mind them," Bonne said loyally, leaving the bench and coming to Lianna's side.

Lianna sighed. "I wish everything I said didn't sound like a general's command. I wish—"

Bonne pointed. "Your husband comes with his harp."

Surrounded by boisterous men, his eyes bright with reflected firelight and hearty drink, Rand strolled across the bailey. His long, strong legs bore him at an easy gait, while children skipped around him, begging for a song.

With a heart-catching grin, he stopped before Lianna, pointed his toe, and swept into an unsteady bow.

He rose. "What be my lady's pleasure?"

Warmth spread through her. He stood with legs splayed, harp in hand, exuding a dashing masculinity. Desire snatched her breath, and pride lifted her heart. "'Tristan and Isolde'?"

"'Tis a fitting lay." He seated himself on the ground, the fire at his back, his hands caressing the harp strings as he adjusted the pitch.

He began to sing in his clear, noble voice. Beckoned

by the spell of his art, people gathered around him. He sang of Tristan, a man captivated by his tragic love for Isolde, a knight rent asunder by devotion to his lady and duty to his king. Happy faces grew pensive as Rand sang the sweet, mournful ballad of love and loss.

> A man, a woman; a woman, a man:
> Tristan, Isolde; Isolde, Tristan.

A chill stole into Lianna's heart. How like the legendary Tristan her husband was. The lovers of old turned their backs on the world, only to find their charmed garden rife with evil and sorrow. Would Rand, like the hero in the ballad, turn away from external claims? Tristan's king had stabbed him from behind. Stricken by grief, Isolde had joined Tristan in death. That they loved without caution, without compromise, was their downfall.

By the time Rand finished, the eyes of besotted men and love-struck women swam with tears. Lianna blinked fast and swallowed hard against emotion.

She wrapped her arms around her stomach and pondered the awed response of her people. When she made a request, they obeyed with alacrity. But when Rand sang to them, they wept with fervor.

If ever forced to choose between lord and lady, England or France, she suspected they would follow their hearts. They would follow Rand.

Her eyes locked with his. Gentle fingers stroked tender chords from the harp. She sent him a tremulous smile and murmured a word of praise for his art.

Beside her, Bonne cried quietly into her apron.

"Come, sweet," said Jack Cade, holding out his arms

to her. "I'll kiss your tears away."

Bonne looked at Lianna. Seeing a woman's longing in her maid's eyes, Lianna said, "Go. I have no need of you tonight."

Bonne and Jack slipped away. Mothers bundled sleepy children off to bed, inebriated knights slept where they fell, and other couples slipped off into the night. Like layers being peeled from the hot core of the bonfire, the people fell away, leaving behind only Rand, Lianna, and the dying embers.

"Well," Lianna said quietly, "your triumph is complete."

He smiled. "All my battles should be so easily won." His fingers stirred the tendrils at her temple. "You look tired. Beautiful, but tired."

"Not *too* tired," she said, holding her arms out to him.

He led her to their chamber, laid her gently on the bed, and turned to bank the fire. She reached to remove her shoes; he pushed her hands away and did the task himself. Then he removed her clothes and his own and lay beside her.

The lambskin covering gently abraded her skin as she moved to extinguish the bedside candle.

He caught her hand, pressed his lips to the pulse at her wrist. "Don't," he whispered, his eyes grazing her nude form.

He'd looked upon her hundreds of times, yet she felt the heat of a blush in her neck and cheeks. "I look like an overripe pear," she said, running her hand up his sinewy arm.

He nuzzled her neck. "Ah, but a most interesting sort of pear." Soft as gossamer, his mouth moved lower, to the heavy globes of her breasts and the gentle rise of her belly. He looked up. "The babe stirs," he said wonderingly.

Framing her face between his hands, he regarded her intently. "Lianna, there is nothing more beautiful to me than the sight of your body, ripe with our child."

She wove her fingers into his hair and brought his face down for a kiss. As their lips melded, love burned fierce and steady in her heart. Nothing mattered now—not the English king, not the feud between Burgundy and Armagnac, not the impending threat of war. Overcome by love and desire, she probed his mouth with her tongue, caught at his lips with her teeth, skimmed her hands down the majestic length of him.

He lifted his head. "My God, woman, what are you thinking, that you could kiss me so?"

A smile started in her heart and unfurled on her lips. "I'm thinking that . . ." She faltered. "That . . ." The words her heart yearned to speak caught in her throat. Swallowing, she burrowed her face in his neck. She'd vowed to make her love conditional, dependent on Rand's renouncement of King Henry.

Yet longing snared her in the selfsame web she sought to spin; she was fast becoming helpless to deny Rand anything he asked. If he bade her to hand her castle over to Henry . . .

"Could it be," he murmured, his thumbs drawing lazy circles around her breasts, "that you love me, that someday—"

"I know." She forced a laugh past the emotion thickening her speech. "Someday I'll tell you about it."

Briefly, disappointment darkened his eyes. "Then show me. . . ." His hands circled her ample girth; with one easy motion he positioned her atop him. "Show me what's in your heart."

A sigh slipped from her as he pulled her close, showering her hair over his neck and shoulders. Willingly, sparing no thought for France, she offered herself to him.

"Shamed!"

The Duke of Burgundy's voice echoed like dark thunder in the privy chamber of Bois-Long. "I am shamed," he shouted.

Lianna stared at him from her seat by the fire. Rand rose and crossed to Burgundy's side, taking the duke's hand in greeting.

The two men were a study in contrasts. Tall, upright, and golden, Rand smiled a confident welcome. Stooped, dark, and angry, Burgundy planted his leather-gloved hands on his hips.

In a flash of insight, Lianna recognized corruption in her uncle's hard eyes, twisted mouth, and wary stance. At the same time, Rand's goodness, his openness, his faith, shone like a jewel against the black velvet of Burgundy's fury.

A subtle movement of Rand's head jarred her from her contemplation. "Will you have wine, Uncle?" she asked softly.

"Aye, and plenty of it."

Bracing both hands on the arms of her chair, she levered herself up and trundled to a sideboard. In the past weeks she'd grown so big that every movement demanded concentration. Yet even though it was December and her confinement drew nigh, she played the role of chatelaine with aplomb.

She poured wine into a silver cup, walked to the fire,

and pulled a red-hot poker from the embers. She drowned the heated point in the wine, turning her face from the pungent steam as the liquid sizzled fiercely.

Burgundy seated himself and sipped the wine. Rand helped Lianna back to her chair, then turned to her uncle. "Tell us, Your Grace, of the peace you made at Arras."

Burgundy scowled. "'Tis no peace at all, but an outrage. A stain upon the House of Burgundy."

Concerned, she leaned forward. "Uncle, were you not able to salvage some concessions?"

He waved his hand; the ermine cuff of his robe fluttered. "The Armagnacs credit themselves with my defeat," he said coldly. "Compiègne, Soissons, Laon, St.-Quentin, and Peronne have fallen. Artois teeters on the brink." His face hardened. "They've backed me into a corner, forced my pen to their treaty, banished me from Paris, punished my loyal followers."

Lianna asked, "What of the Dauphin Louis?"

Burgundy closed his eyes, sucked a long breath through his nostrils. "My son-in-law has forced me to promise no alliance with England, on pain of losing my fiefs."

Rand and Lianna glanced at each other. "Then there's hope," she murmured. But when she looked at her uncle, he'd opened his eyes. A fearsome light glimmered there.

"The Armagnacs are fools," he muttered. "They should know a cornered lion fights more fiercely than one who is free."

"You, cornered?" Rand said ironically. "It's not a sight I'd choose to see."

Burgundy set down his wine cup and parted the folds of his cloak to reveal the nettle and hops emblem sewn on his tunic.

Unthinking, Lianna reached for Rand's hand and

squeezed it. The significance of the device stood out clearly to her: *I will sting all those who cross me.*

"Tell us of the promises wrought," said Rand.

"I made promises I shall never keep." The duke leaned forward, took his cup of mulled wine, and drained it. "Had they treated honorably with me, I might have reconsidered my plans with the English king. But Armagnac leaves me no other choice now."

"No choice but to support King Henry?" asked Rand.

"Aye."

Lianna dropped Rand's hand as if it were a live coal. For months she'd denied the English threat and hoped that the power of their love, not Henry, would command Rand's loyalty.

Now she felt locked in a tug-of-war, her love pitted against the strength of the Duke of Burgundy and the King of England, with Rand in the balance.

Burgundy seemed oblivious to her anxiety, to the nervousness that squeezed her, leaving her breathless. He relaxed slightly, leaning back in his chair and crossing his legs at the ankles.

"'Tis well you didn't await my return before taking Bois-Long," he said to Rand. "A most clever ploy, that. You rounded up Gaucourt's men like cattle to market."

"I did what was necessary."

"You did what many, myself included, would have deemed impossible." Burgundy slapped his thigh. "Imagine, a mere thirty bowmen against seventy armed knights. I would have liked to witness Gaucourt's humiliation."

"Why? 'Twas . . . painful, actually," said Rand.

"You've a heart softer than mine, then."

Lianna nodded. "Few have a heart so sturdy as yours."

"And the siege," Burgundy continued, warming to his

topic. "Already the bards sing of the swine of Bois-Long."

"French bards?" asked Rand, raising an eyebrow.

"Everyone favors a good story. The dauphin's latest tax levy has made him unpopular in some circles. That his pigs fed an English household seems only right and meet."

"A French household," Lianna burst out. A knot of tension formed in her back, subsided, then returned with renewed force. Rubbing her spine, she said, "Uncle, you speak as if my home were an English island in French seas."

"Is it not?"

She could not speak; claws of agony ripped over her back. She scowled, conquering the pain. Bois-Long was slipping from her control. Frustration drove her to her feet and sent her stalking the length of the chamber.

"English and French blood will soon be united," said Burgundy, eyeing her distended profile.

She kneaded the muscles of her back. Suddenly she felt something loosen inside. Her eyes widened, and she gave a little cry. Rand bounded from his chair and hurried over. Staring down in embarrassment at the pool of warm fluids gathering at her feet, she said, "S-sooner than you think, Uncle."

"A day and a night!" Rand bellowed, pounding the wall of the passageway with his fist. "All her women will tell me is that her travail goes hard."

"That is all they *can* say, my lord," Jack replied. "They keep your lady warm and comfortable. What more can they do?"

Rand glowered at the closed door of Lianna's chamber. Wearied by lack of sleep and a burden of worry, he felt as if he'd been chewed up and spat out by a fang-toothed creature.

His knuckles savaged by impotent pounding, he dropped his hands limply to his sides. A rushlight on the wall hissed softly, accentuating the stillness.

"The screams I could endure," Rand said raggedly, rubbing the stubble of his beard, "for I knew she fought. But this thick, unholy silence..." His body sagged against the wall. "It plagues me like a canker."

"Perhaps she sleeps, my lord."

"Perhaps she..." Rand shook his head, swallowed hard. No. He would not even think of that. "I'm through waiting."

"My lord, 'tis a woman's burden..."

Ignoring Jack's admonitions, Rand stalked down the hall. He reached for the door latch. The callused, sun-browned hand of Father Batsford closed over his.

Rand jumped back. The cleric had arrived silently, his brown garment rendering him nearly invisible in the dim passageway. "What do you here, Batsford?" Rand demanded.

"Your wife's maid, Bonne...summoned me." The priest's hand moved into the folds of his robe, but not before Rand saw what the priest tried to conceal.

A vial of oil, such as holy men used in shriving the doomed.

"No." His voice came out a harsh, tortured whisper.

"My lord, surely 'tis but a cautionary—"

"No," Rand said more loudly. "Begone, Batsford. I'll not have you reciting your death chants over her."

"But—"

"Begone!" His shout rang down the corridor. The priest hurried away toward the chapel.

Wild panic shredding his insides, Rand yanked open the door. His eyes adjusted, and he picked out the shapes of Bonne, Mère Brûlot, and Ermengarde, the midwife, who hovered over the curtained bed.

Three female gasps greeted him. Mère Brûlot recovered first, scuttled across the room, then shrank back in fear. He saw himself reflected in her wide, frightened eyes. Briefly he gave a thought to his appearance—disheveled hair, half-laced tunic, unshaven face.

"My lord, you must not be here. She is—"

"My wife." His strides eating up the distance to the bed, he shoved aside the curtain.

And froze.

Lianna lay still, her head arranged precisely in the middle of a satin pillow. Her hair had been carefully combed, and her features lay in perfect, peaceful repose. Her hands, damp-looking, the nails broken, were folded neatly over her breasts, just above the motionless mound of her belly.

His heart skipped a beat. His soul recoiled. Moving like a child's wooden toy, he knelt beside the bed.

Dead. His Lianna was dead. And all the dreams of a lifetime with her.

"No." The tortured denial rasped from his throat. "No," he said again, his voice gathering volume driven by grief, eyes clamping shut against horror. *"Goddamn it, no!"*

"You see, Bonne," a soft, faraway voice whispered, "he does sometimes curse when pressed to it."

Rand's heart left his body and soared to the rafters. He dragged his gaze to the figure on the bed. The wide, moon-silver eyes of Lianna stared out at him.

"Oh, Jesu, God, and all the saints, thank you," he said, reaching for her hands, bringing them to his lips, kissing them fervently. His exultation was but short-lived, for her hands held the chill of death.

"Leave me, Rand," she whispered. "Let me rest, sleep. . . ." Her eyes drifted shut. He slipped her hands under the coverlet. Her chest barely stirred, as if breathing were too great a chore. He turned tormented, questioning eyes to the women.

Ermengarde was a young women, and robust, but she suddenly looked old and weary. "She labored long and hard," said the midwife, drawing Rand away from the bed. "She spent her strength. It happens this way betimes. The babe is dropped and ready, the mouth of the womb open, but she must put forth the effort. Yet she doesn't. The spirit has given up."

His insides clenched into icy knots. He stood. "So . . ."

The midwife would not meet his eyes. "So the babe dies, and its fluids foul and poison the mother." She spoke so quietly, Rand had to strain to hear.

His hands snaked out; he grabbed the midwife, rending her dress. "Can you do nothing? Nothing at all?"

Mère Brûlot stepped forward and pried his fingers from Ermengarde's shoulders. The older woman placed her hand protectively over Ermengarde's. "We be lucky to have such a practitioner to attend your wife. You'll not see Ermengarde stretching the parts and harassing the patient, plaguing the baroness with clysters and catheters."

"Cease your prating," snapped Rand, "and tell me what can be done."

"Your lady's fate lies in the hands of God."

He spun away, stalked to the window. He unlatched the shutter and jerked it open, then gripped the iron grating. Sunlight flooded the chamber and streamed over his face, his shoulders, the bed behind him.

Although pain and fatigue had rendered her weak and hopeless, Lianna felt her heart trip rapidly as she stared at her husband. Her mind separated from the travail and fixed on that image. He looked like an angel standing there, his strong arms outspread like great wings, his body haloed by a golden glow, his hair a shimmering crown.

In the early hours of her travail, she'd tried mightily to respond to the pains and the midwife's urging. Yet now she sought only peace and a release from the tearing agony. Tired . . . she felt so tired that mere sleep could not assuage her weariness. No, she needed something deeper, more lasting. . . .

Sunlight and silence filled the room. Her tongue edged along her dry, cracked lips. She tried to speak, but the effort proved too much. She could only watch the bright image of Rand at the window. So few, she thought, her eyelids drooping, are granted the mercy of such an enthralling final vision.

Ermengarde scurried forward. "My lord, the light—"

"Has your darkness served her any better?"

Ermengarde backed away.

Rage, heated by the fires of frustration, boiled hard and hot in Rand. This was no enemy he could vanquish in battle; no one stood responsible for this monstrous deed. His head began to pound. No one . . . but he. Oh, God, he thought, full of self-loathing, I brought her to this with my lust for her body, my ambition for an heir. He hated himself at that moment, almost as much as he loved Lianna.

Still clutching the window grating, he sank to his knees. Anything, he thought wildly. He would give anything he possessed, endure any torture, gamble the surety of his soul, to preserve her life. He'd turn his back on England, on King Henry himself, if only she would rise delivered and alive from the birthing bed.

The silver-gilt undersides of the clouds reminded him of her eyes. Suddenly he remembered those eyes, narrowed in accusation on their wedding night. *I look upon a scoundrel and a betrayer.... You love only your usurping sovereign and your foul ambition to steal my castle.*

A new and horrifying thought skewered him with the force of a lance. What if her death were retribution for his sins?

You forced me into a marriage I protest, you hold me against my will, you keep me guarded by your lackeys....

Pride and ambition clung to him like an indelible stain. Oh, Lord, he thought, Lord, I recant my sins, I commend myself unto you, body and soul. Only let her live. Let her live.

"My niece surprises me," said a low, calm voice. "I thought her tempered of stronger steel than this."

Rand whirled around and fixed a fierce glare on the Duke of Burgundy. "Is that all you will say of her?"

Burgundy shrugged. "What more can I say? She was ever a fighter. I thought she'd battle her way through the birthing. Yet there she lies." His elegant sleeve whispered as he pointed at the bed. "Listless, uncomplaining, uncaring. It is not like her." His impassive expression turned to one of knife-sharp anger. "You might do well to *make* her care."

They stared at each other, Rand frantic and despairing, Burgundy ruthless and implacable. Ruthless, aye, thought Rand, yet a close inspection of the duke revealed lines of sleeplessness around his eyes, a minute tremor of his hands.

Suddenly Rand's scrutiny penetrated Burgundy's icy mask. Beneath the callous remarks and haughty attitude lay the truth.

Jean Sans Peur, lord of an empire, hero of Nicopolis, was afraid.

The duke departed, but his last words echoed in Rand's mind: *You might do well to make her care.*

"We cannot let her die," he whispered.

"There is one more thing we can try," said Ermengarde tentatively.

"What?" he demanded. "Tell me."

"Make her walk, have her sit upon the birthing stool as our grandmothers used to do." Ermengarde brightened. "My lord, she wouldn't move for me, but perhaps she will for you. It will bring the pains to a hellish peak, but..."

His heart battered his rib cage. "Fetch the stool." He approached the bed and knelt. "Lianna."

She lay still.

"Lianna, look at me."

She dragged her eyes open. He sought her hands beneath the covers, clasped them, squeezed them hard.

"Tired," she whispered. "I'm tired and cold."

He quelled the urge to cradle her in his arms, to offer ease and sympathy. Instead he placed his face very close to hers. "You've a baby to birth, Lianna."

"No. Too hard..."

"Too hard?" he demanded. The cruel edge to his voice caused Bonne to gasp. "Damn you, woman, this is what you've always wanted, an heir for Bois-Long."

From the corner of his eye he saw Bonne start forward. Mère Brûlot yanked her back, whispering, "Let him be."

"The château..." Lianna paused, moistened her lips.

"The château is yours, Rand. You'll have it whether I live or die."

"So," he lashed out, "you surrender, then. Give up the home you've spent a lifetime defending, the heir you wanted."

"I . . . no choice."

"You've made your choice by lying there helpless. I should thank you. Without you constantly rousing my conscience, it will be easy to give the castle to King Henry." He ignored the piteous whimper that slipped from her. "Will you let the child die? Will you lie there while your father's line fades into obscurity?" She only stared, hollow-cheeked, listless. Frantically he said, "So this is how the Demoiselle de Bois-Long, daughter of Aimery the Warrior, ends her life. Helpless, defeated, willing to put her home in the hands of an Englishman and lay her child in the arms of death."

Bonne protested again. Rand ignored her. He laughed harshly. "I'll need a strong woman for my next wife, to give me healthy sons. Aye, a plump English maid."

"You bas . . . tard," said Lianna.

He continued in a loud voice. "My first action will be to send some of the light cannon and mangonels to King Henry."

Her hands clenched around his. "No . . . no, I won't let you. . . ." She stirred restlessly.

He bent closer. "Fight me, Lianna. Show me your mettle. Fight me, else the artillery goes to King Henry."

"Damn . . . you . . ." She forced the words out between gritted teeth. A red mist of determination flooded her pale cheeks. As if strength poured into her from some untapped reserve, she arched her back and screamed.

The midwife rushed to the bed, flung back the covers,

and rapped out, "Take hold of that swathe band and lift her."

Half dragging her, he brought her from the bed. "Walk," he commanded. Swearing, she stepped forward. Fluids rushed from her. The powerful muscles of her laboring body clamped hard; Rand felt the tension. She gave a screaming gasp.

The contractions renewed, hard and fast. "Take me to . . . the birthing stool," Lianna said, panting.

Ermengarde touched Rand's sweat-damp sleeve. "If you please, my lord, your part is done." Amazed by the profusion of fluids, and a little embarrassed, he turned to go.

"No." Lianna's voice stopped him. She narrowed glazed, pain-ravaged eyes at him. "You bully me into birthing your babe, Englishman. I would have you stay and see this through."

In the next hour, he came to understand what a mercy it was that men were banished from the birthing chamber. He stood holding her hands, watching her body racked by pain, feeling each convulsion of agony as if it were his own. Blood and fluid soaked into the rushes on the floor, wetted his boots.

She seemed to forget his presence but clung unthinking to his hands, digging furrows into his flesh with her broken nails. Her face, sweat-sheened and fiery red, grew stiff with total absorption.

Tears burned Rand's eyes. His warrior's detachment from another's pain served him ill when the pain belonged to his wife, his love.

The pile of soiled cloths by the stool grew. He'd seen men disemboweled, set afire, their heads hacked off, yet the blood and gore of childbirth was a new horror for which he was unprepared. Just when he was certain Lianna would burst asunder with her efforts, she emitted a savage scream. The midwife began speaking rapidly. Rand's tortured mind failed to register the words, his ears the sudden wail.

Then, beaming, Ermengarde held out a bundle of linens.

"Your son, my lord."

He gazed from Lianna's exultant face to the tiny squawling object in the midwife's arms, to the slick crimson-and-purple mass that slid thickly from between his wife's legs.

He took a step, tried to speak, failed. The floor sped up to meet him as he pitched forward in a dead faint.

Chapter 16

Shovels and flails over their shoulders, voices raised in ribald song, the men of Bois-Long marched home from the fields. His voice louder and truer than all the rest, Rand rode a sturdy *haquenée* at the head of the contingent.

Watching from the steps of the great hall, Lianna felt pride filling her heart. In her arms, Aimery, aged seven months, squirmed at the sound of voices and tramping feet.

Anticipation swelled in her breast as Rand dismounted. A sweat-stained tunic clung to his brawny shoulders and arms; a broad smile of greeting lit his face as he approached. The late afternoon sun haloed him with gold.

"How fares my lady?" he asked.

Lianna smiled. "She fares well, my lord."

"And my little warrior?" he boomed, taking the child and swinging him gently in the air. Aimery crowed with delight.

"He's been fretful with teething," Lianna confessed.

"Have you thought more on a wet nurse?" Rand grinned. "I'd not have him biting you on a tender spot."

She lowered her eyes. Even now guilt plagued her when she remembered her reluctance to bring Aimery into the world. "I'll care for him myself," she vowed, and reached for a chubby fist. "His grip is tenacious as a terrier's jaw," she said, laughing. "Thank God he hasn't a temper to match."

She leaned up to kiss Rand's cheek. The salty warmth of his flesh sent desire rippling through her. Aimery's arrival had changed their routine. Hours of leisurely lovemaking had become but wistful memories; they now contented themselves with quick, impassioned couplings, inevitably interrupted by their demanding son. She gave the baby a patient smile.

"I thought to take a ride this evening," said Rand, interrupting her thoughts. "Charbu is in need of exercising." He moved his lips over the soft golden fuzz of the baby's hair. "One day you'll be astride a percheron of the best Norman bloodstock," he told his son gravely.

Lianna laughed. "I'd as lief wean him first."

Rand reached out, caressed her milk-swollen bosom until she blushed. "As to that, the sooner the better." He gave her the baby, bent, and pressed his lips to hers. "I'd best go wash the sweat off me. I wouldn't want to offend Charbu."

"Shall I bathe you?" she asked teasingly.

He lifted one eyebrow. "If you do, I'd as soon forget the ride, or settle for one of a different kind."

She glanced at the westering sun. "'Tis the hour of the woodcock's flight." A thread of yearning underlay her words.

"Will you come along?" asked Rand. "You've not sat a horse since before Aimery's arrival."

She sighed. Her lying-in had been long, her recovery from the birth longer. The baby tugged at her braid. Reluctantly she said, "He'll be crying for his dinner soon."

Rand looked disappointed, yet his smile softened with understanding. "I'll take Jack, then, if I can entice him away from his nightly gambling. He did say he wanted to speak to me on a matter." He kissed her again and strode inside.

She stayed on the steps, smelling the ripening apples in the orchard, hearing the lazy hum of bees in the arbor. A warm contentment stole over her, a sense of belonging. She found the role of wife and mother unexpectedly agreeable; with frightening ease she ignored the fact that, this very month, King Henry had formally declared war on France.

Presently Rand emerged, in a fresh tunic, his hair wet and gleaming. He stopped to take another kiss from Lianna, to give one to the baby, then strolled, whistling, toward the stables.

She stared after him, wishing for once that her maternal duties didn't bind her to the castle.

"I'll take our little Aimery," said Macée, stepping from the hall. "Go, Lianna."

Lianna handed the baby to her. "Am I that obvious?"

Macée nodded, bent to coo affectionately at the child, and looked up. "I know a woman's longing when I see it," she said.

"Oh, Macée." Lianna put her hand on the other woman's shoulder. "You do miss Gervais terribly, don't you?"

Macée's raven hair contrasted with the translucent down of the child. "He's refused to send a *sauf-conduit* to bring me to Maisoncelles. Sometimes I've half a mind to . . ." Her lip trembled. "I'm sure he had his reasons."

Aye, reasons like the wenches he undoubtedly kept, or perhaps even ladies of the dauphin's entourage. Gervais's status with the king's son had diminished since the failed attempt to seize Bois-Long, but Gervais had not given up trying to win support. The dauphin, captain-general of the military, was conducting a progress to marshal troops to protect against the imminent English invasion. Gervais, bent on revenge, followed Louis and at present was in the town of Maisoncelles, some forty miles to the north.

As if seeking comfort, Macée hugged Aimery. "It is easy to hate Gervais for ignoring me. Yet I long for him. . . ." She snapped her fingers. "Damn him, he has the power to make me forget I ever had cause to resent him at all."

Once Lianna would have found such an attitude weak, incomprehensible. Yet now that she'd tasted love, unreasoning passion, and the deep, abiding joy of motherhood, she knew the emotional power one person could hold over another.

The baby grasped Macée's hair in his fist. Laughing, she said, "Why not go riding with your husband?"

Longing tugged at Lianna. "No, Macée. I mislike leaving the baby, even for a short time."

"St. Appolonia's teeth," said Bonne, appearing at her side, wiping her hands on her apron, "I never thought you'd turn out to be such a mother hen, my lady."

"He needs me."

Bonne's stare, heavy with meaning, settled over Lianna. "There is another who needs you, too."

Lianna knew it well. She scowled at Bonne for pointing it out. "Aimery will crave nursing—"

"Nursing!" Mère Brûlot, too, stepped from the hall. "He's sprouted his first tooth. Time enough for a man's meal of oat porridge."

Grinning, Lianna shook her head. "The three of you have been plotting against me."

Bonne said, "You weary of playing the doting mother."

"Never, I—"

"You hold him to your breast, yet your eyes follow the men out to the fields. You dangle baubles for him to play with, yet your hands itch for your pen. You walk the floors with little Aimery, but betimes I think you'd rather walk the battlements with Chiang, discussing your gunner's arts."

Mère Brûlot said, "You are a fine mother. But you are chatelaine and baroness, too."

Torn, Lianna touched her chin. "But—"

"Go on," Macée urged. "Your palfrey will think you are a stranger." The baby chortled and reached for Macée's earbob. "You see," said Macée, "the little one's content with me."

Looking at Aimery, in his glory amid a bevy of admirers, Lianna could not deny the truth. She kissed him, inhaling his sweet, babyish scent, then hurried off to the stables. She stopped in the doorway, captivated by the sight of her husband.

Rand stood to one side of his big, dappled horse, and watched while an eager young groom struggled beneath the weight of a saddle. Jack stood holding the bridle of another mount. He grinned indulgently at the youngster's struggles.

As the boy slung the saddle over the horse's back, Rand

reached out surreptitiously to help. His hand, unseen by the industrious lad, pulled on the girth to ease the cinching of the saddle. Jack and Rand exchanged a wink.

Proudly the boy stepped back. "All's ready, my lord," he piped, folding his skinny arms over his chest.

"And a good job you've made of it," said Rand. He looked at Jack. "Are we ready, then?"

Affection simmered in Lianna's heart as she stepped from the shadowed doorway. "Not quite," she said softly.

Surprise and pleasure lit Rand's face. "Hello, love."

She inclined her head, then addressed the groom. "Saddle my palfrey. I ride with my lord today." She turned to Jack and said in English, "That is, if you don't mind my company."

Jack's face split into a wide smile. "I believe I'll entrust the baron to his lady. I'll find a way to keep myself busy."

Rand lifted an eyebrow. "Wenching . . . or gambling?"

Jack puffed out his chest. "If you please, my lord. You know the former is no longer my occupation. And as for the latter, well, I've no need to gamble, not anymore."

"You don't sound like the Jack Cade I know."

To Lianna's vast amazement, Jack blushed. Deeply, to his ears. Looking down, he shuffled his feet. He removed a tattered drawstring purse and held it out. "It's taken me months, but there you have it."

Rand took the purse and emptied it into his palm. The dim light glinted off a handful of gold nobles and silver francs.

"Is this some riddle?" asked Rand.

"It's the marchet fee. I wish to marry, my lord, and there's your marriage boon."

Lianna gasped. "Bonne?"

Jack grinned. "Aye."

Lianna thought of her blithe, pretty maid, whose penchant for men had made her popular. Would Bonne be content with one mate, and an Englishman at that? "She's agreed to this?"

Jack chuckled. "She demands it, my lady."

Rand replaced the coins in the purse and clapped Jack on the shoulder. "I know not what to say. I never thought you the marrying type."

Jack swallowed. His ruddy face softened into solemn, earnest lines. "All my life I claimed to be seeking a woman I could die for." He stared at his hands, the left one covering the mangled one. "Bonne is not a woman to die for." He faced them squarely, almost defiantly. "She is one to live for."

Rand stood silent for a moment. Looking into his eyes, Lianna saw deep affection for Jack.

"Surely you understand," Jack rushed on. "You, too, nigh made the mistake of choosing the wrong woman. Had King Henry not sent you on your quest, you'd have found yourself wed to that psalm-singing Justine."

"Who is Justine?" Propelled by a chill gust of jealousy, the question leaped from Lianna's lips.

All expression left Rand's face. Jack shrugged. "His childhood love, if you could call her that."

Lianna's cheeks burned. Rand had never spoken of this Justine, whom he'd forsaken at King Henry's order. Questions swirled through her mind, but pride kept her silent.

Still expressionless, Rand thrust the purse at Jack.

Aghast, Jack demanded, "Do you refuse me in this?"

"No. But I refuse the boon." He smiled. "Use your ill-gotten coin to buy a pretty dress for your lady fair. And tell Batsford to start reading the banns on the morrow."

Jack took the purse and held Rand with a look so warm and thankful that Rand scowled. "Save your cow eyes for Bonne," he said gruffly. "Begone, Jack. I would ride out with my lady."

With a shout of elation, Jack left the stables. The groom had finished cinching the saddle on Lianna's ivory palfrey.

As Rand helped her mount, she resisted the questions that tore at her, merely said, "Well. Are we all to be seduced by Englishmen?" She spoke jokingly, but a prickle of nervousness touched her. She yearned to belong wholly to Rand. Yet a small, cold voice warned her not to forget her objective—to convince him to embrace the cause of France.

"'Tis how whole kingdoms are conquered," he said, laughing. "One province by one."

They left the château at a gallop. There was no communication between them; there didn't need to be. They both knew where they were going.

A hush hovered over the place of St. Cuthbert's cross. Blossoming blue flax and lavender wild lilies breathed a fine perfume into the air. Sunlight, touched by the orange fire of evening, slid in long shafts between the leaf-laden branches of ancient oaks and swaying willows.

The cross stood, a stony sentinel framed by high summer splendor. The sight, so laden with memories, set Lianna's heart to tripping. Rand dismounted and helped her down.

He tethered the horses, then turned and held out his arms. Instantly she found herself wrapped in his embrace, surrounded by his strength, his scent, the tender, wordless emotions that seemed to emanate from him.

"It's been so long, Lianna," he said at length, his voice muffled by her hair.

She nodded, his coarse-spun working tunic rough beneath her cheek. "Yet you've never complained."

He smiled against her temple. "How could I, when I saw how consumed you were with nursing and coddling our babe?" He tucked his hand beneath her chin, tilted her face up to his. "The brief, bright flares of our couplings sustained me. Still, I do not deny that I've wanted to love you long, uninterrupted. . . ." He kissed her. The unhurried caress of his mouth on hers, the taste of him, the firmness of his arms around her, fanned her desire until she burned for him.

When he finally lifted his lips from hers, he was smiling. "You had me worried, wife."

Anxiety chilled her passion. She lived in daily fear that he would one day guess her objective. Tilting her head to one side, she affected a playful tone. "Worried?"

"I thought I'd never have you alone again."

Relief revived her desire. Smiling, she slowly began to unlace his tunic. "You thought amiss, my lord."

"I'm glad," he said, bending low to press his lips to the side of her neck. "I'm glad, *pucelle*."

The familiar pet name washed over her like sunshine. With a cry of joy, she threw her arms around his neck and kissed him with fierce, sensual abandon. Her tongue plundered the moist velvet of his mouth, rediscovering secrets he'd taught her so long ago. She moved her hands down his back, tracing the firmness of his muscles. Nearly overcome by the scorching kiss, she pulled away and shed her clothes quickly.

Breathing fast, Rand did the same. But when they

reclined in the soft grass and she clutched him to her, he drew back.

"*Doucement*. I would make love to you at leisure. Who knows when our son will next grant us the chance?"

Each slow caress was a promise, each lingering kiss a pledge of imminent fulfillment. Her insides aflame, Lianna melted willingly into a world of sensation, a world devoid of political intrigue, domestic duties, and demanding babies. Their heated flesh became one, Rand moved sensuously within her and enclosed her with light and scent. Passion crested and broke, first shattering her heart and then making it whole again, brimming with love.

Aye, love, she thought as her body sang to the tune stroked by his tender fingers, and at that moment it was true. For at that moment no doubts touched her, no foreboding about the future assailed her.

As they lay in a soft mist of afterlove, their bodies burnished by the lowering sun, she saw him as a man, not an English knight; a husband, not a foreign invader. Gazing into his calm green eyes, she recognized a gentle glow of adoration, and love-words filled her throat.

She opened her mouth to speak, but he kissed her again, weaving magic around her senses, leaving her mute with wonderment. Only when her body recovered from their loving did she force herself to face the problems he'd nearly made her forget.

Her purpose was to play the siren, not the hapless sailor trapped by a sensuous song. She was in danger of falling victim to the very spell she sought to cast. If she came to love this man too much, she might be lulled into being the compliant Englishman's wife. Blinded by emotion, she might not have the strength to draw Rand away from

King Henry. Yet she must do so—for the sake of her home, for France, for Rand himself. If he clung to an English victory, his dreams would be shattered when the French smashed Henry's army back across the Narrow Sea.

"Are you happy with the way of things?" she asked, folding her hands on his chest and cradling her chin in her hands.

He smiled and mussed her hair. "Supremely. Lianna, when we first met I saw you as bruised, hurting. That I can give you love brings me more happiness than I can say."

God, she adored him. "You'd not change a thing?"

He traced the outline of her torso with his big, warm hands. "I might ask for more time with you." His fingers crept up her thigh, seeking the damp curls there. "More times . . . like this."

"That can be arranged. I've discovered a wealth of eager nursemaids." She leaned up to nibble at his ear. "But otherwise?"

"Otherwise I'd change nary a thing."

She dared push him no further. She sighed and bent to trace his chest with her tongue, tasting him, tasting hope. Tonight he belonged to her, not King Henry, and when the time came, she prayed Rand would favor her.

Hours later, the light of a big summer moon guided them back to the château. Listening to the call of a nightingale, the hoot of an owl, they moved beneath the thick, twisted arms of giant oaks, between the sighing fronds of willows. The river slipped peacefully beneath the causeway, and for the first time ever Lianna forgot to hug her mount and clutch the pommel in fear of the water. Rand's love wrapped around her heart, protecting her from doubt, from fear. Glancing at him, his body erect in the saddle, yet relaxed and sated, she smiled with gratitude. At times such as this she knew a contentment so deep it almost frightened her.

The great hall still buzzed with activity. A quick scan of the room told Lianna that Macée was not present. She was doubtless sitting with Aimery in the nursery.

Jack and Bonne stood surrounded by well-wishers. French and English toasts resounded as horned drinking vessels were lifted high in salutation. Jack's wide, proud smile and Bonne's flushed cheeks gave evidence of their joy.

Rand reached for Lianna's hand. "A fine match," he said, "though I'd never have suspected a French maid could tame my Jack." He laughed. "But then, I never thought a Frenchwoman would steal my heart, either."

Briefly, Lianna wondered about Justine again. She banished the thought. "Would you like something to eat?"

He glanced over at Jack and Bonne. "Let's leave them to celebrate, not steal their thunder."

Waving away a pair of servants, they left the hall and climbed the wide stone staircase to the upper galleries.

Lianna said, "This is the first night I've not seen to Aimery's bedtime myself."

Together they visited the small nursery adjacent to Lianna's solar. The room lay in stillness, the fire in the hearth banked.

A tiny flare of anxiety leaped in Lianna. Didn't Macée know she must sit with the baby? If he cried, no one below would hear him above the sounds of revelry.

Her head began to pound. She glanced at Rand, whose

face had gone taut. Skirting the moonlit form of a leathern chair, they approached the cradle. Lianna leaned down, moved the coverlet aside, and bent to see her son.

The cradle was empty.

Chapter 17

Lianna's world exploded. Glancing wildly at Rand, she saw her own awful terror and guilt mirrored in his eyes. "No," she said. "Please God, no." She pulled the baby's shawl out of the cradle, buried her face in the soft-woven wool, and inhaled the sweet scent of Aimery. She looked up at Rand. "Perhaps he was fretful. Perhaps Macée took him to her bed."

A look of quiet rage flashed over Rand's face as he led her to Macée's room. By the time he wrenched open the door to the chamber, fear had taken a firm grip on Lianna. She gasped. Her hands clenched like claws around the woolen shawl. The hearth was cold, the room empty, the bed unmussed.

Horror drilled a path to her heart. "Sweet Jesu."

Rand strode out of the room. "We'd best alert everyone." Dread and worry built as they pounded downstairs and dashed into the great hall. Lianna's breath came in short, terrified gasps.

Rand burst upon the feast, startling the revelers. "Macée and the baby are gone," he said.

Murmurs of disbelief rose to babbles of fright. Rand found Mère Brûlot, held her by the shoulders. The old woman shrank back. "My lord, she said she'd put him to bed herself. I never thought she'd—"

"When?" he demanded. "When did you see them last?"

Mère Brûlot hung her head. "Hours ago, my lord."

"God, if anything's happened to my son—" He broke off, the fury in his eyes more threatening than words.

Knights and damsels scurried in all directions. Lianna tugged at Rand's arm. "*Nom de Dieu,* we'll not find them here." Sobs ripped from her throat. "Sweet Mary, she's taken Aimery."

He held her tightly. "She'd not hurt him, Lianna. She loves the boy."

Eyes scorched by tears, she blinked at him. "Where?"

"Doubtless she's gone to Maisoncelles to find Gervais."

"Then why do we stay here?" she asked wildly. Together they bolted outside and across to the stables. Macée's favorite mount, a swift roan palfrey, was missing.

"Damn her to hell," Lianna wailed. "He's so little. He'll be cold. The ride will jostle him." She wrung her hands. "He'll need me...."

Rand gripped her shoulders. Behind him torches bobbed; men and castle folk rushed about the yard. "And you shall have him, Lianna, before the sun rises."

She clutched the front of his tunic. "I'm going."

He shook his head. "Go back to the hall."

"Nay, I cannot—"

He shook her hard. "Damn you, woman, can you not for once do my bidding? Think you I cannot find my own son?"

Momentarily stunned by his rough handling of her, she lowered her head. His eyes ablaze with determination, Rand walked off, bellowing orders to grooms and knights.

Lianna paused, but only for a moment. She put her hand over her madly pumping heart. Then, with a quick glance to be sure no one noticed, she knotted the shawl around her shoulders, grabbed a rusty knife from the wall, and led her palfrey into the darkened yard. Unnoticed by the men in the stables, she leaped astride and departed.

Maisoncelles lay forty miles to the north.

One thought hammered in her head. Aimery was gone; she must get him back. As the night-shrouded forest closed around her, she came to know the sound of true terror: the ringing, hissing sound in her ears, the rasp of disjointed prayers from her throat. Damp air sailed over her. She considered its effect on Aimery and urged her horse faster.

Before she'd traveled half a league, she heard a shout. Bending low over the neck of the palfrey, she pounded onward. With each explosive stride, her desperation built.

Low branches tore at her hair and plucked at the shawl knotted at her throat. The sinuous road, faintly lit by the summer moon, echoed with the frantic sounds of hoof-beats.

A horseman gained her side, angled his mount to bar the road, and drew rein. "Rand!" she gasped, and tried to maneuver around him, but he snatched her reins.

"Go back to the château, Lianna," he ordered.

His words were a meaningless jumble of sound. She

tried to jerk the reins from his hand. "Let me go. I'll not sit idle while my son is in danger." She pulled great gulps of air into her lungs, tightened her legs around the palfrey as the animal sidled and bumped against Rand's percheron.

Jack Cade galloped up. He showed no surprise at seeing her. "It's about time we caught up with her," he remarked.

She kept her angry, fearful eyes trained on Rand. "If you wish me to turn back, you'll have to force me."

He glanced at Jack, who shook his head. "Not I, my lord. No good comes from getting between a lioness and her cub." He eyed Lianna, who sat her palfrey with defiant strength. "She rides as well as most men."

Rand growled an oath. "Leave the task to me, Lianna. Have I not outwitted Gervais before, won two bloodless battles?"

She glared. "Macée has several hours' lead. You're wasting time arguing."

Swearing again, he dropped her reins and spurred his horse. Jack and Lianna followed.

The mounts devoured the distance at a bone-crunching pace. The bouncing made her milk-filled breasts sore. Tortured by images of Aimery being taken on the same jostling ride, Lianna set her jaw against a scream. They flew northward, crossing bridges over the rivers Authie and Ternoise. Night gave way to the dull gray of a fog-shrouded dawn. The forest thinned to cultivated fields. In the distance, the spires and walls of Maisoncelles etched the hazy horizon.

Nom de Dieu, thought Lianna, what can be Macée's purpose? Did she, in her barrenness, mean to claim Aimery for her own? Or worse, did she hope to earn Gervais's love by taking the child hostage? That her son might be part of some mad plan added a hideous edge to her terror.

Full of wariness and trepidation, the travelers approached the Porte de Blangy, the south gate to the city. Farmers and peasants, awaiting the trading day, eyed them curiously. Rand addressed the fat, sleepy gatekeeper. "Have you seen a woman, dark, riding a good horse? She had a babe with her."

The man blinked. "Not since I took my watch."

"Open the gate," he said. "We've urgent business within."

The gatekeeper shrugged indolently. "Nothing's so urgent it can't wait for the church clock to ring prime." He glanced at the sky. "Another twenty minutes—"

"Is too damned long," growled Rand. Shoving his hand into his tunic, he pulled out several silver *niquets* and tossed them at the man's feet.

Greed flashed brightly in the gatekeeper's eyes. He darted a look at the farmers and said regretfully, "I've strict orders. The Dauphin Louis bides within, and rules must be observed."

Lianna pushed forward. "Will you deny entrance to Burgundy's niece?" she demanded.

He looked startled, then said, "We're not a Burgundian town." And in that instant she felt the full impact of living in a France divided by warring nobles.

Glancing at Rand, she saw patience drain from her husband. His face darkened; his hand moved with unseen speed to the pommel of his sword. "You'll take my coin," he said with soft menace, "or you'll bear my steel."

The gatekeeper leaped to do his bidding.

"The dauphin, eh?" said Jack, looking about as they

rode toward the center of town. "Wonder what he's doing here?"

"Doubtless trying to drum up support to oppose Henry."

Lianna bristled but said nothing. Politics mattered not to her, not with Aimery in danger. Guilt, borne on a chill wind of recriminations, gusted through her. She should have known better than to think Macée had given up all loyalty to Gervais. She should never have entrusted the baby to her. And—God forgive them both—she and Rand should not have dallied the hours away making love.

After crossing several more grasping palms with silver coin, Rand learned the location of the lodging house where Gervais Mondragon kept rooms.

They found the house in a narrow, offal-strewn street. Morning fog twisted through the alley. Eyeing the crumbling, water-stained structure, Jack grumbled, "Mondragon's come down in the world since the pigs."

"He'll come down farther when I've had done with him," said Rand. He stopped his horse. Turning, he fixed Lianna with a gem-hard stare. "This time you will heed me." He gestured at a stone arch, overgrown with sweet-scented creeper vines. "Wait in that courtyard while we go inside. Keep the horses out of sight. They're too valuable to display."

She swallowed hard, nodded.

"Lianna . . ." He reached for her hand and squeezed it. "I want you to promise me something. If things go ill, you must ride with all speed for Calais."

"Calais! But it's another forty miles north, and an English stronghold at that." She tilted her chin up. "I'll go nowhere without my son, and I'll not ride into the arms of my enemy."

His expression fierce, he said, "Who is your enemy now, Lianna? The English, or the Frenchman who holds our son?"

She bit her lip.

"Promise me."

"I . . . Yes, my lord. I promise."

He kissed her hard. She tasted the salt of her own tears and wondered when she'd begun crying. "Have a care, Rand," she said tremulously. "And bring back our son."

His smile seemed forced, but the tender look in his eyes comforted her. "I shall," he said.

Daggers drawn, Rand and Jack approached the house. The chained power of rage and fear tautened Rand's muscles, overcame the weariness of his nightlong ride. He strode to the door, tried the latch, and found it bolted. A powerful kick splintered the old boards and rusting iron.

He and Jack stepped into gloomy silence. The odor of a dead fire and stale beer pervaded the air. Casting his eyes over dark corners, rickety steps, and an ash-strewn hearth, Rand saw no sign of Gervais, nor heard a baby's cries.

Yet his warrior's instincts warned him of danger. The air smelled of old wine and desperation. The back of his neck itched. Scarcely daring to draw breath, he tightened his hold on his sword hilt.

An infantile whimper drifted from the back of the house. The sound wrapped around his heart and fired his blood. Moving carefully so as not to spin his spurs, he walked to the ladder.

To his right, shadows flickered. To his left, a sword

rasped from a sheath; metal flashed. Rand moved to lunge.

The cold steel of a pair of blades formed a cross at his throat. He froze. From the corner of his eye he saw two burly men pressing Jack against the wall.

"Welcome, my Lord of Longwood," said the venom-laden voice of Gervais Mondragon. "We've been expecting you."

Her heart lodged in her throat, Lianna waited beneath the weatherworn archway. She longed to edge closer but dared not leave the horses. Time dragged; each passing second stretched her nerves to an intolerable limit. Were Gervais and Macée alone with the baby? She prayed they were.

But Gervais had left Bois-Long with a war-horse and a suit of Florentine armor. The trappings of a knight were worth a small fortune, enough to hire rough mercenaries.

Lianna's stomach churned. Bent on indulging their lust, she and Rand had given Macée plenty of time to plan her flight. She could have pilfered the coffers of the treasury. Or, with Bonne busy celebrating her betrothal to Jack, Macée might even have helped herself to Lianna's own jewels.

Battling an upsurge of anger and dread, she fought the impulse to march down the street and into the house. That Gervais and Macée had absconded with riches meant nothing compared to the priceless treasure they'd stolen. Lianna wove her fingers into the fabric of the shawl. They'd taken Aimery.

To keep from sinking into despair, she tried to focus on the activity of the awakening town. Women threw open shutters and called to one another across the alleys. Costermongers wheeled carts through the streets, singing the praises of their fresh vegetables. A man reeled from a tavern and paused to urinate against a house. Scolding, a crone in the window above doused him with a bucket of water. The drunkard shook his fist and ambled away. Children spilled from the houses, chasing hoops or balls. Lianna strained to hear Aimery's cries.

She heard the metallic clink of spurs instead. Fearful, she craned her neck to peer over a furrier's pelt-laden cart. Two knights approached. Please God, not now, she thought.

Their *cottes d'armes* bore the gold fleur-de-lis, and their plumes were dyed a deep, rich blue. The costume marked them as royal knights of the House of Valois.

She shrank into the lee of the archway. A year ago the sight of French soldiers would have filled her with hope and confidence. But now she saw them through distrustful eyes, eyes that probed beneath the colorful trappings and cocky gait. These men had the hard mouths and ruthless air of soldiers accustomed to extorting respect through bullying.

Their searching eyes found her. Rand's warning about the horses rang in her ears. She stepped out into the street.

The first to reach her was a rough-featured man of middle years, with sparse gray hair and narrow eyes. The other might have been near her own age. Yet little youthfulness clung to him; the flesh of his jowls hung loose about a cynical, dissipated face. He looked as though he'd been up all night.

Pretending to lower her eyes, she watched the men through the pale skirts of her lashes.

"Good morrow, demoiselle." She was surprised that the younger man spoke first rather than deferring to his elder.

"Good morrow." She dropped to a half curtsy.

"Lower, demoiselle," the older man snapped. "Would you insult your dauphin?"

Her eyes gaped wide. She stared at the Dauphin Louis in mingled awe and disappointment. This overweight, cynical young man was heir to the throne of France?

"Well?" grumbled the knight.

She sank into the deep obeisance reserved for those of highest royal rank.

"Rise, demoiselle."

He spoke through his nose, yet thick, unattractive lips muffled his words. Louis's voice, she thought as she stood, hardly suited a prince royal. "God save the dauphin," muttered a passerby. Louis puffed out his chest.

"She has manners enough, after prodding," said the knight. He subjected her to slow, narrow-eyed scrutiny. "And looks, too, Your Grace. Shall we bring her along for bed sport? God knows there's little else to do in this puny town."

Her hand strayed beneath the shawl, fingers wrapping around the knife in her belt. She stood motionless, battling a fresh surge of fear for the baby, for Rand, and now for herself.

"Not just looks," said the dauphin, considering her lazily "but a rare and true beauty. What is your name?"

"Bel . . . Lianna."

"Speak up, girl."

"Lianna, from the town of Blangy." The dauphin knew of Aimery the warrior, for bards still sang of the deeds of her father. And—yet another warning stole into her mind—Louis was married to Margaret, Burgundy's daughter and Lianna's cousin. After the sham peace at Arras, the dauphin would not be kindly disposed to a Burgundian.

His opaque eyes shuttered whatever thoughts he might be having. "You've the look of a *pucelle de campagne* about you," he said.

Grateful for her homespun smock and age-worn shawl, she nodded. "I am but a simple country maid." Almost without thought she imbued her words with a peasant's drawl.

"Your first visit to Maisoncelles?"

"Aye, Your Grace."

Louis glanced at his companion. "Perhaps, then, we should be certain your visit is a pleasant one."

A high, thin wail pierced the air. Lianna lurched forward; the dauphin gripped her arm. "Not so fast, girl."

Her gaze snapped to the tall, narrow house down the street. The broken door framed Jack Cade, who stumbled out, clutching a swaddled infant in his arms.

Dense crimson blood stained Jack from throat to thigh.

Lianna screamed. Ignoring the dauphin's harsh inquiry, she wrenched from his grasp and raced down the street.

She yanked the howling baby from his arms. Frantically she checked Aimery to be sure he was unhurt. His little fist batted at her chin. The blood, she realized, was Jack's. An intolerable mixture of relief and terror rushed over her.

"Jack, where is Rand?" She tried to peer into the house but saw only darkness and a low, open doorway in the back.

His face gray, he sagged against the door frame. "My lady . . . you must . . . away. . . ."

"Rand—"

"No . . . hope." Jack's words sounded as faint as a wisp of fog. "Rand held them off long enough for me to take the child and run. One life for two. Save . . . yourself and the boy." Blood trickled from the corner of his mouth. "Horses . . ."

"What is amiss, demoiselle?" The Dauphin Louis had appeared behind her. He took one look at Jack and his face paled. He drew his sword and stalked into the house, followed by his companion.

Lianna started after him. Jack grabbed her arm. "No," he pleaded. "When they see . . . *that*, our lives will be forfeit."

"But Rand—"

"No, goddamn it!"

The oath, bellowed in defiance of his body's weakness, jolted a chilling awareness through her. She knew then that Rand was dead. And she knew his death would be for naught if she did not seize the chance to flee.

Leaving a piece of her soul behind, she half dragged Jack to the horses. The baby still cried. By the time they reached the courtyard, Jack could no longer speak, could only curse in brief bursts of sound. He batted her hand away when she tried to stanch his wounds—a deep cut to his shoulder, a split lip.

"Go . . ." he choked. "Cal . . . Calais." He nodded up the street at the Porte de Calais.

"I want to go home," she whispered.

"Home . . . isn't safe," Jack rasped. "You told Rand, you vowed. . . ."

"Yes," she forced out. "I'll keep my final vow to him. But you must come with me, Jack."

"I've another road to travel." He stumbled to his horse. "I promised Rand. . . . You take his horse."

"What promise?" she demanded.

"To return to Bois-Long . . . hold the ford for Henry."

For over a year she'd labored to prevent that. Yet now it didn't seem to matter; nothing did.

Shouts rang from the street. Goaded by urgency, she ceased arguing with Jack. He allowed her to help him onto his horse. Clutching at the pommel, he rode back to the south.

Her mind numb, her hands shaking, she knotted her shawl into a sling for the baby, mounted, and lifted the reins.

She stopped in midmotion. Rand's big horse stood placidly by a cistern. She tried not to imagine Rand as she'd last seen him—strong, vital, determined to get his son back. Yielding to such visions was to embrace uncontrollable agony. The baby keened loudly. She had not the luxury of time for despair.

She leaned down from the saddle, took Charbu's reins, and led him from the courtyard. Aimery calmed and stopped crying, but Lianna's nerves screamed with tension. The Calais gate lay to the right; to reach it she'd have to pass the house where Rand had died.

Pray God the dauphin and his man had left. Her eyes trained on the broken door, she started up the street.

Paler than ever, the dauphin appeared in the doorway. A crowd milled, exclaiming over the pool of blood on the stoop. Two beggars haggled over a blood-soaked tabard. Horrified, she recognized the white-and-gold cloth of Rand's *cotte d'armes*.

Her heart in her mouth, she watched Louis's eyes take in the horse she rode, the percheron she led, the child, the stains of Jack's blood on her shawl.

He lifted his arm and seemed about to speak.

"Oh, please, Your Grace, detain me not." The plea fell from her lips.

The king's son stared at her for a measureless span of time. Then, in an unexpected and unspoken leap of agreement, he jerked his head in the direction of the Porte de Calais.

Witch, they called her in Agincourt. Sorceress, madwoman, they said in St.-Omer. The villagers of Ardres dubbed her a pale gypsy. No woman of virtue would travel alone in such a bedraggled state. No sane female would chase off, with such lethal ferocity, those who admired her horses. Surely, proclaimed the wagging tongues of all she passed, surely this stranger had been stricken by the darkest face of the moon. Bunches of garlic, wreaths of bitter vetches, charms to ward off the evil eye, appeared on the doors of the houses she passed.

Wrapped in a dense mist of shock and agony, Lianna drove her horses at a merciless pace. Heedless of what was being said of her, heedless of all save the need to protect her son, she pushed the mounts until exhaustion nigh claimed them both.

The sentry at the south gate of Calais clearly didn't believe she was the Baroness of Longwood, but fear and pity compelled him to let her enter.

The city of Calais, batted for decades between England and France, was a curious mixture of both cultures. French peasants sold wares to English soldiers; all spoke in an odd bastard tongue of randomly combined English, French, and Latin.

The Earl of Warwick lived in the warden's palace near the center of town.

Warwick's sergeant-at-arms eyed her with open distaste. "Begone, demoiselle. You've no business at the palace."

Bone-weary, numb with grief, and slightly stunned that she was actually turning to an Englishman for help, she said, "Tell the earl that the Baroness of Longwood wishes to see him."

The officer stared.

"Do you not know the name?"

"I know that Enguerrand of Longwood defeated the Sire de Gaucourt and took Château Bois-Long in a single afternoon, and without shedding a drop of blood. I know that later he foiled a siege of starvation." He spoke with hushed reverence.

"Would you then deny entry to his wid—" Her voice caught on the word. She swallowed hard. "His wife?"

His gaze probed her weary face, bloodstained clothes, the sleeping infant in her arms. Reaching into her girdle, she removed her knife and handed it to him. "I mean no harm."

He nodded curtly. "The earl will see you. But not in that condition."

She sent him a weak smile of gratitude.

Attended by two maids who fussed over her and the baby, Lianna bathed, nursed Aimery, and donned a borrowed gown of blue linen. One of the maids offered to tend the child while Lianna visited the warden.

Hugging Aimery protectively, she demurred. "I'll keep him at my side."

Carrying the milk-drowsed baby, she followed an attendant to Warwick's chambers. As they walked beneath a cloister, they encountered a tall blond knight who in passing reminded her so poignantly of Rand that her composure nearly collapsed.

Not now, she told herself sternly. Sheer force of will had kept her from complete despair. That, and a deep, painful determination to honor Rand by protecting his son.

Richard de Beauchamp, Earl of Warwick and Warden of Calais, rose to greet her. Merry, intelligent eyes studied her as he took her hand to raise her from her curtsy.

"My sergeant-at-arms warned me to expect an awkward, beggarly girl."

"I'm sure that's exactly how I looked, my lord Beauchamp. I've been traveling since late last night."

He gazed fondly at the infant, who had been lulled back to sleep by the long walk through the palace.

"I'd heard Longwood had an heir."

Maternal pride surged in her. "Aye, we were blessed."

Warwick took her hand. "Come. I'd not have you standing there swaying from exhaustion." He led her to a dais furnished with a table and chairs. A servitor brought wine and bread.

She sipped the wine but found no appetite for the bread. "I need your protection, my lord."

"From . . . ?"

"Gervais Mondragon. His wife took my son to Maisoncelles, and . . . gave him to Gervais. Rand fought him. . . ." Like a shroud, an image of the bloodied tabard settled over her.

"Good God, you left Bois-Long unprotected?"

She thought of the deep river and high walls of the

château, of Chiang and his guns. "It's secure...for a time."

"Your husband...?" Warwick spoke gently, as if he'd guessed the truth and were loath to force her to speak of Rand.

"Gervais and his hirelings killed him." As she related the story of the fight at Maisoncelles, her voice sounded hollow. Her eyes were dry, and she realized that all through her forty-mile ride she hadn't cried for Rand. Tears could not begin to express the horror and grief of losing the man she loved.

Warwick closed his eyes, sucked in his breath, then expelled it in a long, weary sigh. "Henry and all England will suffer the loss," he said. "I am deeply sorry, my lady."

"I wish to return home," she said, her voice thin with longing. "But I cannot travel without an escort. Gervais is certain to be looking for me."

Warwick's mouth drooped slightly. "You know not how much you ask, my lady."

"Surely you can spare a few men—"

"I cannot." Pain and vexation flickered in his eyes. "Calais is but an island in a hostile sea. It is all I can do to hold the city against the tide of French armies. The dauphin, Boucicaut, and d'Albret are marshaling the nobles of France to foil King Henry. To send even a handful of men from the garrison would lay the city open to attack."

"I am an Englishman's wife," Lianna said with a pride she'd never thought to feel. "Surely you will honor my husband by escorting me home."

"My lady, what you fail to understand is that Calais is but one corner of an empire that spans from Ireland to Aquitaine. I cannot risk dividing my forces."

"Then I shall risk the journey alone," she stated, and started to rise.

He covered her hand with his. His palm felt warm, slightly damp. "Wait, my lady. I did not say I won't help you, only that I cannot give you an escort."

She stayed seated but regarded him suspiciously.

"I'll see that you're taken home by sea. Supply ships arrive regularly from England. I'll persuade one of the captains to take you to the mouth of the Somme."

Fear exploded in her. She could barely countenance a row across a moat. "Nay."

"But a journey by sea is far safer and—"

"I will not sail, my lord," said Lianna. The mere thought of a voyage on the vast, churning Narrow Sea set her insides to quaking. She hid the shame of her terror behind a facade of anger. "I will travel overland—by myself if I must."

Looking baffled and annoyed, Warwick said, "I beg you, my lady, to consider my offer. If you are so determined to return to your home, why do you refuse this logical solution?"

Her fear was not logical. Yet she could no more combat it than she could change the direction of the tides. Even the bitterness of self-disgust could not change her mind.

"I simply . . . cannot take ship, my lord."

His lips tightened in annoyance. "Not even if it means a safe, timely return to your home, your son's home? The home your husband fought for, the child he died for?"

In that she found her strength. In love. It was the one thing more powerful than her dread of water. She knew then that she could—she would—board an English ship and take her son home. With her love for Rand as her talisman, she would conquer her fear.

Grief and gratitude flooded through her. Oh, Rand, she thought, if only you knew how strong my love for you has made me. Regret nipped at the heels of that thought. If only I'd told you about it.

She faced Warwick through a haze of sorrow. "Very well, my lord," she said quietly, "I will sail to Bois-Long."

During the week of waiting for an English vessel to appear, Lianna enclosed herself in a tight cocoon of misery. Although treated as an honored guest in the warden's residence, she kept to herself. Hours crept by as she sat with the baby by a solar window, looked past the thatched or slated rooftops of the town, and stared at the gray, changeless Narrow Sea.

Rumors of King Henry's invasion trickled through the residence. He was at this moment marshaling his forces at Southampton. Lianna listened to the gossip with unfeeling detachment. Rand, sent by Henry to hold the ford at Bois-Long, was dead. The pretender would not find Rand's widow so obedient.

An attendant came one morning to tell her that an English ship had arrived and that the captain had agreed to take her to the Somme. In another hour someone would fetch her and the baby. She glanced down at Aimery, asleep in the wooden box that served as his cradle. Soon she would be home. The thought made her feel painfully empty.

Despite the detachment she deliberately cultivated, fragmented images drove like flaming arrows into her mind.

Rand, a godlike, unconquerable figure towering over her that first day they'd met. *Don't be afraid of me, pucelle. . . .*

Rand, his face opening into that magical, mesmerizing smile. *I think I love you.*

Rand, seated beneath a canopy of budding larch boughs, a baby rabbit nestled in his big hand. *I'd break a hundred lances if the deed could banish the sadness from your eyes.*

Rand, his face a study of solemn disapproval of her gunnery. *Honor and humanity will never be outmoded, Lianna.*

Rand, bestowing deep, searching kisses. *I want to fuse my soul with yours, Lianna, to make you forget where you end and I begin.*

Dry-eyed, she embraced the past. She longed for the damp comfort of tears to salve her shattered soul. Instead she sat staring out the window, wrapping herself in memories and misery.

"Lianna . . ."

The whispered word sounded so real that she felt certain her mind had finally come unstrung.

Only when she heard her name a second time did she dare to believe the voice was not the product of her fevered longing.

She turned.

He smiled.

In one sweeping glance she took in the tattered, blood-stained figure in the doorway. With one exultant movement she jumped up and ran to him.

"*Rand!*"

Chapter 18

"**I** can't do it." Lianna's eyes darted to the steep gangplank, towering masts, and fluttering sails of the English cog *Bonaventure*. As she watched her palfrey and Rand's percheron being led up a plank into the ship's hull, her mind rebelled against stepping aboard.

"Lianna, my sweet, you must." Rand pressed his lips to Aimery's head. An hour after his miraculous reappearance, he seemed much more himself—clean-shaven, hale, and strong. Yet shadows still hovered beneath his eyes, a slight limp corrupted his gait, his body appeared leaner, harder, carved by a close brush with death.

"It's the only way to return safely," he said.

Scarcely daring to believe he'd come back to her, she clung to him. "Please, Rand, we can ride to Bois-Long. You'll keep us safe, I know you'll—"

"You've too much confidence in me, Lianna." He cradled both her and the sleeping baby in his arms. "The villages between Calais and the Somme are rife with French armed parties. By now Gervais must have realized his foolishness in leaving me for dead. He and his hirelings are likely combing the countryside for us."

Her hands gripped the fabric of his tunic. "I'm afraid to take ship. You know of my fear and the reason for it."

He brushed his lips over her brow. "I know, love. Yet you were willing to sail in spite of your fear—Warwick told me so. You would have faced down your fear to honor my memory. Will you do less for me now that you know I'm alive?"

An unspoken question flowed beneath his words. He was asking for more than her agreement. He was asking her to abandon a fear of a lifetime to prove her love.

"I'll go," she said faintly. Her throat tight, her hand clutching Rand's arm, she trod the narrow plank leading on board. Feeling sick, she kept her eyes from the shifting water, closed her ears to the hiss of sand-heavy waves.

Minutes later they sat together in a cramped cabin in the high sterncastle. The baby napped on a narrow bunk while Lianna perched at the edge, her fingers clenched into the homespun ticking of the pallet.

Fear churned beneath the surface of her hard-won composure. The cog shifted gently, inevitably, and her terror nearly boiled over. Dark images stole into her mind— images of her mother's swollen, waterlogged face.

She tensed; Rand clasped her tightly. As if sensing her frantic thoughts, he pressed his lips to her temple.

"Your face is as white as bleached linens."

She turned her face to his chest, inhaling the scent of sun and wind that clung to him. "Perhaps I'd not notice so much if you told me all that's happened these eight days."

She felt his grin against her temple. "This past hour you've seemed more interested in touching, not talking, wife."

A blush warmed her cheeks. "I dared not question how you survived." She pulled back and searched his face. Her stomach listed at the tenderness shimmering in his eyes. "Why did you—and Jack—allow me to believe you'd been killed?"

"Because you never would have fled to Calais without me. And because . . ." Grimacing, he flexed his injured leg. "My survival was hardly a certainty at the time. I only narrowly escaped capture because Gervais left me for dead. The Dauphin Louis did not find me in the house because I'd fled just seconds after Jack emerged with the baby."

"But I heard them say they'd found a dead man."

"One of Gervais's hirelings."

"Why didn't you follow me sooner?"

"It was all I could do to hide myself behind an ash heap at the back of the house. I couldn't have sat a horse."

The thought of him suffering made her voice tremble. "Then where did you go?"

Silent laughter shook him. "To a whorehouse."

She practically leaped out of his arms. "To a *what*?"

He laughed aloud then. "The ladies were quite skilled at nursing. And—God be thanked—they asked few questions."

She touched his bandaged thigh. "They dressed your wound well. I should be grateful." Yet she eyed him suspiciously.

"I was hardly in a condition to misbehave," he said.

"Still . . ." She'd heard of women who sold their favors, but she'd never met one. It was inconceivable that the act that between her and Rand seemed as solemn as a sacred rite could be performed for profit. "What were the ladies like?"

He shrugged. "As human as you or I. A bit more jaded, perhaps, a great deal more practical."

"I'm grateful," she said resolutely. "We must send them a boon for their kindness."

He chuckled. "That would be a most unexpected source of payment," he said, chuckling. Then he sobered. "What of Jack?"

"He rode for Bois-Long."

"Pray God he and Chiang will be able to defend the château should Gervais try anything," said Rand.

"Do you think Gervais will attack?"

"I know he wants to. But he'll need a small army, and I wonder if the dauphin will grant him that."

"Aye, Gervais has certainly diminished in Louis's esteem since the swine incident." She thought to tell Rand of her encounter with the dauphin, about the restraint Louis had shown in not foiling her escape.

But before she could speak, the sound of muffled thunder penetrated the cabin.

With a little shriek of terror, she fell against Rand. "Oh, please," she said, half to herself, "please, not a storm. I could not manage a storm."

The sound growled again. A heavy thud reverberated through the ship's timbers; shouts and a tattoo of running feet ensued. Through her panic, recognition niggled at her. "Cannon fire," she said.

Swearing, Rand took up the baby, folding the shawl over Aimery's head. The child awoke and whimpered as they scrambled through a hatch and emerged on deck.

"Clear the way," bellowed the first mate. He cursed, spied Lianna, and stopped short. The sailors, agog at having a noble lady aboard, paused to stare. "Beggin' yer pardon, my lord, my lady," said the mate. "But you'd best hie below. We be under attack."

Lianna's eyes fastened on the ship bearing down hard from the south. The red oriflamme of St. Denis and blue pennons bearing the lilies of France fluttered at the masthead. She recognized an eight-pointed gilt star adorning the capstan.

"I know that ship," she said.

Sparks and smoke belched from the vessel's broad side. A cannonball careened into the water, falling but a few yards short of the *Bonaventure*. An endless expanse of gale-whipped water stretched ahead. Her heart began to pound.

Rand and the first mate stared at her. "What is it, Lianna?" asked Rand.

"*L'Étoile de l'Est,*" she explained fearfully. "The *Eastern Star*. Remember, Chiang told us of it." She turned to the mate. "'Tis no common cog, but a war machine from the East. The French captured it when..." Her voice trailed off. The less said of Chiang's long-ago mission, the better.

"It's a French warship?" asked the mate.

"Yes," said Lianna. "And thanks to your king's declaration, England and France are at war."

The menacing round eyes of a dozen cannon peered from the ship's sides. "My lady," said the mate, "take the child and get below."

She reared back. "And be there when we sink? No more would I get below than I'd fly up into the rigging."

The warship's cannons spat another round of fire. She raised her voice above Aimery's wails. "Christ, she's a death ship. That's fifteen-pound shot. She'll make a sieve of this cog." She turned to Rand and hugged him, both their bodies curved protectively around the squalling infant.

"Give the spritsail a little sheet," bellowed the first mate. "Lay your backs into the tiller, lads. The enemy ship is weighted with bronze and lead. We can outrun her!"

Looking fearfully over Rand's shoulder, Lianna glanced at the setting sun. The huge golden orb lay dead ahead. "But we're sailing away from France," she protested.

"Damned right," answered the mate. He looked back at the *Eastern Star*. The warship drove toward them, plowing white crests aside so that the waves at her bow resembled a set of bared teeth. "We won't stop until we reach England."

Dazed and stumbling, Lianna clutched at Rand's arm and descended the gangplank. When her feet met English soil, she nearly crumpled from relief and despair. The French warship had chased them halfway across the Narrow Sea; a fierce gale had pushed the *Bonaventure* the rest of the way.

"Where . . . in the world are we?" she asked faintly.

Rand's mouth twisted in an ironic smile. "In West Sussex. Not ten miles from my boyhood home of Arundel."

"Holy Mary." His home, she thought, and looked at the sere meadows, the distant greening hills. This place had been Rand's home until he'd left to claim Bois-Long as his barony. She wondered if he hid a twinge of yearning behind that wide smile, those twinkling eyes.

"Aye." He glanced down at the baby in his arms. "It seems I've come full circle."

"Now what?"

"The captain won't hear of taking us back to France, not with the weather so bad and that unholy warship prowling the Narrow Sea." He looked around the sleepy fishing village, then at the planks astern, where sailors were busy guiding their horses out of the hold.

"We'll ride to Arundel," said Rand. "From there, I'll inquire about passage to Picardy."

"Beggin' your pardon, my lord." They turned to see an elderly man sitting at the wharf, his lap draped with a much-mended fishing net. A pair of bright blue eyes, framed by weather-beaten flesh, shone in the morning light. "I'd not be goin' to Arundel, not with a babe."

"Why not, sir?" asked Rand.

"There's plague in the village."

Instinctively Lianna moved closer to Rand and the baby. She touched Aimery's hand; his little fingers gripped hers with that strength that always surprised her.

"And you'll not find another ship 'twixt here and Portsmouth. Every worthy vessel's been commandeered to join the king's fleet at Southampton."

A study of the nearly deserted port confirmed the news. "Have Arundel and his knights gone?" Rand asked. The fisherman nodded.

"When do they sail?"

"A week hence, maybe."

Rand hesitated only a moment. "I must join them."

Fear and dismay twisted through Lianna. Oh, God, he

was going to war against France. "No," she said, "no, you cannot—"

"Elsewise we'd have to bide here for weeks, perhaps months."

Her hopes wavered. "Can we not find a trading vessel?"

He gestured at the sailors making their way to the village tavern. The seamen spoke animatedly among themselves. "Soon all merchants will have heard of the *Eastern Star*," Rand said. "None can match her guns."

"But we cannot take Aimery on a war fleet," she protested.

"Nor can I take my wife," he said gently.

She gasped. He gripped her shoulders. "You and the child must stay in England, while I go to France and Bois-Long."

"Never," she said immediately. "You cannot expect me to bide idle in England while my homeland is being invaded."

Tension thickened the air. He searched her face. "I've seen that formidable look before. Very well, you may come with me, but Aimery stays. We shall foster him."

Disdainfully she glanced at the tumbledown inn, the seedy town. "What do you mean, foster him?" she said indignantly. "I'll not let anyone here raise my child."

"I know of a convent." He held her with a steady gaze. "St. Agnes's. Justine Tiptoft is a novice there."

Lianna froze.

"Justine can foster the babe for a few weeks, until it is safe to bring him home."

Bells of denial clamored in Lianna's head. Give their child to Rand's former ladylove? "I will not leave him."

"I agree, 'tis folly. You'll both stay at St. Agnes's."

She bit her lip.

"I'm afraid we have no other choice," he said quietly. "Justine is a woman of good character."

"You would know," she snapped.

"Jealous?"

"Of course not."

"She'll care for the babe as her own."

As well he would have been her own, thought Lianna, had I not seduced a knight-errant in a spring glade. Always I am forced into an untenable position; always I must choose between two ills. Damn Henry, whose horror of being labeled a usurper's son made him blind to human emotion. Damn Burgundy, whose lust for power made even his niece a pawn in his hands. And damn Rand, for thinking his former love an apt nursemaid for their child. She forced her words past the grief and doubt clogging her throat. "I will meet this Justine Tiptoft."

Tense and unhappy, she took the baby and waited while Rand saddled their mounts. Then they set off to the west, skirting the castle and village of Arundel.

Rand breathed deeply of the familiar brine-scented air. A lifetime had passed since he'd last ridden this way, past wind-dried grasses and short, brushy trees. It seemed so much longer than a mere year and a half. The man who had once crossed these fields and fens was a different person from the man who now led his wife along the rock-studded road.

High in the north loomed the oak-topped knoll where he'd once sat with Justine, burying memories of war beneath the balm of his music and her gentle presence. Below the town lay the pond where he'd fished for perch, all the while listening to Justine reciting from her book of hours. They passed a hedgerow beneath which, as a fumbling, callow youth, he'd taken his first kiss from her.

Rand looked upon these things and felt . . . nothing. He sensed no kinship with that idealistic young man. So much had changed, and changed so wonderfully.

A cold tremor seized him when he recalled how he'd resisted the task the king had foisted on him. He'd nearly followed his heart, not his mind, and disobeyed Henry. He might never have met Lianna . . . and she would be under the Mondragons' influence.

Fondly he glanced down at the baby—heir to a castle Rand had never wanted—cradled in the crook of one arm, and then at his wife. She rode with a queenly air, head up, back stiff, eyes straight ahead. The attitude spoke volumes of the way she faced not just riding through a foreign land, but all of life. She was a fighter to her very heart, with a warrior's boldness and energy. Still, she embodied the best of a woman's innocence and simplicity. Pride and affection spilled through his veins and brought a smile to his lips.

Beyond Arundel lay a tiny roadside chapel built of chalky stone and roofed by thatch. Thoughtful hands had kept weeds and briars from growing over the burial place of his parents.

He drew rein and signaled for Lianna to do the same. "What is this place?" she asked. "'Tis well tended."

"I would have you see this," he said. He dismounted, helped her from her horse, and led her into the cool chapel. Bemused, Lianna took the baby from him and stood in the doorway while her eyes adjusted to the dimness.

A brass effigy bore the flat, serene images of a knight and his lady, their faces impassive, their fingers entwined.

Rand lit two candles, placed them in sconces near the altar, and knelt facing the effigies. Lianna moved to his side and stood watching him. In the flickering light, he was a study of a man of action at rest. His strong features, reflective now, were intensified by the extraordinary radiance in his eyes as his closed lips offered up a silent prayer. My husband, Lianna thought, swallowing the lump of emotion that had suddenly gathered in her throat, was no sinner cringing before God, but a nobleman communing with heaven. She touched his shoulder; he looked up at her.

"My parents," he said simply. "They used to ride out to this chapel to be together. I thought it a fitting place for their effigies."

She nodded. Putting out a finger, she traced the letters spelling out the name Marc de Beaumanoir and Anne Marne. "Your grandparents," she murmured to Aimery, who stared round-eyed at the candle flames. She touched the familiar motto that was etched on the brass: *A vaillans coeurs riens impossible.*

"'To valiant hearts nothing is impossible,'" she said softly. "Yet your father was nineteen years a prisoner at Arundel."

"His wedded wife would not ransom him."

"Why?" asked Lianna.

He shrugged. "She found a lover, had a child by him, and let the estate fall to the French Crown."

"But your father was a count, a landholder. Did he not yearn to return to Gascony, to reclaim what was his?"

Rand smiled. "He had something infinitely more precious here." His hand covered hers and carried it to the image of Anne Marne. "He had the woman he loved."

Lianna lowered her eyes. "They lived as man and wife?"

"For nigh on eighteen years. They died within months of each other."

She knelt in silence, absently stroking the baby's brow. A thought pushed into her mind. Marc gave up on his French wife, took an English lover. When the English were driven from France, might not Rand do the same? Swallowing hard, she banished the notion and forced herself to ask, "Have you missed Arundel?"

The solemn mood seemed to have left him. He grinned. "No, Lianna. Not since I met you. Nor will I ever."

His statement lifted her spirits. They left the chapel and rode on, reaching the convent of St. Agnes in late afternoon. A laywoman took their horses and bade them wait in the courtyard.

Dreadful anticipation gripped Lianna as she sat holding her child and waiting to meet Justine Tiptoft. A mouse, Jack Cade had called her. A girl, Rand had corrected. Lianna kept her eyes fastened on the cobbled surface of the yard while a nun went to summon Justine.

A soft, feminine voice and trills of childish laughter rang through the square.

Lianna looked up. A procession of children approached. In their midst walked a young woman wearing a coif that shaded a wide, pretty smile and bright, twinkling blue eyes. A breeze molded her gray habit against her generous curves.

Not a mouse, Lianna thought instantly. Nor yet a girl. Justine Tiptoft. Lianna's heart plummeted. So this was Justine. Justine, whom Rand had loved when the Demoiselle de Bois-Long was but a hated obligation.

Her gaze sought Rand. He wasn't looking at her. He smiled and held out his arms to Justine, who moved into his embrace with a familiar ease that turned Lianna's stomach to stone.

She's a novice, Lianna thought feverishly. She'll be a

bride of Christ; she has no hold on Rand. Still . . .

They kissed briefly. Lianna tried to tell herself it was a kiss of friendship. Rand stepped back, took Lianna's hand, and brought her forth.

"Jussie, this is my wife, Lianna. And our son, Aimery."

Jussie? Lianna resisted the impulse to scream. Jussie was a pet name, a lover's name, spoken with obvious ease.

"Hello, Mistress Tiptoft," Lianna said formally. She expected the soft loveliness of Justine's face to harden, her smile to fade. What must she be feeling, facing the woman who'd stolen Rand from her?

Justine's smile broadened. "Please, call me Justine, or better, Jussie." Merry blue eyes swept Lianna from head to toe. "You're beautiful," she said, "and your baby looks like an angel." She glanced at Rand. "You've been blessed, Rand. Truly."

His hand glided to the small of Lianna's back. "Aye," he said, his voice gruff with sincerity. "More richly than I deserve. Jussie, we've come to ask a great favor of you."

"Of course, Rand."

Nom de Dieu, thought Lianna, the woman was certainly biddable.

Justine turned to the group of children. "Go help Sister Frances in the orchard," she instructed. "I'll fetch you at vespers." She made a shooing motion with her apron, and the children scampered off.

Quickly Rand explained what had come to pass, how they had come to be there, and what they wished of Justine.

"I'll care for your Aimery as my own," she promised, reaching out her arms. "The lamb. Let me hold him."

In spite of herself, Lianna felt confidence in Justine's words, her actions. The orphans in her care were clean, well fed, and cheerful. She handed the baby to her. Aimery stared curiously at Justine and waved a fist at her coif. "He favors you, Rand," she said. Lianna scowled. Quickly Justine added, "He has his mother's chin."

A relieved sigh gusted from Rand. "It will only be for a few weeks," he said.

Uncertainty clawed at Lianna. Justine was everything Lianna was not. She was compliant where Lianna was argumentative; her sunny temperament contrasted sharply with Lianna's seriousness. Justine was simpler, and softer. Softer, aye; she'd never borne the burdens of a chatelaine, of a country torn by war.

Rand turned to Lianna. "I'll see that our horses are fed and watered, and make an offering to the abbess for the baby's keep," he said. "Doubtless you'll want to speak to Jussie at length about caring for Aimery."

Peevishness crept into Lianna's voice as she said, "Of course."

Baffled, he shrugged and walked toward the tithe barn. He paused and looked back at the two women. Lianna's jealousy had come as a shock to him. Lord, what a needless emotion. Didn't she realize he could never have felt for Jussie what he felt for her?

He smiled to himself. Jussie had once fit him well, like a hat shaped by years of wear. Lianna was so much more complex, so changeable. She challenged him, made him want to be a better man for her sake. Squaring his shoulders, he vowed she'd find contentment under English rule.

Justine stared thoughtfully at Lianna. "Come. I hope to ease your mind about leaving Aimery with us."

They sat on a curved stone bench in the shade of a

pear tree. Aimery crawled contentedly in the soft grass at their feet. "How old is your son?" asked Justine.

"Nearly eight months."

"Is he weaned from the breast?"

Lianna blushed at the frank question. "In part, yes."

Justine nodded. "The first few days might be hard on you both. Yet I've had luck with honey teats and a wine-skin of goat's milk for nursing. Your Aimery is sure to thrive here."

Lianna heard herself describing, in anxious maternal detail, the baby's sleeping habits, the likes and dislikes that made her child unique. "He does favor a soothing song at bedtime," she concluded. Her throat tightened with pain.

Justine's eyes softened with memories. "I would expect as much from Rand's son. He does play the harp so beautifully. Did he ever sing to you of Héloïse and Abelard?"

Jealousy formed a curl of bitterness around Lianna's heart. So Rand had shared love songs with Justine. What else had he shared?

You are my first, my only.

Could he have lied? No, not Rand. And yet . . .

"Lianna." Justine's sweet voice intruded on the appalling thought. "I suspect you know Rand and I once planned to wed."

"'Twas not my choice to take him away from you," snapped Lianna. "In fact, I did everything in my power to avoid marrying him."

Justine looked surprised. "You did not take Rand away from me."

"Aye," Lianna forced out, "for in his heart he never left you."

Justine shook her head vigorously; the white coif bobbed. "How can you think that? Jesu, he never held me in his heart. He never truly belonged to me." She clasped Lianna's cold hands with her warm ones. "We could have married years ago, yet we didn't. We both claimed we wanted to wait until Rand's campaigning with the Duke of Clarence was done." She spoke with confidence and bore herself with dignity in spite of the drab gray novice's robe she wore. "I think we both knew that we simply weren't meant to marry."

"Yet you planned so long—"

"Only because my family wished it so fervently. To Rand, I was someone to care for, to protect, much as he was always protecting a stray cat, a bird fallen from the nest. But you . . ." Justine looked deep into Lianna's eyes. "You are someone he can love, someone who won't be lost in the broad, strong shadow of him." Her gaze was clear and steady. "Has he ever given you cause to think him untrue?"

"No," said Lianna quietly, remembering the honesty of his emotions. "Never." For a long moment she stared at Justine. She wanted to hate the girl but found her wholly likable. She wanted to find flaws but discovered only good qualities.

Justine opened her arms and Lianna moved to return the embrace. "You must think me a jealous harpy," Lianna confessed.

Justine laughed. "I think you a woman who loves her husband."

Lianna glanced down at Aimery, and her eyes filled with tears. "But how can I love his ambition to open my home to English invaders?"

"If he did not have that ambition, he'd not be the man you love."

Lianna snatched up the baby and hugged him. He grabbed for her chin. "Why can't he just—" She bit back her wish for him to embrace the cause of France. The notion suddenly seemed petty, impossible.

Justine reached over and stroked Aimery's cheek. "Don't force him to choose, Lianna. Please. He's a man of great heart, but that heart can be broken."

Lianna gulped back tears. She'd found her son only to leave him with a stranger. She'd sought to turn Rand away from King Henry only to find him determined to join the English invasion.

Chapter  19

For many long moments since she'd climbed from a bobbing tender onto the crowded deck of the *Trinité Royale*, Lianna stood frozen with terror. The rough, cannon-plagued crossing to England had hardly prepared her for the voyage she faced now. Leaving her son had opened a well of misgivings inside her, rendering her cheeks pale, her face expressionless.

Rand stayed at her side, his hand drawing warm, soothing circles on her back. "Easy, love," he said. "We're on the king's own ship; no ill can befall us."

The lump of misery in her throat held her mute. She stared at Spithead harbor. The sun, bright as a new coin, gilded the sails of fifteen hundred warships.

"'Tis the greatest fighting force ever to leave English shores," Rand said. Then his excitement seemed to dim. "I would to God we'd not had to leave Aimery."

Lianna nodded and wrapped her arms around her roiling stomach, the palms of her knotted fists weeping with sweat. She fixed her eyes on the capstan adorned with a huge scepter bearing the fleur-de-lis. In displaying the lilies of France so prominently, King Henry shouted his objective to the world. Her gaze flicked to a carving on the deckhead: a gold leopard wearing a crown of silver. And, looking at the armada crammed into the harbor, she admitted for the first time that an English victory was possible. God, could her uncle of Burgundy have been right all along?

Noblemen strolled the decks; some paused to greet Rand and stare at Lianna. She bit her lip. "They think me weak."

Rich mirth rumbled in Rand's chest. "My love, they think you beautiful." He gestured at a portly nobleman who stood astern with his household knights. "When Edward of York saw you, he all but dropped the loaf of bread he was eating."

She studied the Duke of York. Burgundy had told her of him. A scheming ex-traitor who had once led a revolt against the king's father, Henry Bolingbroke, York had managed to insinuate himself back into royal favor. Distasteful of the man's self-serving nature, she looked away.

"You say so to be kind." Irritation edged her voice. "A man half-blind could see my . . . my fear."

"You bore yourself like a queen," he said. "Lianna, you do make me swell with a husband's pride."

"I doubt I'll inspire such admiration in your king."

Gulls screeched and flitted through the mastheads. On the decks milled a company of nobles, priests, artisans, yeomen, and mercenaries who anticipated battle with an eagerness that distressed Lianna. Irish warriors, wild of hair and beard, their skin tattooed, ran to and fro. The crack archers of Sir Thomas Erpingham sat fletching arrows. She studied the great guns and siege engines lashed to some of the decks. The men who would operate those machines behaved for all the world as if they were embarking on a fine adventure instead of a mission to kill and conquer.

"By my faith, Longwood, I'd heard you and your lady were aboard!" Lianna turned to see a handsome, big-boned man. A jeweled broach with the arms of Lancaster identified him as a royal personage. His broad, welcoming smile as he yanked Rand into a hearty bear hug identified him as a friend.

"Lianna, this is Thomas, the Duke of Clarence and King Henry's brother."

She curtsied respectfully but could not keep the irony from her voice when she remarked, "This is not your first voyage to France, Your Grace."

Thomas struck his chest, feigning a broken heart. "And I was going to admire your wife's looks. But that voice . . . her accent puts me in mind of lilting breezes over the Norman fells." Taking her hand, he placed a fervent kiss in her palm.

"Is this your way," she asked, extracting her hand to touch a finger to her chin, "of evading my remark?"

Thomas grinned. "A man can always try." He studied her face closely. "At least your quick tongue keeps me from envying Rand too much. I prefer that my women concern themselves only with domestic matters."

"I'd gladly do so," she said, "but your brother the king has forced me to turn my attention to political affairs."

Thomas nodded. "I do pray for a better outcome than

my last voyage four years ago. I pray this conquest ends in peace for both our countries."

"France *is* at peace—"

Clearing his throat, Rand encompassed the fleet with a sweep of his hand and hastily changed the subject. "Lord Scrope must be lamenting the state of the royal treasury."

Thomas's face paled. "My God, you haven't heard, then."

"Heard what?"

"Scrope is no longer the king's treasurer." Fury lent a harsh edge to Thomas's voice. "He and Thomas Grey, together with Henry Percy and Oldcastle, revived the intrigue against my brother. They sought to put the Earl of March on the throne, but March lost his nerve and confessed all to Harry."

"My God, Scrope was one of the king's closest friends."

"As of twelve days ago, he is a headless corpse," said the duke. "As are all who dare attempt to defy my brother."

Despite the warmth of the August day, Lianna shivered. Her plan to ask Rand to turn from King Henry did not seem so simple now. If Henry had shown no mercy to a lifelong friend, how much more ruthless would he be toward Rand?

The strong, bracing arm of Clarence interrupted her thoughts. Walking between her and Rand, he led them toward the center of the top deck. "Come," he said. "Harry seems to have left off his praying for a moment. He would see you now."

A small crowd in the center of the deck parted. The young man in their midst looked unremarkable at first glance, but on closer study Lianna recognized the aura of power that emanated from him like heat from a fired cannon.

Although he wore a crown, he needed no outward sign to identify him. His confident demeanor and the fire in his eyes marked him clearly as Henry of Monmouth, Prince of Wales, Knight of the Bath, Duke of Cornwall, Earl of Chester, Duke of Lancaster and Aquitaine, King of England—and of France, if his goal were indeed fulfilled.

The blood-red eye of a fabulous ruby winked from its setting in the state crown of Henry V. Rand knelt in obeisance. Reluctantly Lianna followed suit. Henry's shoes, she noticed, bore two familiar devices: the leopards of England and the lilies of France. This monarch could well crush both kingdoms beneath his ambitious feet.

She raised her head, keeping her gaze steady, hiding the resentment and trepidation that welled within her.

Henry held out his hand. "Baroness."

She took his hand but could not bring herself to kiss it. She inclined her head and murmured a greeting. Henry gave her a thin, cold smile, then turned a look of inquiry on Rand.

Lianna barely listened to the conversation as she formed an impression of the man whose command had so altered her life. She'd expected a self-centered monster, an imperious usurper, an uncaring plunderer of the poor. Henry seemed none of these things. He sat quiet, impassive, as he listened to Rand's tale.

Briefly Rand explained how they had come to be in England. Respectfully he asked for passage back to France.

With a nod Henry accepted the story, then turned and subjected Lianna to a long, grave moment of speculation.

"You would sail to France on one of my warships?"

"I would reach my home by whatever means, Your Grace."

The corners of his mouth tautened in satisfaction. "I would expect such determination from Burgundy's niece."

She took a deep breath. "I would be lying, Your Grace, if I pretended that I approve of my uncle's alliance with you. His brothers, the Duke of Brabant and the Count of Nevers, are of like mind. France is our country, sovereign unto itself."

A flash of ferocity glinted in Henry's eyes. "Then why should I bear you home, my lady?"

Rand sidled closer to her, pressed his warm hand into the small of her back. "Because, Your Grace, she is my wife."

Henry heard murmurs from the gathered nobles. He lifted one eyebrow, the stern control of his mouth momentarily lost in a sudden quirk. His gaze passed over the handsome pair before him. Despite his own scant seven and twenty years, he saw them as infinitely, unbearably youthful. The girl's face remained composed, her attitude respectful, yet he recognized unease in the vulnerable fullness of her lower lip and yearning in the silver depths of her eyes. She would be a fighter, aye, this lass with the blood of Jean Sans Peur flowing in her veins.

Henry turned to her husband. Longwood's face was a study of quiet dignity, never pleading, yet a request for indulgence haunted those green eyes. The man has changed, Henry thought. He's no longer the monkish knight I dubbed at Westminster, but a man of new strength and self-assurance.

Rand moved closer to his wife and assumed an un-consciously protective stance, one hand at her back, the fingers of the other knit with hers.

An unaccustomed softness welled in Henry's heart, a softness heated by a subtle flare of satisfaction. He'd sent Rand forth to claim a bride and a castle. Rand had done both. But he'd found more than that. He'd found love.

Aye, the bond was written on their achingly young faces, in the fingers twined together between them, in the way the girl leaned slightly into the lee of her husband's shoulder. But was the bond strong enough to keep her from treachery?

When Henry spoke he addressed Rand, yet his gaze stalked challengingly over his whispering counselors. "Aye, my lord, I'll allow your wife to sail with us."

As an uproar of indignant protests resounded, the girl smiled for the first time. Not the gushing, overblown smile of a courtier, but a sweetly understated bowing of her lips.

"Nay, Your Grace," said his cousin Edward, the Duke of York. Edward's fleshy face reddened with resentment. "Your own interdict against women and camp followers forbids it. By your very proclamation any female found among the men is to have her arm broken."

"The interdict is meant to deter prostitutes, cousin," Henry snapped. "It does not extend to noble ladies."

"But the seamen will never suffer her presence, sire. Sailors be a superstitious lot. They consider a woman unlucky."

Henry bristled. York was a fence straddler whose loyalties shifted as easily as the breeze off the Narrow Sea. Henry tolerated him only because the support of the House of York was so vital to all of England. "Enough, cousin. You'll say no more on the matter."

"But, sire, what if she's a spy for the French?"

"Then she's better off with her English husband."

York's jowls quivered. "I demand that—"

"Silence!" Henry's command fell like an ax blow. Edward tossed a smoldering look at Lianna and lumbered off across the deck. Others followed more slowly, their grumbling stifled by fear of the king's displeasure.

Henry walked to Rand and Lianna. His special attention, he knew, would shelter them from resentment better than a shield of iron. Aye, he needed to protect them, for he needed that causeway.

"Thank you, Your Grace," said Rand.

"I wish I could say I acted out of sheer indulgence for the bond you two share." His eyes flicked to Lianna in time to see a startled look cross her face. "But it was more than that. I wish for you to remember that I could have refused."

She moistened her lips. "I shall remember, Your Grace." Suspicion flowed beneath her words. A less perceptive man might not have recognized the veiled indignation. Yet Henry of Monmouth was nothing if not perceptive.

"You are indeed of Burgundy's blood," he said in admiration and annoyance, "no matter what you may think of his politics." He saw her hand tighten around her husband's, and apprehension reared suddenly in his mind.

He dropped a visor of indifference over his features to hide an unsettling notion. He had not reckoned on the idea that Rand could be lost to a Frenchwoman. Now he had to admit the possibility. He'd once had Rand's loyalty, but now this impossibly beautiful niece of Burgundy had his love. Burgundy's niece . . . The idea twisted around his thoughts. Jean Sans Peur would be quick to make use of so compelling an emotion as love. Would his kinswoman do the same?

Reluctant but determined, Henry forced out, "You understand that I must deal harshly with disloyalty."

"Your brother told us of Scrope's treason." Lianna lifted her eyes to his. A challenge gleamed in that silvery gaze. The Baroness of Longwood was his adversary, and Rand the prize.

"I do hope," said Henry, "you'll not ignore that lesson."

As one, they stiffened. Anger, as brief and vivid as summer lightning, flared in Rand's eyes. Yet Henry felt no answering ire, not even when Rand inclined his head and said, "I understand, sire. Royal indulgence is a double-edged sword."

As oarsmen propelled the *Trinité Royale* out to sea, Lianna battled panic. "I should have stayed," she gasped. "God forgive me, I should have stayed with Aimery." Miserable, she folded her arms, cradling her milk-swollen breasts.

"You cannot go to him now," Rand said, his voice soft with sympathy. "But soon. We'll be back within a few weeks."

"It will seem an eternity," she murmured.

Several feet away, Henry stood facing the distant quay where his stepmother, Queen Joanna, and her priests kept up an endless chant. "Jesu mercy and gramercy," he muttered, and turned his gaze toward the east and south, toward France.

Lianna's heart lodged in her throat as she watched the monarch raise his arm, signaling the master mariner.

A trumpet blared; drums beat.

On the *Trinité* and all her sister ships, sailors scrambled up the rigging while others hauled at the staysails. Canvas snapped and cords sang through the pulleys.

Cannon fire grumbled from somewhere off to the right. Lianna clung more tightly to Rand's arm. "Fools," she muttered in French. "The harbor is far too crowded to be firing the guns. They ought to know better than to—"

"Fire!" High in the rigging, a lookout screamed the warning. "A Dutch ship is afire!"

To the stunned company on deck, the conflagration appeared as a distant swirl of smoke among hundreds of lurching masts.

More explosions resounded. "Her gunpowder stores have blown!" yelled the lookout. "She's set two other ships afire!"

The *Trinité* came about. Bracing herself against Rand, Lianna glimpsed the burning ships. Screaming men and panicked horses dove from the vessels. Some men found boards and barrels to cling to; others sank with terrifying speed. Choking with horror, Lianna buried her face in Rand's tunic.

Behind them came a husky whisper: "A bad omen. A bad omen indeed. I did say 'twould be so."

Rand spun around, glared into the broad, fleshy face of Edward of York. "Keep your thoughts to yourself," he snapped.

"Your French wife casts a pall on the venture."

Seeing Rand's big fists double, Lianna pressed closer. "He means to provoke you. Don't let him."

"I'll hear you apologize to my wife, Your Grace."

"Ha! I am a man of honor." York's corpulent body

quivered with indignation. "I speak no false apologies, especially to a Frenchwoman."

"You've a high opinion of yourself," Rand lashed out. "My God, treachery clings to you like a disease. All know of your part in the rebellions against the king's father."

"I am in the royal favor now," York snarled. "Harry has given back the titles Bolingbroke stripped from me. You would do well to remember my position." York looked at Lianna again and opened his mouth as if to speak. Then, glancing at Rand's clenched fists, the duke seemed to think better of risking another slur. Muttering, he spun and disappeared behind a jumble of barrels lashed to a stanchion.

The lookout called again, this time his voice ringing not with terror but with wonder. "Swans! The swans of Lancaster!"

Lianna looked up, the back of her head against Rand's chest. Borne by the wind, the flock streaked eastward, great wings outspread, necks stretched long. The swans appeared glaring white against the brilliant azure of the sky. Sick with foreboding, Lianna watched until her eyes ached, and then she turned away.

In deference to Lianna and despite protests from York and some of his cronies, the Baron and Baroness of Long-wood occupied a cramped but private sterncastle cabin.

"What think you of King Henry?" Rand asked.

"He is ... kingly." Her eyes were deep and wide. "I know well what manner of man your king is. For he is cut from the same cloth as my uncle of Burgundy. Both fabrics are woven with keen judgment, determination, and ruthlessness."

Rand nodded. Based on a single meeting, she had

delved to the ambitious heart of King Henry.

"In allowing me to sail with the fleet, he has put me in his debt." She stared into Rand's eyes.

Something in that searching look caused a sudden chill to seize his heart. "What is it, love?"

"Rand, what do you owe to King Henry?"

The measured deliberation of her words told him she'd pondered the question more than once. "I am sworn to uphold his right to the crown of England. . . ." He drew a deep breath, knowing his next words would smother the flare of expectancy that shone in her eyes. "And France."

The light died. Rand pulled her against him, weaving his fingers into the silken strands of her hair. Cradling her head to his chest, he said, "Lianna, we both knew it would come to this choice. Soon I will have to deliver Bois-Long into King Henry's hands."

And soon, Lianna thought miserably, I will have to stop you. Even as she snuggled against him and sought the forgetful comfort of his embrace, she knew she could not open the ford to the English army. These invading multitudes must not cross the Somme and unleash their fury on all of France.

She drew a deep breath. The waiting and hoping had ended. The time for a covenant had arrived. Pulling back, she held Rand's eyes with hers. "Do you love me?" she whispered.

Surprise softened his expression. "Have I not told you so a thousand times?"

"Tell me again," she said almost desperately.

He laid his lips upon her brow, her mouth. "I love you, Lianna. I love you, as the lily loves the sun and the dew."

She placed her hands on his cheeks and framed his face. And I love you, her heart said, but she did not speak the words. Could not. For she could not love the lions of England. She hauled in a long, steadying breath.

"Do you love me enough to . . . turn away from King Henry? To keep the ford closed to the English army?"

He jerked his head away as if her hands had become white-hot brands. Bitter agony seared his lungs as he sucked in a deep breath. She reached for him again; he pulled away.

"My God," he rasped, "my God, I cannot believe you would ask treason of me."

She pressed her lips into a line of anger. "Is it any worse than the treason you have forced on me?"

"Henry raised me from bastardy, gave me lands, a title."

"He almost got you killed."

"That was Gervais's doing. Gervais, who lays claim to Bois-Long because of the intriguing you did with his father—who is, I might add, now dead because of his plotting."

She reared back. "How dare you blame me for working to preserve the sovereignty of France? Damn you, Rand, I've given you my home, an heir. Will you give me nothing in return?"

"Would you have me dishonor my vow of fealty?" he shot back. "What of honor, Lianna?"

She swallowed. She was asking him to turn traitor, to give up the integrity that was the very essence of the man she'd fallen in love with. "The alternative is allowing France to fall to the English," she whispered.

"Henry beheaded Scrope, his lifelong friend. What do you suppose he'd do to me?"

She glared. "Henry won't kill you. The French will kill

him. He'll have all he can do to flee with his life."

Rand touched her cheek and stared deep into her eyes. "I will not turn from Henry. Is my love not enough?" he asked.

Her silence was answer enough.

Images haunted his mind. The past year had been a gilded dream. Her warmth, her ardor, her acceptance of him, had all been an act. Each sunny smile, each evocative caress, had been a calculated thread in the web of manipulation she'd spun. God, he'd been a fool for deluding himself. He'd believed she loved him, despite her stubborn refusal to admit it.

"Bitch." He spoke the word with deadly quiet menace.

Looking oddly fearful, utterly beautiful, she bit her lip. "What did you say?"

"*Salope.*" He repeated the slur in her own tongue.

Her head snapped to one side as if he'd struck her. He gripped her shoulders, fingers biting into her flesh. It felt strange to handle her harshly, strange and distasteful.

"It's all been a lie, then, hasn't it, Lianna? Your sweetness, your affection. You thought to use my love, to hone my affections like a blade, then have me beheaded for treason."

"No, I don't want your death."

"Admit it, Lianna." He put his face very close to hers and wondered if she could see the sickness of disillusionment in his eyes. "Admit that you only acted the loving wife to lure me into your web of deceit."

"I thought that if you loved me as much as you claim, you'd not want to hurt me by giving my home to King Henry."

"*Our* home," he roared, "or have you forgotten that?

Love is not a weapon to be tested like one of your cannons."

"You're afraid of tests, aren't you, Rand?"

Her soft, agonized query wrapped around his throat, gripped him in a stranglehold. "What of you, Lianna?" he demanded. "Neither will you put aside your allegiance to France for the sake of love."

Tears trembled on her lashes. "I never asked for you, Rand. I did all I could to avoid marrying you."

Her tears tore at his heart. He forced an edge of steel into his voice. "I loved you, Lianna. I loved you when you were nothing, a girl carrying a gun—"

She covered her ears and shouted, "You're afraid, because you've been exposed. You've proven that you put your loyalty to King Henry above your love for me."

"As you put your loyalty to France above your love for me."

Her tears spilled over. "I never said I loved you!"

Agony tasted like bile in his throat. "It is because I love you that I am loyal to Henry," he insisted harshly. "You've seen his force. Within a few weeks he will rule Normandy and Picardy, if not all of France." He stood. He had the urge to pace, but the cramped quarters would allow little movement. "It would have hurt less had you been honest, Lianna, and fought me as you did in the beginning. What pains me is that you lied. You let me love an illusion."

Her eyes held a wide, bruised look he had not seen in many months. Wanting to hate her, he left the cabin.

The English vessels nosed into the estuary of the river Lézarde and dropped anchor at the Chef de Caux, just west of the fortified shipping town of Harfleur.

The fleet bobbed just as quietly. King Henry signaled a council of war by unfurling his royal banner at the masthead. His brothers, Thomas of Clarence and Humphrey of Gloucester, his cousin Edward of York, two bishops, and eight nobles, Rand among them, gathered for the meeting.

"We'll lie at anchor until the morrow," said Henry. "All troops will stay aboard while a reconnaissance is made. No plunder," he reminded them. "No harassing the peasants. No raping women"—here a pointed look at the lusty Edward of York—"and no excesses. The people of Harfleur are my people. 'Tis God's cause we serve, not our own greed."

Rand took a deep breath and grimaced. The stink of brine and rot from the marshes corrupted the warm air. The lasting pain of Lianna's deceit ate bitterly at his soul.

"You and your wife will leave within the hour," Henry said to Rand. "Her presence is a distraction, you understand."

Rand nodded. Already Lianna's beauty and her strength in standing up to King Henry were legendary among the men of the fleet. But those admiring soldiers could know nothing of her hardness, her scheme to lure her husband from England.

"Ride hard for Bois-Long and hold the ford for me," Henry said. "The success of this venture depends on our making that crossing, Rand."

Henry's hand lingered long on Rand's shoulder—so long that Rand felt the heavy weight of duty, the burden of promises wrought a lifetime ago. He looked hard into the king's eyes, the eyes of a man who might have died had Rand not gone a-harping and stumbled into intrigue that night at Eltham long past. They clasped hands, and the king's eyes, the eyes of a man who might have died had Rand not gone a-harping and stumbled into intrigue that night at Eltham long past. They clasped hands, and Rand studied the long, elegant fingers of the king. The hand that had knighted him with a sluice of water and a blow of the sword.

Rand thought of Lianna, with her wide, sad eyes, her impossible demands.

"I will hold the ford for you, sire," he said.

"God speed you on your journey, my lord."

The hundred miles from Harfleur to Bois-Long passed in a blur of misery for Lianna.

At Fécamp, at an inn that was little more than a hovel, they learned that the royal sanity had returned; King Charles had ordered preparations for war. And Lianna discovered Rand was capable of silences so interminable, she wondered if he slept in the saddle.

At Arques, while being ferried across the river Béthune, they learned that Henry was expected to land at Boulogne, that Charles d'Albret, Constable of France, had ordered the nobles to gather a fighting force. Rand discovered that Lianna could ride as hard and uncomplaining as a seasoned soldier; her will defied the punishing pace he set for them.

At Gamaches, while sheltering in a convent, they learned that royal tax gatherers had begun to sweep the populace in great earnest, and that Burgundy had refused to join the Armagnac resistance and retired to his palace in Liège.

Rand realized that, despite Lianna's mandate that he abandon the English cause, he still loved her.

Lianna realized that, despite Rand's insistence on holding the ford at Bois-Long, she still loved him.

At the end of the third day, long shafts of sunlight streamed over the towers of Château Bois-Long.

Lianna glanced at Rand, caught him watching her. She knew his thoughts, for they mirrored her own. One way or another, this war would end. How can we live with one another when the fighting is over?

"We're home," she said quietly.

"Home," he repeated in a flat, hollow voice. "I thought this castle a home . . . once."

Pain burst in her chest, for his comment rang with agonizing truth. It had been a home when they'd presided together at table, made unabashed love in their chamber, birthed their son in pain-filled joy. It had been a home when they'd exclaimed over Aimery's first tooth, planted a cherry tree together, fallen asleep in each other's arms.

Now the baby lay far away. The fact that his parents were together was but incidental, for in their hearts they were worlds apart.

"It is still my home, as it has always been," Lianna said quietly. " 'Tis you who would make Bois-Long an English bastion."

"Only to prevent it from becoming a French ruin."

Two pairs of eyes clashed. Two pairs of determined hands clenched.

And as they entered the château, two hearts died a little.

Chapter  20

Working in the counting house, Lianna made a calculation on her abacus and entered the figure in her ledger. Two weeks had passed since they'd returned to Bois-Long. The crop yields this season were improved as a result of Rand's administration. One finger brushing thoughtfully against her chin, she went back to her books. How often she had completed this task without a second thought. At one time the myriad duties of a chatelaine had filled her days. But with the baby gone and Rand turned from her, a great, empty hole lay at the center of her life.

She was learning that the loss of love was more painful than its lack.

Out in the tilting yard, Rand realigned the quintain and urged Roland to ride at the target. Then he turned to study a mock duel between Piers and Jehan. At one time the manly arts of combat had answered all of his needs. Yet now, deprived of his son's presence and his wife's love, he yearned for the healthy cries of Aimery and the soft comfort of Lianna's arms.

He was learning that an imperfect love was preferable to no love at all.

The figures for the eastern tract of rye were missing. Lianna set aside her quill and corked the ink salver. Rand would know the figures; he kept records as careful as her own. But lately he'd been loath to answer even simple questions.

Jagged pain seared her insides. Her son was an ocean away. She and her husband were on opposite sides of a war. Although she bore no outward signs of strife, unhappiness scourged her from within, creating deep, invisible scars.

Thrusting back her chair, she rose and walked purposefully to the tilting yard. She gestured to Rand; he walked toward her. The men ceased their drills to stare curiously. The tension that had reigned at the château was too all-pervading to be hidden. Ignoring the onlookers, Lianna said, "I would speak to you of the rye yields."

His face expressionless, he led her to the garden. Bees droned lazily in the honeysuckle. The flowers of late summer bloomed in sunbursts and clusters of wild color.

He taught me to love the beauty of flowers, she thought achingly. Swallowing, she said, "I need the figures for the yield."

"I'll have Batsford bring them to you." Rand cleared his throat. "Is that all?"

Their gazes clashed. Her throat filled with tears of agonizing love. "Please," she said, unable to stop herself, "please, don't open the ford to King Henry."

Pain ravaged his face. "You ask the one thing I cannot give." Reaching out with an unsteady hand, he caressed the pale tendrils of hair at her temple. "Let the army cross unheeded, Lianna," he urged. "You are my wife. No Frenchman will think ill of you for doing your husband's bidding."

Angry and disappointed, she snapped, "I care naught what others say. I could not live with myself if I did not try to stop Henry's death march."

"And I could not live with myself did I not try to help him win the crown of France."

"So we are still at an impasse," she stated coldly.

"Aye."

She gulped back tears. Was this chilling stranger the man who had pledged to love her? Did all they had shared mean less to him than his promise to King Henry, and less to her than her loyalty to France?

"This war will be over one day," she said. "How, then, will we live with one another?"

He blinked. The ice of anger left his eyes, replaced by a deep sadness that tore at her heart. "That depends on how much we love, Lianna. And how much we can forgive."

Lashed by agony, she struck out with ill-considered words. "I can neither love nor forgive a man who places a usurper's ambition above his wife and son."

"Nor can I love or forgive a woman who would ask her husband to turn traitor."

She burst into tears. Cursing softly, Rand caught her against him. "Jesu, Lianna, we both say things we do not mean. Can we not try to find some accord?"

"No," she sobbed. "No, Rand, we cannot."

In the hall that evening, as Rand and Lianna presided over supper, unspoken recriminations hung thick in the air.

Edithe, bearing a mazer of mead, spilled the drink on Lianna. "Must you be so clumsy?" she snapped as the sticky honeyed wine seeped into the bodice of her gown.

The girl bristled. "Doing figures all day makes the mistress testy," she muttered. "Ought to pay more mind to that husband of yours—"

"*Nom de Dieu,* hold your tongue!" Lianna commanded.

"Go back to the kitchens, Edithe," Rand said. He eyed the coiled tension of Lianna's hands, which gripped the edge of the table. "Quickly," he added. He moistened a napkin in a finger bowl filled with lemon water and began methodically cleansing her gown. "You should not have vented your spleen on Edithe," he murmured. "'Tis obvious your anger is at me."

The presence of the entire household prevented her from slapping his hand away. Tight-lipped and smoldering, she suffered the gentle strokes of his cleansing in silence.

If only, she thought wildly, her heart would be still, too. But Rand's hand, wielding the cloth, moved leisurely and purposefully over the stain. His touch branded her with fierce yearning; his mild yet knowing smile fired her blood.

"Enough," she said through gritted teeth. "I'll send the cursed gown to be laundered."

"I'd be glad to help you out of it." His eyes fixed on her bosom. His fingers grazed the crest of her breast.

Cheeks scorching, she pulled away. A swift, mortified glance told her the entire household had been watching.

The timely arrival of an English herald spared her further embarrassment. Travel-stained and breathing hard, he approached the high table and bowed. Lianna held her breath and prayed he'd come to announce the withdrawal of the English.

"How goes the siege?" asked Rand.

"Passing well. A party led by our king's brother, Thomas of Clarence, seized a French wagonload of armaments."

Rand smiled.

"But the Sire de Gaucourt marched into Harfleur with three hundred men-at-arms."

Lianna smiled.

"Have Henry's miners set up emplacements for the great guns?" asked Rand.

"Aye, the *King's Daughter*, the *Messenger*, and the *London* are all in place."

Rand set his jaw in grim satisfaction.

"French counterminers must be at work," Lianna persisted.

"Alas, they've clogged the tunnels with rubble."

She gave a smug nod.

In the ensuing weeks, similar reports punctuated the waiting.

English guns belched a rain of rock and iron upon the town walls.

French soldiers and citizens hastened to mend each gap.

Green wine, spoiled water, and illness plagued the English army.

The Burgundy-Armagnac feud still festered. Jean Sans Peur had made an insincere offer to send reinforcements to his son-in-law the dauphin; Louis, in fear of Armagnac reprisals, had refused and stayed in the town of Vernon.

King Henry sent a desperate challenge to Vernon, offering to settle the question of succession by personal combat with the Dauphin Louis.

Predictably, the dauphin ignored the challenge. Louis's refusal sapped the fighting spirit from the beleaguered citizens and soldiers of Harfleur.

On 22 September, the town surrendered unconditionally.

Sickness and siege had reduced Henry's mighty force to nine hundred men-at-arms and five thousand archers.

But those hardy survivors meant to embark on a *chevauchée* to Calais, seizing every town and castle they passed.

Lianna confronted Rand one night in late September. "I want my son back," she said.

A shadow darkened his face. He ran a hand through the golden mane of his hair. "It's still not safe. Henry's army is three weeks' march from here. I am not free to leave, and I'll not disclose Aimery's whereabouts to anyone else."

"You promised I'd have my baby back within a few weeks."

"Lianna, I could not know the siege would take so long."

"But I thought you'd keep your promise to me."

A shaft of pain glinted in his eyes. "I miss Aimery, too. But I'll not endanger his life to have him with me."

Sudden shame gripped her. Rand loved Aimery as much as she did. But he might never bring her son back if Henry retreated with his diminished army. Angry, she lashed out, "Aye, you mustn't let something so unimportant as your son interfere with your plan to give his inheritance to Henry."

Fear and anxiety widened the gap between Rand and Lianna.

The time of waiting became a form of slow, silent torture.

The first week crawled sluggishly into the second.

During the third, Bonne and Jack approached the high table where Rand and Lianna sat in their usual ice-cold silence. "We marry in two days," said Jack. "We'd like you to sing at our nuptial mass."

"Both of you," Bonne added.

"I couldn't," Lianna said faintly. "My art is poor—"

"I've heard you sing, though not lately," said Bonne.

"Will you do it, my lord, my lady?" Jack asked. He looked for all the world like a begging child.

Rand and Lianna exchanged a glance. Wordlessly they agreed that their difficulties must not taint the happiness of Bonne and Jack.

"We'll sing at your wedding," said Rand.

Tapers bathed the chapel in mellow light, gilding the faces of Jack and Bonne, who had just spoken their vows. Batsford, who in deference to the solemnity of the occasion had shed his sportsman's garments, wore a sweet, pious expression as he bestowed a final blessing on the young couple.

All eyes turned to Rand and Lianna. She'd thought it would be easy to sing with Rand, but Jack and Bonne had requested a singularly meaningful song.

They wanted their love celebrated with the "Song of Songs."

Lianna moistened her lips. Their harps, carefully tuned beforehand, sprinkled resonant notes over the hushed chapel.

They began to sing, trading refrains, voices mating, even though their hearts lay miles apart. Lianna's voice trembled as she looked into Rand's eyes and sang.

> Thy love is better than wine:
> I am the rose of Sharon,
> And the lily of the valleys.

Rand answered more forcefully, but beneath his noble tones lay a foundation of emotion.

> My beloved spake, and said unto me,
> Rise up, my love, my fair one, and come away.

The words and melody brought memories surging to Lianna's mind and wistful vibrations to her voice.

> By night on my bed I sought him whom my soul
>   loveth:
> I sought him, but I found him not.

Rand's voice rang with private pain.

> Thou has ravished my heart . . .
> Whither is thy beloved gone,
> My beloved is gone down to the garden,
> To the beds of spices and to gather lilies. . . .

Their voices rejoined, and in the final moments of the song the company in the chapel ceased to exist for them. They were once again in the secluded bower where they'd first met.

Set me as a seal upon thine heart,
For love is strong as death;
Many waters cannot quench love,
Neither can floods drown it.

Lianna felt the hot splash of a tear upon her shaking hand. She lifted her pain-filled eyes to Rand and saw that he, too, had been touched by the timeless words, the haunting melody. The tender, tortured expression on his face, the uncertain, jerky movements of his body as he came to stand by her side, echoed feelings too long suppressed.

For a suspended moment, no one moved or spoke. Suddenly Father Batsford broke the silence by gathering both Bonne and Jack in his arms and proclaiming a fervent wish for their future happiness. The celebrants pressed around the altar, babbling good wishes and praise for the beauty of the bride.

Hemmed in from all sides by well-wishers, Rand and Lianna lacked the privacy to say what was in their hearts. Rand had but time to utter one word before they were jostled apart.

"Tonight," he whispered, and Lianna felt the promise like a shower of warm rain after a long drought.

Rand yearned for the dim retreat of Lianna's chamber. Could they forget their differences, share themselves without politics intruding? He damned well meant to try. Would she be waiting for him? Aye, he reassured himself, the dew-soft look in her eyes had been answer enough.

Frustrated, he eyed the men in the great hall. News of King Henry's imminent arrival weighed on anxious minds. The French household knights, grappling with torn loyalties, had been edgy and combative with their English counterparts.

Tempers, bolstered by excessive drinking at the wedding feast, flared. The behavior of the men obliged Rand to remain in the hall until all the revelers collapsed of drunkenness or fatigue. Ordinarily the task of maintaining order fell to Jack, but tonight he'd retired early with his bride.

In one corner Piers and Simon sang a bawdy song; Jehan and Chiang scowled at each other over a chessboard. Watching the game, Dylan and Roland seemed to be having a reasonably civil discussion. Godfrey, Giles, Neville, and Peter Finch cast draughts with three Frenchmen.

Rotating the stiffness from his shoulders, Rand decided that tempers had calmed enough for him to retire. Filled with unbearable anticipation, he walked to the wide stone staircase.

A shouted oath brought him swinging back around in time to see Roland's fist barrel into Dylan's stomach. The Welshman stumbled back, upsetting the chessboard.

Bellowing, Jehan surged up and aimed a blow of his own at the reeling Welshman. Instantly alert to their comrade's plight, Piers and Godfrey leaped to Dylan's defense.

"Oh, lamb of God," muttered Rand, and stalked back into the hall.

A faint scratching at her chamber door brought Lianna bolting to her feet. She'd considered and discounted at least a dozen phrases of welcome and explanation and had no idea what to say to Rand.

The dancing and feasting and well-wishing had kept

them apart throughout the evening. For that she was oddly grateful; the fragile accord they'd struck during the wedding song might have been shattered by a careless remark, a second thought.

The scratching came again. How formal we've become, she thought sadly. She almost wished he'd kick down the door, as he had when she'd barred it to him that long-ago night. Or better, she wished he'd simply stride confidently into her room, a man certain of his wife's welcome.

She opened the door. The tremulous smile dropped from her face. Her caller was not Rand, but Jufroy.

"I thought you'd been assigned to watch the gate," she said, not bothering to keep the disappointment from her voice.

"I was, my lady." Jufroy's rough features creased with agitation. "But you've a . . . visitor. He awaits you at the water gate, and bids you to come alone."

"I receive no visitors in secret," she snapped. "If someone wishes to see me, let him come to the hall."

Nervously Jufroy sketched the sign of the cross. "The man who wishes to see you . . . sent this."

Frowning, Lianna took the bundle, unfurled the cloth, and gasped. Carefully laundered and mended, it was one of Rand's tabards, the one he'd lost during the fight at Maisoncelles.

Her heart skipped a beat, then began slamming wildly against her rib cage. "Does my husband know of this?"

"Nay, he's still occupied with the men in the hall. A fight broke out—"

"Say nothing to Rand," she said. "I'll get my cloak."

Hurrying down a flight of uneven stone steps, Lianna reached the visitor's side and sank into a deep obeisance.

Louis, Duke of Guienne and Dauphin of France, stood alone in the inky shadows of the water gate.

When she rose, recognition flashed in Louis's eyes. So, she thought without surprise but with a chill of foreboding, he remembers me from Maisoncelles.

"Cousin," he said. "I hope you'll forgive me for coming alone and in secret. I thought it best not to ask the hospitality of an English household."

She didn't believe for one moment that he was alone; the night shadows around the river whispered and shifted with a force that mere breezes couldn't impart. Nor did she credit Louis's reason for not appearing in the hall. Obviously he wanted no chance of becoming a hostage in an English household.

"You . . . are welcome, Your Grace," she said automatically.

"Your loyalty pleases me. Why did you not reveal yourself in Maisoncelles, Belliane? I'd have been pleased to make the acquaintance of my dear wife's cousin."

She cleared her throat. "Circumstances did not permit—"

"Never mind." He waved his hand. Moonlight limned his features and picked out a handsomeness buried beneath flesh fed by overindulgence. "You've had reports of the siege?"

She nodded. "The town surrendered to King Henry, and he is leading his army north, to Calais."

"He means to ford the Somme here."

She swallowed hard, nodded. "There was talk of an English advance guard at Blanche-Tacque, but I understand Marshal Boucicaut outmarched that force."

"You understand correctly." A tight smile tugged at the corners of the dauphin's mouth. "Boucicaut littered the Blanche-Tacque ford with chevaux-de-frise and left the river guarded by a sizable force. So . . ." Louis eyed her through a rippling veil of shadows. "That leaves Bois-Long as Henry's only hope."

Dry-mouthed, she stared down at the moon-washed surface of the river. Ordinarily the sight discomfited her; at the moment the dauphin's face seemed more forbidding.

"Belliane . . . Look at me, cousin." Though soft, the request rang with the timbre of royal command.

She glanced up. Long before he spoke, she knew what he would ask. Silently she pleaded with him not to make the demand.

Heedless of her internal strife, he said, "I want you to tear down the causeway so the English army cannot get across."

Horror raked over her senses. She took a step back. "My husband means to keep the ford open."

"Open to what?" he demanded. "Surely you've heard of the condition of Henry's army. His men are sick, starving, dying by the score. The march of triumph he planned has degenerated into a funeral procession. He's finished, cousin."

"Can you be so certain?" she asked faintly.

He lowered his voice and said, "The Dukes of Alençon and Bar have joined forces with Bourbon and Berry. The King of Sicily has arrived with his own men. The Duke of Brittany has pledged twelve thousand men. The Count of Richemont brings five thousand lancers." Lianna sagged against the wall. Louis leaned closer yet. "Burgundy, plague take him, is off at a christening feast in Tournai. But his brothers, the Count of Nevers and Antoine, the Duke of Brabant, will uphold the Crown. Even at this moment Constable d'Albret's army lies just north of here, ready to smash the straggling English to a bloody pulp. Archers," Louis snorted. "What can a handful of lowborn archers do against the might of French nobles?"

"'Twas English archers, Your Grace, who conquered Bois-Long."

"Trickery," he retorted. "Longwood waited until the knights were trapped in the jousting lists."

Before she could pause to ponder the source of Louis's knowledge, he spoke again. "Cousin, I've revealed secrets tonight that not even my own captains are privy to. I come because I want Henry thwarted, aye, but I come because you are my kinswoman and I'd not see you suffer for your husband's mistakes. Doing my bidding will spare not only you, but many lives as well."

"If the English prevail, Rand will be beheaded for disobeying the king."

"You speak an absurdity," snapped Louis. "Look at the facts, Belliane. Henry's force has dwindled to five thousand, and most of those archers. France has five times that many, trained warriors all. When Henry is crushed, not even my intercession will spare your husband. But you can avert his death if you do as I ask."

Indecision tore at her. Could she trust the dauphin? Could she, even for the sake of France, betray Rand? She asked, "And what do you suppose my husband will do, sit idly by and watch the causeway being destroyed?"

"I leave it to you to dispense with him. You're a resourceful woman. You have until sunset tomorrow to do the deed."

"And if I refuse?"

They stared long into one another's eyes. Lianna could not help but compare the dissipated Louis with the spare strength of King Henry. Louis, who at nineteen had already gone to fat, whose penchant for fleshpots and feasting already tainted his reputation. A chill went through her at the thought that the crown of France would one day rest on this man's head. This man, whose father was a lunatic. Would that Louis possessed a tenth of Henry's shrewdness, his heart. . . .

"Have you forgotten Maisoncelles?" the dauphin asked softly.

Her eyes narrowed. She remembered that frozen moment outside Gervais's lodging house, when Louis could have detained her and the baby but instead had waved them on to Calais.

"I cannot do it," she said helplessly.

"You can. You will. Tomorrow at sunset, one of my captains will bring a small force to garrison the château. If you value your husband's life, you'll see that he's well away from here by then."

"Your Grace, you know not what you ask. Rand would never—"

"Then don't tell him." For the first time, Louis touched her. He placed a cold, moist hand under her chin and brought his fleshy face very close to hers. "Belliane." His voice dripped with a sickeningly soft note of threat. "I know where your baby is."

Stifling a scream of denial, Lianna raced up the steps from the water gate. Louis had said nothing more; after issuing the soul-shriveling words, he'd melted away into the shadows.

He hadn't had to say more. The dire promise, coupled with the ruthless mention of her son, had turned her from indecisive bystander to reluctant conspirator.

She had little time to wonder how Louis had come by such information. Surely his spies roved everywhere, had perhaps tracked her from Maisoncelles to Calais to England and back. In the wake of that thought came an unexpected and shattering yearning to disobey, to abandon her plan to interfere with Henry's crossing, and keep Rand's heart. But she must obey or face peril to her son.

Rand, she realized bleakly, was lost to her. What healing they'd achieved at the wedding was doomed to become a blistering wound again once she executed her plan. He'd despise her for tricking him, but she could live with his hatred more readily than she could bear his death.

Ducking through a small, stout door in the garden wall, she raced to the counting house, scratched a desperate note to her uncle of Burgundy and sent a scurrier to Tournai. If anyone could get to Aimery before the dauphin's lackeys, Jean Sans Peur could. Then she went to find Chiang, whose help would be vital to the success of her desperate plan.

The ruby tinge of dawn streaked the sky by the time she returned to her chamber. The fire in the hearth had burned to cold ash, and shadows hung in the room.

Wearily brushing a strand of hair from her brow, she found a wine bottle at the sideboard. Without pausing to pour, she put the bottle to her lips and took a long drink.

"I've been waiting for you."

The bottle slipped from her fingers and crashed to the floor. Blood-colored wine seeped into the rushes. Slowly she turned toward the curtain-draped bed.

Fully clothed, hair rumpled, eyes shadowed by fatigue, Rand reclined on the lambskin coverlet.

Oh, God. In her panic she'd forgotten he was coming to her room. Her heart in her mouth, she watched his eyes flick over her disheveled hair, the mud-spattered hem of her gown.

"I . . ." Her throat dried. "I . . . was called away. Mère Brûlot took sick after the feast, and I went out to the orchards to fetch her some medlar fruit."

"I asked around the château. No one had seen you."

"Jufroy was sleeping at his post when I passed by."

"I see."

She twisted her fingers into the fabric of her dress. "I waited for you, too," she said, "before I had to leave."

The ghost of a smile hovered on his lips. "The men became unruly. I couldn't leave the hall until I was certain they'd not kill one another." Swinging his long legs over the side of the bed, he rose and came to her side. "I daresay their tempers will cool once they see we've reached an accord."

She nodded. "We have . . . reached an accord."

"No more talk of treachery?"

"No more." She forced the lie past trembling lips.

"It will be for the best, Lianna. I promise." Gently he plucked at the laces of her surcoat and brushed the garment from her shoulders. He bent to kiss the skin revealed by the square-cut bodice of her tunic. "You taste of fresh breezes."

Guilt stung her soul. "Aye, I was a long time searching for the medlars."

"You should have fetched me."

"I knew you were busy in the hall." Terrified that her duplicity was stamped on her face, she flung her arms around his neck. "I just want to forget, Rand. Forget that the English army is south of here, that the French are gathering in the north. . . . Oh, Rand," she whispered fervently against his neck. "I want to shut the world away. Make me forget."

His searing kisses wrapped her in a powerful enchantment. His gentle motions as he carried her to the bed fanned a flame of long-suppressed desire. Burning in the intimacy of his embrace, she shook loose the shackles of betrayal Louis had forced upon her. I'll have this time with my husband, she vowed fiercely.

"I've missed you, wife," he said.

"As I've missed you."

Hungry for him, she tore at his clothes. Laughing, he helped her dispense with hosen, tunic, and smallclothes; then he lay beside her.

She turned on one side to look at him. The beauty of his naked form, the tenderness in his eyes, melted her soul. Yet even through a mist of passion, unslaked these many weeks, she understood what he could not.

This was their last time. They'd never love again, for she was doomed to slay his love for her.

Desire and regret brought her surging into his arms and turned her kisses from merely warm to blazing hot. He gasped as she laid her body into his, pressed him down on the bed, and anointed his flesh with kisses. She dared not speak, for tears burned her throat and sobs would betray her if she spoke her heart. A dark, calculating voice inside her warned that if she blurted her love to him now, he might suspect her coming treachery.

Deprived of the chance to voice her devotion, she let her hands, her mouth, her heart, speak. She showed him with burning kisses, hands and lips finding every intimate part of him. Hard muscle overlaid by sun-bronzed skin yielded to her caresses. Every scar and sinew impressed itself on her memory. Like a mantle of silk, her hair trailed over his body. Desperate with love, she coursed downward, filling her hands and then her lips with the pure, male essence of him. Rand moaned low in his throat and tried to bring her back to his lips, but she continued tasting and touching, making every caress a bold statement of her adoration.

"Lianna, no more," he gasped. "It's been too long; you push me too—"

"Hush," she murmured, bending over him. "Let me. . . ." She wanted to give him this memory of her, so that perhaps when the sting of her betrayal had dulled to an ache, he might remember her with something other than hatred. Perhaps they might fuse a covenant in their hearts, fan a flame that would never die. She branded him with her mouth, pouring all the adoration she felt into the searingly intimate kiss.

Rand's muscles went taut. He nearly reared from the bed. "I . . . Oh, God, Lianna . . ." Love and awe radiated through her; ardor had demolished his self-control, and she felt his ecstasy as if it were her own.

He dragged her into his arms, hugged her fiercely. "Witch. You've left me weak as a spent arrow."

She forced a smile. "I . . . wanted to please you."

"You have." His hands played over her. "Now it's your turn to be pleasured."

With false brightness, she pulled back and said, "I've an idea."

His thumbs circled her breasts. "So have I."

She drew a deep, steadying breath. "Let's meet by St. Cuthbert's cross, where we first loved. You'll be my knight-errant, and I'll be your *pucelle*."

"Henry could arrive any day now."

"So he could, but not today. Dylan's last report placed the English army thirty miles to the south." She nibbled at his neck. "Stores are set by. All is in readiness. We've nothing more to do but wait." She kissed him full on the mouth. "Let's enjoy the waiting, Rand."

"God, I've no quarrel with that."

"Meet me in the glade. I want sunshine and soft breezes, just as we had when our love was new."

He smiled and touched her hair. "I had no idea you were so sentimental, *pucelle*."

"You've melted me into a puddle of sentimentality," she declared, and prayed he didn't recognize the tears in her voice. Reaching out, she caressed him temptingly. "Please, Rand."

Yearning flared in his eyes. "Very well, we'll ride out together after matins."

"Oh, no," she said quickly. "We must arrive separately, at the hour of the woodcock's flight, as ever we used to. Indulge me, husband. I've had so little joy in my life with Aimery gone."

Tenderness softened his eyes. "What can I say? Of course I'll meet you."

The sun burst fully over the horizon as they dressed. Rand hummed snatches from the "Song of Songs," and the words hammered painfully in Lianna's mind.

Rise up, my love, my fair one, and come away.

Away, she thought bleakly, not to a tryst, but to a trap.

His gaze idly following the forays of a young leveret, Rand leaned against the stone cross and let the warmth of a mild autumn seep into his bones. At last, he thought,

Lianna was his again. He'd thought her lost to him, but this morning she'd proven him wrong, and proven it with a sensual power he'd only suspected before.

If only she would hurry. Remembered pleasure heated his blood. His heart quickened. Aye, his heart. He should have been listening to it these weeks past, instead of obeying the dictates of anger and resentment. Where was she? He'd waited nigh on half an hour; surely she'd be here soon.

He smiled. Through the day, she had busied herself with Chiang and spent a long time in conversation with Bonne. Doubtless the women had much to discuss on Bonne's wedding morn. Soon he would ask her what lay beneath her change of heart. And he promised he'd not let her regret her decision.

A twig snapped. The leveret bounded off into the forest. Rand leaped to his feet, muscles tensed, hand at the hilt of his sword.

He looked around. Long shafts of sunlight stalked the shadows of the larches and sighing willows. The smell of humus and autumn leaves wafted on the air. Yet beneath the earthy scent lurked a faint odor that did not quite belong in the idyllic setting. The smell of horses . . . and of danger.

God, why hadn't he noticed it before? His preoccupation with thoughts of Lianna had dulled his warrior's senses. Alarmed, he drew his sword and strode to his horse. Charbu's nostrils flared and quivered; his legs tensed. The percheron, too, seemed to sense a new unseen presence.

Slowly, attuned now to his surroundings, he untethered the horse. Muttering a calming word to Charbu, Rand drew his dagger. This could be a two-handed fight.

Leading the percheron to the edge of the glade, he eyed the tall upthrust of limestone that hid the path to the Norman cliffs. The dull thud of a footstep sounded. He glanced to the right, toward Bois-Long.

His palms grew clammy. He was trapped, and Lianna was riding into the snare.

In sudden decision he leaped onto his horse. But before he could spur Charbu homeward, a small army clambered over the hill.

Rand was about to test Charbu's speed when a voice called, "Hold, my lord."

Stunned, Rand dropped from his mount. "Chiang! What do you here? What . . ." His mouth dried. Not just Chiang, but Jack Cade, Piers Atwood, Simon and Dylan, Batsford and the others. A silent tally revealed that all nine Englishmen from Bois-Long stood before him.

"What jest is this?" Rand asked in annoyance. "Will you all follow a man to a tryst with his wife?"

"My lord, I've grave news," said Chiang. The regretful note in his voice, the cautious look on his face, raised a prickle of alarm on the back of Rand's neck.

The men looked too strained, too apologetic. And they moved too close for Rand's comfort.

"By my troth," he snapped, "will one of you speak?"

"My lord," said Jack, "we are barred from the castle. By the time we guessed the trick, every gun was trained on us. . . ."

The muffled thunder of an explosion rent the air. Birds sped aloft on a whir of wings. Rand stared above the treetops to the north. A plume of smoke surged high over the distant château.

Horror eclipsed all thought save one. He grasped the pommel of his saddle. "Jesu, Lianna—"

"Stop him," someone shouted.

The weight of ten determined men dragged him down. The thud of a well-aimed blow to the temple stunned him. He reeled, lashed out wildly with his sword. Someone wrested the weapon from his grip.

"We cannot let you ride to your death," said Jack.

Another blow, and darkness closed.

Chapter  21

Tension squeezed Lianna's insides into knots of iron. She prayed Chiang was holding Rand and the English soldiers in safety. She prayed Rand would understand, that he'd not hate her for what she'd done. She prayed her urgent missive to Burgundy had resulted in a passage to safety for little Aimery.

Standing atop the barbican, she stared at the wreckage of the causeway, which for generations had spanned the deep, wide river Somme. Once, the bridge had been an avenue to the long woods and water meadows to the south. Now all that remained were twisted splinters of oak, pieces of wood whirling seaward on a path that had no return.

She'd packed the charges herself, seen to their placement beneath the bridge supports, and ordered the wary and baffled household knights to ignite the slow matches.

Then, with the gate closed, people and livestock confined to the safety of the inner ward, she'd seen the stout structure reduced to kindling.

"How could you?" Bonne's face, streaked by tears and drained of color, was a picture of accusation.

Lianna took Bonne's hands in hers. "Do not censure me. Too much is at stake. The dauphin himself gave the order."

"Saint Louis's dysentery take the dauphin! My Jack is gone. We had not even a day to live as man and wife."

"Bonne, he'd be a dead man if Chiang had not tricked him and the other Englishmen away from here."

"But King Henry—"

"Is finished." Lianna derived less satisfaction than she'd expected from that fact. "The English force has diminished to less than six thousand, and those sick and starving. Constable d'Albret is but a few miles north of here, ready to smite the English advance. Jack's life would be worth not a sou if he were discovered here."

"You . . . you're serious."

"Aye, Bonne." Lianna clasped her maid's shoulders. Bonne smelled of the dried rosemary and lavender that had so recently been sprinkled on her marriage bed. "We both know what it is to love a man. To put our selfish wants aside to protect him."

"You've stolen his honor by not allowing him to stand and fight!"

Lianna's hand flashed out and struck Bonne on the cheek. "Damn you, don't you understand?" Regret rushed over Lianna as the maid's face crumpled. Hugging Bonne, soothing her reddened cheek, she said, "Forgive me. Please. I was angry because you speak the truth."

Bonne nodded miserably. "Where are they now?"

"Safe with Chiang. He'll hide them until the English

retreat to Harfleur. Rand and Jack will come to understand that I had no choice." Aye, thought Lianna, say it often enough and it will be true.

"What happens now, my lady?"

A chill seized Lianna. If Henry retreated, he might call Rand back to England. She'd never see her husband or son again. Drawing a deep breath, she banished the thought. "The dauphin is sending a small force to garrison the keep."

"To repel the English when they arrive?"

"I trust in Henry's wisdom. When he sees that the causeway is impassable, he'll turn back to Harfleur."

"Pray God he does. But what if he fights? And what if Rand and Jack are with him?"

"Chiang will see to it that they aren't. Henry's goal is to reach Calais. He'd not risk his small army to take so minor a prize as Bois-Long." She had wanted this all along, but victory left her hollow.

Trumpets blared. Lianna and Bonne hurried to the postern gate, which overlooked the moat-wrapped north side of the keep. Household knights and castle folk formed an anxious cluster in the bailey. As Lianna passed, resentful whispers drifted to her ears. Rand had been their lord, and they knew only that she had betrayed him.

She nodded to Jufroy. With a grinding of axles and chains, the iron portcullis rose. She stepped beneath the archway. Duty compelled her to assume a welcoming stance. These were her countrymen; they'd come to protect her home from foreign invaders. Yet apprehension thrilled through her veins.

Armor glittered in the sunlight. The scarlet oriflamme of St. Denis fluttered on a pennon borne by a herald. At the rear rode a woman. *Nom de Dieu*, thought Lianna, did they bring their wives, or their whores? At the head rode a knight, his plumed helm marking him as captain of the force of some thirty men. The captain wore no *cotte d'armes,* only a plain tabard over his breastplate. Tapping her chin in consternation, Lianna realized the dauphin would not send his best men; those knights would await the higher glory of field combat.

The captain rode to the edge of the moat, waved a hand to form his men into a single line. Then he crossed the bridge and stopped before Lianna.

"Well done, my lady," he said, his voice echoing within the metal basinet. A gauntleted hand reached up and opened the visor.

Shock, rage, and then an icy sluice of terror washed over Lianna. She stumbled back, clutching wildly at a brattice thrusting out from the wall.

"Sweet Mary," she gasped. "Gervais."

Awareness crept on light feet over Rand's senses. The effort of dragging his eyes open proved too great, so he lay still. The cawing of rooks and the cry of gulls added to the cacophony of pain in his head. Kitchen smells and the odor of stale cider wafted from some nearby source. A ringing at his temple reminded him of the blow that had felled him.

That blow... His muddled mind sought an answer. He didn't remember doing battle, but... his own men had felled him, because... because...

Realization detonated in his brain. Because the causeway had been destroyed. Henry's desperate march to Calais would be thwarted.

Rand yanked open his eyes and struggled to prop himself up. Blinking at the dim, dust-sprinkled light, he scanned the roughly furnished room. A twig broom had swept patterns in the dirt floor. A black-and-white cat mewed and padded to his side. He was in the town of Eu, at the inn of Lajoye.

Cursing softly, he tried to rise. The swirling pattern on the floor began to spin. He dropped back and craned his neck to peer through a low-beamed doorway. Two figures sat whispering at a table across the room.

"What the hell am I doing here?" Rand growled. His own voice thrummed like hammers in his head.

Both men turned. Rand found himself squinting at the anxious faces of Jack Cade and Robert Batsford.

"Well?" Rand demanded, ignoring the pain.

They hurried to his pallet. Hand shaking, Jack offered a clay mug. "Drink this, my lord, while we explain."

Peevishly, Rand started to refuse the drink. But his mouth felt dry, so he took a deep gulp. The liquid tasted pleasantly of honey and wine. He drained the mug and let the comforting warmth of mead seep through his veins. His scowl deepened. "Speak, Cade, and it had better be good. How long have I been here?"

The priest and the archer exchanged a long glance. Jack swallowed. "All day, my lord."

Sick fury welled up in Rand. He grasped the flask Batsford held and sucked it dry of the remaining mead. On his tongue he detected a subtle herbal tinge.

Batsford leaned forward as if in protest, but Jack pushed the priest aside. "We had to detain you, my lord, else you'd have gone charging back to Bois-Long."

"As any man of honor would have done." He scowled fiercely. "Did not even one of you try to protect the ford?"

Jack flushed. "We could have made a foolhardy attempt. And would have lost our lives and the ford as well."

Rand sat upright and tried to ignore the spinning of his head. "I'm going." The room tilted; the faces of Jack and Batsford blurred.

"Hold, my lord," said the priest. "We're awaiting a report from Chiang. He's gone back to the château to reconnoiter the area. No sense in riding headlong into God knows what."

"*Chiang.* I thought him loyal. Was the destruction of the causeway his doing?"

"Remember, he was with us when we found you, my lord."

Dust motes leaped and shimmered before Rand's eyes. A hideous thought began to form; he fought it. "But Chiang must have planted the charges," he said almost desperately.

Jack stayed silent. Batsford grew preoccupied with the falconer's cuff he wore beneath his priest's robe. Rand stared at his men until Jack's face swam into focus. Finally Jack spoke. "My lord, Chiang didn't plant the charges."

Images rocketed into Rand's tortured mind. Lianna, her gown streaked with river mud, feeding him a lame excuse about an errand to the orchard. Lianna, promising to meet him at the hour of the woodcock's flight. Lianna, making love to him as if it were the last time.

"It was the last time, damn her!" Rand bellowed.

Faces taut with pity, Jack and Batsford studied him. Jack said, "Your wife had no choice, my lord. Chiang said the Dauphin Louis came to her in secret, ordered her to destroy the causeway and garrison French troops at Bois-Long."

A strange dullness seeped over Rand. "And she obeyed."

"I believe the dauphin made certain threats."

Fear bounded into his mind. "What sort of threats?"

"I'm not sure, my lord. But Chiang said the baroness is in no danger."

Rand tried to struggle to his feet. His limbs trembled, his stomach lurched, and sweat broke out on his brow. "We'll see," he said through gritted teeth, "about French troops at Bois-Long."

"My lord, you mustn't go there," said Batsford. Nervously he began toying with the scourge that belted his robe.

"You cannot," added Jack.

Reeling, Rand seized the mug, sniffed it, and flung it away. Sickness and rage clouded his vision. "What the hell was in that mead?"

Shamefaced, Jack stared at the floor, at the empty mug. "Tincture of poppy."

"Damn you, Jack." But even as Rand spoke, he began sinking back on the pallet.

"Forgive me, my lord." Jack's voice was soft with regret. "I feared to detain you by trickery, but I feared even more what would happen if you went back to Bois-Long."

His body rendered helpless by the numbing effect of the opiate, Rand closed his eyes. Sleep beckoned, promising respite from the bitter sense of betrayal.

Oh, Lianna, he said silently, slipping into darkness, I thought our love meant more to you than this.

"I thought he meant more to you than this," said Guy.

"I had no choice," Lianna said, repeating the defensive

words for perhaps the hundredth time, now to the seneschal. Rebelling against Gervais's insistence on double rations of wine for the French soldiers, Guy had sought out Lianna and demanded to know why she'd opened her husband's home to these undisciplined marauders.

"But my lady—"

"Hush," Lianna whispered. Moments after Gervais's arrival, all had been summoned to the great hall. The household knights, shamed, furious, and outnumbered, had been disarmed by the newcomers. Already the dauphin's men clamored for food and ale. "I cannot risk explaining now."

"In the past your lord husband had no trouble dealing with Mondragon."

Lianna thought of the dauphin's threat to Aimery. "I had another matter to consider, Guy." Catching his mutinous look, she added, "I'll speak to Gervais about the wine."

Marauders, she thought as she surveyed the boisterous knights in the hall, was too mild a term for the self-serving Frenchmen. These soldiers were hardly the finest flower of French chivalry. Most were as rough as felons, as hardened as mercenaries.

She jostled her way through the crowded hall, touching the dagger hilt protruding from her girdle when a man's ribald joke darkened to a lusty threat. She reached Gervais at the high table, where he sat conversing with some of his men. Macée, looking smug yet oddly ill at ease, hovered at the edge of the group.

"I would speak to you in private, Gervais," Lianna said in a commanding voice. Without waiting for a response, she marched through the screened passage to the privy chamber.

Moments later Gervais arrived, his wife hard at his heels. "Do not flatter yourself," said Gervais, "that I jump to do your bidding. But I'm as anxious as you to renew our acquaintance, Lianna." Smiling, he held out his arms. In the flare of a standing candle he looked handsome, earnest, his brown eyes warm, his face sincere. At one time she had been taken in by that trustworthy look. Now she knew a serpent lurked behind the congenial smile.

She glared at him. "How did you convince the dauphin to let you come here? What lies did you tell?"

"I merely offered my services," Gervais said. "Surely you've not forgotten there's an invasion afoot." He glanced from side to side. "Where are Rand and his men?"

"The dauphin said nothing about making my husband stay to suffer your revenge."

The look on her face must have shown Gervais that she'd tell him nothing about Rand's whereabouts. He shrugged. "It matters not. King Henry is sure to retreat to Harfleur, taking your cowardly husband and his motley archers with him."

Anger sizzled through her veins. "He is not a coward. He—" She broke off. Like Gervais, many would think Rand had deserted rather than fight. The rumor was sure to cut straight to her husband's valiant heart. Oh, Lord, she thought, what have I done?

"And the Chinaman?"

She narrowed her eyes. "Chiang is gone, too."

Another shrug. "I always figured him for a traitor. A pity, though; I should have liked to turn his guns on the English." Gervais slid a calculating look at Lianna. "Of course, your own skill could serve the cause of France."

She almost laughed. France, in the form of the dauphin,

had threatened death to her son and sent a company of brigands to her home. "No," she said.

"Oh? Are you saying you don't wish to see Henry return in defeat to England?"

She chewed her lip. "I want peace, Gervais. I just want peace. And you'd best think twice before you send your knights to do a gunner's job. Explosives are dangerous in the wrong hands."

Macée, whose bleary eyes indicated she'd availed herself of plenty of wine, gave Lianna a simpering smile. "Aye, we mustn't use explosives, not with the baby around—"

"Be silent, woman!" Gervais's command resounded in the stone-walled chamber.

Lianna's head began to pound. "Let her speak. The baby?" she repeated incredulously.

"Oh, please, yes," said Macée in a rush. "I've been so worried about little Aimery since Cade snatched him from my arms. I wouldn't have hurt the child. You know how I love him. I want to see him. Is he in his nursery, or—"

"Rants like a madwoman," Gervais said, but his face had gone pale.

Realization bolted through Lianna, igniting a mixture of fury, relief, and dark amusement. "You really don't know where the baby is," she breathed, uncertain whether to laugh, cry, or gnash her teeth.

Macée looked confused. "But we thought—"

A ringing slap from Gervais stopped her short. She stumbled back, holding her wrist to her mouth. Tears shimmered on her lashes. "Oh, Gervais," she choked, "you've hurt me."

Pity, unbidden and unexpected, touched Lianna's

heart. Despite her treachery, Macée now seemed a victim, twisted by the force of her dark devotion to Gervais. She rushed to the woman. "*Nom de Dieu*, you're bleeding—"

"I'll do worse if you don't get out of my sight!" yelled Gervais.

As Macée ran sobbing from the room, Lianna whirled. "You don't know where Aimery is, and neither does Louis."

"All that matters is that you believed him readily enough to obey his command."

She'd betrayed her husband on the strength of an empty threat. Red lights of rage danced before her eyes as she catapulted herself toward Gervais. "You scheming bastard," she hissed. Cursing furiously, she lashed out with fists and feet.

He grunted and swore when her fist landed squarely on his nose, unleashing a stream of blood. With a great heave, he shoved her from him. She flew backward and landed atop a pile of firewood by the hearth. Split logs dug painfully into her ribs, and the impact left her gasping for breath.

A slight tremor of his hands belied Gervais's otherwise calm mien. Stanching his bloodied nose with his sleeve, he crossed to Lianna. She kicked, but he was quicker. His hand shot out, grasped her by the hair. He yanked her to her feet.

"What a fool you are to fight me," he said, his face very close to hers. "Bois-Long is mine, and it can be yours, too, if you would only concede defeat."

"Fool's talk, spoken by a fool."

"I speak reason." He wiped the last trickle of blood from his nose, then insolently ran his hand over her breasts, her stomach. "I've wanted you since first we met, Lianna. Think of it. I'll be lord and you'll be my lady—"

"We are both married to others, you dolt."

"Your uncle of Burgundy has shown that prior marriages need post no obstacle."

A chill eddied through her. The half-mad light in his eyes held dark and fearsome promises.

"You disgust me," she spat.

"You enchant me," he replied. He began lowering his lips to hers. She twisted her head to one side. But his hand in her hair drew her face inexorably toward his.

Just as she steeled herself for the hot, wet assault of Gervais's mouth, the door to the chamber banged open.

Abruptly, Gervais let her go. She fell back onto the woodpile.

"My lord," said a soldier. "An English advance guard approaches."

Pennons fluttering in the warm autumn wind, the vanguard emerged from the woods to the south. High on the deserted gunner's walk, Lianna stood watching. Her heart lodged in her throat as the small party drew near. The vast army that had poured from fifteen hundred ships at Harfleur was no more. Sickness and starvation had reduced the force to a few thousand weary, ill-fed men. The approaching party was smaller still, perhaps a hundred.

To each side of the barbican, Gervais's soldiers made ready to fend off an attack. Their crossbows loaded with razor-tipped quarrels, the archers stood between the merlons. Vats of Greek fire, plundered from Chiang's armory, sat along the wall walk, ready to be lighted and showered on the enemy.

Hearing a noise, Lianna looked down. On the wall walk strode a knight in battle regalia. A flash of gold and white, the leopard emblem upon a *cotte d'armes*, took her breath away. Impossible, and yet...

"Rand?"

Laughter pealed from the dome-shaped basinet. He opened the visor.

"Gervais!" She scrambled down from the gunner's walk. "How dare you wear my husband's colors, his helmet?"

He laughed again. "Since your husband turned tail, I see no reason to preserve his raiments as holy relics."

"You are an abomination."

Gervais's face hardened. He pointed at the approaching vanguard. "That, my lady, is the abomination. A party of raiding foreigners who presume to invade French lands." He shook his gauntleted fist. Turning back to Lianna, he said, "Take some of the knights up and man the guns."

"No. I told you I would not."

"Not even for Bois-Long, Lianna? For France?"

She thought of her husband, betrayed by her and spirited to safety by his loyal men. She thought of her son, a stranger in the keeping of an Englishwoman. She thought of Bonne, pining for the man she'd known as husband for only one night. And finally, she considered her people, batted between Rand and Gervais for nearly two years.

"I have given enough for France," she stated, and turned to watch the advance party. She recognized the white rose standard of Edward, Duke of York. If the powerful noble resented Rand now, he'd despise him when he learned what awaited at Bois-Long.

The party halted some hundred yards distant. A stir among them showed they'd spied the ruined causeway.

"They're within range," said Gervais. "Get to the keep, Lianna." She ignored him.

He snapped his visor shut and signaled to his master archer. The master raised a hand. A swarm of quarrels leaped from the battlements and drove toward the English party.

Screams tore through the air. Two men fell. One lay motionless; the other floundered like a beached fish.

The crossbowmen reloaded their bows.

"No!" Lianna gasped, and ran toward the archers.

"Get away from the wall," Gervais ordered.

She tossed her head. "Not until you cease this attack."

The archers didn't have to shoot again. The Duke of York reined in his horse and gestured angrily at Gervais. A white flag of truce went up.

"Excellent," said Gervais, and she heard the smile in his voice despite the concealing visor. "He knows better than to play the fool. Bertrand!" Gervais shouted to his herald, who came scrambling to the battlement.

"You're to take a message to the English. Tell them they'll find no safe ford on French land. Tell them they'll hie to England if they value their hides."

The herald gulped and nodded nervously. He glanced down at the river; Lianna knew he was wondering about crossing the swift waters in a rowboat.

"A moment, Bertrand." Gervais opened his visor, removed a gauntlet, and fished beneath his breastplate. "Tell the English captain to give this to King Henry."

Lianna gaped in astonishment at the object Gervais placed in the herald's hand. A gold-encrusted emerald, a leopard cut into its glittering depths. Minutely engraved around the edges was the motto *A vaillans coeurs riens impossible.*

"But that's Rand's," she said in useless protest.

"Aye, so I guessed," said Gervais with a malicious grin. "'Twill confirm Rand's shift to the French side."

Lianna lunged at Bertrand, tried to grab the talisman and fling it into the river. Like talons of steel, Gervais's gauntleted hand wrapped around her arm and hauled her back.

"A pity to relinquish a bauble of such value," he said. "Still, I'd have King Henry know exactly who is responsible for destroying this ford."

With clumsy movements Rand saddled his horse. The men had certainly prepared his betrayal well. They'd brought his armor and Charbu's, and their own mounts and weapons. The one item they'd left behind was his *cotte d'armes.* No matter, he thought darkly. This was no time for the vanity of martial colors.

"Please, my lord," said Jack, "wait for Chiang before you embark on anything rash."

"Damn it, Jack, your accursed potion kept me abed for another day and a night. King Henry's army is marching into a trap, and you dare bid me wait? If you wish to malinger here, you may, but I am going to warn the king."

"I'd not advise it, my lord," said a voice from behind. Rand and Jack turned. Chiang stood in the stable-yard.

"Damme, it's about time you got back to us," said Jack. "What news? Did you see my Bonne?"

Chiang's shoulders sagged. "No. The knights of Bois-Long have been disarmed, stripped of power." Rand shifted impatiently, and Chiang hurried on. "Henry's advance guard arrived to find the causeway destroyed. One man—a knight of the House of York—was killed by an arrow. Another was wounded."

Rand swore and gripped the pommel of his saddle.

"Wait, my lord, that's not all." Chiang drew a deep breath. "Gervais Mondragon and thirty knights of the dauphin occupy Bois-Long."

Fury clamored in Rand's brain. For a moment he stood still, silent, forming a picture of Lianna opening the château to the scheming Frenchman. "Damn her," he whispered.

"She had no say in the occupying force," Chiang added.

"Nor will she have a say in what I plan for Mondragon," Rand muttered. Once again he moved to mount his horse.

Once again Chiang delayed him. "You've not heard the end of it. Mondragon wore your *cotte d'armes* when he mounted the attack. He sent an amulet with your motto to King Henry, so it would look like a gesture of fealty to the French."

"Amulet? What . . . ?" Rand had almost forgotten the gift. Nearly two years earlier he'd hurled it into the woods. Oh, God, had Lianna found it in the glade? Found it and presented it to Gervais to serve as evidence of Rand's treason?

"Christ," said Jack. "The king will think . . ."

"That I've betrayed him." Rand sagged against his horse.

Chiang nodded grimly. "You've been declared a traitor, an outlaw, my lord."

A sentence of death would have caused Rand less despair. His honor was all he had left after Lianna's betrayal.

That his countrymen believed him a traitor would stain not only his reputation, but that of his blameless son.

He raked his fingers through his hair. "What is Henry's plan?"

"He'll march until he finds a place to cross the Somme. I ranged inland and found that most of the fords have been destroyed and littered by rocks and timber. The causeway at Voyennes still stands."

"But that's sixty miles upriver. They're starving already. This will cost days."

"Worse," muttered Chiang.

"What?"

"The French army is gathered on the north bank. They'll keep pace with the English and foil any attempt to cross."

Rand stood numb and silent. Lajoye's grandchildren frolicked in the hayloft. In the dooryard, Marie chased a scrawny rooster. Waves beat a relentless tattoo on the sea-bitten rocks.

"There is one thing we can do to help," said Rand.

Jack's jaw dropped. "Us? We're but ten men—"

"Eleven," said Chiang.

"—poorly armed," Jack finished.

"No man with his longbow and a quiver of arrows is poorly armed. We'll go after the French. Perhaps if we distract them with sallies and night forays, it'll give Henry a chance to get across the river."

Slowly his men gathered around them. Piers and Dylan waxed their bowstrings. Batsford crossed himself. Simon arrived, burdened with Rand's armor. Peter Finch, Neville, Godfrey, and Giles emerged from the inn with sacks of foodstuffs supplied by Lajoye. Rand studied his men, each in turn. "I've been branded a traitor," he said, his throat taut with pain. "If you choose not to follow me, none shall think ill of you."

"We're with you, my lord," declared Jack. Murmurs of assent rose from the others.

"Very well. A force as small as ours should have no trouble swimming the horses across the Somme. The French army may be large, but even a giant can feel the sting of a bee. And then..." Rand's voice lowered to a grim whisper. "I'll deal with Mondragon...and my wife."

Chapter

Amoonless midnight wrapped Lianna in a dark cloak of secrecy. A ceaseless hiss of autumn rain covered the sound of her footsteps. Unnoticed by the men-at-arms, who had indulged in extra rations of wine as a reward for their performance against the English, she crossed the rain-slick courtyard and stole through a low door leading to the water gate.

She wore a stableboy's hooded tunic and breeches and carried her wooden sabots in her hand. The hilt of a dagger protruded from her belt. Carefully folded within the belt was a cache of gold and silver coin. In her other hand she held a sack of provisions, for her journey could take days.

Pressing her hand against the wall to keep from slipping on the steps, she slid her feet into the sabots and descended to the river's edge. This was where she'd been forced to betray Rand; from this same place she intended to launch her quest to save his honor and his life.

Briefly she glanced up at the battlements. A naked pole rose against the dark sky. She turned away. Rand had raised the banner of lilies and leopards to proclaim himself lord of the keep; Gervais had ripped it down.

The rain-spattered river appeared inky, fathomless. Tremors of fear started in her belly and radiated out to her limbs. With clumsy movements she untied a small rowboat from its hidden mooring in the tall, plumed reeds. But fear of another sort steadied her resolve. Rand's life was in danger, and for him she would brave the cold currents of the water.

Mud sucked at her feet. Stifling a groan of dread, she got into the boat and took up the oars. The bobbing motion set her teeth to chattering; determinedly she clenched her jaw.

The château had one "dead" wall, a spot that couldn't be seen or defended from above. Her hands, slick with cold rain and the sweat of fear, gripped the oars. Keeping to the shadow of the dead wall and praying that the rain would keep the sentries inside the barbican, she began to row. Blisters rose on her palms, but the discomfort seemed minor, for each oar stroke, each lift of the boat, blew a rush of terror through her. These waters had claimed her mother's life, but if she turned coward now, Rand would pay the price. Focusing on that thought, she plowed across the river.

On the opposite shore she clambered out of the craft. Her breath rasped in short, uneven gasps. Her limbs gave way to the weakness of relief. She fell to her knees and felt the solid ground beneath her. Then, forcing herself to regain control, she rose and plunged into the dark, dripping forest toward the boggy headwaters of the Somme. New unease gripped her. How far had the English marched since being driven from the ford?

Ten miles or more, she gauged three hours later, when her rain-soaked feet and weary legs threatened to give way to fatigue. She located the mired path of the English army. War-horses and baggage tumbrils had plowed a road along the looping river, leading inland.

Lord, she thought, what manner of commander was Henry that he could drive his sick and starving men so far, so quickly?

The river ran wide, deep, and muddy, offering no ford. To draw her mind from discomfort, she concentrated on Rand. Pray God Chiang's tinctures would detain him. She needed time to reach Henry, to explain that her husband was a victim of betrayal—by Gervais, by the Englishmen, and by his own wife.

The sound of masculine voices penetrated the hiss and spatter of rain. She stopped, pushed back her hood, and stood rooted, listening. A burst of laughter. The whinny of horses.

Yet the sounds seemed to be coming from the north bank. Had the English managed to cross?

Pulling her hood up again, she hurried on. She noticed flickers of light. Soon she recognized the shapes of tents and pavilions, glowing from within. There were so many. She'd not thought the English so numerous or well-provisioned.

At closer range she heard the voices clearly and made out the devices on the tents.

French words, French devices.

The noisy, well-equipped army across the Somme was French. The forces of d'Albret and Boucicaut were shadowing the English, matching them mile for mile, waiting to slaughter them should Henry dare to ford the river.

Dizzy with fear, she continued on and found the English army just beyond the deserted town of Abbeville. In contrast to the rowdy and confident French forces, this army huddled in dismal quiet in the burned-out shelters of the wasted village.

She backed under the shadows of the dripping trees. Would Henry receive her? Aye, he must. Drawing a deep breath, she stepped onto the muddied road.

"Who goes there?" Oddly, the voice reminded her of Darby Green, who'd lost his head to a French blade. The speech was thick with the accents of England's northern shires. A man appeared out of the gloom. "Who are you, boy?"

She glanced down at her stained breeches and wooden clogs and decided not to waste explanations on the sentry.

"I am no boy, but a woman, and I would speak to the king."

"A woman, eh? He takes no whores on march."

"I am no whore, either," she said. "Where is the king?"

The man grasped her arm and pulled her toward the camp. "You'll see the king when my master deems it right and proper."

"And who is your master, sir?"

"His Grace, the Duke of York. And he's abed."

York. Her heart sank. Forcing a note of command into her voice, she said, "Then rouse him."

The watchman yanked her toward a firelit shelter. Ducking beneath the stubble of half-burned thatch, he spoke briefly to a man stationed at the door. The man entered the dwelling.

"Christ," grumbled a thick voice. "Food is rationed. Now sleep as well?"

Lianna was ushered inside and thrust before the corpulent and suspicious duke. Of all the ill luck, to find herself at the mercy of the man who blamed her for the burning of three ships at Southampton, the man who had been turned away from Bois-Long at the cost of one of his men.

"For this," grumbled Edward, rubbing the front of his wrinkled smock, "you rouse me from my sleep?" A smoky torch flicked shadows across his florid face.

Summoning all her courage, she let her hood fall back. "Your Grace, it's Lianna, Baroness Longwood."

He scrambled to his feet and wiped his eyes with his fist. "So it is," he sneered. His darting glance fastened on her belt. "She's armed, you idiot," he said to the sentry. "I'll see you flayed for your neglect."

White-faced, the sentry scurried forward. Before he reached her, she yanked the dagger from her belt. "Here." She handed it over. "I mean you no harm." She held still, praying her cache of money was safe.

"What's in the sack?" York demanded.

"Food, Your Grace."

"I'll have that as well." Setting the items aside, he said, "You make bold to come here, after your husband has defied Henry and caused the death of a man from my household."

"Your Grace, my husband did not defy his king," she said quickly. "He meant to hold the causeway for the English army."

"Think you I'm fool enough to credit that, when I saw Rand commanding French crossbowmen? Shall I believe him innocent when I held in my own hand the amulet Henry gave to Longwood?"

"That was a ruse enacted by Gervais Mondragon, who has garrisoned Bois-Long in the name of the Dauphin Louis."

A shuffling sounded from without. A soldier burst into the room, saying, "The advance scouts have found a ford at Voyennes. If we cut across the loop of the river between Chaulnes and Nesle, we can beat the French to the—"

"Hold your damned tongue, varlet!" Edward bellowed. "You speak too freely, plague take you." Chastened, the man-at-arms glanced at Lianna, then scuttled away.

Torchlight carved menacing shadows on York's beefy face. "You've heard all. Know you what that means, Baroness?"

Lianna knew, but she held silent and still.

"I must make a prisoner of you."

"Damn it, York, I'll not have it, I say," snapped King Henry. His features lighted by the heatless sun of early morn, the monarch glanced contemptuously at the manacles on Lianna's wrists. "Remove those at once."

"But, Your Grace, we cannot risk freeing her," said Edward. "Her husband has turned traitor and is yet at large, and she overheard the plan to make our crossing at Voyennes."

Battling the fatigue of a sleepless night, Lianna faced the king. "I would answer these untruthful charges."

"And I would listen, my lady."

With painful candor she related the dauphin's secret visit, his urgent order, his veiled threat. She described how she and Chiang had lured Rand and others from the château.

"Then I blew up the causeway," she finished bleakly.

York snorted in disbelief. Henry frowned at his cousin, then said to Lianna, "*You* blew up the causeway, Baroness?"

She nodded. "I set the charges myself. My household knights lit the fuses." She swallowed hard. "Then the dauphin's captain rode in." Lowering her eyes, she said, "Before God, I'd never have done it had I known Louis's threat to my son was a bluff, that Gervais was his captain."

Henry's face softened ever so slightly.

"Transparent lies, all of it," muttered York. "One should expect as much from a woman of the House of Burgundy. Doubtless she was taught equivocation from the cradle."

She clenched her hands. The cold iron of the manacles was but a passing discomfort compared to the bite of York's insult. Burgundy would neither commit to an alliance Henry badly needed nor join the French in mounting their defense.

"Her story makes sense," said Henry to the duke.

"You would take her word over mine, cousin?"

"I would seek the truth."

"I have given you that, sire. I have also given you more than a thousand men at muster, two hundred men-at-arms, and seven hundred horse archers."

"And I paid you handsomely, cousin," snapped Henry.

Angry red suffused Edward's cheeks. "Might I remind you, sire, of things that cannot be bought, such as the support of my vassals in the north? Yorkshire is more important to the Crown than a small barony in Picardy."

"They are all important if I am to unite England and France."

Wisely, York made no reply.

Her face a careful blank, Lianna looked up at King Henry. Deep in his eyes she read the uncertainty of a man whose dreams of glory had been shattered by privation and sickness, a man who knew well the sting of betrayal. How could she expect him to believe her, a Frenchwoman loyal to King Charles?

He asked, not unkindly, where Rand was.

She glanced quickly at York. Rand's enemies grew in number day by day. "I do not know, sire."

"He is at Bois-Long," York insisted. "Did I not give you his amulet, which he sent as a token of his defiance?"

"Then why the devil would his wife be here?" Henry asked in exasperation.

"Obviously he realized our campaign would succeed, and sent her to save his neck with her lies."

"The amulet fell into Gervais's hands," Lianna insisted.

Nearby, mounted men and foot soldiers formed up to resume the march. Henry said, "My lady, give me your parole that you won't try to escape. Then I'll have the shackles removed."

She drew a long, unsteady breath. "I cannot. For were I not in chains, I'd be obliged to break my word of honor."

Respect crossed Henry's face. "You could have lied."

She shot a resentful look at York. "I have never lied to you, sire."

Trumpets blared. Looking distracted, Henry said, "If you will not tell me where Rand is, then I cannot help you." He eyed her regretfully. "Until I discover the truth, we must detain you. You'll ride under guard with the baggage train."

Miserable, manacled, and despairing, Lianna traveled with the English army, past Amiens, Crouy, Piquigny.

The men subsisted on hazelnuts and berries gathered as they plodded through the misty woods. Between fitful naps snatched in the cart, she pondered escape. Chains restricted her movements and made stealth impossible. York himself held the key and guarded it as carefully as he guarded the king's chancery seal. And if she were to get away, where would she go? The man she hated and feared occupied her home. The man she loved and trusted was lost to her forever. Grimly she conceded that she had no choice but to stay with the English army.

A few men, northerners from the House of York and friends of the soldier killed at Bois-Long, sidled close to leer.

"I smell a traitor's whore," one of them sneered.

"Aye, but we'll soon bring Longwood as low as she."

Rodney, the carter, cursed and waved them away. It was a measure of Henry's discipline that overall she was treated with deference by the baggage guards, chaplains, musicians, and lads who rode on occasion with her.

The mighty French army rode apace, yelling insults across the river, promising to capture Henry and parade him through the streets of Paris. They said they were painting a special tumbril to transport him on a march of shame.

She felt no kinship with the Frenchmen who mocked her captors. Those haughty lords, she conceded reluctantly, would not treat a female prisoner with the deference the English extended.

Each evening, as Henry made his rounds to encourage the men and laud them for their tenacity, he paused with a word for Lianna.

"I sent a scout to Bois-Long, my lady," he said one night when they stopped in the empty town of Boves.

"He'll not find Rand there."

The king offered her a handful of hazelnuts. Glancing at the carter, his face carved gaunt by hunger, she said, "Give them to Rodney, Your Grace. I've eaten."

Henry's eyes told her he knew better. Smiling slightly, he gave the food to the carter.

"How different you are from the nobles of France," she said.

"How so, Baroness?"

"You dress as a commoner, while the French knights sport feathered panaches and glittering martial colors."

Henry grinned. "I do have the means and the mien to glitter like Polaris when the occasion calls for royal pomp. You may be sure that, when the time comes, the French will see my colors, and bow down to them."

His confidence disarmed her. How could he believe his ragged and spiritless army still had a chance against the overwhelming numbers of Frenchmen?

"At present," the king continued, "I must concern myself with preserving my armor from rusting in this accursed rain." He squinted through the mist. "The circumstances of my birth do not entitle me to empty vanity. I would have it said that Henry Fifth earned the right to rule." He stared at her thoughtfully. "Are you having doubts about the French nobles?"

Her eyes hardened. She glanced down at her ironbound wrists. "Not about the rightness of their cause, Your Grace. Only about their arrogance." She paused, recalling the French armed parties that rushed in from time to time to harry the English army. The disorganized *écorcheurs* did little harm. Had they but adequate leadership, the invaders would now be but a bloodstain seeping into the chalky terrain of Picardy.

She tossed the thought aside and said, "The French nobles doubtless consider your army unworthy of a fight."

"Your countrymen will be happily mistaken in treating my campaign so lightly."

She agreed. As would the bickering lords if they but knew the skill and determination of the intrepid English king.

Turning the subject, she asked, "Your Grace, how can you still doubt my husband? Was he not the man who spared you and your brothers by denouncing the Lollard plot to murder you?"

"Henry Scrope served me well, too. Yet he turned on me."

And was executed for it, she recalled with a shiver. "But Scrope was a weakling seduced by promises of wealth, of higher station, greater influence—"

"Your husband," Henry snapped, suddenly angry, "was seduced by a more powerful force than that. The young fool loves you, Baroness. And you are loyal to France."

"I am devoted to peace, Your Grace, be it from the leopard or the lily. I am bound to defend my husband's honor."

"As I am bound to punish a traitor, if traitor he be."

"Monjoie! À St. Denis!" The lethal French battle cry rang through the woods, startling the English army and halting their plodding pace.

"Enemy knights!" bellowed a soldier, running through the ranks. "They're riding down from the garrison at Corbie."

Rodney reined in his team. Chains dragging, Lianna pulled herself up, standing on tiptoe to see the bridge.

Beside her, young Johnny, son of Sir John Cornwall, scrambled for a view.

"At last," the lad breathed. "The French show their colors." The azure and gold of the French lilies joined the sanguine oriflamme of St. Denis in a dance upon the wind, high above the gleaming helms of the French knights. "Cowards!" the boy shrieked. "White-livered bastards!" He turned to Lianna. "Quick, my lady, what is the French for bastard?"

"Just hush up and watch. You might learn something."

Johnny, who regarded her with a mixture of awe and admiration, rested his chin on the side of the cart.

The archers formed up and loosed their arrows, but the knights ranged too close and the arrows flew over the heads of the oncoming French. During the skirmish, Lianna discovered in herself a deep well of fear. She was afraid for the English, afraid for her husband and son, and afraid for herself should the French prevail and find a woman among the enemy.

One archer, trying desperately to draw his longbow, met death beneath the iron-shod hooves of a war-horse. More horses, mired to the hocks in mud, reared and charged unimpeded into the English ranks. *"Nom de Dieu,"* said Lianna, sickened by the bowmen's screams of agony, "they ought to avail themselves of a chevaux-de-frise."

Johnny looked at her curiously. "What mean you?"

"My uncle of Burgundy saw the Sultan Bayard use the tactic at the Battle of Nicopolis. His archers planted a fence of sharp stakes to stop the cavalry advance." She pressed her cheek to the side of the tumbril and wondered why the lives of English bowmen mattered to her. All life, she mused, thinking of Rand, of Aimery, was precious.

"We're finished," Johnny said in a hollow tone.

She noticed a stir among the French knights across the river. To her astonishment, one fell, his neck skewered by an arrow that had penetrated the gorget of his armor. Two others flopped from their destriers and floundered in the mud.

Confused, she sought the source of the assault of arrows. The English archers could not have felled those three; the range and angle were all wrong.

"Hail Mary," breathed Rodney. "The French are being harried by archers on their own side of the river." Movement, as insubstantial as shadows, rippled through the distant woods.

A fourth knight fell. Plagued by more phantom arrows, his comrades retreated to the garrison. By the end of the skirmish several Frenchman had been taken prisoner by the English.

Lianna frowned. "But who . . . ?"

A crackle of laughter grated above the shouts of soldiers and the screams of horses. A vivid stream of profanity, stunningly familiar, followed the laughter and then faded.

Lianna collapsed in the cart, laughing and weeping with relief. "Jack," she gasped. "'Twas him, I know it." She lapsed into rapid, inarticulate French while Johnny and Rodney stared at her in confusion.

When she'd regained control, she considered telling Henry that Rand and his men had foiled the French attack. But York, not the king, visited her that evening. Edward considered her his own prisoner and doubtless meant to demand a ransom from Burgundy once they reached Calais. Rand, she decided, catching York's vindictive glare, was safer in anonymity, at least until her husband's innocence could be proven.

She pretended to ignore York; he pretended to ignore her. Johnny, bedazzled by the grand duke, told him of the Sultan Bayard's chevaux-de-frise at the Battle of Nicopolis. York pointedly dismissed Burgundy's heroism at that battle. Instead he cited the valor of the King's father, Henry Bolingbroke, who had also fought in the war against the Turks.

King Henry did not come the next night, either, for he was busy instructing his archers to sharpen long poles. York, ever anxious to garner Henry's favor, took full credit for the idea of the chevaux-de-frise.

"What day is it?" asked Rand, blinking at Batsford through a mist of predawn drizzle.

The priest yawned, flexed his legs, and frowned at his sodden boots. He thought a moment. "Friday, October the twenty-fifth. The Feast of Saints Crispin and Crispinian."

Rand sighed and rose wearily from his bedroll. A canopy of willows afforded little protection from the ceaseless rain. His flesh, encased for days beneath layers of rain and sweat-soaked clothing, was beginning to shrivel.

He roused the other men, and they formed a circle beneath the willow. While they ate a meager meal of biscuit and dried beef, Rand looked upon them with affection and pity.

Batsford, with his unique combination of piety and camaraderie, had acted as spiritual guide, urging the men onward when weariness, despair, and fear threatened to sap their will to forge ahead with the guerrilla attacks on the French army. Jack's foul-mouthed commands took up where Batsford's pious words left off. Simon, hardened by privation yet still a lad, cared for his lord's armor as if the pieces were the crown jewels. Dylan, Piers, Peter, Neville, Godfrey, and Giles fought in a back-to-back unit that had become as lethal as a siege engine. Chiang, mysterious and silent, had joined the mismatched brotherhood. Midnight blasts from his cannonlike handgun had sobered forever many a drunken French soldier.

Lianna's betrayal, provoked or not by the dauphin's threats, had made outlaws of these simple, steadfast men. They'd be justified if they deserted. Rand would not blame them if they fled to English-held Harfleur to take ship to homes they'd not seen for nigh on two years.

Yet they stayed. They stayed and rode hard through forests and fens, doing what they could to plague the advancing French army. Like an ungainly shadow, that huge force loomed between King Henry and the fortified city of Calais.

"Henry's army is but a mile east of us," Rand said quietly. "We'll see pitched battle today."

Ten pairs of eyes fastened on him. "At last," Jack breathed.

Rand took up a stick. "Here," he said, pushing the end into the wet ground, "is Maisoncelles." The name of the town tasted bitter in his mouth, for at Maisoncelles he'd nearly lost his child, his wife, his life. "To the north and west lies Agincourt. I saw its keep when I climbed to the top of yonder rise. The village to the east is called Tramecourt." He etched more marks on the ground. "A valley lies here, with woods on either side. It surrounds the road to Calais."

"The ideal battlefield," Jack mused.

"Aye, but for whom?" asked Dylan. "Thirty thousand

of France's finest, or five thousand starving English?"

"I'm going to fight for Henry," said Rand. "You are free to stay clear of battle if you so choose."

"Stay clear?" snorted Jack. "I've ridden my goddamned tail off keeping up with this march. I've spent a hundred arrows a day playing cat-and-mouse with the French army. Think you I'd turn away now, my lord?"

The others vehemently agreed.

"But how can we join the fighting?" asked Simon. "When Piers sneaked into the English camp, he heard that the Duke of York is out for your blood. Edward holds you responsible for driving him away from Bois-Long."

As he had for over a fortnight, Rand fought down a rising tide of bitterness. Piers had also learned that Henry had sent a scout to Bois-Long. The scout had not returned; perhaps Henry would never know that Gervais Mondragon, not Rand, had driven off the advance guard.

As for Lianna... He tightened his grip on the stick. Chiang swore she'd acted out of fear for the baby and for Rand himself. Yet even were her motives so noble, she'd betrayed her husband. She should have consulted him, should have known he'd have found a way to defend the château and see to the safety of Aimery. But she'd acted alone, disdaining Rand's abilities.

He stabbed the stick into the soft ground. "Once the fighting starts, we'll attach ourselves to the left flank of Henry's army." He glanced at the ten mounts and the two big packhorses, cropping dispiritedly at clumps of salt grass. "What better way to prove our loyalty to the king?"

They finished their breakfast. Father Batsford offered prayers and heard confessions. Rand spoke quietly of the sins he'd committed, sins of pride, sins of foolishness.

Batsford waved his rosary in annoyance. "My lord, your 'sins' bore me. You were dubbed the Spotless by your fellows at Anjou. You've borne the title well."

Rand shook his head. "Then why did I allow myself to be duped by a woman and branded a traitor by my king?"

"Is it a sin for a man to love, to trust?"

Rand shrugged. "It matters not. We'll likely all be dead by evening."

"An encouraging note on which to conclude," said Batsford dryly. "Come, my lord. Arm yourself and we'll be off."

While the archers busied themselves with waxing bowstrings and notching arrows, Chiang prepared charges for his long handgun. Simon brought forth Rand's armor. As the squire fastened the lacings, straps, and buckles of breastplate, faulds, and cuisses, Jack Cade sidled near. Grinning, he made a game of tossing his sharpened dagger at a nearby tree trunk. The dagger found its target with breathtaking precision.

"You're well practiced," Rand remarked.

"Aye, they took my fingers but not my aim."

Rand winced at a sudden pinch of pressure on his arm. "Have a care, Simon," he said. "You've made a tourniquet of my vambrace."

Jack chuckled. "Such is the discomfort of one destined for glory. Remind me never to become a knight."

"The arm piece used to fit," said Simon.

"Our lord has grown," Jack remarked, and went to retrieve his dagger.

Some hours later, encased in the armor Simon had so carefully protected in waxed cloth, Rand led his men forth. Their horses climbed a ridge that loomed some three hundred feet above the triangular valley he'd surveyed the day before.

Lifting his visor, he squinted through the mist. At first he saw only the distant forest. Then a metallic shimmer caught his eye. He realized that he was looking, not at a row of trees, but at three huge columns of heavily armed Frenchmen.

"God have mercy," Jack said. "'Tis a forest of metal."

Beyond the close-packed host, the French army rolled outward, like steel-draped hills, as far as the eye could see. Lances bristled in the gray morning sky, and ducal standards rode a rising wind. The French wore colors of eye-smarting beauty, as lethal and lovely as Rand's French wife.

Cavalry, foot soldiers, and crossbowmen surrounded a menacing array of gunnery. Bitterly Rand wondered if some of the wheel-mounted arblasts, light cannon, and bombards had been supplied by Lianna.

What was she doing now? Shut up in her fortress and testing her guns? Holding Henry's scout prisoner so the king would never learn the truth? Rand fueled his battle lust with the anger brought on by his thoughts.

A metallic rattle brought him swinging around. There stood Chiang with his bullets and powder, his exotic face drawn into an expression of deep sadness.

"Are we both thinking of Lianna?" he asked.

Chiang nodded.

"You served her nearly all your life. Yet now you side with her enemy."

Chiang looked from side to side and spoke in a low voice. "My lord, blood ties are strong."

Rand's helm crashed against his gorget as he looked up. "What?"

The Chinaman tightened his fist around the barrel of his gun. "If I'm to shed my blood, let it be for my father, Henry Bolingbroke, and my half brother, Henry the Fifth."

Shock barreled into Rand's chest; he nearly stumbled. *"You're Bolingbroke's son?"*

Chiang nodded. "When Bolingbroke was fighting the Turks, he lay with a Chinese slave, who bore him a son."

"My God," said Rand, "so that was why you were bound to help Bolingbroke seize the Crown from Richard Second."

"Aye. I thought it time you knew, my lord." Hefting his gun, Chiang walked away. In a daze of astonishment, Rand stared after King Henry's brother.

Dylan distributed the last of the arrows to the archers. The little Welshman's hands trembled as he worked.

"My lord," asked Simon nervously, "is victory as impossible as it seems?"

"Nay, Simon. The French have forgotten the lessons of Crécy and Poitiers. They follow an antique battle plan that relies on sheer might and disdains the skill of the archers." He dropped his visor. "They've chosen a foolish position to make a stand. The trees on either flank hem them in so that our target is narrowed to that one muddy valley."

"We've buried our arrows in smaller targets than that," Piers boasted.

Grinning, Jack struck the boiled leather of his breastplate and said, "The smaller the target, the bigger the wound. Let's go kill the prissy bastards."

A stir to the right caught Rand's eye. Several hundred

yards distant, the English army gathered at the far end of the ridge. Knowing that his ability to join the battle depended on anonymity, he motioned for his men to halt beneath a concealing veil of low branches.

The king appeared at the head of his pitifully small army. Although bareheaded, he was fully armored. His *cotte d'armes*, covering his chest, bore the leopards of England quartered with the lilies of France. His men formed into one line, four deep. Henry stood at the center, York on the right, Lord Camoys on the left. Erpingham's archers gathered in triangular formations on either side and between the main thrusts.

The English had no reserves. None except Rand and his followers—one a bastard prince, one a priest, one maimed, one a boy, and all scared.

Behind the lines, at the fringe of the Maisoncelles woods, wagons full of baggage and wounded men formed a park—ill protected, as Henry had not the men to spare for a proper guard. Two boys, one hooded, the other bareheaded, peered from the high side of one of the carts. The trumpeters of the minstrel band sat with their instruments lowered. The deployment of the army was carried out in mist-thick silence.

Royally proud as only a king can be, Henry sat a white horse. He raised one arm; the royal banner with the arms of Our Lady, the Trinity, and St. George unfurled above his head.

In the valley below, some of the French were sitting on the ground, eating and drinking as if battle were not moments away. Others jostled for a frontal position. Ever jealous of their own glory, they quarreled. The arguments made a stark contrast to the quiet order of the English. Rand wondered if Gervais were among them. Then he discounted the notion. Mondragon would likely lurk at the rear, hoping to steal his share of the victory after the danger had passed.

Henry placed a basinet on his head. A crown of rubies, sapphires, and pearls marked his rank. He spoke. Rand could not hear the words, but he knew the way of Henry with soldiers. The archers gripped their longbows tighter; the mounted men sat straighter in the saddle. As if by heavenly design, the sun emerged from the clouds and shed a weak light on the field.

Erpingham tossed his baton in the air and shouted, "*Nestroque!*" The marshal's age-old command belled out through the ranks. The bowmen shouted in response.

King Henry then gave the formal cry of battle. "Banner avaunt! In the name of Jesus, Mary, and St. George."

The three tight divisions, dwarfed by the boundless steel wall of the French, marched forward. Archers ran ahead, planting a wall of sharpened stakes.

"What the devil are they doing?" Dylan asked.

With a wry smile, Rand said, "Putting up a fence."

Jack nodded sagely. "The horses have more sense than their riders. They'll shy away from the stakes."

"Or be impaled upon them," said Rand. He reached down and stroked the well-tended coat of Charbu.

The king, York, and Camoys dismounted and came on with drawn swords.

Provoked by the brazenness of a ragged army a fraction its size, the French horsemen galloped around from the wings, flooding like a sea of steel into the gap between the woods. Roars of "*Monjoie! St. Denis!*" filled the air.

"It's time," said Rand.

"God save us all," said Batsford.

"Death to the goddamned French," said Jack.

They cantered down the ridge to join the left flank. Without his martial colors, Rand blended into the ranks of mounted men-at-arms. As he rode, his mind and heart worked in wild, urgent cadence. Certain that death awaited him this day, he embraced his memories. He thought of his son, felt the firm, trusting clench of Aimery's tiny fist about his finger. He thought of Bois-Long, taken from him by a woman's treachery. Yet even now he remembered days of sunshine and nights of splendor, and love for Lianna blazed high in his heart. Somehow, her devotion to France dulled the sting of betrayal. She'd defied him, yet in knowing her, making a life with her, sharing all with her, he'd become a better man. Aye, he'd go to his grave loving Lianna.

Chapter  23

Standing in the baggage cart at the top of the ridge, Lianna watched the battle in horror, awe, and disbelief. The chevaux-de-frise, hidden by mud from the French horsemen, took the knights by surprise. Sickened, she saw horses spitted and disemboweled by the sharpened stakes. Beasts screamed, wheeled, and bucked their armored burdens into the mud. Founts of blood sprayed over the bowmen, drenching them with glorious, hideous color. Entombed by metal, helpless without their pages, the fallen knights met death beneath the blows of English clubs and maces.

Through the next charge, the bowmen kept up a relentless threefold drill of *Notch! Stretch! Loose!* delivering a razor-tipped hail into the ranks of the French.

Still the French nobles came on, swarming into the valley, bearing down with all the speed they could coax from their overburdened destriers. Packed too close to swing a sword, they folded in on one another, trampled their fallen comrades.

Use the guns, she thought in silent frustration. But the arrogant lords had jostled the gunners to either side of the ranks, thus robbing the artillery of a satisfactory field of fire. The crossbowmen, too, had been squeezed aside by disdainful horsemen. Some archers doggedly grappled with cranequins and clinches, gaffles and winders. But their antique bows proved no match for the quick and deadly English longbows.

The crash of steel on steel punctuated the whine of arrows. The slaughter, she thought, sounded like the din of a deadly smithy. She glanced over at Johnny. The boy's face was white, his mouth rimmed by taut lines of fear. Lianna guessed what gripped his mind. The gory reality of pitched battle did not match the flowery tales of valor sung by the bards.

A fresh wave of French knights charged. Some managed to evade the bloodied spikes of the chevaux-de-frise and engaged the English soldiers. She looked at the left flank, where the fighting was most vicious. A tall knight, devoid of an identifying tabard, stood surrounded by four Frenchmen. Even in his suit of steel the man moved with the ease and grace of a dancer. A powerful thrust sliced into the mail beneath one foe's arm. Even before blood welled from the wound, the English knight pivoted to deflect the blade of another. He met blow after blow with magnificent courage and unflinching valor.

Deep within Lianna, an undefinable feeling strained. At first she felt only a sense of admiration for the personal bravery of the lone knight. But as she studied his tireless, calculated movements, she knew it was something more.

Recognition exploded in her mind.

"Dear God, 'tis Rand," she whispered.

Johnny regarded her curiously. "My lady?"

Raw terror left her speechless. The battle was no longer a fight between French and English, archer and horseman. The combat had shrunk to a fight between the man she loved and the French knights intent on killing him.

She tried to pray but could find no coherent words. She dared to hope but could find no promising thoughts. She clung to the side of the cart and watched Rand battle for his life.

Blades, maces, and battle-axes sliced and swung at Rand. His armor was dented in dozens of places. Two more Frenchmen fell beneath his blade, but Lianna could see his energy flagging. The split-second timing that had served him so well only moments ago had suddenly become imprecise. A mace clanged against his basinet. He reeled wildly.

"Help him!" she screamed at the archers who fought nearby. But those not similarly engaged were busy making prisoners of the fallen French nobles. They'd not trade their hard-won booty for the life of one nameless English knight.

Rand recovered from the blow and surged forth. More Frenchmen fell beneath his lethal blade. Just as relief made an inroad into Lianna's terror, a new column of mounted French entered the pocket of fighting. Lances lowered, voices raised, they came on with soul-wrenching speed.

Sobs tore from her throat. She tried to scramble from the cart, but the chains shortened her reach. Unable to witness Rand skewered by a lance, she ground her fists into her eyes.

A burst of dark thunder brought her gaze back to the

battle. The lead horseman had flopped from his saddle; the others galloped away in panic. The men on foot scattered, leaving Rand standing alone, his bloodied sword hanging at his side. Searching through billows of smoke, Lianna made out the small figure of a man running toward Rand. Instantly she identified the gunner's helm and long handgun as Chiang's.

"Sweet Holy Mary," she breathed. Chiang, her friend and confidant, had thrown in his lot with the English. The shift in her master gunner's loyalty bothered her not at all, for Rand was safe. He shouted something to Chiang, and together they plunged down toward the valley and disappeared from view.

"He fought," said Johnny with quiet awe, "like a legend."

Questions seethed through her mind. Did Rand's presence mean the king had found him, forgiven him? Or had her husband joined the battle in anonymity? Finding no answers, she tried to locate him on the field. But now all she could see were the growing piles of dead and wounded, the groups of prisoners.

The French lay floundering, crushed, dying in the mud. Archers, seized by blood lust, threw down their bows and took to stabbing their fallen adversaries between rivets, plunging daggers into visors. Noblemen were dragged off by sergeants in charge of ransoms. The captives, stunned speechless, were deposited by the baggage park. Just fifteen minutes before, these cocksure lords had been eating and drinking and, between toasts, taunting the puny English force.

The mounds of dead towered higher than a man's shoulder. Already carrion crows circled overhead. The mud was stained red and reeked of blood and sweat and fear. English soldiers, Welsh bowmen, and Irish warriors butchered with a savage jubilance that chilled Lianna's heart.

The Duke of Alençon stumbled toward King Henry and held out his sword in surrender, sobbing, "I yield! *Ayez merci*, I yield!" Lianna sagged with relief; perhaps the slaughter would end now. Yet a blood-crazed English knight stepped between Henry and Alençon and rived the duke's head from his shoulders.

The fighting continued.

Lianna was shocked to note, from the changeless position of the sun, that only a half hour had passed. The tiny English army had made a vicious advance into the French ranks. Soldiers scrambled over mountains of dead. The archers, in an orgy of victory, looted. One bowman sliced the fingers off a wounded man, doubtless to get at his jewels, but also in reprisal for the French threat to maim all archers.

The battle lines faded into disorganized pockets of fighting. Rand was nowhere in sight. Looking about, Lianna became aware that the men guarding the baggage park had gone off to join the fighting and looting. She thought to flee, but shackles and horrified fascination held her still.

A howl sounded from behind. She whirled to see a mounted French knight leading a rabble of peasants toward her. The knight wore Rand's *cotte d'armes*.

Gervais.

A scream gathered in her throat; the keen edge of his blade suddenly laid across her neck held her silent. From the corner of her eye she saw Johnny knocked senseless. He sank onto the sacks of grain and utensils.

"The woman's mine," bellowed Gervais from behind

his visor. He dismounted; his gauntleted hand rifled the contents of the cart. In greedy triumph he held up a gold crown and King Henry's chancery seal. "These as well. 'Twill be a high insult. Do what you will with the rest."

Baggage boys were summarily tossed aside. Eager hands took horses, caches of gold and silver. Lianna scrambled from Gervais, but the manacles made her clumsy. She fell over the side of the baggage cart.

"You never should have left," said Gervais. His steel-encased hand snatched at her. She shrank from him, stumbled.

Caparisoned in light armor, and thus unencumbered, he captured her easily and hauled her to her feet. His fingers bit into her upper arms. She looked around in panic. Not far away, knights wearing the colors of York had gathered around the prisoners. One or two Yorkists glanced her way, mildly interested. Doubtless they believed Gervais an Englishman and didn't realize what he was about.

Breathing hard, he said, "Do you come docilely, Baroness, or shall I sling you across my saddle like the article of baggage the English have made of you?" He cuffed Johnny, who was shaking his head groggily.

"I'd sooner see you in hell," she spat, then clenched her teeth against the pressure of his bruising fingers.

Johnny, recovering from the blow, leaped over the side of the tumbril. "Leave go of her," the lad yelled. Brief as lightning, he lashed out at Gervais. A dagger glittered in the cloud-filtered sunlight. Blood spurted from Gervais's shoulder, drenching the stolen tabard.

"Whoreson!" he bellowed. His free hand swung wildly. Johnny fell. Then, jerking Lianna into his arms with bone-jarring force, Gervais ran toward his horse.

Terrorized beyond reason, she screamed the name of her beloved. *"Rand!"*

Somewhere at the fringes of the disassembled left flank, Rand fell still. His heart gave a great lurch. The sudden feeling of dread that washed over him had nothing to do with the two dismounted knights he was fighting. Both were battle weary and not entirely sober; almost casually he had been trying to batter them into yielding.

But the sound, faint as a wisp of breeze-borne smoke, set his nerves on edge. His heart always heard, no matter how faint her cries. He turned toward the baggage park.

At the site, he saw a hooded youth struggling with a knight. Then the hood fell back, and moon-silver hair spilled over narrow shoulders.

Lianna.

He felt as if an iron fist had driven into him. "Sweet lamb of God," he gasped. Unthinking, he deflected a blow.

A knight wearing Rand's own *cotte d'armes* dragged her away from the carts. Rand knew with pure dread that the imposter was Gervais Mondragon.

A mace slammed against Rand's basinet, and deep ringing sound blotted out all save the burst of pain. Reeling, he lashed out wildly with his sword. The flat of the blade met armor; the impact reverberated up the length of his arm.

His vision cleared. Through the slits of his visor he saw the two knights advancing, one wielding a sword, the other a mace. Fear for Lianna drove all thought of mercy from his mind. His blade sang a note of deadly menace and sliced cleanly into the gorget of the mace-wielding warrior. The man babbled a curse, sank to his knees, and pitched into the mud.

The other man, swinging deftly, came on.

Rand heard Lianna scream again.

He thrust; his opponent parried. Seconds flew by.

"I'll take him," yelled a familiar voice. Jack bounded up. He'd discarded his bow in favor of knightly weapons retrieved from fallen Frenchmen. Rand experienced a moment of anxiety; how would Jack fare against a trained knight?

"Just go, damn your eyes!" Jack bellowed.

Running as fast as his steel-encased legs would allow, Rand crossed to the baggage park.

Manacles clanging against the imposter's breastplate, Lianna hammered at her captor. Her small fists seemed impossibly fragile against the steel wall of armor.

Roaring with fury, Rand bore down on Mondragon. He grasped Lianna and sent her hurtling back. With his sword tip, he lifted the visor. Gervais glared, hard-eyed and red-faced.

"Yield or die," said Rand.

"I . . ." Gervais swallowed.

Rand flicked the blade to Gervais's throat. "You'll squirm on my sword like a bug on a pin."

Mondragon's weapon clattered to the ground. "I yield," he spat bitterly.

Rand noticed the jeweled piece swinging from Mondragon's baldric. "The crown," Rand said through clenched teeth. Cursing, Gervais surrendered it, and Rand shoved the object into his own baldric. He began pushing Gervais at sword point toward a group of guarded prisoners.

Over his shoulder Rand addressed Lianna, who followed hard on his heels. "What do you here?" he demanded.

"I sought the king," she said. "I wanted him to know you did not betray him."

Rand's breath caught in his throat. He longed to believe her; his heart told him she spoke the truth. His eyes fastened briefly on her iron-bound wrists.

"The Duke of York made me a prisoner," she said. "He's convinced you turned traitor." Her weary, lovely face lit with hope. "But we have Gervais now. He's proof of your loyalty."

Gervais swore.

Trumpets blared in the distance. Lianna stopped short. "'Tis my uncle's refrain."

Alarm raced through Rand's veins. "Damn Burgundy! If he's violated his promise to remain neutral, the French could yet win the day."

Lianna pointed to the north. A knight leading a host of horsemen raced toward the battlefield. "Not Burgundy; 'tis Uncle Antoine of Brabant."

Seizing the second of preoccupation, Gervais turned and ran for his horse.

Rand lunged after him.

"Rand, wait!" Lianna's scream brought him wheeling back around. "Help him." Her eyes, wide with horror, were fastened on the field. She pointed a shaking finger.

Jack Cade lay on the ground, disarmed, rolling from side to side in an effort to evade the downthrusts of his opponent's sword.

Forgetting Mondragon, Rand hurtled across the field. He arrived just as the knight's blade made another stab at Jack.

The blade sliced into Jack's side.

Rand beheaded the knight with a single stroke that bore all the savage force of his horror and grief.

He plunged to his knees beside Jack. Heart pounding, teeth clenched, Rand extracted the blade.

Jack winced and swore. He turned his head toward the twitching body of the fallen Frenchman. "That bastard . . . won't be toasting victory tonight, my lord."

"Hush, Jack, save your wind." Rand looked down at the fount of crimson spurting from Jack's side. "Surgeon!" he bellowed, looking about wildly. Cold inside and out, he flung off his gauntlets and cradled Jack's head. "Hold on, my friend. . . ."

Jack's face had drained to gray. His eyes fluttered shut. "Goddamn, I think I'm dead."

"Nay!" Rand yelled. "I'll not let you go. I'll not face Bonne's wrath when she learns you died fighting my battle."

Jack dragged his eyes open, and a long shadow crossed his agonized face. He squinted up, past Rand. Turning, Rand spied King Henry several yards away. Behind the king ran a French soldier. The man wore battered armor but no helmet. In his hand he swung a death-spiked mace.

A warning leaped from Rand's throat. The mace came about in a lethal arc, driving toward the young king's head. Just as Henry's death became a certainty, his pursuer stopped, stiffened, and crumpled boneless to the ground. The hilt of Jack's dagger protruded from his throat.

Rand turned in disbelief to Jack. Propped on one elbow, Jack smiled weakly. "Took my fingers," he said in a thready voice, "but not my aim."

Rand looked up to see the embattled figure of the King of England. Recognition blazed in Henry's dark eyes. He stared coldly at Rand, then at Jack. "What is your name?" he asked.

"Jack . . . Jack Cade."

"You saved my life, Jack Cade. I would to God I could offer you something of meaning for that."

"Victory," breathed Jack. "Meaning enough, sire,"

Henry lifted his sword and touched the flat of the bloodied blade to Jack's shoulders. "In the name of the Father, and of the Son, and of St. George, I dub thee knight."

Jack twisted his head in Rand's lap. "I thought," he said faintly, "I told you . . . remind me never to become a knight. Can't take . . . all that goddamned honor. . . ."

"Jack." Tears streamed down Rand's face. "Oh, God, Jack, if ever knighthood were deserved . . ." He looked up and met Henry's gaze. Rand knew why the king had made the gesture. Common soldiers were buried in mass graves; knights were transported to England for burial in hallowed ground.

"So you've come to fight, Longwood," said Henry in an icy voice. "But for whom, I wonder, do you do battle?"

"The traitor has turned to France," bellowed a furious voice. The Duke of York lumbered up. He snatched the crown from Rand's belt. "Longwood stole this from the baggage cart."

Henry's face drained to white. "Jesu, Rand, I did fear you'd betray me."

The king's fury bit at Rand. "I betrayed you not. Mondragon took the—"

A herald came running toward them. "Sire!" Spying Jack, the herald sobered and made the sign of the cross. "Sire, the Duke of Brabant is mounting another assault."

Cursing, York hurried toward the prisoners.

Henry glanced at the woods, then back at the French captives at the baggage park. Rand followed the king's gaze over the wealth of discarded weapons on the field.

"Sweet Mary," said Henry, "the prisoners outnumber their guards. If they revolt and take up arms, we'll be surrounded."

A litter arrived; tenderly Rand laid Jack upon the canvas bed. "Jesus, I'm a knight," Jack muttered. Unexpectedly, a hint of color had returned to his face, a glimmer of brightness to his eyes. Rand started toward the hospital pavilion, but a stir at the baggage train stopped him short. The prisoners had begun to harass their guards.

"Surrounded," Henry repeated. Determination hardened his gaunt face. "All prisoners are to be slain." Glancing at Rand, he read the shock on his face. "What choice have I?" he asked defiantly. "We are outnumbered, and Brabant is moving." He hurried off to give the dreadful order.

The command echoed through the ranks. The English soldiers showed disbelief, then resentment at losing their battle prizes, and finally a wild blood lust as they began to carry out the order.

The idea of slaughtering the disarmed prisoners filled Rand with disgust. Then he thought, *Lianna*. Shock waves rang through his mind. Lianna was a prisoner of the Duke of York.

Surely the order didn't extend to a woman, and yet . . . Who could say how far this madness would go? He raced back to the baggage park.

Calling up every bit of his soldier's hardness, he armed his heart and his mind against the pleas for mercy, the growls of vengeance, the grinding of weapons thrust through armor, through bone. Blood filled the air with bitter scent and slicked the ground beneath his feet. Shoving aside an archer poised above a French knight, Rand found the cart where he'd left Lianna.

She was gone. In terror he scanned writhing bodies and halted running men. No one had seen her. Oh, God, had Gervais captured her after all?

"My lord." Rand turned to see the young son of Lord Cornwall. "I heard you asking about the woman."

Rand grabbed his shoulders. "Have you seen her, lad?"

The boy's bruised face paled. His lip trembled. Fleetingly Rand wondered what scars this carnage would leave on the youngster's tender heart. "The men of York," said the boy. "They took her. . . ." He jerked his head toward the wasted village of Maisoncelles.

His heart hammering with fear, Rand raced down the ridge.

Lianna shrank against a half-ruined building. Face white, eyes wide, she looked like a ghost as she recoiled from two men whose emblazoned tabards bore the white rose of the House of York.

A bellow of rage tore from Rand's throat as he lunged forward. Swords drawn, the knights spun to face him.

"Let her go," Rand ordered.

"She's a prisoner. The king said—"

"My blade says leave her be!"

"They but carry out a royal command." The Duke of York arrived, his corpulent body clumsy beneath the weight of armor.

"Churls! Varlets!" Rand yelled. "Think you the king's order extends to women?"

"It extends to all prisoners hale enough to wield a weapon. Begone, Longwood. My men have a duty to perform."

"You'll slay me first." Rand thrust at one of the men.

"Hold! Hold, I say!" Shouts rang through the ranks. "The king has rescinded his order. Brabant is down. His men are retreating!"

Lianna's breath whooshed out as she sagged against the building. "Uncle Antoine . . ." she breathed. Rand cast off his basinet and scooped her into his arms. Trembling and cold, she lay limp in his embrace. Over the top of her head he spied York's angry face.

"So," said Rand. "You've been cheated out of revenge."

"Be not so certain," Edward spat. "I'll see you slain for a traitor; and your French wife burned as a witch."

Lianna's trembling abated. Gently Rand set her down. He had much to say to this wife of his, but not now, not with the battle still raging and this angry noble glaring at them.

"Why don't we settle both charges right now, Your Grace?" he asked. "By personal combat."

Lianna gasped. York's face darkened. A flash, pale as the underbelly of a fish, flickered in his eyes. Fear, thought Rand. He's afraid.

"I'll see you in hell, Longwood, before I sully my blade with your flesh," said York. Calling for his knights, he hurried off to join the last of the skirmishes. Almost immediately the portly Duke of York engaged the weary Charles d'Albret in hand-to-hand combat.

"Coward," Rand spat. "He's a fat buzzard picking over the remains of a carcass."

"Rand, come away," Lianna whispered urgently. "We are both in danger here."

"I've run long enough," he said. Still angry, still confused, and still numb with the horror of almost losing her, he kept his voice flat and emotionless. Drawing his dagger, he began to pick at the lock on her wrist. "Take one of the captured horses," he ordered. "You're to go to your uncle in Liège."

"But I can't—"

"For once you'll do as I say, damn you!"

She bit her lip. "Is Jack . . . ?"

"He was still alive when they took him off to the hospital pavilion."

"Thank God. Rand—"

Shouts rippled through the ranks. York was dead, unwounded but smothered in his own armor.

Rand felt relieved that his budding enmity with York had never had a chance to flower. Then he felt ashamed of that relief, for York would be mourned as a man who had marched, and fought bravely, and died a hero. While Rand . . .

"In the name of the king, I arrest you."

Rand and Lianna turned. Facing them were four burly, battered knights, all wearing the white rose of York. One of them wept freely, his face streaked by blood and dirt and tears. Another bore a wilted plume in his helm, marking him as a sergeant-at-arms.

Rand gave a half smile. "What's this? The battle draws to a close, and from all angles it appears I've fought for the winning side."

"From all angles it appears you've been a timeserver."

"Your brazen taunts sent our lord to his death," said the weeping man.

"You're to be taken to Agincourt castle, and there placed under arrest."

Rand felt Lianna stiffen beside him. Dread reared high in his heart. He had a swift, vivid memory of King Henry's cold stare. "On what grounds?" he demanded.

"Treason."

Chapter  24

"I don't believe this." Rand let his head drop back against the stone wall of the cell. Finding the surface cold and beslimed, he jerked forward. The iron shackles binding him to the wall tore at his wrists. "By God, I don't believe this." Footsteps sounded outside.

"Nor does King Henry, I trow," came a familiar voice. The door hinges grated. Robert Batsford stepped into the room. A torch in his hand illuminated his ravaged features.

"Batsford!" Rand sat forward; the chains rattled. "What of Lianna?" he asked urgently. The last he'd seen of her, one of York's men had knocked her, screaming, to the ground.

"She is unhurt, though they still detain her. They know of her skill, her cunning, and will not risk setting her free until . . ." The priest seemed loath to finish the thought.

Rand asked, "Jack . . .?"

"In the hospital pavilion. His wound was not so grave as it appeared. No vitals were cut."

Relief gusted from Rand in a great sigh. "The others?"

"Gone, my lord. I know not where. There is such confusion in battle. All have scattered."

Rand sat silent for a moment. "I still don't believe this," he said.

"King Henry is deeply dismayed by the turn of events. In his heart he knows you well, knows you'd not turn traitor."

"Then why the devil am I shackled here in the dark, when the others are celebrating victory and counting their ransoms?"

"The evidence, my lord. The king wants to believe you innocent, but the evidence tells a different story, especially with York's embellishments. His lackeys add their tales of treason to what is already known."

"What are they saying?"

Batsford set his torch in a brattice, squatted beside Rand, and rocked back on his heels. "York claimed he saw you on the battlements of Bois-Long, driving his advance guard away."

"Undoubtedly Gervais, wearing my *cotte d'armes.*"

The priest nodded. "Would that we'd had time to bring your martial colors when we fled Bois-Long."

"Would that you'd let me stay and keep the French devils out," Rand said darkly.

Batsford cleared his throat. "Then there's the issue of the amulet Henry gave you."

"The accursed thing fell into Gervais's hands months ago."

"We might have discounted York's accusations, but for

today. The incident at the baggage park was truly damning."

"Gervais again," Rand growled out, remembering. "He wore my colors when he led the peasants in that attack."

"One of York's men recognized the tabard and swears you were the perpetrator."

"But the king himself saw me on the battlefield."

"Others say when you realized Henry would win the day, you shed your colors to hide the deed. And when York gave Henry the crown from your belt—"

"Jesu, I took the damned thing back from Gervais!"

"The Yorkists swear this is not so. The king must heed them or risk losing their support." Batsford sighed. "Duke Edward lived dishonorably, but died a hero's death. His kinsmen are clamoring for your blood, my lord. They say you drove him to that last charge against d'Albret."

"He had just ordered my wife to be slain, damn it!"

"You are the only one who seems to recall that." Batsford lowered his eyes. The flame of the torch bathed his stooped figure in smoky light. "There has been bad blood between the Houses of York and Lancaster ever since Bolingbroke took the throne. Henry can ill afford to offend the Yorkists."

"And the next Duke of York is sure to oppose Henry if he feels his father has been dishonored." It was beginning to make hideous sense to Rand.

"Aye."

"And Henry will forfeit the life of a minor noble to appease the Yorkists."

"Aye." The priest's faint whisper wavered like a wind-bitten flame.

Coldness welled inside Rand, but the chill had nothing

to do with the dank, mildew-laden air of the cell. "Father," he said, eyeing the slumped, shaking figure of the priest, "why have you been sent to me?"

Slowly Batsford lifted his head. Tears streamed down his face and sobs racked his chest. "Almighty God, Rand, you know, don't you?"

Rand's teeth began to chatter. He clamped his jaw. "Tell me."

"I've come to see you shriven," Batsford whispered. "And to see to your last request."

"Now? Tonight?"

"Aye. You're to be..." Batsford moistened his lips. "The execution takes place on the morrow. It's to be carried out before the march to Calais."

"You've been drinking," Lianna said, glaring accusingly at the priest.

Robert Batsford shook his head and glanced over his shoulder at the guard who lurked nearby. Batsford reeled forward. Something thudded on the ground near Lianna's hemp-bound feet. Unable to see the object in the moonless dark, she scowled. "You stumble about like a sot," she said, lifting her hands to point at him. Like her ankles, her wrists were bound with rope, and she was tethered to the same baggage cart on which she'd ridden to the battlefield. Her iron manacles had been removed and placed upon some hapless French prisoner.

"Believe me, my lady," said Batsford, "I have never been more sober in all my life."

She eyed him suspiciously. "How fares my husband?"

Batsford swallowed. "He's not been harmed. But he stands accused of treason." Briefly the priest related the evidence against Rand. "The king fears losing support in the north, and so he must appease the Yorkists."

Disbelief and fear washed over her. "But Rand once saved Henry's life. My husband shadowed and distracted the French army all during the march from the Somme. He fought with valor today. Henry loved Rand well."

"But he loves peace in his kingdom more."

"So much that he'll credit the vengeful lies of York's partisans?"

"The unity of York and Lancaster means much to him."

"But it's all a mistake. I'll go to Henry myself and tell him so." She turned to address the guard.

Batsford raised a hand, stopping her. "I have tried already, my lady. But if Henry wouldn't listen to an English priest, why would he heed a Frenchwoman?"

"Because I speak the truth."

"Speaking the truth cannot refute the hard evidence of the amulet, the *cotte d'armes*, the crown found on your husband's person."

Panic rose like bile in her throat. She set her jaw and forced herself to calmness. "What of Cornwall's son? He saw Gervais."

Batsford shook his head. "The lad went on to Calais with an advance party. Besides, do you think the Yorkists would allow him to speak freely?"

Thinking suddenly of her uncle of Burgundy, she nodded in agreement. "Nay, they'd keep the boy from telling the truth." Touching her finger to her chin, she murmured, "I must do something to convince the king. I need irrefutable evidence." Then, snapping her fingers, she said, "Gervais."

Batsford stared. "My lady?"

"Gervais holds the key. If we bring him forth, with the *cotte d'armes* and the chancery seal he stole..." She pounded her thigh with her bound hands. "That's it, Batsford! 'Tis simple. The tabard even has a distinctive tear. Johnny stabbed Gervais during the struggle."

Batsford brightened, but only for a moment. He studied the ground. "We've no time, my lady."

She barely heard his hoarse whisper; her mind was racing ahead. "Why not?"

"Your husband is to be beheaded at noontide tomorrow."

Horror rose in her breast. She brought her hands to her mouth, stifling a scream. "Nay," she breathed. "Oh, God!"

Batsford nodded miserably. "At dawn, a guard will come to conduct you to Rand's cell in Agincourt castle. He asked"—Batsford gulped—"to see you one last time."

She began to tremble violently. Oh, Rand, she thought. She remembered the coldness in his eyes, the bitterness in his voice, when he'd come to save her from York's men. His hatred had been real, yet she recalled his defense of her, his willingness to die protecting her.

"I never had to chance to tell him I loved him." Tears streamed from her eyes. "He . . . he always said I . . . I'd tell him about it."

Batsford spread his arms and enclosed her in the rough warmth of his woolen robes. She poured her sorrow and despair into his shoulder.

The guard cleared his throat. "Father," he said gruffly but not unkindly, "you're needed at the hospital pavilion."

Batsford squeezed Lianna hard. "You're shaking, my lady." He stared at her with an intensity she didn't understand.

"Think you I'd bear the news calmly?" she demanded.

He placed his hand under her chin and lifted her face. The guard's torch flickered over the priest's features. Batsford looked stern and beautifully holy.

"Father." The guard's pikestaff thumped impatiently.

"I come anon," said Batsford over his shoulder. "Only . . . you'll have to help me to the hospital pavilion. I've a rheumy ankle, and this damp weather plagues me to the bone."

The guard shrugged. "As you wish."

Batsford made the sign of the cross over Lianna. "Remember, my lady," he intoned formally. "If your knees knock, then kneel on them."

Vaguely, absurdly, she thought it an odd time for the sportsman-priest Batsford to suffer a sudden attack of piety. As he and the guard walked away she wondered why he'd lied about his ankle. Though spry, he walked as slowly as an old man. The thoughts flitted through her mind, insubstantial as the night mist that lowered over the field.

Reality barreled into her heart. Rand was going to die tomorrow.

She couldn't have stayed on her feet if she'd tried. Her shaking legs gave way, and she sank to the ground. Her knee struck a hard, sharp object.

Recalling that Batsford had dropped something— probably a vial of holy water or oil—she groped about in the dark.

Her fingers closed around the iron hilt of a small dagger.

Her heart started to pound. "Sweet Jesu," she breathed. Now she understood Batsford's cryptic words, his lie to the guard. "Thank you, Father," she breathed.

Her fingers and toes ached as she furtively cut her tight

bonds. She ignored the pain, crouched beside the baggage cart, and studied the trampled terrain. Darkness shrouded the battleground from view. But the rank smell of blood and spilled entrails wafted on the night breeze, ghastly evidence of the slaughter that had taken place that day. The rhythmic rasp of gravediggers' shovels grated on her taut nerves.

Firelight flickered in the distance, illuminating the pavilions and tents where King Henry and his army celebrated their stunning victory. Resentment welled in Lianna. When the French heralds had surrendered the day to Henry, he'd named the battle Agincourt and proclaimed triumph for God and England. He might well celebrate, but did Rand's unjust fate weigh on the royal conscience?

She tore her gaze from the fires of victory and studied the black silhouette of Agincourt keep. Rand was in there, awaiting death. She yearned to go to him but resisted. Her own path lay behind, to the south. In darkness.

At the edge of the abandoned village of Maisoncelles, horses seized from captured and fallen Frenchmen were corralled. A guard sat indolently at the gate of a crude pen built of rubble, broken timber, even some of the bloodied stakes the archers used in their chevaux-de-frise.

She gulped a deep breath of the misty night air and stepped from the shadows.

The guard jumped up and angled his pikestaff at her. "Who are you, boy?"

She studied him briefly. Doubtless he was not a favored soldier; elsewise he'd not be relegated to guarding the horses while his comrades drank the night away.

"Please," she said softly. "I've come to buy back my husband's horse."

The guard eyed her skeptically. "Such matters are to be settled with the king's sergeant of ransoms."

She tried to quell her impatience. "But wouldn't you rather settle the matter of the horse right now, sir?" She opened her palm. A pair of gold angelots glinted dully. Seeing his fingers clench and his eyes narrow, she hastened to add, "Aye, you could well overpower me and steal my coin, sir. But I could just as well scream accusations. Your king does not approve of unregulated thievery."

The guard snatched the coins. He tested the temper of one between his teeth. "I don't give my complicity cheaply."

Fighting a pounding sense of urgency, she produced a silver franc.

He took this as well, opened the gate, and led her into the pen. She moved silently among the horses, measuring the assets of the various mounts. This one had a bit-hardened mouth; that one had lost an ear in the battle. Scanning quickly, she saw a familiar high-arched neck, a distinctive blaze on a noble face. "Charbu," she breathed, and hurried to the percheron.

"This be your husband's horse?" the guard asked.

Tears welled in her eyes. She'd been prepared to lie, to lay claim to any likely-looking beast that could take her to Bois-Long. She hadn't dared hope to find Rand's horse among the captured animals. Charbu nuzzled her shoulder.

"Yes," she said. "Yes, this is my husband's horse."

"Still got his trappings." The guard eyed the tooled leather of the saddle, the finely carved wooden stirrups.

She slapped a last coin in his hand. "That should take

care of the saddle." And keep you in fine wine for years, she added silently.

"Go quietly," he warned. "If an alert sounds, I'll deny all knowledge of our exchange."

She nodded, led Charbu out of the corral, and shortened the stirrups to accommodate her height. Resisting a reckless impulse for haste, she mounted and set the percheron to a quiet walk, entering the shadowy, river-fed forest.

Only when the swishing current of the river Ternoise masked the noises of the woods did she dig her heels into Charbu's sides. The war-horse surged forward, his long strides eating up the army-trampled road. She bent low over the thick, stretching neck. The wind rushed over her and blew her hair.

Thoughts of Rand pounded through her head. His last request had been to see her. To forgive her, or to lay a final curse on her? She wouldn't be there to find out. What would he think of her absence? Bitter and betrayed, he would doubtless suppose she'd abandoned him once again. But she had to risk hurting him this time, for his life hung in the balance.

During the headlong ride, her mind worked at breakneck speed. Bois-Long lay forty miles to the south. Charbu, fleet and strong, could cover the distance in three hours. But that fact failed to allay her fears. Once she reached the château, she would have to subdue the dauphin's knights, find Gervais, capture him, and bear him back to Agincourt.

And what of Aimery? She experienced a deep, shuddering dread that her son was yet in danger. Gervais had fastened his ambitions on Bois-Long; he would naturally want to eliminate the heir to the château. Lianna prayed her desperate letter to her uncle of Burgundy had borne fruit.

A pale moon rose. Beneath all her hideous thoughts lay a frantic sense of urgency. If she could not bring proof of Rand's innocence by noontide tomorrow, her husband would die.

Through the shadows, she recognized the long woods and water meadows of Bois-Long. Like a warrior spurring his horse to a final charge, she nudged the percheron to an all-out gallop. They shot through the last stretch of forest and burst into the clearing north of the château. She reined the horse to a halt. Charbu stood quivering, blowing loudly as she dismounted and tethered him to a tree. Briefly she collapsed against his sweat-slick neck. She'd arrived. But the difficult part of her journey lay ahead.

She touched the dagger stuck in her belt and started cautiously across the clearing. A rising wind sent shadows rippling over the tall, damp grass. The movement terrified her; if Gervais had sent *hobelars* out to scour the area, the scouts would surely find her. Bowing low, she moved into the inky shadow cast by the walls and towers of the castle.

The river, diverted to form a moat around the north face, slipped past in menacing silence. Parting the wind-dried reeds, she craned her neck to study the causeway. Like half-fallen sentinels, the bridge supports stood parting the current, creating fathomless whorls in their wake. Closer in, the more sluggish moat was alive with water lilies and darting insects. The bridge was drawn up; the boat she'd used to leave Bois-Long was gone.

A deep eddy of resentment swirled within her. This was her home, the seat of her ancestors, yet like an unwanted guest she must seek entrance by stealth.

And between her and home lay a dark span of water.

Glancing up, she spied movement on the wall walk. With a sinking heart she realized that sentries patrolled. Only a short time ago they'd disdained security measures against the puny English army. Now, in the wake of Henry's victory, the overconfident French finally perceived a real threat.

Lianna crouched, frozen, until the sentry moved on. If he followed the logical pattern of surveillance, his rounds would take him another quarter hour before he returned.

Drawing up all the nerve and courage she possessed, Lianna took off her sabots and slid down the bank to the muddy fringe of the moat. Her toes mere inches from the dark water, she hesitated. Although she battled a current of fear, she could not draw her mind from a sudden terrible vision of her drowned mother's colorless, waterlogged face.

Like an animal shying from a fire, she drew back and thought, This I cannot do. I'd brave the flames of hell before I could bear this. But an image of Rand swam into her mind. Rand, noble, loving, betrayed... and doomed.

A vaillans coeurs riens impossible. His motto roared in her ears. To valiant hearts nothing is impossible.

For love of Rand and Aimery she'd crossed the Narrow Sea.

But those voyages had not required her to immerse herself in inky, breath-stealing water.

She must cross. She must. Her fear of water was her private demon, to be slain by her devotion to Rand. Calling up all the love in her heart and all the determination of her will, she stepped into the moat.

Coldness seeped around her feet and ankles; terror flooded her belly. Damming the tide of fear, she stepped lower. The muddy shelf at the water's edge gave way, and she lost her foothold. She bit back a scream.

Like death-cold fingers the water crept over her body, her face, her scalp. Choking, limbs flailing, she fought her way to the surface.

Cool air rushed over her. She had but time for a single, life-giving gulp before sinking again. A liquid shroud closed over her. Every instinct told her to turn back.

Yet some rational part of her mind stood away from the panic. She remembered seeing the boys of the castle swimming, their sleek, nude bodies darting effortlessly through the water.

Gaining the surface for another breath, she attempted to duplicate those movements. She kicked, parting the water with a stroke of her arms. Plants caught at her, dragged her down. As she struggled, the torrent of fear sluiced over her again.

But Rand's life depended on her fording the moat. New power, born of love-given bravery, flowed into her limbs. *Rand*. Her mind shouted his name with every kick of her feet, every stroke of her arms.

At last her knees sank into the mud at the opposite bank. Lianna burst from the water and scrambled to the base of the wall. She lay sodden, gasping and praying, weeping as fear ebbed into relief. She trembled, but forced her hands and feet to obey. She stood and glanced up at the wall walk. Oh, God, had the sentry heard the splashing?

Moving with unsteady caution, she crept below the

drawn-up bridge and approached the steps to the water gate.

A man emerged from the reeds at the water's edge.

Terrified, she shrank against the wall and stood frozen. She drew her dagger. The flash of steel brought the man to a halt. White teeth glinted as he grinned. In dread she recognized one of the dauphin's knights.

"So you're back, Baroness." Almost casually his hand shot out and grasped her wrist, squeezed until the knife fell from her numb fingers.

"Please," she said. "Please, in the name of mercy, sir—"

"I'll have no mercy on an Englishman's whore," he growled. Pressing her against the wall, he pawed at her breasts. "A wet tunic suits your charms, my lady." He leaned down and bit at her lips. He smelled of sweat, tasted of old wine. Revolted, Lianna jerked her head away and kicked at him.

He swore and shook her hard, rattling her teeth. "You'll be sorry you did that, Baroness. Gervais had plans for you. He taunted his wife with them each night. He's vowed to cast her aside, take you as his lady. But I believe I'll be the first to sample you." Groping hands and wet lips engulfed her.

Lianna screamed. Over his shoulder she saw still more men; a frantic tally revealed nine dark, ominous shapes. Oh, God, she thought, one I might survive, but nine . . . A whimper escaped her.

The knight spun around, wielding Lianna's knife.

"Surely you'd not attack a man of the cloth," said one of the men. A dull thud sounded; the knight crumpled.

Trailing mud and water, Lianna flung herself at him. "Father Batsford! Sweet Mary, I thought you were Gervais's man." The others surrounded her. Jack winced as she hugged him. "Oh, Jack, forgive me, I forgot your wound," she said.

He waved his hand. "*Sir* Jack Cade, if you please. And I'll not let a French pinprick stop me."

"Lower your voice," said Chiang. Lianna stared at her master gunner, loyal in secret to the English monarchy all these years. She could summon no anger at him. Urgently she motioned them up the steps. How they had come to be here did not matter; that she had their help meant everything.

Silent as shadows, they entered through a low door in the garden wall. "We must get to the armory first," she said.

"We're outnumbered at least three to one," said Simon.

"So was King Harry," Dylan whispered.

Jack muttered something to three of the others. They slipped along the wall, climbed to the upper battlement.

With cold, remorseless certainty Lianna knew the sentries were dead men. The blood price of Gervais's treachery grew dearer by the moment.

"I'll fetch Bonne," said Jack, and moved toward the keep. "She'll know what Gervais did with the tabard and seal."

Crossing the bailey, they passed the kennels. One of the alaunt hounds whined and pawed at the gate. With a quiet command Lianna hushed the animal and thanked God her familiar voice forestalled a chorus of howling.

They entered the armory and moved through the silent gloom of weapons and armor. The smell of sulfur grew sharp as they neared the alcove where Chiang performed his alchemy. He struck flint and lit a candle. His narrow eyes made a quick assessment of the room. "Good," he whispered. "They've left it untouched. We'll need all the firepower we can concoct."

"You've a plan?" asked Jack from the doorway. He and Bonne stepped into the room. Lianna rushed to hug her maid.

"My lady!" Bonne cried. "Oh, my lady, are you all right? You're soaking wet. Here, I've brought you a dry smock and some shoes." The maid wrung her hands. "Gervais swore you, Rand, and Aimery were dead. We've been all aggrieved."

Lianna took the clean garment. "Save your worry for Rand."

Bonne hung her head. "Jack told me. We'll help you, my lady. By St. Wilgefort's beard, we'll help you."

Jack had taken the men into the main room of the armory. Hurrying, Lianna shed her wet clothes and donned the ivory-colored smock. She fidgeted while Bonne scrubbed her hair dry with a towel. Then they both entered the armory.

She turned to address the men in a quiet voice. "We need Gervais, the *cotte d'armes*, and the chancery seal he stole."

"He's abed," said Bonne. "The things are in his chamber."

Jack reeled slightly; she hurried to his side to support him. "We'll get Mondragon, my lady," Jack promised.

Lianna put a finger to her chin. "But we cannot leave the way we came, not bearing a prisoner. It's too risky, too slow."

"No matter what we do," said Piers, "the French knights will likely be down around our ears."

"If we're to meet the enemy, then let it be on our own terms." Lianna paused; she had just referred to French soldiers as the enemy. So they were, as was any man who impeded her rescue of Rand.

Turning to the men, she sketched out her plan.

Dawn had come, and Lianna had not. Rand stared at the gray half-light that filtered through a grate high above.

He tried to understand why she had not allowed herself to be brought to him. Batsford had promised. But Rand had spent the night alone, with hostile guards outside.

Perhaps they hadn't let her come. He sank deeper into despair. Perhaps Lianna had stayed away because she did not want to stain herself with a man looked upon as a traitor. God, was her love so thin, so shallow?

Would that he could shrug off his own love like an outgrown shirt. But he couldn't hate her. He'd come to understand that she'd been as powerless as he in the struggle between their warring nations.

Incensed, he forced his mind to other matters. What would happen to his land, his rank? Would his title, not two years old, be attainted? Would his barony fall to Gervais, or would Henry send yet another Englishman to wed Lianna? Oh, Christ, he thought, and what of Aimery? Rand would never see his son grow into the flower of manhood. But perhaps that was a blessing, for all Rand had to leave him was a legacy of treason. He prayed Aimery would one day learn the truth and forgive his father.

His men...Rand wondered what had become of them. They'd followed him from England, conquered a castle with him, and fought by his side. Yet now, in his hour of greatest need, they'd forsaken him. Even Robert Batsford had not returned.

Regrets poured over Rand. He thought of Darby Green, dead in Rand's service, his head on a French pikestaff. He thought of all the men he'd killed in his bloody career, men he'd snatched from families that needed them, all for the sake of a young king's ambitions. Jack had given his hand and perhaps his life; Chiang, a king's secret son, had given his loyalty; and now Rand was about to give his head. And all the glory would go to the greedy Yorkists. Chivalry *was* an empty spectacle. Lianna had told him so once. He should have listened.

But today he would make the ultimate sacrifice to the ideals of knighthood. He squeezed his eyes shut and recalled a beheading he'd witnessed at Anjou. The axman had missed the victim's neck and cut into the skull. The victim had whispered, "Sweet God have mercy," before two more blows finally severed the neck. Even then, tenacious sinew had still bound head to body. Sawing with his blade, the axman had cut it.

Rand shivered. God, don't let the axman be some butcher. And please God, let me die well.

His head fell back against the wall. Through the hiss of fear in his ears he imagined Lianna singing, her voice like an angel's. Most men, when faced with imminent death, remembered all the women they had held in their arms and loved.

But for Rand there had been only one.

The gray ghosts of dawn haunted the horizon by the time all was in readiness. As a cock crowed, Lianna stood by the well in the center of the bailey. Glancing about, she saw her comrades lying in wait for the signal. None, and she least of all, knew whether the signal would herald victory or death.

High on the wall, two men stood ready at each main gun—only instead of being turned toward the outlying fields, each cannon faced inward, pointed at the spot where Lianna stood. Chiang ran from gun to gun, checking charges and angles of aim.

She turned toward the keep and fastened her eyes on a cruciform arrow slit in a stairwell. Hurry, she thought. Please hurry. Just as the first weak light appeared, so did the signal. Robert Batsford's knotted scourge dangled from the arrow slit.

So. Jack and Batsford had managed to subdue Gervais. Now all that remained was to flush out the French knights.

Gulping a deep, fearful breath, she lowered her gunner's torch. The slow match smoked, fizzled, and died. Cursing under her breath, she tried again. The flame failed to catch. Frightened now, she bit her lip in concentration. If the knights were alerted too soon, they'd stop her. Hands shaking, she touched the torch to the fuse a third time. At last the match caught and burned toward the monstrous concoction of charges.

Flinging down the torch, she lifted her skirts and ran with terrified speed toward the battlements. Taking the stairs two at a time, she reached the wall walk just as the bombs detonated.

Smoke and sparks rocketed skyward. The noise of the explosion ripped through the air like hellish thunder. Stables, kennel, and stockyard came alive with the sounds of animal panic.

Soldiers poured from the barracks; castle folk streamed from the keep.

The discharges continued in a fearsome series of loud cracks. Lianna's eyes stung; her throat burned. Smoke roiled through the yard, and someone shouted that he'd been blinded. Wailed prayers and frightened pleas rose from the crowd.

When the blasting ceased, Lianna ran back down to the bailey. Choking, she fought her way across the blackened and smoldering ground. A few of the charges had failed to detonate, but they'd managed to bring out the French knights.

A gust of wind parted the smoke. As the sulfurous fog thinned, Lianna heard a collective gasp.

"She comes from the dead," someone called. Others made signs against sorcery and sank to their knees. Lianna could well understand the gesture; Gervais had told them she was dead. To the stupefied crowd it must seem she'd appeared by magic, on a swirl of smoke.

A jostling movement caught her eye. Struggling, sputtering, and sporting a livid bruise on his face, Gervais Mondragon was dragged forth by Batsford and Jack.

He spied Lianna, cursed viciously, and bellowed to his men: "Stop them, you fools!"

The men started forward.

"Do so at Mondragon's peril," came a commanding voice from the battlements.

As one, the crowd in the bailey glanced up. Looking regal, Chiang stood high on the gunner's walk. Four round iron eyes glared at Gervais. Jack shackled Mondragon's hand to the well sweep; then Jack, Batsford, and Lianna hurried off.

"One move," Jack growled, clutching his wounded side. "One move, and those guns go off, and you're porridge."

A fearful murmur rippled through the crowd. Macée,

robed in scarlet, tried to run toward the well. "Gervais! Oh, God—" Cursing, Guy held her back.

Batsford held a cloth-wrapped bundle. "Lord Rand's *cotte d'armes*," he said triumphantly. "And the chancery seal."

"Form up," Jack yelled at the soldiers. "You're to be locked in the granary."

The French sergeant planted his feet. "We obey no sniveling English cripple."

Jack brandished his maimed hand. "*This* cripple holds your fate." Four heated iron bars lowered toward four touchholes.

"Hold!" Gervais's voice vibrated with fear. "God have mercy, do as he says. I order you to obey the Englishman."

The man glared at Gervais, then at Jack. "I bow to no lowborn archer." He whipped a dagger from his baldric.

Quicker by half, Jack drew his own blade. No sooner did Lianna see the flash of steel than the blade sank to the haft in the Frenchman's chest. He fell, dead.

"*Sir* Jack Cade," Jack said fiercely. "Now, to the granary with your smelly hides."

The men, prodded by Dylan and Jack, filed away.

Lianna turned to the household knights. Jehan and his men stood uncertainly before the stables. Some had known her all her life, others had served under Aimery the Warrior, all had sworn fealty to her husband. Yet they were French; they'd supped at Gervais's table.

"We're with you, my lady," said Jehan. "Mondragon disarmed us. The dauphin's knights treated us like scum."

She sent him a grateful look, then darted a worried glance at the brightening sky. "Four hours to noontide," she said. Could they reach Agincourt before the executioner's ax fell?

Jehan shouted orders; grooms scurried to the stables. Jufroy hurried to raise the portcullis and lower the drawbridge.

Bonne assumed a bossy air. "The baron will return soon, and he'd be loath to see you idle. Haul away this mess." The maid, now a knight's lady, spoke with new authority. "We must prepare a feast. Oh, and Roland, fetch that Englishman from the cellar."

Henry's scout, Lianna recalled. Thank God Gervais hadn't killed the man.

Jack and Bonne walked with her to the gate. She hugged them both. "See to that wound, Jack."

He nodded and stepped away. "Just bring my lord home."

"And get the remaining charges out of the bailey."

Gervais, lashed to a saddle, his horse's reins in Batsford's capable hands, glared at Lianna. "Fool. All Picardy could have been at our feet. We could have been good together, you and I."

"Nothing that you have touched could ever be good," she retorted.

"Gervais!" Hair unbound, red robe fluttering, Macée raced across the bailey. She threw herself against his horse, her hands clutching at her husband.

Lianna expected him to dismiss his grasping wife. Instead he leaned down as far as his bound hands would allow and accepted her long, fierce embrace. A woodcock chirruped.

Impatient to the point of desperation, Lianna signaled to Batsford and cantered across the drawbridge, into the northern woods. Chiang and the English scout accompanied them. They paused to loose Charbu from where she'd tethered him.

As they rode through the awakening woods, she prayed they'd reach Agincourt in time.

Gervais stared stonily ahead. But something gleamed in his dark eyes—something that sent a shaft of fear streaking through Lianna.

The sun stood high and cold, directly overhead. Rand's guards, hardened by the day of slaughter that had preceded this day, showed no emotion as they led the prisoner from Château Agincourt to a muddy clearing.

Mutters of "traitor" and "bastard" rippled through the ranks of men who had gathered to witness the execution. The vilest catcalls issued from a large contingent standing beneath the standard of the white rose of York.

"Enguerrand Sans Tache," came a bold, contemptuous voice. "Today we'll see this field spotted with your traitor's blood."

Rand ignored the taunt as he passed the king. Pale and strained, Henry said, "Rand, I'm sorry." He looked suddenly very old. "I didn't love you as well as she."

"Justice must be served this day," said a Yorkshireman.

Rand stood silent as a priest chanted in a monotone. The executioner, his garb black, his ax shining, waited by a makeshift block, freshly cut from the Tramecourt woods.

Rand felt no fear; he was beyond terror. Instead he felt empty, washed clean of all emotion.

As the priest droned on, Rand wondered again at his utter aloneness. He'd wanted to see Lianna, to make his peace with her before he died, but she'd robbed him even of that.

Vaguely he became aware of a stir far away, in the ranks. They're all clamoring for my blood, he thought. Was yesterday not enough for them? He glanced at the king. A herald appeared; Henry and his councillors retreated to the rear of the crowd. The Yorkists pressed closer. Amazing, that they still had stomachs for another killing only a day after the slaughter of some eight thousand men.

Rand craned his neck to see the fields and woods one last time. But the outside world was already closed off to him by the forest of blood-hungry men who formed a circle around him.

He closed his eyes. Above the relentless droning of the priest, he heard distant shouts, the pounding of hoofs. More spectators. Few had cared that he'd lived, yet it seemed hundreds wanted to see him die.

Hands gripped his shoulders. He opened his eyes. The executioner stood before him.

"Your collar, sir," said the hooded man, touching the opening of Rand's tunic.

Rand reached up to help. For the deadly blade to rive a clean cut, his neck must be bared. A shiver passed through him as he felt the caress of a cool autumn wind on his flesh. "I have no coin to pay you the customary boon," he said.

"I've been paid."

Rand wondered whether his death were to be financed by the Yorkists—or by King Henry himself. "Make it a clean cut, will you?" he muttered.

The priest's voice and the rolling timbre of a drum rose in crescendo. "Have done already," called a Yorkshireman. The executioner gestured at the block.

Determined to die well, Rand stepped forward and

knelt before the block. The axman's assistant put a hand on his back. To steady my body for the blow, Rand thought. He uttered a brief, disjointed prayer for absolution. With an absurdly misplaced sense of annoyance, he noticed that the noises around him had risen. Not even a moment of respectful silence would mark his passing.

Then he became aware of movement; voices penetrated the loud surge of blood in his ears. Someone shouted, pleaded . . .

A trick of the wind or of his own feverish imaginings made him feel a sudden and unaccountable jolt of life. That voice, that lilting, female voice. His heart always heard, no matter how faint her cries.

The heavy hand left his back. Rand glanced at the axman. Although a hood masked the burly man's face, Rand sensed hesitation in the wary stance, in the loosened grip on the ax.

"Let her through," someone said. "God's mercy . . ."

The executioner looked over Rand's shoulder. Seized by unbearable hope, Rand shot to his feet.

He turned.

She smiled.

Like an ivory-robed vision, her silver hair streaming, she burst through the ranks of men. Adoration and astonishment unfurled in Rand as she came catapulting, weeping, laughing, into his arms.

"I love you, Rand," she declared. "I love you. I've come to tell you about it."

His heart bursting with joy, he held her fiercely. She smelled of fresh winds and woodlands, the fragrance soothing after the dankness of the cell. Bending his head, he kissed her deeply, thoroughly, with a desperation that left them both breathless.

"Ah, *pucelle*, you choose the oddest moments to do my bidding. Say again that you love me."

"I love you," she breathed. "*Je t'adore*. I'll say it in a thousand tongues."

He looked upon her and for a moment saw the cautious girl she had been when they'd first met. In the next instant he saw the woman she had become—strong, decisive, and now able to speak of love as easily as she spoke of guns and wars. He touched her cheek. A sublime peace invaded his soul. Love seemed to spill from her like sunbeams; her smile had the power to bring the gods to earth. He'd carry that image of her into eternity.

"I love you, Lianna. Now I can die well, knowing you have answered my dreams. Tell Aimery for me, when he's older . . ."

She reared back. "*Nom de Dieu*, you will not die at all. I did not risk my life only to hear you vow to die well!"

Confused, he studied the depths of her moon-silver eyes. "Would that I could tell you elsewise, but—"

"Come away from this gruesome place." She tugged at his sleeve.

He eyed the circle of soldiers. Some looked relieved, others resentful. Rand said, "My love, I am not free to go."

"You are, my lord," called a bell-toned voice. Like ebbing waves the men fell back, creating a cleft in their ranks to allow King Henry to pass. Batsford and Chiang hurried in his wake.

Face pale, Henry approached. Flouting protocol, he wrapped Rand in a brief, fierce embrace. "By the holy rood," Henry breathed. His voice trembled with unaccustomed emotion. "And to think I nearly let this injustice be done." He stepped back but still held Rand's hand, grasping it like a lifeline. "Much folly has been committed at Agincourt," he said. "I won a battle, but what does it mean? That I am King of England and France?"

Lianna gasped softly. Henry must have heard, for he turned to her, his face mild. "France will always be France, no matter who wears her crown." Taking her hand as well, he joined it with Rand's. "Kingdoms may be traded. But not hearts."

Rand had then, among the loud bursts of disbelief and joy that clamored in his head, a clear sense of the king's humanity, his fallibility.

But when Henry stepped away, his face was washed clean of emotion. Only close inspection revealed glints of residual horror in his dark eyes. Gravely he nodded to Lianna.

"Your wife, my lord, has seen justice served. She— with some divine intervention, I presume"—he sent a wry look at Batsford, who flushed deeply—"managed to break her bonds and ride to Bois-Long, where with a force of only ten men she gained entrance." He held out his hand. In it lay the chancery seal. "She brought me this, and your *tabard* as well—the one Mondragon wore."

Stunned, Rand stared at her. For the first time he recognized the shadows and pallor of fatigue on her face. "Lianna, how did you get in?"

She tilted her chin up. "I swam the moat."

Love and pity surged through him. He knew well what that perilous swim must have cost her, and yet she had braved her terror of water for him. "Oh, *pucelle* . . ."

One of York's men said, "Could the woman not have

fabricated this evidence? Surely her husband owns more than one tabard."

Henry eyed the man coldly. "Not one marked by Mondragon's blood, blood that matches the wound he took in the skirmish at the baggage park."

"Treachery from a French whore," the man maintained.

Henry drew himself up. "And the chancery seal?"

The man ducked his head and retreated.

Henry gestured toward a wagon fort formed by a circle of baggage tumbrils. Gervais stood in the middle of the circle. "Mondragon just dictated a full confession to a scribe." With a satisfied air Henry turned to Chiang. "I marked your gunner's art during the battle yesterday. Who are you, and why did you fight for England?"

Rand held his breath and squeezed Lianna's hand. She sent him a perplexed look.

Chiang bowed. "I am Chiang, Your Grace," he said in clipped English. "I gave you my service to fulfill . . . an old obligation."

"You must tell me of this," said the king. "Perhaps there's a place for you, as my master of artillery."

Disappointment shadowed Lianna's face. "He'll leave us, I think." She took a deep breath. "'Tis fitting, somehow."

"More than you could know," Rand murmured. He watched as the brothers put their heads together and spoke of glories to come for the House of Lancaster. "Princes both," Rand said, "but only one will be remembered by the chroniclers."

"What riddle is this?" asked Lianna.

"I'll tell you about it sometime, love." Pulling her against his chest, he rested his chin on top of her head. Sensing an end to the day's drama, the crowd of soldiers began to drift away. Rand saw Gervais, alone, slumped between the carts.

"King Henry seized much gunpowder from the French," Lianna said, pointing to one of the wagons. Barrels marked with the letter *B*, signifying St. Barbara, patron of gunners, were crammed into a cart.

"I'd not worry, love. You'll keep Bois-Long in gunpowder for years to come."

"Pray God we'll not need it."

A ruby flicker in the woods caught his eye. A banner of black identified the rider.

"What the devil is Macée doing here?" Rand asked.

Lianna turned to watch. Riding at perilous speed, Macée burst from the forest and dismounted before her horse had even slid to a halt. Her face pale, her voice screeching something incomprehensible, Macée ran toward the wagon fort.

In one hand she held a jumble of linen-wrapped and wood-spined rockets; with the other she grabbed a torch from its stand by a pavilion.

Comprehension burst in Lianna's mind. She recalled the unexploded charges left in the bailey. "Stop her!" she screamed, running toward Macée. Macée couldn't know one of the carts was laden with powder.

Rand pounded past, roaring at Macée to stop, bellowing at the men to take cover. Chiang snapped a warning at King Henry. Fearfully, the English soldiers hurried away.

Eyes blazing, the red-clad woman whirled.

Lianna gained Rand's side. "Macée, don't! You know not what you do!"

For a frozen moment Macée hesitated. Then with a defiant toss of her head she screamed, "You have overpowered men with your gunnery. Why shouldn't I?"

She threw the charges under the wagon.

"Macée, don't," Gervais yelled in a ragged voice. "I didn't mean—it wasn't our plan to—"

Reckessly, her eyes glittering, she put the torch to one of the rockets. The explosion sent a plume of smoke skyward and touched off the barrels of powder.

Lianna crashed against Rand's chest, and together they fell. Rolling, he shielded her with his body.

Wood splinters, broken weapons, grain dust, and bits of torn iron streaked through the air. A last, furious flash burst from the wagon fort. Wounded men groaned; frightened soldiers cried out. Rand drew away from Lianna. "Are you hurt?"

She shook her head. "King Henry—"

"I'm safe," said Henry, behind them. He gestured grandly at Chiang. "Thanks to the quickness of my master of artillery."

As the evil-smelling smoke began to clear, Lianna forced herself to look at the blackened remains of the wagon fort. Nothing save charred tatters of scarlet remained of Macée. Gervais lay still, lifeless, his incinerated body curled inward. Lianna buried her face in Rand's shoulder and wept.

"I hate myself for feeling relieved," she whispered.

"Gervais's treachery brought them to this."

"But Macée . . ."

"Hush, love," he said. "She was past helping. Did you not see the madness in her eyes?"

A gust of wind furled the smoke across the field. The blast of a clarion rent the horrified silence.

Lianna's heart shot to her throat. "'Tis my uncle of Burgundy's salute."

His voice tinged with irony, Rand said, "He always comes when the smoke clears."

A contingent of knights in polished armor, led by the glory-draped figure of Jean Sans Peur, rode into the encampment. A white flag of truce fluttered over the Burgundians' heads.

"He must be coming to parley with King Henry."

"He'd best do so," said Lianna, starting forward, "for he's proven himself no Frenchman."

The king's councillors gathered to meet the duke, but Jean Sans Peur rode straight to Rand and Lianna. Through the mist of smoke she saw that a woman on a gray palfrey followed him. The woman cradled a baby in her arms.

"Sweet Jesu," Lianna breathed. Arms outstretched to receive their son, Rand and Lianna ran past King Henry, past Burgundy.

Lianna clutched Aimery to her chest while Rand embraced them both. The baby, absent for nearly three months, crowed with delight. He'd grown stronger, more like Rand with his noble features, more like Lianna with her stubborn chin. His tiny hand clutched at Lianna's finger.

"Thank God," Rand said hoarsely. "Thank God he's safe."

Elated warmth flowed through Lianna. "He's cut two more teeth," she cried. Parting the folds of the baby's shawl, she noticed a sewn-on emblem of a nettle and staff. Burgundy's device. She looked over Rand's shoulder at her uncle. "You received my message."

A wry smile fought for control of his thin mouth. "Your mother still stinks of sulfur, lad," he said to the child. "The men of Longwood must have a weakness for the abominable scent."

Rand laughed. "So they do. Either that, or they are forced unto it. Thank you for bringing our son."

His monkish features softened to smiles, King Henry stepped forward. "Welcome, Your Grace."

The duke dismounted. "What think you of my niece now, Harry?" Burgundy asked, fiercely proud.

"You've heard?" asked Henry.

"Aye, already the tale races through the countryside."

Henry nodded. "The bards will sing of her courage for years to come."

Lianna swallowed past a sudden lump in her throat. "Of yours, too, sire," she said in conciliation. "You'll be remembered as the king who united the lily and the leopard under one banner."

Henry smiled at her and Rand. He touched the baby's cheek. "And under one roof," he added. Together, he and Burgundy walked off, to make their peace and their plans.

Rand wrapped his arms around his family. "Henry has conquered a kingdom," he said.

"And you, husband, have conquered my heart."

He grinned. "I wonder who waged the harder campaign."

She shrugged, raised up on tiptoe to kiss him. "That," she said airily, "is something we shall leave for the bards to decide."

Afterword

Henry V's astonishing triumph at Agincourt brought him such a fierce reputation that never again did the French engage him in a major battle. In 1420 the Treaty of Troyes secured his betrothal to the French Princess Katherine and made him Heir and Regent of France.

Jean Sans Peur, the Duke of Burgundy, was murdered by agents of the dauphin in 1418.

Henry's nine-year reign ended in 1422 when, at the age of thirty-five, he died of dysentery. By 1461 England lost its foothold in France, for Henry's military imagination and strategic genius were never equaled.

Susan Wiggs is the author of five novels and one children's book. She attended school in Brussels and Paris, and has traveled extensively in Europe, North Africa, the Soviet Union, the United Kingdom and Mexico. She has a master's degree from Harvard University, and is currently a teacher in Texas, where she lives with her husband and daughter.

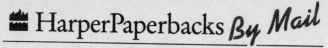